The Festival of
Earthly Delights

The Festival of Earthly Delights

a novel

Matt Dojny

DZANC
BOOKS

www.dzancbooks.org

The characters and events in this book are fictitious. Any similarity to real persons, living or dead, is coincidental and not intended by the author.

NEW POSITION: "Goldfish Jump" © Andrey Matyuk/Dreamstime.com; "Goldfish Jumping Out of the Water" © Mikael Damkier/Dreamstime.com.

THE ABSENT PRESENT: "Leaf Face" © Karuppasamy .g/Dreamstime.com; "Marine Life" © Philcold/Dreamstime.com.

YOUR FINALE VOYAGE: "The Voyage" © Spectral-design/Dreamstime.com; "Fireworks" © Freevectordownload.com.

Cover design and illustrations by Matt Dojny
Book design by Steven Seighman

ISBN: 978-1-936-87369-2

First edition: June 2012

ART WORKS.
arts.gov

*michigan council for
arts and cultural affairs*

This project is supported in part by an award from the National Endowment for the Arts and the MCACA.

Printed in the United States of America

10 9 8 7 6 5 4 3 2 1

TO SPY

THE FESTIVAL
OF EARTHLY
DELIGHTS

Our company will do its very best to advocate your own, personal sentiments and emotions. PUCHAI FANCY NOTE LTD.

> A new position falls into the hands of one who, living, dreams.
> IT WILL COME TRUE

#1 BOYD DARROW
HOME KWAN HOME
MAI MOR

February 19
8:23 AM

Dear Hap:

A new position falls into the hands of one who, living, dreams.
I bought this notebook in the airport when we arrived in
Puchai, and, instead of keeping a journal—which always feels
lonely and pointless to me—I've decided to write you a letter.
IT WILL COME TRUE.

Ulla and I are in the Central Dakhong Railway Station,
waiting for the 12:13 train to Mai Mor. The station is rumbling
and hot and cavernous and painted floor-to-ceiling in volcanic
orange. Ulla has wandered off in search of a bathroom and I'm
sitting on a bench, guarding our bags. And—where are you?

For some reason I imagine you lying on your back in a field,
sipping from a can of beer, surrounded by animals: ducks and
snakes and wolves and cats and hummingbirds and rabbits.
Maybe even a cow, standing in the shade of some nearby trees.
They're all just kind of hanging around, ignoring each other.
Even the ones that are natural enemies.

Then you sit up and make a circle with your thumb and
forefinger and look up at the sky, and you can see me through it.

9:46 AM

Our flight from Newark was seventeen hours and twenty-
three minutes, non-stop. Ulla took a pill and was unconscious
for most of the trip. I spent my time playing solitaire and

drinking tiny bottles of Boodles gin mixed with *Puchalicious*-brand tamarind soda. After a while, I put away the cards and opened up our *Pocket Adventure: Puchai!* guidebook. I'd meant to read it before we left, but had never quite gotten around to it. From the introduction:

"The Kingdom of Winks" is a phrase that conjures many images: Saffron-robed monks and tantalizing bar-girls—sun-drenched beaches and moss-encrusted mountains—the exotic nightclubs of Dakhong and the picturesque rice farms of Hattanai Province—world-class hotels and soft-adventure experiences in the jungle. Puchai may be miniscule in size, but irregardless, this charming country offers a myriad of cultural and sensual contrasts for the visitor on holiday. Whatever you seek, Puchai's scintillating blend of age-old tradition and modern amenities makes for the most unique holiday available to date. Truly, this land of contradictions—by turns zestful and tranquil, resplendent and subtle, soulful and hedonistic—never fails to delight your senses… and/or your spirit.

The Puchanese are a mischievous and happy-go-lucky people who are sure to greet you with a wide smile and their trademark "wink" of the eye. Puchai isn't known as "The Kingdom of Winks" for nothin'! Winking back at them is a sure-fire way of saying, "I like you, too. Thank you for welcoming me to your country. I'm really excited to be here, and I look forward to experiencing everything it has to offer!"

I put the guidebook down and rested my forehead against the window, barely able to keep my eyes open. The sun was rising and I watched the clouds—thin and feathery and edged with pink and gold—slowly creep across the purplish sky, coming together as if to form characters in some forgotten language. And then, like a film reel stuck on a frame, their motion abruptly ceased. My heart hammered in my chest when I saw that they'd taken the shape of six enormous letters.

My own surname, written across the sky in fire.

The airplane's engines had come to a complete stop, and we were hanging silently in mid-air. I continued staring out at my name, now grasping its meaning: the plane was about to crash, and in a few moments I would be dead, along with everyone on board.

I glanced around at the other passengers—wondering if each of them saw their own name in the clouds—then squeezed my eyes shut. I was hoping to see highlights from my life flashing by in rapid succession, but all I saw was empty blackness. And then, as if you were sitting in the seat behind me, murmuring the words into my ear—I heard your voice.

Jungle honey.

I opened my eyes with a start. Ulla was awake now, shrieking wildly. Turning to her, I grabbed her wrists and said, "*Don't panic. Everything's going to be all right.*" My voice had shot up an entire octave, wobbly and sharp, and it seemed obvious that I was lying—that everything was not, in fact, going to be all right. Ulla's palms were damp and sticky and her shirt was stained dark brown, as if she was already covered in blood. I looked into her face and said: "Goodbye."

Ulla stared at me with a mixture of confusion and alarm. Several other passengers were watching us closely. She glanced around at them, then leaned in close. "Are you okay, Boyd?"

I looked out the window. The sky was clear, the engines were humming, and the plane was moving steadily through the air. "Weren't you just screaming?"

"I screamed because you were flailing around in your sleep and spilling soda all over the place," said Ulla, taking my pillow and rubbing it in her lap.

I searched the sky one more time. "I saw—I mean, I thought that we were going to…" I felt my eyelid give a little twitch as the passengers around us began to whisper to one another. "Never mind," I said, pressing my hand to my eye.

Ulla patted my arm. "Just a bad dream."

Our plane was now making its descent into the soupy yellow smog that hung above the city of Dakhong. I saw that we were passing over a railroad junction, and instinctively I lifted both my feet off the floor—either for good luck, or to ward off disaster. I forget which it is.

A driver hired by Mai Mor College was waiting for us at the gate, holding a paper plate with "MR. + MRS. DARROW" scrawled across it. His rendition of my name was reminiscent of the DARROW in the sky—it almost looked like the same handwriting—and the similarity made my stomach tighten.

Ulla and I changed dollars for *prik* at the airport, and then we were driven to the train station in a *pini-mini*—a small, noisy, three-wheeled vehicle that looks like a cross between a rickshaw and a Vespa. We rode through the industrial outskirts and entered the traffic-clogged streets of downtown Dakhong, inching past a succession of skyscrapers, markets, exotica clubs, shantytowns, and temples (which are known as *mâdans*, Ulla informed me—she finished reading the guidebook weeks ago). Blue-black fumes poured out of the tailpipe of the *pini-mini*, and by the time we reached the train station, I felt another one of my out-of-body experiences coming on.

After some difficulty, we managed to purchase two one-way tickets to the town of Mai Mor. I'd wanted to spend a few days looking around Dakhong, but Ulla is eager to settle in before she starts her new job. She's been hired by Mai Mor College's Faculty of Theatre Drama to help organize and stage-manage the big talent show (the Expo *Taang*) that's held in conjunction with the town's annual "Festival of *Taang Lôke Kwaam Banterng Sumitchanani.*" My own job prospects are sketchy, although Ulla's new boss—Mrs. Haraporn Leekanchanakoth-Young—suggested in her letters that I might be able to work at the English-language school run by her husband. I'm anxious to start earning some *prik*: I owe Ulla nine hundred and eighty-three dollars for my plane ticket here.

I'll bet I can guess what you're wondering at this point, Hap: What are Ulla and I doing here? Why Puchai?

There are a lot of reasons. One reason we left New York was because Ulla had harbored romantic ideas about moving to a foreign land ever since her junior year abroad in Luxembourg. Another reason was that—apart from my freelance job designing brochures for the Department of Public Health and Mental Hygiene—I didn't have much going on back in the city, and I thought that a change of scenery might do me good.

And another reason I wanted to leave home, if you really want to know, was the White Sikh.

I call the White Sikh "the White Sikh" because he's a white man who is a follower of the Sikh faith. I also call him the White Sikh because I don't like saying his actual name—Shawn Talbot-Singh—aloud. He was Ulla's boss at Gelder & Ventry, and, not too long ago, I learned that Ulla and this Sikh—a married man in his mid-40s, with three young children—had been meeting up in the stairwell during their lunch break for a daily make-out session.

After this revelation, Ulla and I went into a tailspin that lasted for several weeks, though we never broke up for more than an hour at a time. When I had to go to the Catskills for Maury's wedding in January, Ulla decided to join me at the last minute, and we ended up having an unexpectedly fun time together—it was as if our problems vaporized as soon as we left the city limits. On the drive home, Ulla informed me that she'd heard about a job opportunity in Puchai, and was seriously thinking about applying. We discussed it for a while, and after a stretch of tense silence, she asked me if I'd like to go with her.

You said: *Let's do it.*

Over the years, I've gotten used to hearing your voice in my head—prodding and cajoling me, as if you were looking over my shoulder, judging every decision I make. Usually I'm pretty good at ignoring you. This time, though, an idea occurred to me: as an experiment, I'd try doing exactly what you told me to do, and see if my life improved. The thought of traveling to some small random foreign destination with Ulla terrified me for a lot of reasons. But maybe that was why I had to go. Things couldn't get much worse.

I forced my lips to move before my brain could second-guess itself. "All right," I told Ulla. "Let's do it."

Half an hour later, I asked: "Where's Puchai?"

11:02 AM

Still waiting for the train. I don't feel very well right now, probably due to the sleep deprivation, carbon monoxide inhalation, and gin consumption, along with the fact that I haven't eaten anything for several hours. There's a food stall near our bench where a man is frying batches of something in a silver skillet—they look like oversized hush puppies. A woman in a dress stitched from sackcloth is standing next to him. She has a large pink basket balanced on her head, and she's yelling "*Fae-dong! Fae-dong!*" at the top of her lungs, as though calling to a dog, or a small child. I've been watching her and thinking about buying some of whatever she's selling. It seems like a daunting task, and I'm tempted to just sit here and starve for a while longer—but I can hear you saying: *You're hungry. You have money. She has food. How complicated could it be?*

Wish me luck.

11:58 AM

Before approaching the snack-sellers, I skimmed our *Puchanese Language Dictionary* (which is just a hand-bound stack of mimeographed pages that Ulla bought from a kid at the airport). The English-language section didn't follow the traditional rules of alphabetization as far as I could tell, but I figured out how to say "one" (*tûan-nâa*) and "please" (*gà-roó-na*).

I turned to Ulla and said, "*Tûan-nâa fae-dong gà-roó-na.* One bag of deep-fried food, please."

Ulla flipped through the *Pocket Adventure* guide. "There must be a list of phrases in here. Let me see if it says how to order something."

"That's okay," I said. "I'm just going to go for it."

As I approached the woman, I saw that she was delicately picking her nose with one hand and holding her other hand in front of her face—to shield her actions from public view, I guess—while effortlessly balancing the basket on her head. Once I'd reached her, I cleared my throat and said, "Hello."

The woman spun around, removed her finger from her nose, and let out a startled, high-pitched gasp.

I pointed to her basket. "Um… *tûan-nâa… fae-dong… gà-roó-na?*"

Grimacing, she stepped backwards, clutching her goods protectively. "*Gà-roó-na?*"

"Yes, please. *Tûan-nâa. Gà-roó-na.* Thank you." I gave her a big, friendly wink.

The woman watched me wordlessly, straining her neck forward, then said something to the man behind the fryer. He laughed and made a suggestive movement with his hips. "*Fae-dong gà-roó-na?*" he repeated, smirking.

I took out my wallet, thumbed through my fresh wad of *prik*, and randomly selected a rumpled bill with an image of laughing peasants flying kites. I wasn't sure how much it was worth, but it was small and yellow and undistinguished-looking. I thrust it towards them and said, with confidence, "*Tûan-nâa fae-dong!*"

The man snatched the money from me, held it up to the light, then broke into a broad, toothless grin. I smiled back and nodded serenely. He brought his hands to his forehead, bowed, then reached into his smock and counted out my change: sixteen light-blue bills and nine small coins.

The woman took a step towards me, put her hands on my shoulders, and, with a shy smile, pulled me down until our faces were at the same height. It felt as if we were about to share some kind of intimate moment, and I found myself wishing that I'd taken the time to read more about the local customs. And then— in one deft motion—she removed the basket from her head and placed it onto mine. I reached up reflexively and steadied it as the woman fell to her knees, pressing her chin to the floor.

"Wait, no—I don't want to buy the whole thing." I tried to lift the basket off my head, but it was surprisingly heavy and began to slide out of my hands, so I re-balanced it and said, "Listen,

I'm sorry, but there's been a misunderstanding." I turned to the man, who was sorting the money in his apron. When I caught his eye he looked down and puffed out his cheeks. "No," I said quietly. "No, no, no." The woman was rocking back and forth on the ground, murmuring to herself. I suddenly felt dizzy, and knew that I had to go sit down.

As I walked back towards Ulla, I carefully balanced the basket on my head and avoided making eye contact with any passersby. Ulla was reading the guidebook and listening to my Walkman, and for a moment I considered ditching the basket somewhere—but then she looked up, and it was too late.

I lowered myself into a squatting position, gingerly placed the basket on the bench, and said: "*Tûan-nâa fae-dong gà-roó-na?*"

12:36 PM

The interior of this train is a mishmash of different styles: ornate brass luggage racks, Modernist plastic seats, turn-of-the-century light fixtures, and orange leatherette walls printed with a subtle Op art pattern. It's like an old World's Fair prototype for the Locomotive of Tomorrow. When I climbed on board, struggling with my basket, the passengers gawked at me as though I held a baby dolphin in my arms.

After consulting the dictionary, Ulla determined that I should've used the word *tiân*—which is defined as "one [single discrete groupings]"—as opposed to *tûan-nâa*, which means "one [entirety of groupings]." Also, I should've said *bpròh* ("please") instead of *gà-roó-na*, which apparently means: "to please [bringing satisfy with touch, eating, feelings]."

"So," I said, "according to you, I told that woman: 'I want to pleasure your entire basket'?"

Ulla was quiet for a moment, then asked how much money I'd given them. I reluctantly told her, and, after doing some calculations, she informed me that I'd paid about $67—approximately one-fifth their annual income. The light-blue bills that they'd given to me as change were worth about twelve cents apiece.

I opened one of the bags, plucked out a snack, and popped it into my mouth. It was crunchy on the outside, with a moist center that tasted like walnuts and garlic, but also like French fries and mint. It was delicious. I immediately ate another, and, after some prodding, Ulla tried one. We went through the whole bag in about a minute.

When we were finished, Ulla asked, "What are these things called again?"

"*Fae-dongs.*" I belched, and tasted a strange new flavor rising up from the back of my throat. "Let's remember that name."

8:12 PM

I'm sitting on an overturned black plastic trash can outside the door of our new home. Ulla's inside sleeping—due to the twelve-hour time difference, we're both exhausted—but I'm feeling pretty wired, so I'm out here drinking a beer and writing to you.

When we arrived at the Mai Mor station this afternoon, we got off the train and sat on a bench out front and waited to be picked up by someone from the Faculty of Theatre Drama. The station is a lonely sort of place—just a small concrete ticket office flanked by a dirt parking lot. After twenty minutes, a white van appeared on the horizon and came to a stop about thirty feet away from us. Stenciled on its side were the words:

FACULTY OF THEATRE DRAMA

"*Finally*," Ulla said, getting to her feet. "Now, Boyd, don't forget—" She pointed at the silver band on her ring finger and smiled at me. "We're newlyweds."

Ulla had read in *Pocket Adventure* that a man and woman aren't supposed to live together in Puchai until they're married. Because the Faculty of Theatre Drama is providing housing for us, she's afraid that our relationship status might cause a problem, and so she's told Haraporn that we're husband and wife. I wasn't crazy about this idea, but Ulla and I went to St. Mark's Place and bought a matching pair of silver bands for ten bucks each. It still feels strange on my finger, yet also gives me a kind of illicit thrill.

A young woman in a tight pink taffeta gown emerged from the van and surveyed the empty lot. When she spotted us, she began making frantic motions with the back of her hand, as though shooing us away.

"She wants us to get back on the train?" I said.

"That's how people wave in Puchai—backwards," Ulla explained, hoisting her bag. "You seriously need to read the guidebook. What I want to know is, why is she dressed like she's taking us to the prom?"

The woman was rail-thin, with frizzy bangs framing her angular, giddy face. She wore high heels and teetered uncertainly on her skinny legs like a newborn flamingo. As we approached her, she patted her sternum and made a noise that sounded like the mewling of a cat. We later determined that she'd been introducing herself to us—her name is *Miaw*.

Miaw stepped to one side, and a short, cylindrical woman in a tent-like purple dress and matching Reeboks emerged from the van. The broad swath of white that ran through the middle of her black hair gave her an Indira-Gandhi-like air of authority, and I knew that this must be Ulla's new boss: Mrs. Haraporn Leekanchanakoth-Young.

Haraporn looked me up and down, then said, in a scolding voice: "Mr. Darrow, you are extremely tall!"

"Hi." I extended my hand. "You must be Haraporn."

"In Puchai, when you greet a new acquaintance, you do the following." Haraporn pressed her palms together, lifted them to her chin, and bowed. "This is called *hai*."

"*Hai*." I mimicked her bow.

"Very good," said Haraporn. "But you do not need to say *hai* when you do this."

A stocky, squinting man appeared from the driver's side of the van and took our bags from us. He was dressed in an unadorned gray uniform that made him look as though he held some kind of low-level governmental position: postal worker, maybe, or park ranger. He pointedly avoided my gaze, but when I handed him the *fae-dong* basket, he glanced at me with a look of intense curiosity.

The interior of the van was freezing cold and filled with a distinct and powerful odor—a mixture of turpentine, sour mash, and halitosis. As we began to drive, Miaw took Ulla's hand in hers. She held it for the duration of the trip.

Haraporn turned around in her seat and said, "It's wonderful to finally meet you both. This is your first time to our country—true?"

The smell in the van grew more intense with every passing moment, and I began to breathe shallowly through my mouth. In a choked voice, I responded: "True."

Haraporn smiled and leaned closer to us. "How do you enjoy Puchai? It's very beautiful—yes or no?"

"Oh, yes," said Ulla. "Very beautiful." She took a gulp of air and looked at me, and I bobbed my head in agreement.

"And the people?" Haraporn asked. "They are friendly?"

"Extremely," I said.

Ulla nodded. "We haven't really met very many people yet."

Haraporn smiled modestly. "People are very friendly here," she said. "Truly."

I heard the scratch of a lighter as the driver lit a cigarette, exhaling a cloud of sweet-smelling white smoke that floated back into our faces. Ulla put her hand to her nose and widened her eyes at me. I hesitated, then began to roll my window down.

"Please, do not do that," said Haraporn. "The air-conditioner is switched on." She pointed at the vents. "We will lose all our coolness."

"Sorry." I rolled the window back up. Ulla continued to stare at me imploringly, so I added, "It was just..." I made a vague gesture towards the smoke.

"Ah, is the cigarette a bother?" Haraporn turned and said a few sharp words to the van driver. He glanced at me in the rearview mirror, his eyes cold and flat, then lowered his window and flicked the cigarette outside.

"And the food of Puchai?" said Haraporn, turning back to us. "Is it delicious to you?"

"I hear that the local cuisine is very delicious," I said.

Haraporn ran her tongue across her lips. "You must sample the *uluka pai mong*, the crunchy infant bird with the pineapple sauce that they sell in the market. *Uluka* is like a… what do you say? A baby owl. We say: *pêt!*"

"The owl is a pet?" said Ulla.

"No, no! *Pêt* is the word meaning: 'delicious.'" A bright laugh escaped from Haraporn's lips. "Ah, and before I am forgetting, I have something for you both. A welcoming gift." She gave us a wink and passed back a large plastic bag.

Before I'd even gotten the bag open, the awful stench had grown ten times stronger. Holding my breath, I glanced inside and saw that it was filled with what looked like several monstrous avocados that had been spray-painted bright orange. My whole face began to pucker, but I quickly un-puckered it and looked up at Haraporn. "Thank you," I said.

"You are welcome to them."

"What are these, exactly?"

"It is called *garong*. It is 'Queen of the Fruits' in our nation. Very, very *pêt*. But with a powerful smell, yes? I find it to be very rich and tempting, but I am led to believe that, to some people, it is disagreeable. An odor like old men who are sick in the clinic."

I tied the bag tightly shut and put it under the seat. "I can't wait to taste them."

"If you like, we could peel one now and—"

"Actually," I said, "that reminds me, I wanted to ask you— what does *fae-dong* mean?" I twisted around and retrieved a bag of the snacks from the basket. "These things," I said, passing them up to Haraporn.

She glanced behind and arched an eyebrow. "You purchased an entire *brà-boong* of *fae-dongs*?"

"It was an accident."

"I see." Haraporn looked dubiously at the bag. "*Fae-dong* is a *malchak* word. I believe that it means: 'fried object'?"

"What's *malchak*?" asked Ulla.

"*Malchak* are a type of people. Nomads from the hills who live in Puchai, but are not Puchanese. They are considered *pônge*—alien. Similar to the little green men in your country." Haraporn squinted at the snacks and wrinkled her nose. "The *malchak* are always eating food that is cheap and unpleasant. This may be something like the gland of an animal, with a coating of rice flour and then cooked in lard."

Ulla inhaled sharply. "*Glands?*"

"I don't think that's what they are," I said. "They're sort of crunchy, like a nut, but soft on the inside. Would you like to try one?"

Haraporn smiled and nodded her head, then deposited the bag into my lap. "So, Ulla—we are pleased to have you assisting us with the planning of the Expo *Taang*."

"I'm excited to get started," said Ulla.

"You will be assisting Miaw with much of the labor. Miaw is the Secondary Adjunct Secretary to Faculty of Theatre Drama. She has had great experience with the Expo *Taang*, and can explain various aspects to you."

Miaw, who had been staring out the window, perked up at the sound of her name. She nodded uncertainly and gave Ulla's hand a quick squeeze. "Expo," she said.

"Miaw is very scared about speaking English," said Haraporn. "Ulla, you must help her to speak it with you. It is important for the Faculty of Theatre Drama."

"Of course." Ulla turned to Miaw, who was once again gazing out the window, humming under her breath as she stroked Ulla's hand.

I cleared my throat and said, "Haraporn, in your letter to us, you had mentioned a possible job here for me?"

"Yes. My husband, Samuel, is the founding father of the Young English School. He can certainly give you English-teaching work. Samuel is a *gareng*, like you."

I furrowed my brow. "A *gareng*—as in... 'Queen of the Fruits'?" Ulla shot me an alarmed look, and I quickly added, "Sorry, I'm not sure I understand what you mean."

Haraporn chuckled. "*Garong* is the fruit. *Gareng* means... 'pale outsider.'" She clasped her hands together and said, "I will make an interview for you with Samuel very soon. Please remind me: what kind of work did you do before you come here? What is your trade?" Haraporn stared at me with great interest, as did Ulla.

"I don't exactly have a trade, *per se*. I've held a variety of different—"

"Boyd works for my father," Ulla said.

"Ah!" Haraporn smiled. "Very fortunate. The familial business."

"Mm-hmm," I said. It was true that I'd spent a week working for Ulla's dad over the summer—painting the office where his dental practice is located—but I wasn't expecting to have the position waiting for me when I got back to town.

"When the father and the husband can work side by side, it is a special gift," Haraporn observed. "You two are newly-wed, correct?"

"Very newly," I said. "This trip is sort of our honeymoon."

"*Honey-moon*." Haraporn sighed. "A lovely expression."

Ulla's mouth twitched into the shape of a smile. "Honeymoon," she repeated, pronouncing it as if she wasn't sure what it meant.

The van made a sharp turn down a gravel driveway, pulling up in front of a ranch-style house surrounded by a grove of slender yellow fruit trees. A ping-pong table stood on the front lawn, and irregular squares of blue slate led to a lush vegetable garden off to the side.

"All right, then," said Haraporn.

I reached out and rested my hand on Ulla's knee, transfixed by a vision of our new life in Puchai. I could see the two of us sitting together at that ping-pong table, talking and laughing and eating a leisurely breakfast; I could see us walking together hand in hand through the grove of trees, collecting swollen fruit from the ground, peeling it and feeding it to one another; I could see us together in the garden, on our knees in the dirt, harvesting the vegetables that we'd grown. I could see us starting over here, and being happy.

"So, this is where we'll be living?" I said. I hadn't meant for it to be a question, but I'd begun to doubt myself as soon as I spoke the words aloud.

"Oh, no!" Haraporn said. "This is *my* home."

"Ah," I said. "Of course."

"It's very pretty," murmured Ulla.

"Miaw will now escort you to your lodgings." Haraporn *hai*-ed us and climbed out of the van. "I'm very content to meet you, Darrows! I think you will be excellent replacements."

Before I could ask her what she meant, she'd already slammed the door shut.

On our way back into town, Ulla, Miaw, and I quietly stared out the windows as the van edged its way through throngs of bicyclists and food-hawkers and livestock. We turned down a wide dirt highway, and soon the buildings gave way to grassy fields dotted with overgrown, rusting structures that looked like roller coasters abandoned in the previous century. We crossed a bridge spanning a brown, fast-moving river lined with clusters of metal shacks, then took a left at a hand-carved wooden sign that read—in English—*WELCOME TO MAI MOR COLLEGE.* Beneath that, the words "*WE ARE LEARNING!*" were stenciled alongside a logo of a turtle balancing a globe on its back.

Miaw suddenly started yelling and wildly flapping her arms. The driver cursed and slammed on the brakes, and Miaw hopped out and ran around to the front, disappearing from view for a moment. When she stood up, she was cradling a small green turtle in her hands.

She climbed back into her seat and placed the turtle gingerly on her lap, stroking its shell as its legs clawed at the air. "Remind me," I whispered to Ulla. "What's the deal with the turtles here?"

"Tortoises," she said. "Not turtles. And everybody worships them. Very random."

A few minutes later, we pulled up in front of a single-story apartment complex with a sign on its front lawn that read:

HOME KWAN HOME NO.3

The exterior of the building was painted cornflower blue, but a lot of the paint was peeling, revealing a layer of yellow underneath; from a distance, *Home Kwan Home No. 3* gave off a faint greenish glow, and it reminded me of that old falling-down motel at Stinson Beach we stayed at that one time. (Remember—the place run by the crazy-eyed hippie who performed an a cappella imitation of a Ginger Baker drum solo for us?) Next to the building's entrance was a Volkswagen-sized wooden statue of a turtle, draped with strings of flowers and yellow Christmas lights. Haphazardly piled around its base were dozens of smaller statues: tiny ivory turtles, cheap plastic toy turtles, stone turtles, a turtle made out of wrought iron, a turtle carved from a bar of soap, and others that I couldn't begin to describe. Miaw set her turtle down on this pile, and I noticed that several living turtles were crawling among the effigies.

Miaw went over to a covered altar next to the shrine, lit a stick of incense, and murmured a few words. Then she picked up a canister filled with ivory chopsticks, knelt on the ground, and began to shake it violently, tilting it until the chopsticks started to work their way out. When one fell to the ground, she inserted the chopstick into a small hole in the top of the altar. As she pushed it down, a one-inch-by-one-inch drawer slid open on the lower left corner of the altar's façade, and, at the same time, a panel popped open on the side of the altar, revealing a set of small numbered drawers that looked like a library card catalogue. Miaw retrieved a fingernail-sized key from the front drawer, then inspected the numeral engraved on the end of the chopstick. She located the corresponding numbered drawer, unlocked it with the key, took out a piece of paper, read it, replaced it, and stood up. I asked her to explain what she'd been doing, but she just blinked at me and shook her head.

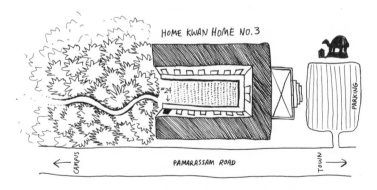

Ulla and I followed Miaw and the driver around the side of the building to a door-lined courtyard that faced out onto a small forest. A scabby, wolfish dog with matted white hair lay on the grass, eyeing us as it gnawed on something that looked like a horse's hoof. We stopped in front of a door marked #24, and Miaw took a large key ring out of her purse and began to sort through it, humming to herself as she attempted to unlock the padlock. After trying every single key on the ring, she turned reluctantly to the driver. They argued briefly, then he dropped our bags to the ground and stalked off.

The man returned thirty seconds later holding a tire iron. Ulla and I exchanged a glance and took several steps back as he pointed the iron straight above his head, and then—in a wide, graceful arc—brought it crashing down against the door. We inched forward and inspected the results: there was a fist-sized gash in the wood, but the lock itself remained pristine.

The driver rolled his shoulders back, closed one eye, then raised the bar in the air again and swung with all his strength. As Miaw gasped and cooed and muttered, the driver battered the door until there was a sharp *clang* and the lock clattered to the ground.

He picked up the lock and handed it to me. Though his breathing was labored, his face was more impassive than ever. I looked down at the twisted piece of metal in my hand and closed my fingers around it. "Thanks," I said, wondering if he was waiting for a tip.

"That man just demolished our door," Ulla whispered.

The driver winked at Ulla, lit a cigarette, and disappeared around the corner of *Home Kwan Home No. 3* without a word.

Miaw pressed the keys into my hand. "Welcome to Puchai," she said, then bowed to us and hurried after him.

As I watched Miaw go, Ulla took in a series of short breaths. "Do you think that thing is rabid?"

The white dog on the grass stared at us intently, sniffing the air to catch our scent.

"Probably not," I said, taking Ulla by the hand. "Let's go inside."

*   *   *

Our new home looks like a cross between a college dorm room and a hospital waiting area—an anonymous space, the kind that no one is meant to spend much time in. The cinderblock walls are painted glossy white and are crawling with tiny darting lizards the color of margarine. A pair of twin beds are in the corner, spaced slightly apart; two chairs and a glass coffee table sit beneath a window facing the courtyard. The lights are dim and fluorescent, there's no telephone, and the only indications of a kitchen are a fridge, an electric wok, and a toaster oven.

"*Home kwan home*," I said, flopping down on one of the beds. "Why can't we sleep together if we're supposedly married? This is like *I Love Lucy* or something."

Ulla surveyed our new surroundings, her hand lingering on the doorknob. She looked like a child trying to decide whether or not to cry.

"Hey, Mrs. Darrow," I said, giving her a backwards wave. "Come over here."

Ulla sat down next to me on the bed. I put my arms around her and pulled her toward me and kissed her on the mouth.

"The guidebook says there's at least sixty types of poisonous reptiles in Puchai," Ulla murmured. She was staring over my shoulder, wide-eyed.

I looked up at the small lizards running back and forth across the ceiling, then turned to Ulla and said, "Screw the guidebook," and stuck my tongue into her ear. She pulled away and slapped me lightly on the face, and I put my hand on her stomach and kissed her again. Then I ▓▓▓▓ my ▓▓▓▓ and she ▓▓▓▓ a ▓▓▓▓▓▓. I ▓▓▓▓ my ▓▓▓▓ a little further ▓▓▓▓ ▓▓▓▓, ▓▓ing the ▓▓▓▓▓ ▓▓▓▓▓▓ of ▓▓ ▓▓▓▓ until I ▓▓▓▓ her ▓▓▓▓▓▓. I ▓▓▓▓ my ▓▓▓▓ and Ulla continued to stare up at the ceiling, but then she ▓▓▓▓ her ▓▓▓▓ and ▓▓▓▓ ▓▓▓ ▓▓ close to ▓▓▓▓. I ▓▓▓ ▓▓ ▓ ▓▓▓▓▓▓ and ▓▓▓▓ ▓▓▓▓▓

▓▓▓▓▓ not to ▓▓▓—it had been a ▓▓▓▓ ▓▓▓, and I was
a little ▓▓▓-▓▓. Ulla ▓▓▓ed down in the ▓▓▓ until her
▓▓▓▓ ▓▓ed my ▓▓▓▓, and began to ▓▓▓ ▓▓▓▓▓▓ ▓▓
all around ▓▓ ▓▓. I moved ▓▓▓ ▓▓▓ ▓▓ and ▓▓▓▓ my
▓▓▓ on her ▓▓▓ and ▓▓▓ it ▓▓▓▓ so her ▓▓▓ would ▓▓▓
over ▓▓▓ ▓▓▓▓. She ▓▓▓▓ ▓▓▓ on her ▓▓▓ as she ▓▓
and ▓▓▓▓▓ until I ▓▓▓. I ▓▓▓▓▓▓ Ulla in ▓▓ ▓▓▓ and we lay
there for a while, not ▓▓▓▓ ▓▓▓▓. Then she roused herself,
▓▓▓▓▓ her ▓▓▓▓▓▓, and ▓▓▓ ▓▓ ▓▓ ▓▓▓. I kissed her
again and she drew back and narrowed her eyes at me.

"Hey," I said, touching her face. "What's the matter?"

Ulla wiped her lips with the back of her hand. "Sorry. You
kind of taste like cigarettes, and—" She laughed, wrinkling
her nose. "*Fae-dongs.*"

I opened my mouth to say something, then closed it
as Ulla stood up and looked around the room. "Can you
believe this place?" she said. "Don't even *tell* me that's our
only closet." As she began unpacking her things, I lay back
and watched the yellow lizards crawling on the ceiling. I
found myself wondering if the guidebook might not be
right after all.

February 24
11:42 PM

Dear Hap:

Ulla has started her job at the Faculty of Theatre Drama. So far, her duties consist of reorganizing the filing system and teaching Miaw to speak English. I'm still at loose ends—Haraporn's husband is out of town, and for the past several days I've just been sitting around *Home Kwan Home*, killing time. Ulla's asleep right now and I'm outside on my trash can perch, surrounded by smoldering mosquito coils. I keep hearing sinister rustling noises coming from the woods, but there's very little light out here, so I can't really see what's going on. I've made myself a lantern by sticking a candle in a water bottle with the bottom cut out and hanging it from the laundry rack next to our door. It looks like this:

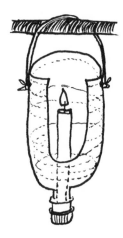

I feel like young Abe Lincoln, reading and writing by candlelight—although, last night, the plastic bottle caught on fire and I had to pour my beer on it to put it out.

One way I've been passing the time has been by reading the guidebook. The entry on Mai Mor is barely a page long:

*Located along Route 17 (a.k.a. "the Friendly Highway") in the heart of rural Northeastern Puchai, the town of **MAI MOR** (pop. 22,576) is a good halfway point between Dakhong and the beautiful hill country of Reoi. The surprisingly opulent **Hotel Tel-Hô** (457-39 Burrarmachai) has modern-style accommodations, a squash court, and luxurious bathing facilities.*

Mai Mor is home to Mai Mor College—the largest education center in Hattanai Province—and is referred to amongst locals as "Turtle Town," due to the unusual number of tortoises that freely roam the campus. The Ngoo-pìk River snakes its way along the outer perimeter of Mai Mor proper, and, though pretty to look at, swimming in the water is not recommended (particularly downriver from the shanties that line its banks).

If you happen to be in the area during the month of April, it's worth checking out Mai Mor's "Festival Day" (the Festival of Taang Lôke Kwaam Ban-terng Sumitchanani). Every year at this time, when the moon is full, the river's resident "ngoo" ("lovely-giant-turtle-monster") shoots red balls of flame up into the night sky to celebrate the conclusion of the local monks' annual retreat. (In actuality, this charming phenomenon is caused by river-gases that combust upon reaching the water's surface.) The festival is primarily an excuse for a 24-hour bacchanalia, and it's de rigueur to party all day (and all night) long. Tradition dictates that festival attendees must dress in wild, often sexually suggestive costumes. Be warned that

another Festival Day ritual involves residents filling balloons
with milk or soda and throwing them at everyone they meet!
The long day ends with the Expo Taang, a "talent show"
that features diverse acts ranging from native-style dance to
goofball comedy skits to yodeling. Bring ear plugs.

The accompanying image is a photo of a turtle resting on
a heap of dead flowers. The turtle has a tiny Shriner-style
fez taped onto its head. Off to one side, a white monkey is
pointing at it and baring its teeth.

Haraporn brought over a pair of bicycles for us—mine looks
like it's from the 1930s and is as heavy as a snowmobile, but
it works well enough. This morning I rode up to the campus
laundry, balancing my bag of dirty clothes on the handlebars.
There was a guy selling bootleg cassettes on the side of the
road, and I bought a homemade-looking R&B compilation
from him called *BLACK-EYE SOUL*. I took it home and
listened to it, and the first track is "Black + White," by Angel
& Mann. It's the one that begins: *Humans—they act so funny*
some days...
    I remember listening to that song on your record player
and picturing Angel and Mann together in the studio, side
by side—in my mind, Angel was a skinny, soft-looking white
guy, and Mann was a muscular black man with an enormous
Afro. (I also remember when you smugly informed me
that Angel & Mann's duets were, in reality, sung by a single
middle-aged Native American woman with a seven-octave
range named Evangeline Little Cloud.) Hearing the song
after all those years gave me a homey sort of feeling, and
I kept rewinding the tape and listening to it over and over
while I folded my laundry and made myself a late lunch of
ramen noodles ("*Sweet & Spice Prawn Egg Flavor*").

Once I finished eating, I grabbed my book and went outside. The air smelled like roast pork and orange soda, along with something else I couldn't quite identify—maybe those fire-retardant pajamas we used to wear. (Do they even still make those?) I sat down next to a turtle sunning itself on the grass and read for a while. At one point, the white dog appeared around the corner of the building and glared peevishly at me for a minute before loping away. Eventually I gave up reading and lay back, shutting my eyes and draping the book over my face.

I awoke to the sound of an explosion that seemed to come from deep underground. I sat up and looked around in confusion—it was so dark that I thought I'd slept straight into the night. Sheets of warm rain began pouring down from the sky, hammering me with such force that I had trouble staying upright. By the time I got inside, I'd already been soaked to the bone. As I changed out of my wet clothes, I discovered a large black ant nestled in my pubic hair. I was about to crush it between my fingers, then reconsidered and set it on a paper towel to dry.

When I looked out the window a few minutes later, the sky was clear and the sun was shining, as if the entire event had been something I'd imagined. I glanced at my watch: I must've slept at least two hours, because it was almost six.

Over the past few days, I've settled into a routine: At 5:30, I walk through campus up Pamarassam, the main road, and arrive at the Hi-Fi Cafeteria by six o' clock, where I meet Ulla for dinner. (The Hi-Fi—an open-air pavilion with a blue roof shaped like a Pringle—offers a multitude of meal options, including: roasted pork, roasted chicken, roasted duck, and roasted squid; translucent green noodles sprinkled with clusters of mosquito-sized shrimp; large purple blossoms floating in a bowl of coconut syrup; and plates heaped with tiny hardboiled eggs that are smothered in ketchup and eaten shells and all. [I remember that you pride yourself on your ability to eat anything, no matter how disgusting. You'd have a field day at this place: there's an entire food stall dedicated to organ meat.] During our first cafeteria meal, Ulla found a dead spider at the bottom of her "Yankee Plate" [fried rice served with a hot dog, a fried egg, melted cheese, croutons, and a side of mayo]— but in general, if you choose carefully, the food's pretty decent.) Haraporn had mentioned that the path through the woods behind *Home Kwan Home* is a shortcut to the Hi-Fi, but I hadn't ventured in there yet. I decided to take it today to make up for lost time.

The path was heavily overgrown, the trees still dripping from the storm, and it felt as if the damp leaves slapping against my face and arms were the tongues of little forest animals, licking me clean. The dirt beneath my feet steamed slightly and gave off a sharp smell of cocoa. Thin shafts of light pierced the thicket, illuminating clusters of tiny white gnats above my head. I opened my mouth, and when the sun hit my tongue, I tasted lemons.

Up ahead, the path forked in two: one trail continued straight, and the other trail—narrower and more overgrown— veered off sharply downhill to the right. In front of this second path a large black dog lay on its side, staring up at me with blank, milky eyes. Its body was malformed, collapsed into itself, as if its organs had been removed and replaced with wads of cotton. Its ears were crawling with black flies, and its pink tongue was clenched delicately between its dull yellow teeth. I stood there for a time, listening to the blurry noise of the wind pushing through the trees and staring at the dead animal as though waiting for it to lift its head and speak to me. Then I *hai*-ed the dog, stepped around it, and continued up the main path.

After walking through the woods for another few minutes, I emerged onto a tree-lined dirt lane and began heading in the direction of the cafeteria. The lane was free of traffic and students, and the only sign of life was a small green-eyed cat moving towards me down the middle of the road. She was a dusky shade of gold, with short hair, tiny feet, and ears like two pink seashells. A purplish discoloration bloomed above her left cheek, as if someone had punched her in the eye. She strode towards me with the confidence of a panther, strange-looking but beautiful. A cluster of dragonflies hung in the air above the cat, pulsing rhythmically and giving off an electrical hum. Craning my neck farther back, I noticed an identical cluster of dragonflies hovering over my own head. The cat seemed lost in thought, unaware of me as she approached—but, just as we passed one other, she turned and did an odd thing: she tilted her head and scrunched up the left side of her face, almost like she was trying to wink at me. At that instant, my heart felt as if it had been shot through with warm milk.

I looked up and saw that the two groups of insects had come together in the air and were swirling over our heads, tumbling and swelling like a pair of colliding stormfronts. A moment later, the cat's face recovered its dreamy, faraway expression, and she drifted on past me down the lane. Up ahead, I caught sight of Ulla standing in front of the cafeteria, arms crossed. I had a sudden urge to turn back and follow the cat wherever she was going.

The next time I looked up, the dragonflies were gone.

February 26
5:32 PM

Dear Hap:

Right now I'm sitting at a picnic table downwind from a grove of *garong* trees, waiting to meet Ulla for dinner. A group of dark-skinned men and women wearing sackcloth robes are collecting the smashed and rotting fruit from the ground. Apart from the nasty odor, I have to admit that *garongs* taste pretty good: once you peel away and discard the scaly skin, inside is a dense, white, pear-like flesh with a flavor that reminds me of Creamsicles. At its core is a heavy, walnut-sized stone. According to the guidebook, some people believe that a mixture of *garong*-pit shavings and tamarind soda makes for a powerful aphrodisiac. Duly noted.

Yesterday morning, I had my interview with Haraporn's husband, Sam Young, at the Young English School. Following Haraporn's directions, I rode my bike straight up Pamarassam and took a left at the Post Office, nearly running over a turtle in the middle of the road. Upon reaching a pit filled with smoldering tires, I turned down a gravel driveway that led to a brown-shingled building with a wooden sign hanging out front that read:

Y.E.S.

As I approached the office, a heavy, oily rain began to fall. I ran up to the door and knocked, holding my notebook over my head in a futile effort to keep from getting soaked. No answer. I knocked again, louder this time, then pressed my ear against the door and heard a muffled voice say something that I couldn't make out. I waited another moment, then turned the knob and stepped inside.

The office was small and windowless and painted a dusty pink, and seated at a wide wooden desk was a middle-aged man I took to be Sam Young. His eyes were hidden behind a pair of green-tinted aviator glasses, and his skin was both deeply tanned and oddly shiny, making his cropped blonde hair and gray moustache stand out in unsettling relief. He appeared simultaneously youthful and elderly, like a wizened little boy. A half-finished puzzle took up most of his desk: a photo-collaged image of *Mont Saint-Michel* floating in outer space. A completed puzzle depicting the *Arc de Triomphe* hung on the wall behind him, mounted and framed in black lacquered bamboo.

I smiled and said, "I hope I'm not interrupting—"

"I'll be with you in a sec." Sam jerked his thumb toward a tiny blue plastic armchair in the corner, the kind you find in kindergarten classrooms. When I sat down on it, I could barely see over the edge of his desk.

"Sorry, I got a little rained-on," I said, glancing at the puddle of water collecting beneath me on the floor. But Sam had already returned to his puzzle.

I ran my hands through my wet hair and looked around. Stacks of faded old paperbacks lined one wall of the office; the opposite wall had a chalkboard with a teaching schedule on it. The names *SAM*, *SHINEY*, *PLASSEN*, and *SLOAT* were written across the top in small, tidy handwriting. Through a door next to the desk, I dimly heard an instructor conjugating a verb for his class. Behind Sam hung a shelf of red-bound books that I mistook for an encyclopedia set until I noticed that every spine bore the identical title, embossed in gold: *ENGLISH FOR EACH.*

The room was warm and stuffy and quiet, and as I sat listening to the lulling sounds of distant traffic and the droning teacher, I found myself getting drowsy. In an attempt to keep from falling asleep in my seat, I bit down on my lower lip and widened my eyes to the full extent possible. At that very moment, the door behind me swung open, filling the room with sunlight, and a girl stepped inside.

I should explain: When I first started writing these letters to you, I was a little paranoid about Ulla reading them, and so, when I wrote that I'd seen an attractive cat walking down the road the other day, I wasn't being 100% accurate. It was a girl that walked past me on the road—a vaguely cat-like girl, but not a cat. And that same girl was now standing in the doorway of Sam's office, smiling at me.

Today she was dressed in a light pink short-sleeved shirt with a rounded tucked-in collar, maroon pants that had a skinny braided belt cinched around the waist, and black slippers. Her hair was boyishly short and dyed the color of copper and was pulled back by two neat barrettes on either side of her head, and she wore a pair of pearl clip-on earrings. Her face was smooth and glowing slightly, as though carved from pink-brown marble, and the planes and contours of her features were organized in a precise but surprising way that made me want to keep looking at them. She had high, rounded cheeks—her asymmetrical grin creating a deep dimple in one, and just the hint of a dimple in the other—and her upper lip formed a small but dramatic lower-case *v* beneath her snub nose. A plum-colored bruise still bloomed beneath her left eye, as it had when I'd first seen her, and I found myself wondering who'd given it to her.

As the girl gazed down at me—sitting there in my undersized blue chair, dripping wet—she tilted her head, and her features briefly mimicked my expression: brows arched, mouth half-open, eyes bulging. I couldn't tell whether she was making fun of me or having some kind of sympathetic reaction. I couldn't think at all, to be honest. When she flashed me another quick smile, I felt the hairs on my arms stand on end like iron filings passing through a magnetic field.

Before I could bring myself to speak, Sam glanced up and murmured, "If it isn't my precious princess."

"I'm not really here, so don't get any ideas," she said. "I just came by to—"

"It's your lucky day. Richie called in sick, and I am otherwise preoccupied, so I need you to go do his class. Room 14-Rabbit."

The girl pointed to the door behind the desk. "I told Gabe I'd meet him after his—"

"Sorry, Shiney. No can do."

"But, Dad!" She glanced at me, then began speaking to her father in rapid Puchanese. Her voice was husky and thick, as though hoarse from yelling, and was an octave lower than I'd expected it to be.

Sam cut her off with a wave of his hand. "No ifs, ands, or buts. I mean that sincerely."

The girl made a disgusted noise, grabbed a copy of *ENGLISH FOR EACH* off the shelf, and hurried out. I watched her leave, feeling bereft.

When I turned back to Sam, he was studying me with a look of intense curiosity.

"Mr. Young," I said, rising from my chair. "Boyd Darrow. It's good to meet you."

Sam nodded vaguely and got to his feet. As we shook hands, I caught sight of a blurry blue tattoo etched into his forearm—it appeared to be an illustration of a skull wearing a furry Russian hat, though I couldn't say for sure. Looking back up at his face, I saw his eyes stare at me curiously through the tinted lenses of his sunglasses, as though I were a dog that had unexpectedly stood up on its hind legs. It was obvious that he had no idea who I was.

"I just moved to town with my wife, Ulla," I said. Sam nodded again, blinking. I added, "She's working at the Faculty of Theatre Drama?"

"Ah, okay. *Right.*" Sam's grip on my hand intensified. "Sam Young." Continuing the handshake a moment too long, he added: "Welcome to paradise, Arrow."

"Thanks. It's 'Darrow,' actually..."

"So—what can I do you for?" he asked, gesturing towards the chair.

I sat down, then lifted myself slightly off the seat to maintain eye contact. "Haraporn mentioned that there might be some job openings here at the school, and told me to stop by this morning for an interview."

"*My* Haraporn said that?"

"Yes."

Sam leaned back and studied me for a moment. "You done much teaching back home? Got your certificate?"

"I don't have a teaching certificate, but I did some tutoring in college."

"You studied English?"

"I was an art history major, but—"

"*Un historian de art*, huh?" Sam smiled indulgently. "Is it fair to say, then, that you're an *artiste*?"

I shrugged. "I took some art classes."

"Ever draw from the nude woman and whatnot?"

"The emphasis was more on a conceptual approach, rather than—"

"You claim to be an artist," he said, leaning forward, "and yet you've *never* drawn from the nude woman?"

"No, I mean..." I sat up a little straighter. "I've taken life drawing classes, sure."

"You could theoretically sit here and draw a lifelike picture of me?"

"I guess, theoretically, although—"

"Why don't you give it a shot."

I looked around the room. "Right now?"

He chuckled. "Don't worry, I'm not going to be doffing my clothes. I'm just interested in a simple facial portrait."

I opened my notebook and took out a pen. "I haven't really done this for a while."

"*No problemo.*" Sam patted his hair with both hands and lifted his chin up, assuming a wistful expression. "Just try to capture my essence."

I stared at him for a long moment, then began to draw. After about twenty seconds, I said, "Do you mind if I start over?"

Still holding his pose, Sam muttered, "Finish it up, Arrow. This is just an exercise."

I filled in the rest of his moustache and handed him the sketch. He peered at it intently, pressing his lips together, then passed it back to me and said, "That's all right. *Mox nix.* You aren't here to teach these people how to draw pictures." He clapped his hands. "How about you provide me with an example of your English."

"Sure," I said. "How do you mean, exactly?"

"Since you've been in my office, Arrow, you've hardly said hi, shit, or boo. I want to hear a *spiel* that will display your powerful grasp upon the English language." He raised his arm in the air as he said this, his fist trembling as though clutching an invisible kite. "Pretend like it's the first day of school and you're talking to your pupils. Try to use a noun, a verb, an adjective, a preposition. Maybe a gerund. *Ding a ling a ling!*" He jerked his chin at me. "You can stand."

I got stiffly to my feet and clasped my hands behind my back, then shoved them into my pockets, then took them out again and let them dangle at my sides like a gunfighter. "Hello, everybody," I said, addressing my imaginary students. "Let me welcome you all to my excellent class. I have come to you today, happily, in order to..." I paused. "To *ameliorate* your understanding of the English language. This will—"

"*Whoa*, Nellie Belle! Amelior-*what?*"

"Um... ameliorate. It means..." As I tried to remember what the word meant, I felt my eyelids becoming heavy again, and resisted the urge to close them and go to sleep where I stood, horse-like.

"You don't need to define it for me, Arrow. I was responding to you like I'm one of your students. 'Huh? Amelior-*which?*' Y.E.S. students aren't here to study for the PSATs. They want to be able to read the cartoons on the back of a soda-pop can, and maybe get a good job, helping people fix their toasters over the telephone. They don't need your two-dollar vocab words to do that." Sam tilted back in his chair. "Continue."

"Okay." I squared my shoulders and said, "I am your new teacher. My name is Boyd. I will be teaching you how to read and write the English language." Sam nodded, and I continued, "I am very happy to be with you today. I have just recently moved here to your beautiful country. My own country is very different from yours. Where I come from, we—"

"Okay, Arrow. We all know where you come from. No need to give us a show-and-tell about the motherland." Sam's face looked tense. "You can take a seat."

"Was that all right?"

"You are *relatively eloquent*." He pronounced the phrase as if it were a foreign expression. "I get it. You can speak English." He put his hands flat on the desk and glowered at them. He remained like this for almost a minute, and I began to wonder if the interview might be over. Then he nodded to himself, coming to some kind of decision, and looked up at me. "Before our business relationship proceeds any further down the primrose path, I'd like to ask you another question that occurred to me during your little speech—just to clear the air." He tapped the side of his nose with his finger. "Do you love your country? The land where you and I were both born?"

"Sure. I'm very fond of it."

"Do you *love* it?"

I nodded gravely. "Yes."

"Well, you know what? I *don't* love your country."

"Oh. I guess it does have its pluses and minuses—"

"*Used* to love it. Yes, sir! Used to love it the best. But now I don't even *like* your country. I hate to use the 'hate' word, but, I *hate* your country. I hate your country because it drafted me and plunked me down into the middle of a hellish—pardon my French here—*clusterfuck* of a war. I hate your country because those pissants in your government wouldn't even let us *win* that war. And then I get back home to your country, and I'm hollered at by kids like you. Kids who smell like linseed oil, with greasy hair hanging down to their butts."

I reached up, running my fingers through my close-cropped hair, and opened my mouth to protest.

Sam jutted his chin out at me and continued, "Not that I didn't have long greasy hair myself back then. We all did. It was the style. That's not my point."

"I understand how you would feel—"

"Let me ask you this: do you plan on returning to your country?"

"Yes. Eventually."

"Will you do me a favor? Can I give you something to take back for me?"

"Sure." I pictured myself knocking on his mother's door and handing her a basket of pineapples. Then I pictured myself in an airport bathroom, swallowing a condom full of angel dust. "What exactly did you have in mind?"

"A little something, about yea big." He held his fingers a few inches apart. "A tiny little bottle."

"Okay."

"Tell you what," Sam said. "I'm going to take a piss in that bottle. I might even eat a bunch of asparagus beforehand, so my piss is nice and fragrant. But don't worry—I'll screw the cap on real tight. You can put it in the pocket of your blue jeans. Then, once you land on *firma terra*, and you disembark from the airplane, take that bottle out of your pocket... unscrew the cap..." He paused. "And then just pour that piss onto the ground."

I bobbed my head, straining to read his eyes through his sunglasses. "Okay."

"Because that's what I think of *your* country. Not my country anymore. This is my country now." He pointed at the floor. "If I could, I'd piss on the ground in person, but I don't have plans to visit there anytime soon; and, unfortunately, my Jimmy Jones isn't long enough to reach from here. *Almost*, but not quite." Then he parted his lips, revealing a set of square white teeth. I'm reasonably sure that he was smiling.

When I didn't respond, he stood up and said, "So—you can do this for me?"

I shook my head slowly, getting to my feet. "Sure."

"Okey doke." He held out a hand. "You got the job."

"That's great." We shook on it, and then I added: "The teaching job, you mean?"

Sam shrugged. "You can have that job, too."

As I walked back to where I'd parked my bicycle, the air felt soft and mild against my skin. I was glad to be out of that office, and glad to be employed. I looked up at the flat blue sky and watched the dragonflies clustering around the power lines, and a hopeful feeling began to gather in my chest.

Then I felt something else—something underneath the heel of my shoe. Something that felt hard and soft at once, as though I'd stepped on an Easter egg. I lifted my foot, revealing a dark and wet and formless lump on the ground. I bent down to get a closer look, then stepped back with a groan.

It was a tiny turtle, its shell split in half, smeared in gore. One of its legs was clawing uselessly at the air.

I stood frozen in place, watching it suffer and twitch, then looked around—the parking lot was empty—and brought my heel down and drove the turtle deeper into the dirt. When I lifted my foot again, there wasn't too much left to see.

I stared at it for a moment longer, watching for any remaining signs of life, then climbed onto my bicycle and pedaled quickly away.

Dear Hap:

Last night, a noise woke me up at around 2 AM. It was a sound so faint that I thought at first I might be imagining it, and I lay there for a while listening, trying to separate it from the other night noises: the sighs of Ulla asleep in the bed next to me, the hushed laughter of girls off in the distance, the sound of the wind dragging itself across the tops of trees. Beneath all of these was a sound that sounded as if it was right outside our door: *thib, thib, thub*. A dull, repetitive sound, like the sound of melting wax dripping into an empty plastic bucket.

I lifted my head off the pillow. At that angle, the sound became more distinct—no longer a dripping sound so much as the scraping of a key trying to find its way into a lock. *Click, click, scratch*. I sat up in bed, my brain buzzing with adrenaline, and the sound changed once again, now sounding like the plaintive door-scratch of a dog. Every time I shifted my head, the texture and amplification of the sound altered, the way a weak radio signal ebbs and flows with the slightest turn of the dial. I got up and walked quietly across the room and crouched down, so that I was now face to face with the sound. When I reached out and placed my palm on the door, the wood felt oddly cold to the touch.

What are you doing?

I jolted and spun around, as if someone had stuck a gun against my back.

Ulla laughed, and repeated: "What are you doing?"

"Do you hear that?"

"Hear what?"

"That noise outside. Listen." As we listened, it now seemed that the night had been leeched of all sound. "It was there before."

Ulla yawned in the darkness. "Let's go to sleep, Boyd."

I sighed, then stood and returned to my bed. "There was a weird sound outside. You really didn't hear anything?"

"I don't think so." Ulla was quiet for a moment. "But I was just having a horrible nightmare. I was in a super-dirty bathroom, and my bare butt accidentally touched the wall." She laughed and added, "You were there, too. You were trying to have sex with me. Ugh."

"Sounds nightmarish."

"No, it's just that the bathroom was so gross… it's hard to explain. I'm not positive it was even you, actually." Ulla pulled the sheet up over her face. "Now I have the heebie-jeebies."

"Because of that creepy noise outside."

"If you say so."

"Want to get in my bed? I promise not to try to have sex with you."

"It's kind of hot for snuggling, don't you think?"

"I won't try to snuggle you, either."

"Okay." Ulla climbed in next to me and rolled over on her side. "You can try to have sex with me if you want. Maybe wait until I fall asleep first. I might like that."

I kissed her on the back of the head and then held my breath and listened for a minute, glancing over my shoulder at the door. "Okay," I whispered. "Let me know when you're asleep."

But she already was.

Dear Hap:

Behind the Hi-Fi Cafeteria is a market with vendors selling grilled meats and paper kites and deep-fried candy bars and *Gong* beer, and along the edge of the market is a street lined with shops and bars and restaurants, including a café called Golden Cowboy Place, which is where I'm sitting right now. I was initially drawn here because of the intricate hand-carved wooden sign out front, and also because it looks like a Wild West saloon you'd see at some run-down amusement park. Ulla and I sometimes stop by after dinner and have a couple of drinks and watch the students criss-cross the bumpy terrain of the market at top speed on their mopeds. It's a good way to kill some time before returning to our small, shadowless room at *Home Kwan Home*.

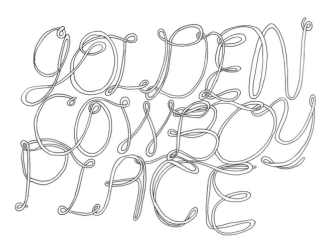

Lately I've been wondering if gravity's pull isn't maybe a little weaker on this side of the planet, affecting the curve of space-time and making the hours pass more slowly. The evenings feel especially long: every night I either sit outside on my trash can and drink beer and read, or sit inside and drink beer and play dominoes with Ulla. We've learned several new variations on the game, including "Seven-Toed Pete," "The Big Clock," and "Chickenhead." Yesterday I realized that I'm on the verge of running out of books, and I felt like a submarine captain discovering that his ship was dangerously low on air.

I sometimes wonder how you experience time, Hap. I remember reading a book once theorizing that a person is like a piece of paper, and time is like a ballpoint pen passing through that paper. The point where the pen and paper intersect is the moment in time that we are currently experiencing:

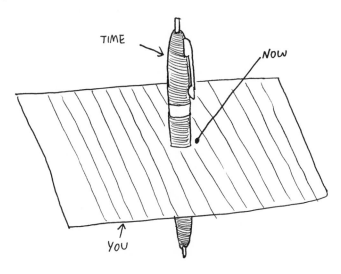

The idea is that the body of time—past, present and future—already exists, but can't be experienced all at once, and so I (the piece of paper) can only experience time (the ballpoint pen) moment by moment, as it passes through me. What about you? Do you experience the ballpoint pen all at once? Or maybe you're a blank sheet of paper, waiting for a new pen to poke a hole in you.

Although Ulla and I haven't been here long, it somehow feels as though we've been living in Puchai for years. I don't start teaching at Y.E.S. for another few weeks, and I'd been planning to make use of all my free time and try to improve myself— learn to cook, study Puchanese, maybe do some pushups—but all I actually do is drink ice coffee and smoke cigarettes and wander around campus, waiting for Ulla to get off work.

Ulla's job isn't what she'd thought it would be—she hasn't yet been assigned any Expo-related tasks, and spends most of her days running errands for Haraporn and making small talk with Miaw. Her excitement about Puchai reached a fever pitch back in New York and has been steadily diminishing since we arrived. There are a lot of small things that conspire to make Ulla unhappy here. She doesn't like the strange smells in the air—the unpredictable mixture of burning plastic and roasting meat and rotting *garongs* and honeysuckle and car exhaust; she doesn't like the lack of a telephone and the lack of a television; she doesn't like the fact that you can't open your mouth in the shower because even one swallow of water could give you the runs; she doesn't like the lizards in our room or the turtles all over campus, constantly underfoot. The one thing she does enjoy is a dessert they serve at the cafeteria: a hot-dog bun filled with soybean ice cream, then smothered in creamed corn.

Our life in Puchai definitely isn't the tropical idyll that we'd been anticipating. I'd imagined the two of us browning our skin in the sun, our bodies becoming lean and muscular from constant exercise and clean living. I'd imagined us making love on a hot, flat rock next to a medium-sized waterfall. I'd imagined all traces of the White Sikh evaporating from my memory permanently.

So far, none of this has happened.

I first learned about Ulla and the White Sikh due to a random occurrence: I was sitting on the subway, reading a book that I'd borrowed from Ulla, when a small square of graph paper slipped out of the pages and fluttered to the ground. Written on it, in Ulla's handwriting, was the beginning of a list:

1. Shetland, not horse
2. Case of Lady burn
3.

I spent a minute re-reading these words and trying to puzzle out their meaning before folding the paper back up and using it to mark my page. I forgot about it until later that night, when Ulla came over to my apartment. We were watching *Wheel of Fortune* and eating overcooked spaghetti when, out of the blue, I asked: "What is 'Shetland, not horse'?"

Ulla regarded me blankly.

"Or, 'a bad case of lady burn'?"

Something changed in Ulla's face, and she said, carefully: "What are you talking about?"

I went and retrieved the piece of paper for her. She squinted her eyes as if the words were written in a language she didn't understand.

"I... I'm not sure what this is," she said.

I took the list out of her hand and studied it. "You wrote it, didn't you?"

"It was just a *joke*." Her cheeks were the queasy pink color of salt-water taffy. "You really want me to explain the whole boring story?"

"What kind of a joke," I said, watching her closely.

"I was talking to Shawn, asking him what he wanted for Christmas—"

"You were asking your boss what he wanted for Christmas?"

"It was at the holiday party. I was just making conversation. He started telling me what he wanted, and I started writing it down. Like, pretending to make a list. We were both just kidding around."

"'Shetland, not horse'?"

"He wanted a Shetland pony. He specified a pony. It was just a joke," she repeated, balling up her fists and pressing them against her chest. Something about this gesture alarmed me more than anything she'd told me so far.

"'Lady burn'?"

"It's a type of whisky." Ulla took the list from me and held it close to her eyes. "I think it should be one word, not two."

She lowered the piece of paper, and I saw that her face was glazed with tears. And that was when she confessed that she and the White Sikh had developed feelings for one another.

I was too stunned to say anything for a while. Then I asked if anything had happened between them.

"No," said Ulla.

"It's better if you just tell me the truth. I won't be angry." I tried to make my voice sound like the voice of someone who wouldn't be angry.

"Absolutely nothing," she said.

Later that night—after going out with her friends from high school, drinking several Black Russians, returning to my apartment, and puking in my bathtub—Ulla admitted to me that, for the past month and a half, she and the White Sikh had been meeting up in the stairwell during their lunch hour and making out. She swore that this was as far as it had gone, and told me she was going to break it off with him on Monday morning. She told me that she didn't understand what was happening to her, that it was as if she'd had a fever, and she felt like she'd become someone else—someone she didn't even recognize. She told me she'd been lost and confused but that this had been a wake-up call, and she was over the whole thing now. She told me that it was never going to happen again.

After that, we went through an extended rough patch: I stopped sleeping, Ulla stopped eating, and we both lost ten pounds. My left eye started twitching spasmodically—so much so that I actually considered wearing an eye patch. Ulla quit smoking and I started smoking again and lost another seven pounds. Ulla dyed her hair dark brown, and I grew a sparse, prickly beard. What really bothered me was that the whole thing was so out of character for Ulla—she was the most practical person I'd ever met, and making out with her boss in the stairwell during office hours was a wildly impractical course of action. If Ulla was capable of this, then the world was a more unpredictable and dangerous place than I'd thought.

During those weeks, when things were feeling hopeless, I often found myself thinking back to the first night that Ulla and I met. It's a story that we'd always enjoyed telling to other people, and it gave me comfort when I re-told it to myself.

It had been an abnormally cold autumn the year that Ulla entered my life, and I was in a bad place: I was supposed to have graduated from NYU the previous June, but, halfway through my final semester, I'd mysteriously lost all motivation to complete my senior thesis paper (*Loplop Introduces Loplop: The Curious World of Max Ernst*), instead choosing to spend my time writing and drawing an improvisational and plotless comic book (*The Beholder*) that depicted the eponymous Dungeons & Dragons character in a variety of humiliating situations. (You probably remember The Beholder from your D&D days—he was the giant floating eyeball, also known as "The Eye Tyrant.")

I'd moved from the dorms into a tiny apartment in Chinatown, and was ostensibly putting the finishing touches on my paper so that I could finally get my degree. However, not only had I been avoiding my thesis, but my procrastination had become so bad that I'd even abandoned *The Beholder*. Instead of concentrating on either of these projects, I'd been spending my evenings taking long hot baths, drinking beer, and slowly making my way through *The Annotated Moby Dick*.

My day job at the time was working for my neighbor, a woman in her mid-fifties named Corrine Hewitt who ran a tiny, lesbian-themed bookshop in the West Village. (The store was called *Her Lavender Reader*, but Corrine once referred to it as *Read It to Beaver* and I was never able to think of it by any other name after that.) Working there turned out to be the best job I'd ever had: Corrine and I would hang around all day smoking cigarettes, playing dominoes, and listening to NPR. On the Friday before Halloween, Corrine informed me she was hosting a party in her home and that attendance was mandatory for all *Read It to Beaver* employees.

I left my apartment that night dressed in Poppy's old houndstooth suit, a Santa Claus hat-and-beard combo, and a set of rubber vampire fangs. Corrine had moved into a loft in Red Hook, and I spent half an hour wandering up and down the unfamiliar streets before I found the converted slaughterhouse where she now lived. Despite my relative lateness, the only other guests were a few older women clustered around a hollowed-out loaf of bread filled with Corrine's Famous Five-Cup Salad (equal parts mandarin oranges, crushed pineapple, mini marshmallows, flaked coconut, and sour cream). I was helping myself to a beer from the fridge when I heard a voice behind me say, "That you, Darrow?"

Corrine was dressed as an old-time newsie in an oversized cap, wool trousers rolled up to the knee, and paisley suspenders, with enormous red freckles drawn onto her cheeks. In one hand she clutched a stack of newspapers, and in the other, she cradled the elbow of a tall blonde girl who looked as if she was waiting for an opportunity to bolt for the door.

I raised my eyebrows and grunted—it was hard to talk through those rubber teeth—and Corrine handed me a paper. "*Extra! Extra! Read all about it!*" The headline read:

FIRST LADY ON THE MOON!

"Boyd Darrow, Ulla Liptauer," Corrine said, grabbing my shoulder and pulling me towards the girl. "Ulla Liptauer, Boyd Darrow. You two are the only younger folks here, so I thought you should meet." She gave Ulla an appraising look, then stage-whispered to me, "Isn't she *attractive*, Boyd?"

Ulla wore a clingy, toga-like sheet, and there were black rubber snakes intertwined with her strawberry-blonde hair. She had an elegant ski-jump of a nose, and large blue eyes that regarded me dubiously.

"*Ice oo eet oo*," I said. Then I lifted my beard, took the fangs out of my mouth, and repeated: "Nice to meet you."

"Boyd, try not to be such a half-wit. Ulla, he's actually very sweet." Corrine tucked in my shirt collar and straightened my beard. "Not a college graduate, technically, but totally drug-free." She pressed my wrist against Ulla's, as if forcing us into some kind of pact, then scampered away.

Ulla watched Corrine depart, and, after considering her other social options, turned back to me. We made small talk for a while: she told me that she studied theater at Barnard, and was currently stage-managing a production of *A Doll's House* that had an all-South African cast and was set in the year 2525. I explained my graduation situation, and told her that I was working at *Read It to Beaver* but was thinking of quitting because I felt uncomfortable about not being a lesbian. She was simultaneously disturbed and impressed by the fact that I worked at Corrine's shop. "I've heard about you," she said. It turned out that she'd come to the party with her professor—the playwright Patreesha B.—who also happened to be Corrine's girlfriend. It was then that I had a fleeting but vivid sensation that Ulla was not just some random girl at a party, but a person who had entered my life for a reason. I asked her if she wanted to sneak out with me and go find something else to drink.

Ulla and I went around the corner to an old longshoreman's bar that was empty except for an old woman playing pinball. As we drank our whiskey sours, Ulla slowly removed her snakes and placed them in a neat pile on the table. When she was done, she tied her hair behind her head with a rubber band, revealing a small silver hoop earring high up on her left ear. For some reason, I felt a warm twinge in my blood when I saw that earring. I listened to her talk about her career goals and her father's new summerhouse in Maine, and as she spoke I stared at her earring and at her pale oval face. Her cheeks were flushed and glowing from the cold, and at certain moments, seen from certain angles, she looked genuinely beautiful; then she would move her head ever so slightly, and appeared strikingly plain. The effect reminded me of that poster that Poppy used to have hanging on the wall in his garage: the illustration of a rabbit that, on second glance, became a drawing of a duck. While Ulla talked, I tilted my head from side to side, watching her change back and forth—*rabbit/duck, rabbit/duck*—until she asked what I was doing and I stopped.

When we left the bar, ghostly streaks of snow were whipping back and forth between the heavy gray buildings, and Ulla and I huddled together as we walked down Van Brunt. Apart from a small black cat sitting on a trash can on the corner, the street was deserted.

"It was very nice to meet you," said Ulla, leaning against the bus shelter. "I'd like you to have these."

She pressed something into my hands. I looked down and saw that she'd given me a handful of snakes.

"Will you do me a favor?" she asked. "Can you put on your costume again?"

I shoved the snakes into my pocket and pulled the Santa mask over my face, combing the beard out with my fingers. "How's that?"

"And the teeth."

I put the fangs in my mouth and posed, arms akimbo.

Ulla studied me thoughtfully. "You're *tall*," she said, then leaned in and kissed me on the mouth, hard. The plastic fangs cut into my gums—I could taste a hint of blood on my tongue—but somehow it didn't occur to me to take them out. I slid my hands underneath Ulla's coat, feeling her warm skin through the thin cotton bedsheet wrapped around her body.

As we stood there kissing in the snow, a black Lincoln Town Car glided quietly past, then braked and backed up until it was alongside us. A small elderly man—neatly dressed in a dark suit and tie, with a chauffeur's cap on his head—got out and walked in our direction. His left leg dragged behind him slightly, as though it had fallen asleep.

The man came right up and stood beside us, coughing noisily into his sleeve. I ignored him, hoping he'd take the hint and leave us alone. He cleared his throat, spat onto the street, and said, "Hello! Excuse me, my friends."

I pulled away from Ulla and looked at the man. I couldn't quite place his accent—it sounded both Mexican and somehow Transylvanian—and he appeared weirdly foreshortened, as though viewed through the wrong end of a telescope.

"Can I offer a ride to you, my friends?" he asked, touching the brim of his cap.

I removed my fangs. "No, thanks."

"Let me tell you this," he said. "I'm a licensed livery cab, and can take you to any borough."

"Look," I said, lifting my beard, "we're kind of in the middle of something right now, so—"

"Sir, it's very cold. It's snowing, and it's not even November yet. Inside my car, it's nice and hot."

I took out my wallet and displayed my last two dollars, hoping to discourage him. "This is all the money I have. Sorry."

"That's fine."

"But... we're going into the city."

"I'm going there anyway." The man gave me a sad smile, as if he were accustomed to passengers being unable to pay him, and I once again had the strange sense that this was all predetermined—that this man had been waiting to deliver us through the cold night to our destination.

I turned to Ulla. "You want a ride home?"

Ulla brushed her hair behind her ear and quietly hiccupped. "Okay. If you think it's all right."

The man opened the back door of the car and we slid in. The interior smelled like chewing tobacco and lavender oil, and Ulla's toga glowed beneath the blacklight that illuminated the back seat. As the man started the engine, the opening chords of "Lover Believer" came blasting out of the speakers:

It's been a long bad road headin' God knows where
And I'm feelin' like Barabbas today
I'm like a big round peg tryin' to stick it to a square
I wanna talk but I got nothin' to say
Lord, I wish my body had...
the spirit of BELIEVING!

I leaned forward and said to the driver, "Just take the BQE to the bridge, and we'll tell you where to go from there."

"All right, then," he said. "You make yourself at home."

"Do I need to tell him which bridge?" I asked Ulla.

"I don't know." Ulla patted the backseat. "This feels like it's covered in rubber," she whispered. "It's like—" She let out several hiccups that segued into a fit of giggles.

"Like those plastic sheets. For bed-wetters," I said, leaning over and kissing her, the music swelling as if we were in a movie:

Well, I wrote my own ticket but I missed the train
Now I'm thinkin' 'bout ending it all
But your warm-blooded lovin's gonna make me insane
Don't you know you are the woman I call
When I want to be with someone...
Who's not ever LEAVING!

I pulled Ulla closer to me and pressed her body against mine. When I closed my eyes, I saw tiny white snowflakes rushing at me through the darkness.

The next time I opened my eyes and looked out the window, we were on Beard Street, driving past a long soccer field. I caught a glimpse of the driver's reflection in the rear-view mirror: he wore a pained grimace on his face, as if he was being tickled and couldn't decide if he liked it or not.

I whispered to Ulla, "Isn't the BQE in the other direction?"

She leaned across my lap and squinted. "We're totally going the wrong way." Smoothing her toga over her knees, she yelled over the music: "We need to get on the Brooklyn Bridge!"

The man flashed a curdled grin and turned down the radio. "I thought you might want to drive around for a while, enjoy the beautiful night. For the mere price of two dollars."

"We don't want to drive around," I said. "You can just start heading toward the bridge."

The driver nodded. "All right, then."

I slumped back into the seat. "He's going to turn around," I told Ulla. "He said so."

Ulla took the Santa Claus mask out of my pocket and tried it on. "Ho ho ho," she said, pushing her face toward mine, the long white beard shining eerily in the blacklight. I closed my eyes and put my mouth on Santa's plump, moist lips.

A few minutes later, I broke away from Ulla and said to the driver: "Hey—can you take us into the city. Please. Now." I didn't recognize where we were, but it wasn't anywhere near the bridge.

The driver stopped at a red light and turned around in his seat. "Tell you what. We'll just go up here to Coffey Street, to avoid the construction. Then I have to go to Myrtle and Throop to make a quick pit-stop. And then we'll go into the city." He reached up and flicked off the blacklight. "Perhaps you'll be more comfortable in the dark?"

I groped my hand blindly along the side of the door, but felt only smooth molded plastic. I thought about how you'd once told me, Hap, that the doors in the backseat of a cop car don't have handles, and how scary it was to be trapped back there.

"Can't you *do* something?" Ulla whispered.

I emptied my pockets, pulling out handfuls of snakes until I found a lighter. In the flickering light of the flame, I glimpsed the door handle and yanked on it. It was locked.

"Sir, take us to the nearest subway right now and let us out there," I said.

The man looked back at me, frowning, and spoke as if to a complaining child. "I need to pick up a client at my nephew's, and *then* we'll go to your house. This client is a wealthy man, with a wonderful collection of antique cameras. You both should become cozy in the backseat in the meanwhile. You'll be delivered presently." He leaned forward and felt around for something on the floor. I thought I saw him pick up a small black shiny metal object, and I felt the blood begin to rush up into my head. The driver weighed the object in his hand, then put it back down and picked up something else: a furry white blanket.

"Spread it on the seat," he said, tossing it back to us. The fur was matted and slightly greasy. "Made from real rabbits," he added.

I dropped the thing on the floor and looked out the window. The streets were dark and empty, and I had absolutely no idea where we were. The man and I exchanged another glance in the mirror. He was sucking on his lower lip, and his eyes were like two ping-pong balls colored in with a black magic marker. I blinked and looked away, feeling suddenly as if I couldn't breathe, and wondered if it was possible to pass out while sitting down. I put my hands flat on the rubbery seat and tried to think of what to do next.

When we recite our story to people, Ulla usually jumps in at this point and tells how I managed to unlock the door at a red light, throwing two fistfuls of rubber snakes into the front seat before we jumped out of the car, and how the driver let out a bloodcurdling series of shrieks that followed us as we ran down the dark wind-filled street, laughing. She tells about how I started singing at the top of my lungs, and how she joined in and sang with me:

Now I understand... I'm a LOVER BELIEVER!
If she runs away from me... I'll GO AND RETRIEVE HER!
'Cuz she's my angel sweet... my GOLDEN RECEIVER!
Girl, I'll climb inside your world... every day.

At the end of the storytelling, Ulla talks about how much she liked my costume and my tallness, and how funny it was when I threw the snakes at the driver, and I always say how happy I was that she wasn't a lesbian, and how nice she looked in her toga. We talk about the small semi-coincidences that conspired to bring us together, and we speculate about what might've happened to us if we hadn't escaped that car. We talk about how, in a certain way, it was the perfect first date.

But, we haven't told that story to anyone for a while now.

Dear Hap:

Since Ulla and I arrived in Mai Mor, we've hardly seen any signs of life around *Home Kwan Home*—for some reason, it's always eerily deserted. I was beginning to think we might be the only people living here. This morning, though, I met a neighbor. His name is Mr. Horse.

I'd just finished eating a late breakfast and was washing the dishes in the bathroom sink when I heard music coming from the courtyard. I went to the window and saw a white-shirted student sitting on a bamboo mat in the grass, playing an acoustic guitar. I decided to go introduce myself.

The student looked up when I opened the door and broke into a wide smile, as if he'd been expecting me. He made the shooing-away motion with his hand, and I gave him a backwards wave and walked over.

"Hello!" he said, getting to his feet. "Greeting." He was slender and bookish-looking, about twenty years old, with an oblong, melancholy face, and floppy black bangs parted carefully in the middle of his forehead. "My name is Ratanankorn Chulalongkorn." He pointed across the way. "I am living there."

"It's good to meet you—Ra... tan... an... ana... korn. I live here." I pointed at my apartment door. "My name's Boyd," I added, *hai*-ing him.

He *hai*-ed me back, then offered me his hand, gripping and bending my fingers as if demonstrating a self-defense technique on me. His pinkie nail was three times longer than his other fingernails.

"If it is simpler, you can call me Máa," he said, releasing my hand. "This is the familiar name."

"Maa?"

"No, no." He smiled again. "That means, 'Dog.' You are calling me 'Dog.'"

"I'm sorry. How do you say it?"

"Máa."

I hesitated a moment, then repeated: "*Maa.*"

"No. You are saying to me, 'Come.' Listen: *Maa.* That means, 'Come.' Now listen: *Mäa.*" His voice rose at the end of the word, as if it were a question. "That means, 'Dog.'"

"Okay."

"Now listen: *Máa.*" This time, he pronounced the word with a low tone at the end. "That means, 'Horse.' That is my name."

"I understand. I'm very sorry."

"That is all right. You do not speak our language yet. You can call me Horse if it is easier."

"No, I'll get it. Maa?"

"'Dog.'"

"Maa. Maa?"

"'Come.' 'Dog.'"

I pitched my voice an octave higher and said, "*Maa!*"

He nodded. "You can call me Horse," he said. "Call me Mr. Horse."

"Okay. Mr. Horse. Thank you."

Mr. Horse invited me to sit with him on his mat. I offered him a cigarette, which he declined, making an apologetic coughing noise. As he began tuning his guitar, I asked, "What are you studying here at Mai Mor?"

"I am a student of the School of Science of Veterinary. Are you too a student?"

"No, I'm here because my girlfriend—wife—got a job at the Faculty of Theatre Drama. She's helping to organize the big show in April. For the Festival of... *Tang*."

Mr. Horse held his finger in the air. "We say: Festival of *Taang Lôke Kwaam Ban-terng Sumitchanani*."

"*Tang... low... kwam... bantern... summitchinanni.*"

Mr. Horse smiled and nodded. "No. *Taang. Lôke. Kwaam. Ban-terng. Sumitchanani.*"

"Got it," I said, shutting my eyes, as if committing the pronunciation to memory. "What does that mean, exactly?"

"Ah... hmm. It is not simple to explain. In our religion, the way to stop from being born and born, again and again, is to lose feeling of *wanting* for the world. Do you know?"

"You believe that suffering is caused by attachment to desires, and you try to achieve enlightenment by letting go of your attachment to this world, thereby breaking the cycle of rebirth—right?" I had just skimmed the *Religious Beliefs* section of the guidebook a few days earlier.

"Yes, you are understanding. We are always living and thinking about how to end desires. But, on the day of Festival of *Taang*, we forget the religion thinking, and make party to enjoy of living on Earth." Mr. Horse looked thoughtfully at a turtle crawling past us on the grass. "In general, 'Festival of *Taang Lôke Kwaam Ban-terng Sumitchanani*' is meaning: 'Festival Day of enjoy the pleasant feeling of this saddest world by being drunken, and kissing the neighbor, and become carried away with dancing to traditional music, before you become dead and do not have body for enjoying.'" He touched his finger to his lips. "How would you say this idea in English?"

"We might say something like, 'the Festival of... *Worldly Pleasures*,'" I said. "Or... I don't know. 'Earthly Delights.'"

"That is good." Mr. Horse played a few chords on his guitar and then grinned. "I called hello to your wife this morning, but she did not wish to speak. She is very shy. And, may I honor you and say, the wife is so handsome and slim! Her face looks bold, like the *ngoo*—the giant river-turtle—and her hair is golden, and her skin is white like the bottom of a fish."

I nodded. "True, true."

"Very beautiful. My skin is dark. Not beautiful. Very ugly." He chuckled ruefully and scratched at his cheek, as if trying to remove the pigment.

"No, your skin is... beautiful also."

"I am sorry, no. Very black and ugly."

"In my country, we have an expression. We say: 'Black is beautiful.'"

"Yes?" Mr. Horse raised his eyebrows. "I was understanding that, in your country, the darker person is not loved. He is as a dog."

"No, that's not—"

"In the films, he is a poor man, and must shoot guns and selling drug to have money for his group of women."

"No, no, no."

"But it is true that the dark skin brings sadness in your land? And I would be hated there?"

"I mean... no. It's not really like that, exactly. For example: people pay money to lie down inside machines with bright lights, as if lying in the sunshine, and they make their skin dark so they can look more like you."

"No!"

"Yes, it's true. You're very lucky. You *always* look tan."

Mr. Horse slowly shook his head. "That is very crazy! Maybe I must visit your country."

"You should," I said. "You'd be very popular there."

"Yesterday, I hear you playing the Angel & Mann song many times in your home—the song like this?" Mr. Horse began to strum the opening chords to "Black + White" and said, "The song about the white man and black man! I would love to hear your English singing of it."

I laughed. "I'm not much of a singer…"

"Please? It would be an honor."

I tilted my head and listened to Mr. Horse play, then said, "Let me think. I'm not exactly sure how it goes." I cleared my throat, and when Mr. Horse nodded to me, I started in, mimicking the deep baritone of "Mann":

Humans… they act so funny some days
They say the world is a hell,
a… foul sty, and… something… hey

Yeah, people… they're always… something… each other
Go to war and fight their brothers
Keep their dum-dum under covers…

Mr. Horse jumped in here, approximating Angel's falsetto:
I having messy
I'm the writing in a sky
Lock up air people,
Learning way to live alive…

And together, we sang:
Black and white, unite!
Black and white, unite!

Mr. Horse:
You a coffee in my tea…

Me:
...I'm the bitter in your greens

Mr. Horse:
I'm a peachy in a cream...

Me:
...You're the killer in my dreams!

I started laughing—I was just making stuff up by that point. "Nice work, Mr. Horse," I said. "You sound just like a Bee Gee."

He bowed his head. "You too have a special sound of voice. It is like the cry of a dog outside the—ah, Mr. Boyd, no!"

I felt my elbow brush against something cold and hard, and looked over my shoulder: I'd almost leaned back onto a turtle on the grass. Mr. Horse bowed to it, mumbling under his breath, then carefully picked it up and placed it on my lap. "We must honor the turtle," he said. "It is spirit protector of Mai Mor. It is very religious."

I gently stroked its shell. "Yeah, they're everywhere. I've never seen so many turtles in one place."

"They stay in Mai Mor town for they understand to be safe, because nobody eat him here." He frowned and added, "Some men say they see the *malchak* eat turtle. But, *malchak* have hearts made of black."

"Nobody seems to like the *malchaks* very much."

"They are—" Mr. Horse made a face as if he'd just swallowed a mothball. "They are *pônge*. They come from the hills, and their skin very dark—more dark than my skin—and they work for job of dig a hole, or sell thing at market, stupid toy, like the box with bug inside. The bug says noise: *ree-pip, ree-pip, ree-pip.* You know this toy?" I shook my head.

"*Malchak* live at Mòk Bòo—the junk-town on river. Do not visit the junk-town, never—very dangerous. The *malchak* are always drink *garong* liquor, and steal, and make violence to you." Mr. Horse gently placed his hand on the turtle's shell. "But most times, *malchak* do not eat turtle. They know they have the curse upon them if eating."

"A curse?"

He nodded. "In old time, the man and turtle live together in Mai Mor with no fighting—always love. But, late in modern time, men forget the tradition belief, and do not care if they kill turtle with a car and then cook it into *pêt* soup. Turtle become to be less, and not many numbers remain. Then, at the time when the college was building in Mai Mor, many bad thing happen to our town. Two big building fall down, and seven men were kill under, plus many *malchak*. Every day, car and bus crash and having violence. One small girl gone from her family, and later find her under river, with cut on the body, like cuts from paper. A bad spirit come on Mai Mor town, and many family exit. But there was one monk of Mai Mor who save us: Mr. Purit Songpole Phammawattaana—the famous man who Expo stage is name for. He talk to town people, tell how we forgot turtle tradition and bring curse on us. Town people have fear, confusion, and they listen to Mr. Purit Songpole Phammawattaana and build the spirit house for turtle—the house here, next to *Home Kwan Home*—and make very beautiful, so turtle spirit will forgive and will live inside spirit house and not make troubles."

"And it worked?"

"Yes. The trouble stop, and the college was finish building, and numbers of turtle begin to grow again in town. Now, man and turtle have strong friendship. All citizens understanding tradition: if men hurt turtle, kill or eat, you have curse. Maybe you not die, but there other ways the curse come at you."

I glanced warily at the turtle on my lap. "Like... how?"

"Oh! There are many different curse." Mr. Horse began to count them on his fingers. "One curse is call 'Great-Pretender.' This is when you see and hear things that no others can see and hear—baby insects made from metal, or the bird with no face. One curse is 'Brown-Eye-Girl,' that is, a need to use toilet when no toilet is near. 'Splish-Splash' is the curse that is to have a small vomit come up into your mouth. For the turtle-killer-man, 'Ninety-Six-Tears' is a curse to have lack when being with any woman, not have enough excitement. The 'Taste-of-Honey' is when man is fast to have *over*-much excitement with the woman—if you understand. And one of the most feared curse is: 'Final-Countdown.' When the turtle-killer plays a lottery, he will get all number perfect, but for final number is wrong. Every time." Mr. Horse widened his eyes. "It will make you to be *crazy*."

"Can you get rid of the curse somehow?"

"The turtle-killer can make peace by offering the gift to spirit house. If a turtle spirit take the gift, then curse is gone. You must bring the Johnnie Walker whiskey, or the fancy pork."

I couldn't help but think about that turtle I'd stepped on outside Sam's office. I briefly considered bringing something for the turtles, but rejected the idea as being too crazy, and too expensive.

"Turtle spirits eat pork?" I asked.

"Yes. If you return the next day, the pork is gone. The turtle will eat it. The spirit is always with a great hunger." He gently removed the turtle from my lap and placed it back on the grass.

The turtle scrutinized me with its flat black eyes, as if memorizing my face, and then turned away.

Dear Hap:

Did you see what happened today? Were you watching? Or maybe you're so far away that it didn't look like much of anything: a swarm of spiders spitting on a cornflake. I wish you'd been there. I could've used your help.

A few hours ago I wandered up Pamarassam Road, trying to decide what to do with myself. Ulla was going out after work to drink beer and eat fried chicken livers with the women of the Faculty of Theatre Drama—apparently a traditional girls'-night-out in Puchai—so I had some time to kill. There was a big group of students walking in front of me, and when they all turned off at the soccer field, I caught sight of Sam's daughter standing on the corner. Shiney. I didn't recognize her at first because she had this funny green visor on her head that made her look like a child dressed as a bookie. Next to her stood a black-bearded *gareng* guy wearing seersucker pants and a tight-fitting green polo shirt with the collar flipped up. He had a Prince Valiant haircut and excellent posture, and was emphatically chopping at the air with his hands as he spoke. The girl didn't seem to be listening to him; she kept taking her visor off and looking inside it, as if double-checking the size, then putting it back on her head. I didn't want them to see me—I'm not sure why, exactly—

so I stood still for a minute or so, watching. Then they turned and began to walk up the hill, and, on a whim, I decided to follow them.

It was now clear to me that they were having an argument. Shiney was a little ahead of the guy, and he gestured at her, palms up, as if saying: *What the hell's your problem?* She stared fixedly down at her visor. The *gareng* stopped walking and put his hands on his hips, but Shiney just kept going, not looking back. The guy glanced around to see if anyone had seen this, and I reflexively stooped down and pretended to tie my shoe. Then he ran to catch up with her, and they walked side by side without speaking for a while.

They passed the Hi-Fi Cafeteria, and I followed them down the dirt road where I'd first seen Shiney last week. A few minutes later they entered the path that leads back to *Home Kwan Home.* I quickened my pace, and when I reached the fork in the woods—the place marked by the dead dog—I stood still for a moment, straining to hear which way they'd gone. I could only make out the sounds of the forest at first: the wind in the treetops, a jabbering bird, and the dry crackle of insects moving among dead leaves. Then I heard a laugh, or maybe a yell. It sounded as though it came from the overgrown trail that led downhill, away from *Home Kwan Home.* I found myself stepping over the corpse of the dog and heading down into the underbrush.

I hurried along the path, treading lightly and occasionally glancing back over my shoulder, as if I were the one being followed. The path snaked haphazardly through the forest, doubling back on itself several times, then grew wider and more clear-cut before abruptly tapering off into a bank of red and purple grass. I could just barely make out a subtle indentation there, like the ghost of a deer trail. It seemed like the end of the line.

I thought about turning around—and then, I thought about you. I pictured you in a forest like this one, hacking at the thicket with a machete. Pushing your way towards the buzzing hive in the distance.

Let's try to go a little farther.

Just then, I heard the sound of a woman laughing somewhere close by. I decided to make myself known to them—tell them that I'd been exploring the woods and had gotten lost. I put my head down and entered the sharp grass, pushing forward and emerging moments later into a clearing. No one was there.

In the center of the clearing stood a small, egg-like boulder, and on either side of the boulder, two new paths began. I crouched and studied the jumble of mud and rocks and grass. I thought I could make out a small footprint pointing toward the overgrown path on the right, and I started down it, charging through clusters of thorny brush that lashed at my arms.

After a minute I arrived at a massive spider web that spanned the width of the path like a lace curtain, and I knew that no one had been walking here recently. The light was beginning to fade from the forest, and I checked my watch: it was almost six. My pursuit of these people now struck me as being pointless, and also vaguely creepy.

Let's just go a little farther.

But I decided to ignore you and head home. It was easy enough to find my way back to the clearing, but the strange thing was, there now were three different paths radiating out from the egg-shaped boulder, rather than only two, and the high bank of grass that I'd emerged from was nowhere in sight. Everything blurred together in the unearthly, greenish glow of dusk—rocks, paths, leaves, grass, trees, sky—and I felt the first hint of panic flutter in my chest.

I selected a path at random and started walking. It was lined with beds of tiny red flowers that I hadn't noticed before, and the ground felt soft underfoot, as if there were heaps of deflated basketballs buried just beneath the dirt. I turned around and sprinted back to the egg-shaped boulder. On second glance, though, it wasn't exactly egg-shaped—it looked more like a half-melted candle. Was it even the same rock? I looked for the other paths. In the dimming light, it was difficult to tell what was a path and what wasn't. I went down one trail that seemed promising until it ended abruptly at a fallen tree. I ran back to the rock and spun around in place three times. I now had no idea which direction I'd come from. I thought about simply staying at the rock, which was my only remaining point of reference—although, of course, that made no sense at all. Now that I looked at it more closely, this rock once again seemed unfamiliar. Was it yet another rock—a third rock? It looked like neither an egg nor a candle. This rock had the shape of a crushed muffin.

You're being retarded. You're not in the middle of the rainforest—you're on a college campus.

"I know," I said aloud.

So just pick a path and follow it until you're out of the woods.

"Fine. I will."

I selected the trail that appeared the most well-worn, and within a few minutes I was walking down some makeshift stone steps built into the side of the hill. They were slick with spring water, and I steadied myself by grabbing onto the trunks of the gray saplings on either side. Eventually the ground became level again, and up ahead, I glimpsed a strip of purple sky through the trees. I began to run towards it.

When I emerged from the forest, I felt dizzy with relief. I was on a grassy ridge that sloped gently down towards the bank of the Ngoo-pìk River, fifty yards below. I realized I was standing on the outskirts of Mòk Bòo—the place that Mr. Horse had warned me about. The place where the *malchaks* lived.

The river ran wide there, the water glassy and blood-colored in the fading sun. On the opposite bank stood a grove of yellow trees, their branches heavy with fluorescent-orange *garongs*. Mossy limestone peaks loomed in the far distance like gigantic statues worn smooth by the weather of the centuries. Three dog-sized bats were inching across the horizon, blimp-like, seemingly suspended by some force other than their slowly flapping wings. The entire scene was bathed in a light that had an uncanny, flattening quality to it, and the air was filled with a fine white mist that made objects appear lit from within. I had the sensation of seeing all things with equal clarity: the grass beneath my feet and the bats above the tree line had equal weight and detail, coexisting on the same two-dimensional plane.

A gray slip of road ran alongside the river, empty except for a drunk-looking chicken and a young girl carrying a bicycle. Old women stood knee-deep in the water doing laundry, dipping pants and shirts into the current and then slapping them indifferently against the rocks. Along the bank were rows of shacks patched together from scraps of painted tin, driftwood, carpet, cardboard, trash bags, furniture, corrugated plastic, and chicken wire. Three naked boys squatted at the river's edge, throwing stones. Men and women lounged on water-stained mattresses outside the shanties, or stood cooking over fires in rusted metal barrels while skinny dogs nervously paced back and forth between them. The scene had an air of unreality and expectation to it, as if the *malchaks* were actors on a movie set, killing time until the next scene.

I retreated into the woods. It was dark in there now, and it took me a few moments of squinting in the half-light before I was able to see the stone path leading back up the hill. Out of the corner of my eye, I glimpsed darting shadows in the branches, and the forest groaned and rustled impatiently. I stood behind a tree and looked out at the *malchak*s and the river and thought about what I should do next.

Here's what *Pocket Adventure* has to say about the *malchak* people:

The "malchak" are an ethnic minority that resides primarily in Puchai's Hattanai Province. Descended from hill tribe peasant-farmers brought to the area—against their will—over two hundred years ago, the malchaks were initially exploited as cheap labor for the gem mines and silk plantations in the region. They are a gypsy-like people who typically live together in cramped and unsanitary "shanty-towns"—jerrybuilt constructions that possess a picturesque, Swiss-Family-Robinson-ish charm when viewed from a distance.

The government of Puchai officially considers malchaks to be "pônge" ("alien"), and therefore the malchak people do not enjoy many basic civil liberties afforded to Puchanese citizens. They have a reputation for being high-spirited and unpredictable, and it's best to give them a wide berth when encountering them in the public sphere. Some people claim that malchaks are relatively harmless, especially when sober. However, many Puchanese can attest to the unpleasant, often violent nature of the malchak character; and, when this is taken into consideration alongside their diminutive physical stature, it might be fair to humorously describe the malchaks as being—quite literally—"nasty, brutish, and short."

As I stood there observing the *malchaks*, they appeared neither high-spirited nor unpredictable, and certainly not violent. They looked peaceful—sort of sleepy, if anything—and nothing like the drunken savages that Mr. Horse had warned me about.

I stepped back out of the woods and tried to orient myself. I decided that if I walked upriver, it wouldn't take me long to reach the bridge and the highway. From there, it was about half a mile to Pamarassam Road. Take the river to the road—sounded easy enough. I said it out loud: "The river to the road."

I made my way along the grassy ridge, sticking close to the forest and glancing down from time to time at the encampment below. The only people who noticed me were two young women who stared wonderingly in my direction, as if I were an antelope passing through their backyard. After a time, the distance between the river and the woods lessened, and there were fewer and fewer shanties. There didn't seem to be any point to staying up on the slope, so I went down and walked on the river road. I started seeing some signs of civilization: a medical clinic, a Post Office, a *pini-mini* garage. Behind a chain-link fence stood a shoddy-looking *mâdan* with an enormous concrete chimney in the back. Thick gray smoke poured out of it, and a delicious smell of baking bread wafted towards me.

At the corner where the river road intersected with the highway stood a low, ugly building that reminded me of Tamalpais High. Next to it, beneath a grove of *garong* trees, ten or so young *malchaks* clustered on the sidewalk, jostling one another as if they were watching a parade pass by. From a distance, the kids looked like a swarm of insects, moving together with a single unified intelligence. It took me a moment to realize what they were so excited about: they were hurling rotten *garongs* at passing cars.

If I'd been in a similar situation back home—confronted with a group of teenage boys on the sidewalk chucking snowballs at taxis—I probably would've gone out of my way to avoid them. Which is what I wanted to do now.

Keep walking. They're just a bunch of kids having fun. Ignore them, and they'll ignore you.

I was about twenty feet from them by now. They were laughing and throwing fruit and bouncing up and down, and as I continued along the sidewalk, straight into their midst, I tried to compose my features into an expression that said: *I'm just a gareng on my way home, minding my own business. I don't think what you're doing is cool, but I'm not judging you, either. It's not really a big deal. Just don't get anybody killed. I'm a visitor from New York City, the "Big Apple," so, believe me, I've seen much worse. I once saw a homeless man stabbed in broad daylight outside of the Howard Johnson's at Times Square. Another time, I saw a beautiful young Indian woman get hit by a taxi and fly forty feet through the air. The very fact that I have the confidence to casually walk among you proves that I'm not somebody to mess with. As you can see, I'm super-tall—almost a foot taller than any of you. Except for that one guy over there. He's pretty tall. You can sense that I'm a respected guest in your country, but you also know I'm not some tourist who's come here to sleep with your women and do your drugs and eat your pineapples and throw my cigarette butts in your rainforests. I'm a teacher—or, at least, very soon I'm going to start being a teacher—and I don't view you as "the other." I know that the same blood runs through all of our veins. You may not have realized this before, but I know that you realize it now, as you look into my eyes: I am not afraid.*

This is the face that I presented to the group of shrieking *malchaks* as I approached them.

Kids just being kids, you said—though, now that I got a good look at them, they were actually a lot more intimidating than your average kid. Their compact, muscular bodies were covered with jailhouse-style tribal tattoos, and woven into their long unwashed hair were bits of string and wire, and many of them had fat hand-rolled cigarettes clenched between their teeth. The closer I got, the more they looked like a gang of post-apocalyptic street urchins.

I was now just a couple of feet away from them—so close that I could feel their breath on my face as they shouted to one another—and yet they acted as if they didn't notice me at all. I picked my way carefully down the sidewalk, trying to avoid the smashed fruit pulp and slippery *garong* skins. When I murmured "*Kraà-yoom*" ("Excuse me") to a group of boys blocking my path, they spun around in surprise, as if a ghost had just spoken to them, and then quickly moved aside.

I found myself wondering how long a walk I had ahead of me. I was pretty thirsty by now, and was looking forward to drinking a beer when I got home. A beer was exactly the thing I wanted most at that moment. A beer and a big plate of *hee-maô* noodles. I wasn't sure if we had any beer in the fridge, and tried to remember if there was anywhere on the way home to—

A sharp, white-hot pain flashed at the base of my skull, and my nostrils were engulfed with a stench that made my eyes water. The pain disappeared almost immediately, replaced by a cool and prickly numbness. I touched my hand to the back of my head and felt something cool and damp there, as though my brains were leaking out. When I looked at my fingers, I saw they were smeared with clumps of rancid fruit-flesh.

I turned and faced the kids. The group grinned with excitement, their eyes darting back and forth between me and an enormously fat boy who stood a few feet away. From the way they deferred to him, I knew that he was the one who'd thrown the fruit. The fat boy was bouncing lightly back and forth like a boxer, his shoulders half-shrugged and his fingers wiggling in the air. My lips moved soundlessly as I tried to think of something to say that he might possibly understand.

The fat boy took a step toward me, leaning in so that his nose almost touched my cheek—I thought for a moment that he was going to try to kiss me. He inhaled deeply, then stumbled backwards, cackling: "*Hot dog*! *Hot dog*! *Hot dog*!"

I stared at him. "Hot dog?"

The fat boy sang, "*Hot dog gareng*! *Garong, gareng, garong, gareng, garong, gareng*!"

Their laughter now contained a hint of wild abandon that made me feel genuinely afraid. I shook my head, standing dumbly rooted in my spot, then rotated on my heel and slowly continued on down the sidewalk. The group fell silent, and I found myself believing that they were unexpectedly touched by my display of quiet dignity, and that, as they watched me walk away, their hearts were filled with a bittersweet mixture of sorrow and respect.

And that was when I felt the stinging impact of a second *garong* explode against my spine.

An overripe *garong* is really the perfect weapon for a juvenile delinquent: its skin is strong enough that it can be picked up and thrown without falling apart, but when it collides with a stationary object, it bursts open, smearing the target with rotten fruit. Simultaneously, at the moment of contact, the heavy pit inflicts a painful injury, like a rock inside a snowball.

I looked back at the group in utter shock. As I stood there gaping, trying to find words to express my outrage over this second attack, the *malchaks* pummeled me with *garongs*. The kids were now crazed, scrambling to scoop the fruit off the ground and fling it at me, chanting *garong, gareng*! *garong, gareng*! *garong, gareng*! until the words cancelled one another out, becoming a hum of white noise that entered my head and ricocheted there, like a firefly trapped in a jam jar, until the pitch and frequency of the hum was identified and then imitated by my own sputtering brain waves, so that they too began to hum in sympathy, as when the vibrations of one tuning fork are passed on to another; and I could feel this hum spreading throughout my body, growing louder and warmer and darker, my face and hands tingling with it, my tongue growing thick and heavy with it, my throat constricting around it—and now, as the inky darkness in my peripheral vision enveloped me, wrapping around me like a black woolen blanket, I found myself giving in to this darkness, even welcoming it, wanting it to drag me backwards and downwards and away from where I stood. I took in a deep, shuddering breath—and then:

I'm lying on a huge flat blanket in the darkness. I'm surrounded by tiny white figurines carved from smooth stone, strung together like charms on a bracelet. I am one of them: the tiny figure of a man, reclining on his side as if posing for a portrait, one leg outstretched, the other propped up, my cheek resting on my fist. There's something small and faraway hovering high above me. A flat black smudge. I can't really see it, but it casts a shadow overhead. The shadow smells like sweat, cigarettes. Lime Old Spice. The shadow wants something.

I blinked several times and let out a groan. Staring down at me, silhouetted against the dark purplish sky, was the upside-down face of the bearded *gareng*. I fluttered my eyelids and tried to remain perfectly still, hoping he'd lose interest and leave me alone.

"Hey." He nudged my shoulder with his shoe. "Dude. You okay?"

"Oh. Hey," I said. I yawned casually and glanced around, as if I'd just been enjoying a relaxing nap on the lawn.

The *gareng* craned his neck forward, studying me. He had a strong, Roman nose, small eyes, and a weak chin hidden beneath an impressive beard. His facial hair was so meticulously groomed that for a moment I thought it might be fake.

"We saw the whole thing from across the street," he said. "Did they hit you on the head with a rock or something? Are you—" He paused, then said with a trace of disgust: "You're not *bleeding*, are you?"

His tone was vaguely accusatory, and I considered closing my eyes again and ignoring him. Off in the distance, I heard a woman yelling, followed by the taunts of the *malchaks*. I lifted my head and saw Sam's daughter shaking her fist at my attackers, who were now huddled together beneath a *garong* tree, laughing.

Shiney turned and strode over to us, pausing briefly to shout a final admonition at the kids. She walked with tremendous poise and determination, her shoulders rolling and her hips swinging in a way that suggested a strength held in reserve—a jungle cat stalking a wounded bird.

"Those little bastards," she said. "Are you hurt?"

"No. I don't think so."

"Do you need help to stand?"

I sat halfway up. My body felt as if it had been hollowed out like a pumpkin and filled with toothpaste. "I think I'll just stay here for another minute."

I introduced myself to them, and the *gareng* crouched down and gave me a weak handshake. "Gabe Sloat," he said.

The girl *hai*-ed me. "I'm Srisuriyokhai," she said. "I'm also called Shiney. You can call me that."

"It's nearly 6:30," Gabe murmured to her. "What should we do?"

"You guys can leave if you need to," I said. "I'll be fine." I glanced over at the *malchaks*, who were still hanging out by the tree, watching us.

"You look very, very white," Shiney said.

I picked some fruit out of my hair. "That's pretty much my natural coloring."

Shiney put her visor on her head and turned to Gabe. "You should go to the show. I'll make sure he gets home okay, then meet you there."

"Will they let me in without you?"

"If they give you any problems, just ask for Pônge."

"Fine. Just try to hurry." He nodded at me and said, "See you around," then headed off towards the river road.

Shiney squatted down by my side. "Have you had this occur before?" she asked.

"People throwing stuff at me?" I considered her question. "Surprisingly, no."

"I meant the unconsciousness," she said, smiling. Shiney's mouth is small and serious-looking, but when she smiles, it doubles in size, spreading across her entire face. And when the smile is pointed in your direction, it's like someone's shining a flashlight into your eyes.

I had to look away from her before I could manage to reply: "Yeah, it's not a big deal. I'm a fainter."

Shiney snapped her fingers. "Wait here," she said, then stood and walked over to the *garong* trees. The kids all scattered, screaming and giggling as if they wanted her to chase them. Standing on her tip-toes, she inspected the branches of one of the trees and plucked off a large yellow leaf, then came and knelt down on the ground next to me. She broke off the stem and tied one end of it into a loop, then crushed the leaf, squeezing it between her fingers until a bit of clear liquid pooled in its center. "Lie back," she commanded. "Turn your head and open your mouth."

I rested my cheek on the grass and Shiney put her face near mine and dipped the stem-loop into the leaf juice, then held the loop up to her face, put her lips together, and blew a stream of tiny bubbles into my mouth. When they landed on my tongue, I started laughing, then coughed. The bubbles tasted both acrid and sweet, like medicine for a child. I began to sit up and Shiney said, "Stay down." I lay back down and opened my mouth and waited. Shiney dipped the loop into the juice again and said, "Relax yourself and let the bubbles coat your tongue. Then mix it with spit and gulp it down." She blew more bubbles into my mouth, and when I swallowed, a cloudy, burning sensation briefly filled my head and then dissipated. Shiney touched my brow with the back of her hand and told me: "Now stay down there for a few minutes. Close your mouth and shut your eyes."

I did as she said. Shiney sat next to me on the grass, and I heard a match strike and smelled cigarette smoke. I tried to lie still, ignoring the tickle of an ant crawling up my arm. The next time I opened my eyes, Shiney was crouching over me, studying my face and chewing on her thumb.

"You're awake." She spat a tiny piece of nail onto the ground and rocked back on her heels. "Are you okay?"

I blinked up at her, still half-asleep, and stared at her black eye. A thought began to take shape in my head.

Shiney sensed my gaze and touched her hand to her cheek. "It's a birthmark."

"Yeah. I see."

Shiney helped me to my feet. "I can find you a *pini-mini*. How do you feel?"

"I feel good. I feel great, actually." I stretched out my arms and held them above my head and grinned at Shiney. "I feel like I just slept for a year."

I feel like a body brought back to life.

Dear Hap:

I was fast asleep by the time Ulla got home last night, so I didn't get a chance to tell her about what'd happened until this morning. She gasped when I showed her the dark yellow bruises that covered my body.

"That's so awful! A group of *children* did that to you?"

"Teenagers." I buttoned up my shirt. "Some of them might've been young adults."

"You poor thing. I can't believe you passed out right there. You're lucky they didn't kill you."

"Some people came and chased them away. A white guy, and a girl." I paused. "Sam and Haraporn's daughter."

"Are you serious? What's she like? I can't even imagine."

I shrugged. "She's about our age. Seems nice enough." I shrugged again. "She's... short." I shrugged a third time. "Fairly nondescript."

Ulla went to the mirror and began brushing her hair. "You really need to go see someone about this fainting stuff."

"It hardly ever happens anymore. I saw a doctor two years ago—they all say the same thing."

"That's not the kind of doctor I meant."

"I thought you didn't believe in shrinks."

"I never said that. I just don't think *I* need to go." Our eyes met briefly in the mirror, and Ulla put the hairbrush down. "My father thought you'd get better here. All the fresh air."

"What, does he think I have TB? No offense, but your dad's a dentist."

"He's an oral surgeon." Ulla picked up her bag and stood looking at me for a moment, chewing on her lip as though thinking about something else. "I'm going to be late," she said. She reached out and gently touched the bruise on my neck, then turned and walked out the door.

Although I didn't really need one, I decided to go get a haircut. I rode my bike to the small barbershop around the corner from Golden Cowboy Place. The barber offered to clean the wax out of my ears with a long, sharp-looking metal rod, but I used sign language to communicate that it wouldn't be necessary. I did, however, allow him to give me a shave, and I left there looking like a freakishly tall seven-year-old who'd been in a car accident. And yet, in spite of this—or maybe because of it—my trip to the barbershop made me feel better.

Now I'm sitting at Golden Cowboy, enjoying a nice hot bowl of sour prawn soup. I can't stop thinking about yesterday, wondering what I should've done differently. I know what you'd say: *I would've fought them all, no matter how many there were, no matter how pointless it seemed.* But is that actually true?

I keep going through all of my possible responses, trying to think what might've been best. I can imagine all sorts of scenarios:

• The fat boy throws a *garong* at me, and, instead of doing nothing, I turn and hit him in the face—an open-handed slap. He kicks me in the spine, killing me instantly. The frenzied *malchaks* rip apart my body, dancing on my corpse. They cut off my head and kick it back and forth like a soccer ball, yelling, "*Garong, gareng!*"

• The fat boy throws a *garong* at me, and I fall to the ground and lie there, perfectly still, as though dead. The kids get scared and run away. I have a concussion but manage to drag myself into the forest. Using the bow-and-drill technique, I start a fire in a large rotting tree stump and then scrape out the charred interior. I curl up inside and remain there for several weeks, hydrating myself by licking the dew from leaves and drinking my own urine. I eat the bark of certain trees, and I eat the gray gelatinous body of a newborn baby sparrow that I discover on the forest floor. Once I'm stronger, I make a poultice for my wound by mashing together wild herbs and spices and mixing these with dirt and spit. A bird of prey comes and sits nearby, watching and waiting for me to die so that it can feast on my carcass. I place some ant eggs in my mouth, and after a time the bird draws nearer and nearer until finally it stands next to me, dipping its beak between my lips and consuming my gift. Now we are friends, and the bird does my bidding. I train it to go and catch small mammals and deliver them to me. I cook these offerings over a handful of pine needles that I've ignited using the tinder-plough technique. I share the cooked meat with the bird, feeding it small pieces that I place in my mouth. After I've completely recovered from my injuries, I check into the Hotel Tel-Hô under a pseudonym and send an anonymous letter to the Mai Mor newspaper stating that Boyd Darrow was last seen walking down the sidewalk toward a group of *malchak* kids, including one uncharacteristically obese boy. The kids are brought into the police station and questioned. They refuse to speak, but then the cops get rough with them, giving them a bitter taste of Third World interrogation techniques. The Chief batters the fat boy's face repeatedly with a damp washcloth full of nickels and says, "Just tell us what happened to Mr. Boyd!" After several hours of this, the fat boy caves and tells the whole story. The kids go to prison for the rest of their lives. The cops drag the river, looking for my body. I am eventually declared dead. Everybody grieves. I become an agoraphobic hermit and die alone.

• The fat boy throws a *garong* at me. Now, let's say that I somehow suspected ahead of time that I was going to be attacked by a group of teenagers, and so, before I left my apartment, I took two small pink balloons and filled them with tamarind syrup. Then I took a hot dog and tied the balloons to it, so that it resembled a penis. I carefully placed this in my underpants. (I am wearing briefs.) When the fat boy throws that *garong* at me, I pause for a moment, then reach down into my pants, grasping hold of the hot-dog-and-balloons. I make a terrifying face and let out a blood-curdling shriek, as if ripping my genitals off my body. Still shrieking, I throw my "penis and testicles" at the fat boy. The balloons explode, soaking him in a shower of sticky red "blood." He shrieks. Everybody is shrieking.

I say to him: "*Hot dog!*" and then continue walking, as if nothing has happened.

You have to admit: this seems like the best possible scenario.

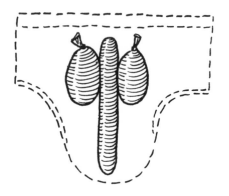

Dear Hap:

Sitting on my trash can. I'm thinking it might be nice to get an actual chair out here. Can't sleep. That noise outside our door—*click, click, scratch*—wakes me up almost every night. It never bothers Ulla. She claims I'm just imagining things. Sometimes I think she might be right.

Mr. Horse was in the courtyard earlier, sitting on the grass with a telescope, an astronomy book, and a flashlight, trying to locate various constellations. He showed me the turtle in the moon. I looked for the man in the moon, but couldn't find it. I think they might see a different section of the moon in this part of the world.

One of my favorite pastimes is asking Mr. Horse questions—he's a great source of information. I asked him about those enormous bats I saw the other day, and he told me they're "flying dogs" (*dtit laa*) and that they come out at sundown to eat the dragonflies. When I questioned him on the subject of his extremely long pinkie nail, he explained that it's for playing guitar, but also has several other uses. He pantomimed picking his nose, picking his armpit, picking his teeth. "And, is good for the girls," he said, scratching at an imaginary female in the air, making cooing noises, then scratching his heart. I'm not exactly sure what he meant by that.

He was lecturing me on the subject of Puchai's beloved king—a handsome, melancholy man who loves cats and is a talented jazz pianist—when I heard a low growl from the far end of the courtyard. Mr. Horse pointed his flashlight across the grass and we saw the white dog standing there, lightly swaying back and forth and staring at us. I told Mr. Horse that I'd been trying to make friends with the dog by feeding it, and asked if it was dangerous.

"Dog is not cruel," said Mr. Horse. "Sometime he say, '*gahhhhrrrr, gahhhhrrrr,*' but not often attack." Mr. Horse made a smacking sound with his lips and then yelled something at the dog. It wagged its tail, then lay down on the grass and began chewing on its foot. "But, I think maybe you should have care," Mr. Horse added. "The Puchai dog think that *gareng* strange to see, and sometime become violent at him, biting your face and feet."

I eyed the dog warily. "Does this one have a name?"

"*Malami.* Meaning: 'broken coconut.'"

Mr. Horse explained to me that Malami was a stray that had been brought into the School of Veterinary Science a few years ago by a graduate student who wanted to determine what would happen if a dog were isolated on a desert island and had to survive solely on a diet of coconuts. Malami was only allowed to eat coconut meat and drink coconut milk. Additionally, the student injected coconut milk into Malami's bloodstream. Malami began to get sick, and eventually a professor decided that the student's experiments should be discontinued, and Malami was set free.

"Who takes care of the dog now?" I asked.

"All the people of *Home Kwan Home.*" Mr. Horse looked back at Malami and said, "Should I summon him? *Judy-judy-judy!*" The dog rose to its feet and stood there, watching us.

"Is Judy his nickname?"

"Nickname? No," he said. "Dogs do not have nicknames." He looked over his shoulder again. "*Judy-judy-judy!*"

"Let me try." I called out: "Malami! *Maa, maa!*" I turned to Mr. Horse. "'Come, dog'?"

Mr. Horse gave me a pained smile and changed the subject. "I see you got new haircut, yes? Very handsome."

"Thanks," I said. "For some reason, whenever I feel bad, my first instinct is to get my hair cut."

"You are sick?" Mr. Horse's eyes widened with alarm. "You are *unhappy*?"

"No, no. I'm not unhappy. Just, you know… it can be hard, adjusting to a new place." As I spoke, I realized that—apart from you—I hadn't had anyone to talk to over the past few weeks. Tentatively, I added: "Sometimes, also, it's difficult to be… married."

Mr. Horse leaned forward and asked, incredulously, "You are not happy with beauty of your Ulla?" He shined the flashlight in my face. "You have no happiness here!"

"That's not true," I said, squinting into the light. "I have happiness here, in general. Puchai's great."

"Your eyes and mouth look *un*-happy."

"Really?" I reached up and rubbed my face, as if trying to massage it into a happier arrangement.

Mr. Horse lowered the light to my throat and gasped. "You are hurt!"

"A little bit," I said, touching the bruise. "I… well, I went to Mòk Bòo."

"No!"

"And a bunch of kids threw *garongs* at me."

"*Malchaks!*"

"I guess."

"I *tell* you!" shouted Mr. Horse, pointing at me. "Never go to Mòk Bòo! Great sorrow!"

"I know. I should've listened."

"They are a bad people! I tell you! No goodness!"

"Hey, can you explain something? One of the kids was yelling 'Hot dog!' at me. What did he mean by that?"

Mr. Horse paused. "Only stupid *malchak* talk."

"'*Hot dog, hot dog*,'" I said, imitating the fat boy's sing-songy voice. "Was it like—'Hot diggity dog'?"

Mr. Horse averted his gaze and mumbled, "Sometime… men say the *gareng* is smelly. Like the smell of hot dog. A hot dog not cooked." He looked up at me and added, "But *I* do not think so, Mr. Boyd."

I tried to imagine putting my nose to a package of cold hot dogs. "It's not exactly a bad smell. Is it?"

Mr. Horse gave a noncommittal shrug. "We are living in a smelly town, in a smelly country of Puchai. Let us talk of smelliness no more." He lifted his head and placed his right eye to the telescope. "Let us try to forget all of the smelly in this world. Let us hold our breath now, and turn our noses up toward the heaven."

March 8
3:05 PM

Dear Hap:
I love angels. Did you know that?
Let me tell you why.

Haraporn invited us to dinner at her house last night, so at
5:30 PM I went over to the Faculty of Theatre Drama to meet
up with Ulla. No one was in the office, and after a minute I
remembered what day it was and walked across the road to
the P. Songpole Phammawattaana Memorial Auditorium—
the open-air theater on the soccer field where the Expo
Taang show will be held. A man dressed as the Cowardly
Lion was onstage, singing "Somewhere Over the Rainbow"
in a shaky voice as Miaw videotaped him and Haraporn and
Ulla took notes. Wednesday is Audition Day.

Once a week, the Faculty of Theatre Drama holds an open
call for Expo *Taang* try-outs. Although the selection process
is merit-based, Ulla says there's a lot of nepotism involved,
as well as subtle political considerations that Haraporn takes
into account. *Malchaks* are not invited to perform in the
show—the rationale being that *malchaks* aren't technically
Puchanese. The show is four hours long and tightly scheduled,
so there's time for a lot of performers, and Ulla's seen all sorts
of different acts so far: stand-up comedy, poetry recitals, a
variety of singing styles (including traditional Puchanese
bailam music, opera, and show tunes) and dancing styles (belly

dancing, breakdancing, ballroom dancing, and traditional Puchanese elbow-dancing); also performance art, juggling, ventriloquism, cooking demonstrations, mind reading, dog tricks, a mime act, feats of strength, impersonations, sports demonstrations, and many more. Ulla has watched a drag queen lip-syncing a Puchanese disco song; a man doing the graveyard scene from Hamlet (pronouncing his lines phonetically); and a local senior-citizen's group that performed a slow-motion Ziegfeld-style dance routine while dressed as *malchak* gem-miners.

Once Haraporn and Ulla narrow the list down to twenty-five performers, Ulla will be responsible for determining the order, spacing them in terms of style and tech requirements. She told me that Mr. Horse came in and auditioned last week, accompanying himself on acoustic guitar and singing "I'm Easy," the Lionel Richie song. Despite my attempts to influence her decision, she said he probably wouldn't make the cut.

When the lion's audition was over, I followed the three ladies out to the parking lot where the Faculty of Theatre Drama van was waiting for us. As we drove down the Friendly Highway towards Haraporn's house, she and Ulla discussed various bits of Expo-related business while Miaw listened intently, nodding at inappropriate moments. I sat back and closed my eyes. I wasn't feeling so great—my head was killing me, and I'd been mysteriously constipated for three days straight. I was just beginning to doze off when I heard Haraporn say:

"Truly, everybody in the Faculty is missing the Talbot-Singhs very much! Have you received any communications from Devasheesh or Shawn?"

I snapped my eyes open and looked around. Haraporn was turned around in her seat, smiling at Ulla. Ulla's face was bright pink and she didn't appear to be breathing.

I leaned forward and said to Haraporn: "Excuse me, but what did you just say?"

Haraporn reared her head back a bit, as if I'd been speaking too loudly. Maybe I had been. "I was asking Ulla about the Talbot-Singhs," she said. "Devasheesh was the woman who performed Ulla's job for the Faculty of Theatre Drama last year. Mr. Shawn is her husband." She raised her eyebrows. "Are you not acquainted with them?"

"Ahh," I said, coughing into my fist. "Hmm."

Ulla blinked several times and peered out the window; she seemed to be considering whether to open the door and leap out onto the highway. In a robotic voice, she said: "Boyd didn't have the opportunity to meet them, no."

Haraporn watched this performance with mild alarm. "I'm… sorry to hear that," she said. "It would be illuminating for Boyd to know the story of their Mai Mor experience."

A wild burst of laughter escaped from Ulla's lips. She quickly pressed them together and rested her chin on her chest. "Yes," she said.

I stared blindly ahead, trying to absorb this new information, turning it over in my mind: the White Sikh had been here, in Puchai—in Mai Mor. He'd probably even ridden in the Faculty of Theatre Drama van, his body warming the very seat where I now sat.

"We all cared very much for Devasheesh and her husband," said Haraporn, smiling wistfully. "And their beautiful children! Giaanroop, Nripinder—and little Dylan, the baby. Devasheesh did many great things with the Expo *Taang* show last year, working closely with our Mai Mor community. Many people say to me: 'Last year was best Expo *Taang* ever!'" Haraporn glanced out the window, then spoke curtly to the van driver. He put on his blinker, did a U-turn, and went down a side street. Haraporn swiveled back towards us and continued, "Mr. Shawn did very much work for the community as well, teaching the *gà-roó-na* girls at the Hotel Tel-Hô. He made a program for them to study English, so they can get jobs working on the telephone and do not have to be prostituting, trading love for *prik*." She chuckled and added, "Everyone say, 'Oh, Mr. Shawn is the best teacher, he is the most handsome!' I always think that Mr. Shawn looks like a film actor—similar to Tyrone Power."

Miaw sighed, "Mr. *Shawn!*"

"Mr. Shawn," I repeated. I hadn't meant to speak his name aloud, but as I did, I felt something stir within my bowels: a throbbing pulse, like a baby goat in the belly of a python.

"Mr. Shawn also worked at Y.E.S.," said Haraporn, "like *you* will be doing, Boyd, when Samuel returns from his conference in Dakhong. That was Mr. Shawn's job in the daytime, for money." The driver made a sharp turn into the driveway and came to an abrupt stop. Haraporn opened her door, then turned back to me and smiled. "During the nighttime," she added, "Mr. Shawn taught the *gà-roó-na* girls, for free."

When Ulla and I entered the home of the Leekanchanakoth-Youngs, we removed our shoes in the foyer and followed Haraporn and Miaw down a narrow hallway crammed with mounted and framed puzzles: a Monet painting, *Notre Dame*, and an image of a little boy on the back of a bicycle clutching an armful of baguettes. We turned the corner and passed through a den where a variety of cultural artifacts—an embroidered shawl, a set of ancient-looking wooden masks, an ivory turtle sculpture—were on display. Only the "*HOOK 'EM HORNS!*" banner that hung above the doorway marred the room's museum-like effect.

Ulla hurried ahead of me, but I caught up to her and whispered, "I need to talk to you."

"Not now," she said. "We'll talk at home."

Before I could respond, I found myself standing in a brightly lit kitchen full of people. The tile walls were covered floor-to-ceiling with assorted cooking-related items, some of which seemed intended for practical use, and some of which were purely decorative (such as the nook dedicated to antique eggbeaters). At one table, four middle-aged men passed around a bottle of whiskey while playing dice; three women sat at another table, slicing vegetables and laughing. Everyone stopped talking when we walked through the door.

Haraporn escorted Ulla and me around the room, introducing us to the other guests. The women *hai*-ed us and laughed merrily, then returned to their business. The first three men we met looked like a trio of aging bus boys, with their matching white button-down shirts tucked into black pleated pants. The fourth man was dressed in a tailored brown suit and blue necktie, and wore a black silk handkerchief diagonally across his face, covering his left eye. He was completely bald, and seemed strangely familiar to me.

Haraporn gestured to him with a flourish. "Please to meet our neighbor, Mr. Phammawattaana. He is the Head Chairman of Faculty of Gemology of Mai Mor College. Mr. Phammawattaana, may I introduce our new guests: Mr. Boyd and Mrs. Ulla Darrow."

Pushing his chair back, the man stood and took my hand, staring at me intently. Then he blinked his eye several times, and said: "Mr. Boyd Darrow, it is very rare and interesting to be making your acquaintance. Haraporn has previously spoken of your arrival within the boundaries of our complicated and magnificent country." Furrowing his enormous eyebrows, he continued, "To be grasping your northern hand in fellowship—a fellowship that maybe had begun in a past life, or maybe continue in a future incarnation, but, surely, a friendship and fellowship that will grow in the present day, during your visit to this home town—yes, I liken the sensation to the body's relaxation after a long period of anticipating the fulfillment of a need." He then released my hand and *hai*-ed me, bowing deeply.

I *hai*-ed him in return, wondering if he had me confused with someone else. "It's an honor to make your acquaintance, Mr. Pham... wanna..."

"Phammawat*taa*na."

The name rang a bell. "Like the auditorium?" I asked.

He smiled gravely. "Yes. The P. Songpole Phammawattaana Memorial Auditorium was so named for the honor of my departed sibling, Purit." There was an awkward pause, and then he continued, "My bosom acquaintances, family members, and select coworkers refer to me by the nickname of 'Mr. Yul.' You may do the same." He ran his hand across his perfectly smooth, shiny head. "Like the famous star of the screen and the stage."

I realized that, apart from the eye-patch, the resemblance was uncanny: Mr. Yul had the same deep-set eyes, oversized nostrils, and fish-like frown as his namesake.

He glanced behind me, and I stepped aside and said, "Mr. Yul, this is Ulla." I gritted my teeth, and added, "My *wife*."

Mr. Yul took both of Ulla's hands in his. "It is a particular honor to now acquaint myself with you, Mrs. Ulla Darrow. Infrequent is it that such pale beauty, combined with nature's grace and glowing thoughtfulness, is present in our district. I will approximate the words of the Lithuanian poet, Juozapas Tveirijonavicius, when I say: '*We have been living in a long nighttime, and thy face is the heated lamp of a distant star that has lowered surprisingly into our dim sphere, creating a summer-like appearance of daylight that thus causes our greatest strengths and weaknesses to stand out in stark relief amongst the limpid shadows of noon.*'" Mr. Yul brought Ulla's hands up to his mouth, as if about to kiss her knuckles, then apparently reconsidered and released them.

Before Ulla could respond, Haraporn clutched her shoulder. "Please, come with me now. I will show you the traditional method of preparing the *bpòot.*"

Mr. Yul offered me a seat, fixed me a whiskey and soda, and rejoined the game. The other men ignored me completely, but I didn't mind—I was in no mood to make small talk. I felt like a ghost observing the living as I watched the men play, sipping my whiskey and brooding on the question of the White Sikh.

After I had a couple of drinks in me, I stood up and walked over to Ulla. She was frowning with concentration and chopping up a small blue penis-shaped vegetable. Nodding to the other women at the table, I murmured into Ulla's ear: "Let's go talk."

She kept her head down, mincing the tuber into smaller and smaller pieces. "We'll talk later."

"Come on."

"No. I'm sorry."

"Give me five minutes. You owe me that."

Ulla sighed, and hesitantly got to her feet.

Haraporn smiled at us. "You are leaving?"

"We'll be right back," I said. "Ulla's going to come and keep me company while I smoke a cigarette."

"Ah." Haraporn raised her eyebrows. "You are addicted to smoke."

"Exactly," I said.

I escorted Ulla to the front door, and we wordlessly slipped into our shoes and stepped outside. There was a light on inside the Faculty van, and I could just make out Miaw's slim silhouette leaning into the driver's window, like a waitress at a drive-in. I stood watching her for a moment, then went around the side of the house to where Ulla waited in the darkness next to the garden.

"Boyd," she said softly. "Listen, I'm sorry—"

"I thought the whole point of us coming to this country was to get away from that bastard."

"Well… it wasn't the *whole* point. Anyway, he's not here now." Ulla moved closer to me and took my hand. "Shawn told me about the *Taang* job, and I really wanted you to come along, but I was afraid you'd feel weird if you knew he lived here last year. I feel so much better now that you finally know."

"Why'd he tell you about the job, if he's supposedly so in love with you?"

She shrugged and murmured, "He was trying to save his marriage."

"So he exiled you from the country."

Ulla glanced over her shoulder. "We should go back inside."

"Is there anything else I should know?"

Ulla stared down at the ground, tracing a triangle into the dirt with the toe of her shoe. Then she raised her head and said, "Boyd, I was—"

"*Mr. Darrow!*"

We looked toward the house and saw Mr. Yul and the men standing under the light by the front door. Mr. Yul gave us the backwards wave.

I turned to Ulla, but she was already waving to Mr. Yul and walking towards him. I swore under my breath and followed behind her.

Mr. Yul bowed to us as we approached. "Mr. Boyd Darrow, may I invite you to attend a brief expedition? We must travel to the establishment of our acquaintance—a Mr. Judy." He spread his arms wide, and for a moment, I thought he was waiting for me to step forward and embrace him. "We need to retrieve the fixings of the Pleasurely Beast."

"I'd like to, but—"

"Sounds like fun," Ulla said brightly. "You go off with the men, Boyd. I'll see you when you get back." She placed her hands on my shoulders and kissed me on the cheek, then scurried inside.

"Excellent." Mr. Yul bowed again. "Please, follow me."

The five of us squeezed inside Mr. Yul's sleek, insect-like car and set out into the night. ("The only Citroën DS model in Hattanai Province," he proudly informed me, revving the engine.) As we drove through the dark along the Friendly Highway, heading away from campus, the men were somber, smoking cigarettes and barely speaking to one another. After twenty minutes or so, we turned onto a road that wound through a barren stretch of fields, abruptly dead-ending at a lopsided house and a long gray barn. Mr. Yul honked his horn and we all got out of the car.

An elderly man materialized in the doorway of the barn, squinting into the headlights. He wore an apron covered in black stains and held a kerosene lantern up to his face. As we approached him, I saw that his teeth and the whites of his eyes were the color of maple syrup.

Mr. Yul said: "Mr. Boyd Darrow, please to meet Mr. Judy."

Mr. Judy and I *hai*-ed each other, and one of the men turned to me and said, "You know—'*Judy*.' Like you calling dog?" In a high-pitched voice, he yelled, "*Judy-judy-judy-judy!*" Everybody laughed at this, except for Mr. Judy, who simply shook his head and walked away.

We followed the glow of Mr. Judy's lantern as he led us into the unlit barn. A heavy odor hung in the air: a rich, sickly sweetness, mixed with the smell of rusted iron. The straw on the floor felt slippery beneath my feet, as if covered with freshly spilled paint. The only sound was of a cow lowing somewhere in the darkness.

Mr. Judy came to a stop in front of a red metal door. When he opened it, the smell intensified, hitting me in the face like a damp mattress. Mr. Judy raised his lantern and walked into the room. We crowded around the door and peered after him.

Lashed to the rafters, swaying gently in the flickering lamplight, was the blood-blackened carcass of a slaughtered cow. It hung upside-down from two thick ropes tied around the stumps of its hind legs, and a yellow plastic trough on the floor collected the blood that flowed from it in thin, steady streams. Its hooves and head had been cut off, and the body was slit down the middle, the milk sack and udders removed. The cow's hide, partially peeled away, hung behind it like a tattered cape. The thing looked like an enormous, misshapen bat hovering in the darkness.

The men pushed forward and gathered around it, murmuring to one another in hushed and excited tones. I backed out of the room, then lowered myself slowly, half-kneeling on the barn floor like a man about to be knighted. I counted to ten and waited for the feeling to pass—that familiar feeling of a gray heaviness and an airy lightness mixing woozily throughout my body. After a minute I got to my feet and staggered along the darkened corridor until I emerged outside.

I sat on an overturned bucket and took a few deep breaths. When I closed my eyes, I felt my body becoming soft, smoke-like, dispersing and mingling with the breeze and the spray of stars above. I opened my eyes and I took out a pack of *Cowpokes* and lit a cigarette—it tasted bad and made me dizzy, but I forced myself to finish it, as if it were medicine.

As I sat there smoking, the men filed out of the barn. Mr. Yul approached me holding several packages wrapped in heavy gray paper, along with a clear plastic bag filled with a thick, black liquid.

"Mr. Boyd Darrow, I did not witness your departure from the scene," he said. "Are you unwell?"

"I just wanted to get some air."

He nodded. "Tonight, we shall dine on the most freshly slaughtered body of a cow," he said, clasping my hand and placing it on the side of the warm plastic bag. "And this is the blood!"

When we got back to Haraporn's house, the women were bustling around the kitchen, cooking and setting the table. Ulla and I exchanged a look, but instead of going over to talk to her, I followed Mr. Yul to the counter and watched as he prepared the meat, grinding it up and mixing it with handfuls of spices and chopped chilies. While he worked he spoke at length about the study of Gemology, explaining how it was an expanding field that needed more bright young *garengs* such as myself. He'd just about convinced me to go back to school for my Gemology degree when I heard the front door slam and the sound of voices in the hall. I glanced over my shoulder and saw two new guests standing in the doorway.

Shiney was wearing tight black high-waisted jeans with holes ripped in the knees, and a white Oxford shirt that looked like it'd once belonged to her dad. The shirt buttoned all the way to the top, *pachuco*-style, and had been re-stitched by hand, with the seams in all the wrong places. Her short hair was wet and combed straight down. Despite the strangeness of her appearance, she looked devastatingly pretty. Gabe loomed behind her, arms crossed, seeming as if he'd rather be anywhere else in the world.

Haraporn stood to welcome them, calling over her shoulder: "Boyd and Ulla! Please come here." When we approached, she encircled us in her arms. "The Darrows, let me introduce you to our Srisuriyokhai. And her friend, Gabriel, whom you may also call 'Gabe.'"

"Hi," said Shiney. "Feeling better?"

"Yeah, thanks," I said.

"The bubbles helped?"

Ulla looked back and forth between us. "Bubbles?"

"You know one another?" asked Haraporn.

"We met the other day," Shiney said. She pointed at my pants. "Are you injured?"

I glanced down. There was a dark red stain on my knee from when I'd knelt on the barn floor. "Oh, that's not my blood," I said.

Shiney laughed. "Every time I see you, you appear dirty."

Ulla took a step forward. "Hi. I'm Ulla. Boyd's wife." She looked Shiney up and down and smiled politely. "I like your costume," she said. "Are you guys going to a... party?"

"It's not a costume. It's just an outfit." Shiney shrugged. "I enjoy making fashion."

"Ah. I see."

"Shiney, you two will be joining us for dinner?" asked Haraporn.

"We'd love to," Gabe said, studying his watch, "but we really just stopped by to grab Shiney's sweater and say a quick hello."

"I think we have time for a bowl of *aa-raam gaeng*," said Shiney.

"Wonderful!" Haraporn clapped her hands together. "Now, I think the *bpòot* are finished steaming. Shiney, come with us. You and I will demonstrate for Ulla the traditional method of cooling them in the bucket of ice-milk."

As the three women walked past me, Ulla whispered in my ear: "*Bubbles?*"

Gabe watched them go, then smirked at me. "You guys are married?"

"Uh-huh."

"Kind of young for that, aren't you?"

"I guess… I just couldn't wait to settle down."

"Hmm." Gabe leaned against the wall and fingered his beard. "So—what *was* Shiney talking about back there? Regarding the bubbles."

"The bubbles?" I reached up to rub my eye, then shoved my hand in my pocket and said, "Well, after you left, I still wasn't feeling so hot, so Shiney did this thing with a *garong* leaf, and she blew these bubbles at me. Some sort of ancient Puchanese cure."

Gabe was quiet for a moment, then said in a low voice: "Did she lie down next to you on the ground, and blow the bubbles directly into your mouth?"

"Not exactly." I shook my head. "Sort of."

"I saw her do the exact same thing once with a sick dog." Gabe scratched the underside of his chin, then studied his fingernails and murmured: "Shiney's always doing stuff like that. Being friendly. Saving cats with broken legs. Putting sick birds into shoeboxes. Etcetera." He raised his eyes and gazed steadily at me. "It's just her friendly nature," he said. "You understand what I mean?"

I slowly nodded. "I appreciated you guys helping me out."

"Hey, man, no problem. That's the way things are here in Puchai." Gabe gave my shoulder a quick, hard squeeze and winked at me, unsmiling. "It's a friendly fucking place."

There was a noisy cough behind us, and a voice said: "Misters Darrow and Sloat, please excuse me for pausing your conversation."

We turned around. Mr. Yul was grinning and holding a large stone bowl. "I have the special *aa-raam gaeng* for your consumption," he announced, lifting the bowl up to my nose. "The 'Pleasurely Beast.'"

The raw beef, mixed with the chilies and spices, gave off a warm odor that was intoxicating yet slightly nauseating—like sticking your face into the armpit of a beautiful woman. It appeared to be quivering, sloughing off the last remaining traces of the slaughtered cow's vitality. I moved my head back, overcome with an irrational fear that it was about to lunge out at me.

Gabe mumbled something about checking on Shiney and quickly slunk away, leaving me alone with Mr. Yul and the Pleasurely Beast.

"Mmm," I said, smiling down into the bowl. "It looks delicious, but..." I put my hand on my stomach, as if I were too full to eat. "I don't think I'll have any right now. Thank you very much, though."

Mr. Yul furrowed his brow and held up a large silver spoon. "Mr. Darrow, I must recommend for you to consume this traditional dish of the Hattanai Province, for purposes of bringing a year of luck and health."

Eat it.

I glanced over at Ulla. She was standing at the table, arms immersed in a bucket of white liquid, watching me with the corners of her mouth turned down. I faced Mr. Yul and said, "I'm sorry. I mean no disrespect, and I'm sure it's very *pêt*—but the cow is not cooked. I am concerned that maybe it could make me sick."

"Sick?" Mr. Yul threw his head back and laughed. "No, no. The Pleasurely Beast will make you *strong!*" He winked and added, in a low voice, "It will give you a strong *love* for your wife, as well." He scooped up a large lump of the meat and presented the spoon to me. "I am insistent."

I took it from him, studying the tremulous portion of Pleasurely Beast.

Eat it now.

Before I could allow myself to reconsider, I put it into my mouth. Mucus immediately began streaming out of my nose, and my eyes filled with hot tears as the spicy meat-paste slid over my tongue and down my throat. Mr. Yul slapped me on the back and shoved a cold cup of whiskey into my hand. I wiped my face off on my sleeve, drank from the cup, and lowered myself onto a wooden chair. A shiver ran down my spine, and a numbing warmth oozed throughout my body. I lifted my head and saw a few of the guests were now watching me closely. I smiled, pounded my chest with my fist, and said, "*Pêt!*"

I wasn't sure, but I think Shiney was watching me, too.

The thirteen of us sat down to eat. The two tables had been pushed together and were covered with an impressive array of food: a large bowl of the Pleasurely Beast; a platter of alien-looking steamed vegetables; a teepee-shaped display of grilled prawns; an enormous black fish wrapped in banana leaves; a plate of crunchy yellow noodles fried with pork and cuttlefish; a salad of green mango and fried eggs; and a clay pot filled with a purplish soup that smelled like the Gowanus Canal. As I filled my plate, Mr. Yul told me to make sure that I got some fish-cheek, which is apparently the most tender and delicious portion.

I was seated between two of the white-shirted men, both of whom politely pretended I wasn't there. Ulla was next to Gabe, discussing the Threepenny Opera; Shiney and Mr. Yul were speaking intently to one another; and Haraporn and Miaw chatted and laughed with the other women at the far end of the table. Since I didn't have anyone to talk to, I focused on eating. Other than the *bpòot* (which tasted like radishes boiled in eggnog and cigarette ash), everything was extremely *pêt*.

I was just swallowing my first bite of fish-cheek when I overheard Haraporn, speaking in Puchanese, saying: "*Blah blah blah* Mr. Shawn *blah*. Mr. Shawn *blah* Mrs. Devasheesh, *blah blah blah* Mr. Shawn.*" Ulla was immersed in conversation with Gabe, but I could tell from her expression that she'd also caught the references to the White Sikh and was studiously ignoring my gaze. From somewhere inside my body, I heard a high-pitched sputter, like the whistle of a wet bottle rocket. Nobody seemed to notice; the entire table was listening to Haraporn now. "*Blah blah blah* Talbot-Singhs," she said. "*Blah* Mr. Shawn *blah*. *Blah blah* Giaanroop, Nripinder, *blah blah* Dylan, *blah blah blah*—Mr. Shawn!"

Two of the women—and one of the men—sighed loudly and said, "Mr. *Shawn!*"

I heard another noise coming from my abdomen at that moment, this one like the melancholy whinny of a horse that's been hit by a car. The man next to me shot a curious glance in my direction, and I sat up a little straighter. Sweat was beading on my upper lip, and I felt a molten, burbling sensation deep within my gut. It was clear to me now I didn't have much time. I got to my feet and put my napkin on my chair.

Haraporn looked up. "Is everything all right, Mr. Boyd?"

"If you'll excuse me," I said quietly, "I was wondering if you could tell me where the bathroom is, please?"

"You have an expression of concern. Are you about to be ill?"

"No, I'm fine. I just want to wash my hands."

"Ah, but you may use the *choon-buri*." Haraporn indicated a finger bowl next to my plate. "The water is scented with essence of the *pi-pi* flower."

"Yes, well, I wanted some… soap," I said. The kicking in my abdomen had become more insistent, and it felt as though the thing inside me was threatening to forego the traditional point of exit in favor of splitting my stomach open and bursting out onto the table.

"The oil of the *pi-pi* has a remarkable cleansing power," said Haraporn, smiling serenely.

Mr. Yul cleared his throat. "I believe that Mr. Darrow might like to enjoy a private function."

Haraporn laughed. "Ah, yes, I knew it to be so! Puchai food is very *seep*, no? *Seep* meaning 'spicy.'"

By this point, the entire table was following the conversation. "The bathroom's down that corridor, on the left," Shiney said, pointing over my shoulder. "The door with the shoes."

I excused myself and hurried, stiff-legged, along the knick-knack-lined hallway to a door that had a pair of high-heeled Dutch clogs hanging outside it. There was no lock on the knob, and I silently cursed the lax security of the Leekanchanakoth-Youngs as I pulled the door shut. A quarter-inch of water covered the tile floor. I cursed the Leekanchanakoth-Youngs a second time as I splashed across the room to the squat-style toilet, shoved my pants to my ankles, and dropped into a crouch.

There was a pregnant pause, and then, with a tremendous shudder, I felt something begin to slowly, gently slide out of my body. It was unnaturally large and abnormally thick and went on and on and on, seeming as if it might not stop until my intestines had unspooled in a heap onto the floor. The violence of the act disturbed me, but I simultaneously experienced an illicit, adrenaline-filled rush that made my head swim. After I finally heard the thing fall with a thud into the ceramic bowl below, I hovered there, savoring an empty-headed moment of blissful calm, and then cautiously turned around to see what I'd created.

The thing was perfectly straight and practically the length and circumference of my arm. It was the color of tar, and its dark, mottled surface gleamed in the fluorescent lights as if it had been shellacked. I gaped at it, aghast, my eyes burning in the wake of its low-tide stench—and then, nodding my head, I gave it a respectful wink. I couldn't help but feel a bit proud to be personally responsible for such a grand and terrifying object.

I looked around for a roll of toilet paper, though of course, there was none—most Puchanese bathrooms don't provide any, due to their delicate plumbing. Instead, they usually offer one of two options: a basin of water with a plastic scoop, with which you're expected to pour water over your backside; or a pressurized water gun attached to the tank, as was the case here. *Home Kwan Home*'s modernized facilities are able to handle toilet paper, so I'd never used a squirt gun before, but I didn't have any other choice now.

I pointed the nozzle in the appropriate direction and very, very gently squeezed the handle. Nothing happened. I squeezed a little harder. Nothing. I squeezed just a little harder—and a powerful blast of water shot out, soaking the entire back half of my body. I swore loudly as I felt the cold, filthy liquid slide down my legs and pool in my underpants. Casting my eyes desperately around the room, I caught sight of a pink-and-gray-checkered hand towel on the back of the door, hanging from two alligator clips screwed into the wood. I climbed off the toilet—my pants still around my ankles—and crab-walked over to the door, splashing through the water on the floor. I took down the towel and, crouching in the middle of the room, began vigorously wiping myself dry.

"Mr. Boyd?" came a voice from outside.

I froze: it was Haraporn. I opened my mouth to respond, but couldn't speak.

"Are you all right?" she asked. "May I enter for just a moment?"

I reached my hand straight out into the air, like a crossing guard halting an oncoming truck, and shouted, "Yes! No!"

"I'm sorry?" The doorknob began to turn. "Yes to come in?"

"NO!" I yelled savagely. "Do *not* come in! But, yes, I am fine!" I took a deep breath, then added, in as level a voice as I could muster: "I'm almost done."

"Very good. I shall wait. I hope you do not have the 'moths in your stomach'?" Haraporn giggled. "That is how we call the diarrhea in Puchai."

"No, no moths," I said, still crouching there, pants around my ankles. It somehow seemed that, if I remained absolutely still, I would be safe. "I'm just… fixing my hair. I might be a few minutes."

"I see. May I ask, when you exit, will you please bring the *àep-sôn* to the table with you?"

"Of course." I looked around the room. "Sorry, what is that?"

"The item on exhibition—a traditional *malchaki-gai* child-shroud that I recently acquired and would like to show to Mr. Yul. It is, as you can see, quite a unique artifact—very old, but never used, and in pristine condition."

I contemplated the crumpled piece of cloth in my hand.

"The… the item hanging on the door?" I asked.

"Yes, that's exactly right."

I gasped and tossed the cloth onto the floor—as though realizing that I'd been wiping myself dry with a rattlesnake— then watched in horror as it quickly grew saturated with water. I snatched it back up and held it, dripping, from one corner.

"I hope to move it to a more prominent place of display in the future," said Haraporn. "However, it does reflect the color scheme quite nicely in there, would you not agree?"

"I…" I paused, then murmured, "I'll bring it right out."

"Excuse me?"

"I said *I'll bring it right out!*"

Haraporn was quiet for a moment. "Many thanks," she said.

I waited until the sound of her footsteps had receded down the hallway, then yanked up my pants, wincing slightly as my wet underwear pressed against my flesh. "*Fuck!*" I whispered loudly. "Fuck fuck fuck fuck *fuck.*"

"Excuse me?" said Haraporn.

Apparently, I had heard someone else's footsteps receding down the hallway.

"Nothing!" I yelled. "Sorry! I was just… forget it."

"Very well." She cleared her throat. "I would like to caution you to be aware of the water on the floor. I see that you chose not to wear the toilet-sandals that hang outside the door."

I looked down at my soaking-wet socks. "I am aware of it. Thanks."

I held my breath, listening, until I was certain that Haraporn was gone, then spread out the *àep-sôn*. As I inspected it, I let out a muted gasp—there was a small but distinct brown streak in the corner of the shroud. A streak that most definitely hadn't been there before.

I ran over to the sink, squirted some liquid soap on the *àep-sôn*, and ran it under hot water for a minute, scrubbing furiously until only the faintest ghost of a stain remained. I wrung as much water out of it as I could, then went and hung it on the alligator clips. I took a step back and considered my work: it looked like a hobo's pathetic attempt at doing laundry.

You're fucked. Get out of here. Climb out the window and bury the shroud in the garden and hitchhike home.

As I walked slowly down the hallway, rehearsing in my mind what I was going to say—*I'm so sorry, Haraporn, there's been a tragic accident, and unfortunately I don't have the money to pay you back right now, but perhaps I could do some chores around your house*—I saw Shiney ducking into a room two doors down. She gave me a sympathetic and slightly embarrassed smile, then began to shut the door.

"*Shiney!*"

She stuck her head back out. "Yes?"

"Could I talk to you a second?"

"Is everything all right?" she asked, her gaze lingering on my wet socks.

I glanced around, then whispered: "I don't know what to do, there's this... child death... item... I forget what it's called—hang on a second. Don't go anywhere." I ran and retrieved the piece of cloth from the bathroom. "This thing," I said, showing it to her.

Shiney pressed the back of her wrist against her mouth and laughed. "Oh, no! The *àep-sôn*! What did you do?" She examined it. "It's extremely wet."

"I thought it was just a cheap hand-towel."

She abruptly stopped laughing and gave me a steady look. "Hardly. It is a traditional *malchak* child-shroud."

I felt my eye begin to throb once again. "I know it is," I said. "I didn't—"

"Are you winking at me?"

"No!" I clapped my hand over the twitching side of my face. "Is there anything I can do? Haraporn's going to kill me if she sees this."

"That's very true." Shiney closed her eyes and was silent for several seconds. Then she snapped her fingers and grabbed my arm. "Come with me," she said. "I have a scheme."

Shiney led me to a room a few doors down from the bathroom. "This is Haraporn's special room," she said, flipping on the light. "It is called the Angel Nest."

The walls were lined with cabinets and shelves containing hundreds, perhaps thousands, of angel figurines: porcelain angels, plastic angels, rough-hewn clay angels, precision-cut crystal angels; angels posing as nurses, angels playing hockey, angels kissing Santa, angels delivering mail in a snowstorm. There were also angel pendants, angel music boxes, angel wind chimes, angel collectible plates, angel snow globes, angel dioramas, angel Christmas ornaments, angel teddy bears; an angel mirror, an angel table lamp, an angel tapestry, and a hand-painted angel-themed Kleenex box. There were cherubs, fairies, *putti*, cupids, seraphim, and wood sprites—and, hanging from the light switch, there was a small Batman action figure that had been spray-painted white. In the middle of the floor stood a black leather office chair in which a visitor could relax and meditate upon the room's contents.

I began to have grave doubts about Shiney's scheme. I said, "I don't understand what—"

"It will make sense in a minute," she said, turning off the light. "Come along."

I followed Shiney to the laundry room at the end of the hallway. She threw the cloth into the dryer and switched it on, then took an iron and ironing board from the closet and set them up as she explained her plan. "After five minutes, you will remove the *àep-sôn* from the dryer. The iron should be heated by then. You will iron the shroud so that it is very flat. When you are finished, return the ironing tools to their proper places." She pointed at the closet. "While you are doing all of this, I will return to the dinner table and tell them that I happened to meet you in the hallway and that I offered to show you the Angel Nest, because it is the most beautiful room in the house. You became very excited when you saw the Angel Nest because you share Haraporn's love of angels."

"I love angels?"

"You believe, as Haraporn does, that we each have a special angel that speaks to us, giving us support and advice if we choose to listen. As you stood in the Angel Nest, you became enchanted by Haraporn's delightful collection, and that is why you have not yet brought the *àep-sôn* as she requested. I will then volunteer to retrieve the *àep-sôn* from you and bring it to Haraporn. At that point, I will rejoin you here in the laundry room. I will inspect the *àep-sôn* to make sure it looks acceptable, and then you and I both will return to the table and present it to her. You will express great admiration for the Angel Nest, and your deep love of the angels."

"Okay," I said, nodding. "Dryer, iron. Angels. Got it."

"Remember, remove the *àep-sôn* in five minutes." Shiney began to leave, then looked over her shoulder and whispered: "*You love angels!*"

I stood watching the *àep-sôn* through the dryer window as it spun, checking my watch every fifteen seconds or so. Time slowed to a crawl, and I fully expected Haraporn to come pounding on the door at any time; but finally, after five minutes had passed, I removed the shroud from the machine. It was warm and almost completely dry. I quickly ironed it on both sides, then held it up and inspected it. All things considered, I thought it looked pretty good.

There was a knock on the door, and my heart skipped a beat before Shiney stuck her head in.

"How is it?" she asked.

"Not bad." I held the shroud by the corners and showed it to her.

She studied it skeptically. "I guess it's good enough."

We started down the hallway, Shiney slightly in front

of me, and as I stared at the back of her head, I felt an overwhelming desire to bend down and press my mouth against her neck. At that same moment, I felt an equally overwhelming desire to rid myself of the wedgie caused by my damp, clammy underpants.

I paused when we reached the bathroom door. "Is it okay if I meet you back at the table?"

"Are you very sick again?"

"No, I—I'll be there in just a minute. I promise."

This time, I took down the toilet-sandals and put them on my feet before entering the bathroom. The fumes that I'd generated during my previous visit still lingered, and I felt compelled to breathe through my mouth as I balanced on top of the wooden shoes and set about removing my pants with one hand, keeping a tight grip on the doorknob with the other. I had just yanked off my underpants when I felt the knob begin to turn beneath my fingers.

"*Someone's in here!*" I said, holding the door shut with all my strength.

I heard Gabe's voice mutter: "I thought you were entranced by the angels."

"I'll be right out."

When I saw that the knob had stopped turning, I released it and quickly climbed back into my pants. I stuffed the damp tightie-whities into a small garbage can under the sink, artfully camouflaging them beneath damp cottonballs and lipstick-smeared wads of Kleenex, and then opened the door.

Gabe was standing there, glowering. "Dude, I'm about to piss my pants."

"Sorry. It's all yours." As I removed the toilet-sandals and stepped aside, I remembered the lingering stench. Smiling apologetically, I added: "Just a warning—I left a real bouquet in there for you."

"Bouquet?" Gabe grunted, then slipped into the sandals and pushed past me.

On my way back to the dining room I ducked into the Angel Nest and flipped on the light. I wasn't in any big hurry to rejoin the party, and if I was expected to wax rhapsodic about Haraporn's angels, I figured that it couldn't hurt to familiarize myself with her collection. A ceramic statue on a pedestal in the corner caught my eye: it depicted a wedding between a nervous-looking dentist and a large, possibly pregnant Tooth Fairy. I was puzzling over this piece when Gabe stuck his head into the room and spoke my name.

"That was no joke about the bouquet, huh?" he said, leering at me savagely. His face was red and his eyes were wide and darting, as if he'd had a run-in with a poltergeist.

"Yeah, sorry."

"All because I tried to establish some boundaries?"

"Boundaries? Sorry, I'm not sure what you—"

"You must be really sick, man." Gabe shook his head with amazement.

"Well… I feel better now, actually," I said, placing my hand on my stomach.

"Just because I'm a recognized scholar in the field of Ethnomusicology—someone who won a Jaap Kunst *and* a Fumio Koizumi—doesn't mean I couldn't kick your ass if I wanted to. I don't care *how* tall you are, bro."

Mystified by the direction our conversation had taken, I decided to keep my response neutral for the time being. "A Jaap Kunst, huh?"

"Is this how you stake out your territory? Show me you're the big *gareng* in town now? I didn't think you had it in you, to be honest. Though, apparently"—he gave an involuntary shiver—"you did." He gathered himself up and added, "I just left it there. I don't give a fuck if they think it's mine."

And then I understood: in my panic over the *àep-sôn*, I had completely forgotten to flush the toilet.

I tried to speak, to explain, but was laughing so hard I could barely breathe. Gabe gazed at me with a mixture of incredulity and fear, as if realizing he was trapped in the Angel Nest with the devil himself. He took a step backwards. I shook my head and said, "No, wait—"

"You're lucky we're not in Connecticut right now, asshole."

"*Connecticut?*" I gasped, and began to laugh even harder.

Before I could say anything else, Gabe spun around and hurried out.

I took another minute to quiet down before leaving the Angel Nest, then tiptoed back to the bathroom, shut the door, and cautiously approached the scene of the crime. Sure enough, there the thing was, right where I'd left it. I flushed the toilet, though I knew full well that it wouldn't go down on its own—and when it didn't, I took a deep breath and proceeded to break the turd apart with my bare hands. After successfully dismantling it, I flushed the toilet several more times, until there was no trace left.

When I walked into the dining room, everybody at the table turned in my direction. Gabe placed his hands on the tabletop, apparently preparing himself for some even more sinister attack. Haraporn stared with dark, suspicious eyes, and Ulla gawked at me as though I'd just emerged from the grave and was tracking cemetery dirt over the rug.

"Boyd?" she said, her voice full of wonder. "Where have you *been?*"

I felt a flare of anger in my chest at the sight of Ulla— I'd momentarily forgotten about the White Sikh. I looked away from her and, taking a deep breath, my eye winking uncontrollably, I shrugged my shoulders and said to nobody in particular:

"I love angels."

March 12
1:32 AM

Dear Hap:

Last night I had a dream.

You and I were kids, and we were flying kites on Mount Tam—me with that red white and blue kite I had, and you with your bat kite. We stood there for what seemed like hours, not talking, just watching our kites moving against the sky. It started to get dark and we went into the clubhouse, although on the inside it wasn't actually the clubhouse, but our home. None of the lights worked so I felt my way down the hallway to my bedroom and got into bed and went to sleep.

Then I was awake again and you were standing over my bed. I could just see the outline of your body in the darkness: there was something wrong with the shape of your head, but I knew it was you. Then my eyes adjusted and I saw you were holding the bat kite up in front of your face—like you did in real life that one time. I said your name. You were making quiet soft noises, sucking air in between your teeth as you clicked them together. The room began to fill with wind.

I woke up with a start, heart pounding. It was after 3 AM, and I'd been woken by a noise. I've gotten used to having my sleep disturbed by noises outside our door, but this was different. This noise was inside the room.

It came from the far corner, where we keep the basket of *fae-dongs*, and sounded like something in the basket that was trying to get out: *skritch, skritch, skritch, skritch*. But not a lizard—the noise was too loud for that. Whatever was making it sounded heavy and clumsy, like a drunken raccoon.

When I turned on the lamp, the noise stopped.

"What are you doing?" Ulla cried, draping her arm over her face.

"Stay there," I said. I slowly got out of bed and edged over to the corner by the window where we kept the broom. Then I climbed up on a chair and waited for something to come at me.

"Boyd, what the—"

"*Shh!*" I climbed down and went to the front door and opened it very quietly. Then I took a breath and poked at the basket with the broom handle. Nothing stirred. I edged the broom handle under the basket lid, took another deep breath, then flipped it up, leaping backwards as I tipped the basket over. Bags of *fae-dongs* scattered across the floor. Ulla screamed.

Nothing was there.

I inspected each of the plastic bags, but didn't see any sign of teeth marks. The next night—tonight—I went to sleep with a flashlight next to the bed. When the noise started up, my eyes snapped open and, before I was even fully awake, I was pointing the flashlight into the corner. I thought I might've glimpsed something—a gray blur, a small yellow eye—but it was hard to say. Ulla yelled for me to turn off the light, and I did. But I couldn't get back to sleep, and now I'm sitting outside. I don't understand what's inside our room. But I have the beginnings of an idea.

I've almost filled an entire notebook, Hap.

I wish I knew how to get these letters to you.

The Absent Present

"Yes I am a Ghost a Haint a Shadow in the rigging Twisting down the Main Mast & up the Misid Mast each night Taunting the cowards that killed Me No none but they see Me & they fear Me more then when I had lived No I shall not let them forget how I was thrown over the Bow & draged under the hull & torn to ribbons apon the barnicles until only bloody foam & sinking skull remained No I wont let them Rest in Peace Yes I shall always be with them Yes Memory makes the Absent Present

BOOK TWO

March 15
11:57 PM

Dear Hap:

I woke up this morning with a mouthful of rubies. I understood that I had to chew them up and swallow them—that it was somehow my responsibility to the Faculty of Gemology—but my teeth crumbled and splintered, and my mouth was filling with blood. When Ulla shook me awake and told me I'd been grinding my teeth again, it took me a while to understand what she was talking about.

After Ulla left for work, I looked out the window and saw that Malami, the white dog, was lying in his spot beneath the palm tree in the middle of the courtyard. I made two bowls of eggs and bread—one for me and one for him—then grabbed a handful of *fae-dongs* and went outside. I stood at the edge of the grass and called, "Malami!" The dog squinted at me, as if trying to remember where he knew me from. I tossed a *fae-dong* near him and called, "*Judy-judy-judy!*" in a high, girlish voice. He seemed to like that. He stood up, looking at me and looking at the *fae-dong*. I tossed another one. "Come, dog! *Judy-judy-judy!*" He wagged his tail, ate the *fae-dongs*, and continued walking toward me. I couldn't be sure, but it sounded like he was growling. I put the remaining *fae-dongs* into his bowl and said, "Good Judy," then hurried back inside.

I scarfed down my breakfast, took a shower, and got dressed. I was scheduled to arrive at the Young English School at 9:30

for my first teacher-training session, and didn't want to be late. To save time, I decided to ride my bike.

I was halfway to Y.E.S. when my brakes jammed on a steep section of Pamarassam Road, throwing me to the ground. I lay there for a moment, staring at the sky as the cars drove past, then carefully got to my feet and brushed myself off. I'd skinned my elbow and ripped my shirt, but didn't have time to go back home and change. I ended up carrying my bicycle the rest of the way.

When I entered Sam's office, he sat hunched over his desk, fiddling with a purple square of paper and muttering to himself.

I cleared my throat. "Hey, Sam. I'm here for—"

"I could do a better mountain fold with a piece of quilted Charmin." He held up the piece of origami. It looked like a moth that had been run over by a car. "This rinky-dinky *koi* paper just breaks my heart. Try a little tessellation, and you wind up with a hunk of garbage." He crumpled it up and tossed it aside, then assessed me over the tops of his aviator shades and grunted. "It appears you lost a fight with a mudpuppy, Arrow."

The yellow dust from the road had coated my sweat-soaked skin and clothes like sugar on a donut. I made a show of brushing off my pants and said, "Sorry, I'm a—"

"Running a bit late?"

"Well, I wasn't, but then my bicycle—"

"Mr. Arrow?"

"Yes?"

"Do you think we tolerate lateness here at Y.E.S.?"

I lowered myself into my little blue chair. "No, sir. The truth is, my bike—"

Sam held his hand in the air, as if inviting me to slap him high-five. "Actually, we *do* tolerate lateness."

"I was—" I leaned my head to one side and blinked. "You do?"

"Lord knows, we don't *appreciate* lateness. However, I had you pegged as a latecomer the moment I laid eyes on you. Know how I knew?" He pointed at me and tapped his forehead. "Like minds think alike. You see, I *too* am a chronically late individual, and so therefore have a certain degree of sympathy, or even—I'm going to use the 'empathy' word here—*empathy* for your situation. Unfortunately, six years in the military failed to rid me of my condition. You ask me to meet you at noon, and—*ding dong!*—I'm knocking on your door at thirteen-hundred hours. Meaning one o'clock in the afternoon, Arrow. An entire hour tardy." He sighed. "You're not the only one acquainted with the pleasures of laggardliness."

I balled up my fists and placed them together in my lap, rubbing the knuckles against one another. "The thing is, I usually have a problem with arriving too *early* everywhere, but this morning, my bicycle—"

"So the word on the street is that you were a guest in my home last week?"

I hesitated, thrown off guard by this new topic. "I was," I admitted.

"Funny thing," he said, studying my face. "My wife has the peculiar notion that, during the course of her little dinner party, you somehow magically decreased the dimensions of her *àep-sôn* by approximately one-sixteenth. If you ask me, the thing looks the same as always, but I feel compelled to officially ask you, man to man: did you monkey with my wife's artifact?"

No, sir. I did not.

I bit down on the inside of my cheek, resisting the powerful urge to confess everything. "No, sir," I said, my throat growing tight. "I did not."

He nodded and wrote something on a piece of paper. "Another thing. Did you happen to leave behind a damp pair of briefs in our bathroom?"

Tell him the truth. If you admit to this smaller crime, it'll give you credibility, and make your previous lie seem more believable.

"Um… yes. Sorry about that," I said. "I had some trouble with the water gun."

Sam drummed his fingers on the table. "It gave the wife a real scare when she found your undershorts hiding in the garbage. She thought it might be some kind of *gareng* perversion thing. You're not perverted, are you, Arrow?"

"No, sir. Not at all. Just the opposite."

"Also, I hear you have a thing for angels," he said, looking at me shrewdly, "and that you were quite smitten with my wife's little nest?"

I tilted my head from side to side and said, "She has some very nice pieces in her collection."

"You think?"

"Well, you know…" I tried to recall an example to cite. "The one with the dentist marrying the Tooth Fairy? That was pretty interesting. And… I liked the Batman angel."

Sam snorted. "I don't get it, but, each to his own. As long as your angel-love doesn't affect your work, I guess it's a non-issue. However—we digress." He consulted the schedule on the wall. "I was going to have you sit in on Shiney's ten o'clock session, but it got cancelled… so, unfortunately, you'll be observing Richie Plassen's class today." He leaned back in his chair, opened the door of the classroom behind him, and yelled, "Shiney! Do me a favor and take this guy to Richie's room!" He waited, and when there was no response, he sang: "*O, where is my wandering brat tonight? O, where is my wandering brat?*"

Shiney appeared in the doorway. Her hair was now dyed a dark bluish tint and stuck up in all directions, as though she'd just rolled out of bed. She wore gray jeans and a tight-fitting pink t-shirt with the neck and arms cut off. Scrawled on it in black magic marker were the words:

dOLPHiN
33 TiMES

"*The chilly wind blows, to the hoosegow she goes!*" sang Sam. "*That's where my brat is tonight!*"

Shiney glanced in my direction, and—taking note of my ripped shirt and dusty pants—broke into a wide grin. "*Ràp-naa lei,*" she said, *hai*-ing me.

Sam stared at Shiney and scrunched up his face. "What's the matter with your hair, girl? And what in the world are you wearing?"

"My class was cancelled, so I changed."

"You certainly did. I'm glad your mother's not around to see you in that get-up." He spat into his palm and reached for Shiney's head. "You *look* like you spent the night in the hoosegow."

"What are you doing?" she squealed, ducking out of his way. "My hair's *supposed* to look like this!"

Sam sighed and wiped his hand on his pants. "Sometimes," he said to me, "I find it hard to believe that this here *non compos mentis* is actually the fruit of my own looms."

*　　*　　*

I followed Shiney outside and around the back of the office to a long green stucco building. As we made our way along a concrete walkway past a row of empty classrooms, I said, "You know—the other night at dinner, I think Gabe and I might've had a misunderstanding…"

Shiney laughed and clapped her hands together. "The giant shit! I heard!"

"I swear, I had no idea I'd left it there."

"Of course! I told him so. Gabe is very paranoid. He also has a morbid fear of human bodily excretions. The shit must've been truly impressive to give him such terror."

"It was a unique specimen," I said, shrugging modestly.

Shiney gave me a sideways glance. "You're reminding me of that comic character who is followed everywhere by a cloud of dust. I think he's friends with a white dog?" We came to a stop in front of a classroom door. "Here we are," she said.

I glanced through the window and saw about fifteen students sitting at wooden desks. A few were idly paging through their books; others appeared to be sleeping.

"By the way," Shiney said, "I think my father believes that your name is 'Boyd Arrow' rather than 'Boy-*duh Dar*-row.'"

"Yeah. I haven't gotten around to correcting him yet."

"Boy-*duh*." She smacked her lips, as if getting the taste of the name. "Do you have a nickname?"

"My brother used to call me 'Droid'—I don't know if that counts. I was never too keen on it."

"We need to think of something appropriate for you. You can't remember the name of that comic character covered in dirt? Is it maybe… 'Dust-Bin'?"

"I do remember his name, but I don't want a nickname based on a filthy cartoon character."

"'Dirt-Cloud'?"

"Does everybody in Puchai have a nickname?"

Shiney nodded. "Your parents give you a nickname when you're born, to confuse the evil spirits. If the spirits don't know your real name, then they can't find you."

"My neighbor's nickname is 'Horse.'"

"And does your neighbor look like a horse?"

"A little bit." I pictured Mr. Horse's long, narrow face and calm, unblinking eyes. "Do you really think his parents called him 'Horse' because he was a horse-faced baby?"

"When I was a girl, my two best friends were named Dent and Fat. Dent is short for Rodent—she had large front teeth. And Fat was called Fat because she was so fat."

"I hate to think what my nickname as a kid would've been," I said. "'Tall-Soft-Boy-Irrationally-Afraid-of-Bees.'"

"You're afraid of honeybees?"

Earn Thousands. Live Your Dreams. JUNGLE HONEY.

"No," I said. "Not anymore."

"Sometimes, the nickname's just a word that the family likes the sound of," Shiney said. "My first lover was a boy named Jar-Lin, which means: 'Handle-on-top-of-the-sticky-rice-basket.'" She chuckled and added, "He was truly well-named." Then she tilted her head to one side and blinked several times, as though attempting to shake some water out of her ear.

"Are you all right?"

"I'm winking at you!"

"Oh."

Shiney sighed. "I've never been able to do it properly."

"It must be hell for you, living in the Kingdom of Winks."

"It's difficult, yes."

I put my hands in my pockets and leaned against the wall. "'Shiney'—how'd you get that nickname?"

"My dad called me Shiner when I was little," she said, pointing at her eye. "Shiner, Shiney." Then she pointed through the classroom window. "And Richie here is called Mr. Dicksplash."

I peeked in at the *gareng* sitting at the front of the room. He was older than I'd expected—he looked at least fifty—and was dressed in Bermuda shorts and a brown tie-dyed shirt, with bushy gray hair tied back into the tiniest ponytail I'd ever seen. (He reminded me, for some reason, of Mr. Kearse—the guy who lived next door to the Costellos and used to garden in the nude all the time.) His head hung forward at an odd angle, as if his neck was broken, and I might almost have thought he was dead if not for the regular rise and fall of his shoulders.

"'Dicksplash'?" I said.

"That's right."

"Maybe I don't want a nickname after all."

"I'm afraid you don't have a choice in the matter."

Shiney opened the classroom door and I followed her inside. She approached the *gareng*, put her mouth next to his ear, and whispered loudly: "Hey—*Richie!*"

Richie jerked his head up and launched into a brief and wet-sounding coughing fit, his oversized Adam's apple twitching spasmodically. He pounded his chest, blinked several times, then focused on Shiney. He wore thick-lensed reading glasses—the kind old people buy at the drugstore—and they magnified his eyes just enough to make them look subtly unreal, as though they belonged to an oversized doll.

"Hey," he said, his gaze moving up and down Shiney's body. He seemed to be trying to figure out if she was a leftover figment of his dream. "What's up?"

Shiney pointed at the clock. "I think your class is in session?"

Richie bobbed his head and moved his lips as he scanned Shiney's chest, reading the words on her shirt. "You know what's really messed up?" he murmured. "I read somewhere that if you touch a dolphin's privates, it'll, like, totally rape you, and you'll die."

Shiney raised her eyebrows and nodded slightly, as if she couldn't quite hear him, then turned back towards me, angling her body away from Richie's line of vision. "This is our new teacher. Boy-*duh* Darrow. He's here to observe."

Richie broke into a wide grin and shook my hand. "Totally," he said. "Awesome. Let's go for it."

Shiney and I grabbed a couple of seats in the back row. I heard someone call my name, and saw Miaw sitting up front, waving at me. I waved back and gave her a big wink as Richie began his class.

"All right. Good morning, team." Richie got out of his chair, perched on the corner of his desk, and fussed with his ponytail. "Okay. Let's all turn to page fifty-three." He opened a copy of *ENGLISH FOR EACH*. "Page fifty-three. Everybody got it?"

The class remained silent. Most of the students were staring nervously down at their books.

"Cool. Today we will be studying..." He held the book close to his face. "...*vocabulary-building riddles*." He looked up. "Now, I don't know about you, but I love riddles. A riddle is a question with a quirky answer. Sometimes it's for children: 'Why did the skunk put the plug up its nose? Answer: Because it wanted to smell electricity!' Or sometimes it's a sexy joke that's especially for grown-ups. 'What is 69 squared?' These are riddles that make us laugh. And laughter is no laughing matter—scientists have proven that three good chuckles a day is the equivalent of riding an exercise bicycle for forty minutes." He wiped some imaginary sweat off his brow. "But there are other types of riddles too. Brain-teasers, such as the infamous classic: 'I walk on four legs, then three legs, then two legs, and then one leg. What am I?' These riddles literally *tease* your brain." He held the book to his face again. "I'll read the first one out loud. '*What Am I?*'" He looked up. "We all wonder that sometimes, right? 'Who am I? Where am I?'" Clearing his throat, he continued: "'I cannot be *smelt.*'" Richie pointed to his nose, inhaling deeply. "Smelling. Smelly. Smelt. You know?"

The class nodded uncertainly.

"'I cannot be *dealt.*'" Richie dealt cards from an imaginary deck. "As in, dealing. Dealership. What's the *deal.* I *dealt* with you, *hombre.*" He glanced at the book. "'I cannot be *touched.*'" He made a movement with his hand as though he was petting a dog. "The Midas touch. Touching an angel. Touched in the head. Everybody knows touching, right?" Richie paused, then read: "'I cannot be *felt.*' So, felt is like... touching. But a little different." He moved his hand in slow circles, as if he was waxing a car. "I *felt* you. But, felt is also like a type of cloth. Like... felt underpants. But in this case, it's a verb. You *felt* me today." He lifted his shirt and tenderly ran his hand across his bare stomach. "So, to recap: 'I cannot be *smelt*, I cannot be *dealt*, I cannot be *touched*, I cannot be *felt*. What am I?'" Richie's head drifted slowly back and forth, as if he was watching fish in an aquarium. "What the heck am I? Anybody have an idea?"

A man in the front row raised his hand. Richie pointed at him and said, "What am I, Bom?"

"Water?"

"*Water.* Maybe so. Can't be smelt, dealt, felt—ah, but you can *touch* water." Richie did a doggy-paddle. "You know. '*Splash!*' Nope, I don't think I'm water." He looked around and pointed to a dark-skinned young man in the back row. "Ooan? Any ideas?"

Ooan whispered to the person next to him, then started laughing. "Is it making…" He lifted slightly out of his chair. "…*poot poot?*"

A few people in the class chuckled nervously. Richie stared at him, then began to breathe loudly through his mouth—*huhn huhn huhn*—as if hyperventilating, though I'm pretty sure he was laughing. "Fun guess, Ooan. But remember: 'I cannot be *smelt.*'" He inhaled deeply and then made a face. "*Pee-yew!* In my country, we have a saying: 'Whoever *smelt* it, *dealt* it.' So, uh—not quite." He looked around the room again, then pointed at Miaw and grinned. Lowering his voice to a sultry purr, he said: "*Miaaaaaw?*"

Miaw giggled and hid her face behind her hands. "No!"

Richie took off his glasses and set them on the desk. Without them, his face looked unnaturally naked, like a turtle with its shell taken away. He tiptoed up to Miaw, covered his eyes with his fingers, then peeked through them, and in a high, warbling voice, said: "Miaw, I *seeeee* you!"

Miaw giggled even more hysterically and slid down in her chair. "Mr. Richard, I don't know!" she shrieked.

Richie sighed heavily. "Miaw. Please. I'm not a 'mister.' Or a 'Richard.' Look at me. Do I look like a 'Mr. Richard'?"

Miaw stopped laughing for a moment and nodded her head tentatively. "Yes?"

"We're all friends here. I call you by your nicknames, so there's no reason why you can't call me by mine: just plain old *Richie*. I also invite you guys to come up with a cool new nickname for me, Puchai-style. 'Gray Panther.' 'Mr. Wizard.' 'The Groove.' Something fun." Richie smiled encouragingly. "Anyways. Miaw, please tell me. *What am I?*"

"Hmm." Miaw shut her eyes and got a dreamy expression on her face. "You are… magic turtle?"

"Magic turtle." Richie whistled between his teeth and grabbed at the air, as if trying to snatch at something flying past. "*Very* creative. That's a thing in your religion here, right?"

Miaw hugged herself and nodded.

"Let's see what the official answer is." Richie put his glasses back on and thumbed through the book. "Wow. Check it out..." His voice lowered to an ominous whisper. "*Darkness. I am darkness.*"

Miaw let out a yelp, then clapped her hand over her mouth.

"You can't *smell* it, *deal* it, or *touch* it. Or *feel* it. The darkness of the night. Or," he said, closing one eye and putting his finger in his ear, "the darkness on the *inside*. You don't know my darkness. It's the human condition."

Richie paused there, allowing his words to sink in. "Heavy stuff. We're really getting into the marrow today." He went and sat down behind his desk. "Let's do another one." He consulted the book, then read:

I am in pain but not in pleasure.
I live in sin but not in joy.
I dwell within a man and woman;
not in a girl or a boy.
What am I?

"All right, guys. This is a toughie," said Richie. "How about we all write down a list of possible answers? Try to be super-creative, like Miaw's 'magic turtle' theory. Dig deep."

As the class set to work, Richie perused his book, turning the pages occasionally. The room grew still. I gazed up at the ceiling fan, watching it rotate. Distant snatches of birdsong floated in through the open window. I heard the hum of a motorbike driving past. The next time I looked up, Richie had closed his eyes and was resting his chin on his chest.

Shiney leaned over and whispered, "I'm going to leave. Are you staying?"

"I think your dad wanted me to observe this whole class."

"Yes?" Shiney glanced at Richie. "All right, then. See you later." She stood up and walked out without a sound.

I looked down at the notes I'd taken. The only things on the page were the two riddles, along with a sketch of Richie's ponytail. Richie had slumped down farther into his seat, and was now making a soft, sputtering noise, like a leaf blower running out of gas.

I picked up my notebook and left.

I spotted Shiney on Pamarassam Road and jogged after her. When I was a few feet away, I said, in as casual a voice as I could muster: "Hey."

She didn't seem at all surprised to see me. "You escaped," she said.

As we walked together up the hill, Shiney filled me in on Richie's backstory: He'd been vacationing in Puchai with his wife a few months earlier, and they were passing through Mai Mor when she developed some kind of problem with her feet and had to go home early. Richie stayed behind to finish up the vacation alone, and by the end of the week he'd found an apartment to rent and had applied for the job at Y.E.S. He now supplements his income by selling marijuana and magic mushrooms to *gareng* backpackers. Shiney hadn't heard him mention his wife lately.

"It's common for *garengs* like him to stay in Mai Mor," she said. "It's cheap, and they get addicted to the hotel bar. The girls." She made a disgusted noise and shook her head.

I thought of the White Sikh. "I know someone who used to volunteer at the hotel, working with the girls. Ulla's old boss. You probably met him. Shawn…" I paused, as though searching for the name. "…Talbot-Singh? He taught at Y.E.S. last year."

"The Sikh *gareng*?"

"Exactly."

"Yes, I did meet him a few times."

I waited for Shiney to continue. When she didn't, I asked, "What did you think of him? Did you like him?"

She shrugged. "He seemed very… *gareng*-ish," she said, vaguely. "Haraporn *loved* Shawn. I think because his face looked like the old movie actor… what's his name? Tyrone…?"

"Power," I said glumly.

We were now walking alongside the large field of scrubby sun-burnt grass that leads to the P. Songpole Phammawattaana Memorial Auditorium. Up ahead, across the road from the Hi-Fi Cafeteria, a crowd of twenty or so students were gathered around a phone booth, yelling and shaking their fists in the air.

"What do you think that's all about?" I asked.

"Today is one of the Special Days—'Spring-Secret Day,'" Shiney said. "The students are performing the annual Spring-Secret ritual of *Rák-Wá-See*."

Special Days are mini-holidays that occur at least once a week here in Mai Mor. (Ulla says if it weren't for the constant interruptions of the Special Days, she could've finished planning the entirety of the Expo *Taang* by now.) Each Special Day has a unique name—*Animal-Friend Day, New-Magic Day, Sundae-Citizen Day, Jungle-Manner Day*— but, for the most part, they're all celebrated the same way: student and faculty members gather on the soccer field to eat ice cream, sing songs, and play badminton. The upcoming Festival of *Taang Lôke Kwaam Ban-terng Sumitchanani* is the most special Special Day of all.

As we approached the edge of the crowd, I stood on my tiptoes, trying to catch a glimpse of what was going on. Two students—a grinning boy and a nervous-looking girl—were being herded into the booth by an elderly, pear-shaped man in a seersucker suit. The old man's hair was dyed black and styled into an impressive pompadour, and something about him seemed a bit off, though I couldn't put my finger on *what*, exactly. It might've been his curious resemblance to Ronald Reagan.

I watched as he removed a small Tupperware container from a sack, carefully lifted the lid, then tossed the container into the phone booth and quickly shut the door. The young couple screamed and began flailing around as if the floor had become electrified.

I took a step forward. "What the hell is going on in there?"

"A giant moth has been released within the booth, and the man and woman must try to snatch it from the air in mid-flight."

I watched the two students writhing inside the glass box as the audience clapped and cheered. "Do you get a prize when you catch it, or something?"

"No. You capture the moth, and then it's over."

The crowd emitted another loud cheer, and the couple tumbled out of the booth, giggling and wild-eyed. The girl drunkenly shook her fist and then flung something into the air. Everyone quieted down for a moment, cooing softly as they watched the enormous black moth flutter away. Then they all raised their hands, begging to be chosen next.

"I don't get it," I said. "What's the point?"

Shiney wasn't listening to me. She was staring at the old man, who was pushing through the crowd in our direction. "I should've warned you," she murmured. "It's just that you're so... *conspicuous*."

"What are you talking about?"

The man now stood a few feet away, shouting at us in Puchanese like an impatient carnival barker. Up close, the subtle dissonance of his appearance was even more intense: his wrinkled face had a queasy sort of softness about it, and something about his body, the way it was hidden beneath his billowy suit...

Then I saw it: the old man was, in fact, an old woman.

"She says that you're a special guest to our country," explained Shiney, "and it would be an honor if you would take part in the ritual."

Sounds like fun.

"Look, I appreciate the offer, but can you please tell her maybe some other time?"

The students were now stamping their feet on the ground in unison and chanting, "*Rák-Wá-See! Rák-Wá-See! Rák-Wá-See!*"

"I don't want to refuse her," said Shiney, raising her voice. "It would be rude."

"It's just, I'm not so crazy about being shut up inside small spaces," I said. But it was too late: the old woman who looked like Ronald Reagan had grabbed our elbows and was dragging us towards the phone booth.

"The other thing is, Shiney, I was actually on my way to meet Ulla at the cafeteria," I said, shouting over the cheering students. "Ulla is extremely punctual—"

The old woman who looked like Ronald Reagan fixed me with an icy glare and said, with an air of finality, "*Rák... Wá... See,*" then shoved us roughly into the phone booth, slamming the door shut.

The booth's interior was quiet and warm and thick with the odor of human bodies. Shiney and I backed into opposing corners and stared down at our shoes. I felt wildly nervous, though I wasn't exactly sure why.

"What happens next?" I whispered.

"The moth will be introduced in a few moments."

"Great." I looked up at her. "Sorry if I smell like hot dogs."

"That's okay," Shiney said, not meeting my gaze. "I don't dislike hot dogs."

I glanced outside at the woman. She was holding a Tupperware container in her hand, and through the semi-opaque plastic, I could make out a large dark shape.

I turned back to Shiney. "Have you ever done this before?"

"Many times, yes."

"Weird," I said, shaking my head. "What does *Rák-Wá-See* mean, exactly?"

"It means..." Shiney looked away and shrugged. "'Snatch-of-Desire.'"

The old woman abruptly pushed the door open, tossed the container on the floor, and yanked the door shut. There was a pregnant pause as Shiney and I stood frozen in place, waiting. I cautiously eyed the Tupperware and whispered, "Maybe it's not *eeeaaaagggghhhhhhhhhhhhhhhhh!*"

A hummingbird-sized moth rose into the air and began desperately hurling itself against the glass walls of the booth.

It brushed against the back of my neck and I let out a yell and fell towards Shiney. Shiney shrieked and laughed and pushed me away and I fell backwards and hit my head against the corner of the booth. Shiney crouched down, waving her hands in the air. "*Ow!*" I yelled. "*Hey! Shiney, get up!*" I tried to crouch down too and yelled, "*Aren't we supposed to catch it?*" and Shiney yelled, "*Yes!*" We both stood up, our knees knocking together, and I reached towards the moth and then recoiled when my fingers touched its hard, bristly body. I gritted my teeth and grabbed at it again and it flew down to our feet and Shiney screamed and pushed me against the wall and held me by the wrists for a moment, shrieking, "*Don't step on it! It's bad luck!*" and I yelled "*I'm not!*" and then the moth began crawling up my leg. I kicked my foot and it flew into the air again and I reached for it, my body falling into Shiney's body, her bare arms pressing against mine, my armpit in her face, the two of us kicking each other's shins and then spinning and pressing together into the corner again, yelling and laughing and grasping, and it felt like I was being touched all over by an enormous soft furry hand, the constant glancing contact of the insect against my skin merging with the sensation of Shiney's body against mine, so that my flesh was crawling with an awful exquisite delight—

And then, almost without meaning to, I had clapped my hands together and I held the moth inside them and I screamed: "*Eeeaaahhhhhhhh!*"

"Do you have it?" yelled Shiney.

"Yes *eehhhhhwwwwwwwww* and it's trying to crawl out *agghhccchhhhhhhh!*"

"Throw it away! Before it bites you!"

"It *bites*?"

"They stick their pointy thing into you!"

"Jesus Christ!" I kicked at the door and yelled, "Hey, lady! Let me out of here!"

Shiney pushed me out of the way and opened the door and we burst outside. I unfolded my hands and the moth clung to my palm as I shook it wildly, until finally it let go, and we all watched as it flew in a dizzy figure-8 above our heads and disappeared over the yellow trees.

Shiney and I stood close together, faces flushed, panting and laughing as the crowd rushed in all around us. I shook my head and flapped my arms and ran my fingers through my hair, as the crawling, touching sensation slowly left my body. The old woman who looked like Ronald Reagan pinched my cheek, and the students were yelling and I waved to everybody and thanked them, as if I was a celebrity who'd just made a cameo appearance in a piece of performance art. I slapped my hands against my chest and then I turned to Shiney and smiled.

And that was when I noticed Ulla, standing at the edge of the crowd, clutching two shopping bags to her chest, staring at us with shock and wonder.

Later on—after Ulla and I walked home together in silence; after Ulla opened the bottle of wine that we'd been saving for a special occasion; after she silently consumed half the bottle, sitting and listening to me explain how I'd ended up in a phone booth with Shiney; after Ulla finally began to speak, saying *Who does she think she is, Sparkles, Sprinkles, whatever the hell her name is, blowing bubbles into your mouth and feeling you up in a phone booth, you're a married man, for all she knows, and she's not even pretty, she looks like a little boy with boobs and a black eye... and you, after all the shit you've given me about Shawn, and your talk about how we're supposed to be starting over here,* Ulla working herself up into a frenzy until, abruptly, the wineglass she held clenched in her hand shattered, blood spraying everywhere—though actually not blood, just red wine, but still, we were both freaked out enough that we gave up fighting and silently retreated to our separate corners of the room—after all of this had happened, when it was late at night and I climbed into bed, I lay in the dark for a long time, eyes open but unseeing, listening to the rustling of the Night Visitor in the basket, and I found myself thinking, over and over:

I am in pain but not in pleasure.
I live in sin but not in joy.
I dwell within a man and woman;
not in a girl or a boy.
What am I?

March 19
8:09 PM

Dear Hap:

I'm sitting outside right now, drinking a bottle of *Gong* beer and smoking a *Cowpoke* cigarette and slapping at mosquitoes. When the wind blows in a certain direction, coming out of the woods, I get a faint whiff of that delicious bread-baking smell. Ulla's inside, reading a magazine. Things are kind of tense between us—due to the White Sikh stuff and the moth episode—but we're not talking about it. Maybe all we need to do is not talk about it for a little while longer, and everything will settle back down to the way it was.

The white dog, Malami—or "Judy," as I like to call him—is at my feet now, creeping me out by sitting stock-still and staring at the forest, as if braced for an attack. I can feel dozens of small eyes watching us from the trees, but when I turn my head and look, all I see is blackness.

Last night I taught my first class at the Young English School.

When I arrived at the office, Sam was at his desk working on a new puzzle: an oil painting of a small, chubby man in full military uniform posing triumphantly on a white stallion, his sword high in the air. *Mont Saint-Michel* had been completed, mounted, and framed, and now hung on the wall behind him.

"Hi, Sam," I said. "How's it going?"

He grunted and continued to gaze fixedly at the blue patch of sky that he held in his hand.

I peered down at his desk. "That's Napoleon, isn't it?"

Sam lifted his head and surveyed me from behind his dark glasses. "That's correct. *Buonaparte* himself. A great, though short, Frenchman. Misunderstood by his women." He studied the picture and nodded thoughtfully. "When I was a younger man, I used to say: 'The French fuck with their faces and fight with their feet.' But now that I'm aged, and have more experience"—he chuckled—"I realize the French might have the right idea."

"Yeah, the French—"

"But enough about the French," said Sam, picking a ruler up off his desk. He held it to his eye, sighting along it like a rifle, then put it back down. "Tonight you'll be interviewing our fresh crop of students. They'll meet you in classroom 1-D. One-Donkey. Your task is to determine each student's degree of E.L.A., Eagle-Lizard-Ape, a.k.a. 'English Language Abilities.' You'll separate them into two sections: B.G., Bravo-Gopher, which is the Beginner Group, and A.G., Alpha-Gopher, which would be...?"

"The Advanced Group?"

"What? No. *Accelerated* Group." He frowned and made a mark on a piece of paper, then continued: "Anyways, you *write* down their names, you *assess* their E.L.A., you *assign* them to a group, and then *report* back to me. Write, Assess, Assign, Report. Whiskey-Ape-Ape-Rabbit. W.A.A.R." He glanced over at my notebook. "It must be nice, having a photogenic memory. Remind me never to play baccarat with you."

"Right, sorry." I took out my pen and quickly scrawled down:

1D-ELA-BG-AG-WAAR

Sam pointed at the copies of *ENGLISH FOR EACH* on the floor. "There are fourteen textbooks there. Distribute them amongst your students. One of them is yours. Take it home. *Read* it. *Learn* it. *Teach* it. R.L.T. Rabbit-Lizard-Tomcat."

"Okay, but how should I—"

Sam slapped the ruler on the edge of the desk. "*Chip chop*, and get thee to One-Donkey!"

Room 1-D was empty when I arrived, so while I waited for my students, I flipped through the textbook. *ENGLISH FOR EACH* looked and smelled as if it had been printed fifty years ago, and consisted of an assortment of stories, songs, pronunciation exercises, and party ideas. I opened the book to a chapter titled *Idiomatic Expressions*. Beneath a photograph of Winston Churchill, the caption read:

IDIOM #1
I'm not fat, I'm just short for my weight.

I spent the next few minutes reading a chapter called *MAKE IT FUN*, which listed a variety of games that you could play with your students:

Blind Monkeys: *Students are paired off, male-female, and blindfolded. The female student shells and feeds peanuts to her male partner. In this game, the teacher is the winner, to witness such a spectacle!*

Cry-baby Wah-Wah-Wah: *Before class, the teacher should secretly take the classroom's "most-popular" student aside and smut his fingers with charcoal. Then, when class is in session, the fun begins! Students are seated in a circle. The teacher makes certain to seat the most-popular student to the left of the* "least-popular" student in class. The teacher starts the game by turning to the student to his right, pinching both cheeks of that student, and saying, solemnly—"Pinchee, no laughee." That person turns to the student to his right and repeats the action. On the next round, the students put the forefinger of one hand under the chin of the student to their right and say, "Chuck-a-luckee." On the third round, they run their fingers down the face of the person to their right, as if that person is crying, and say: "Cry-baby wah-wah-wah." The trick is soon apparent to all but that one unlucky student whose face has been blackened with soot!

Cock-Fight: Two students are selected and have their wrists and ankles tied together with heavy rope. The arms are then passed over the knees, and a broomstick is pushed over one arm, under both knees, and over the other arm. In this position, the students try to upset one another. Whoever is the first to be successful wins a sack of peanut brittle.

Just as I began to wonder whether I was in the wrong room, a tall man with an extremely long ponytail walked in, *hai*-ed me, and sat down. My first student. I introduced myself, and we proceeded to have an awkward, one-sided conversation, during which I unsuccessfully attempted to learn his name. I gave up, and we both fell silent and sat waiting for the rest of the class to arrive.

After a couple of minutes the man stood, *hai*-ed me again, and left, presumably to go to the bathroom. Almost immediately, a familiar-looking older woman came in. I was pretty sure she was the secretary at the Faculty of Theatre Drama—I recognized the lobster-shaped ceramic brooch that she wore pinned to the lapel of her lavender business suit. I told her my name, explaining that I was Ulla's husband. When

I attempted to learn her name, she grew agitated, shouting at me in Puchanese and stalking out of the room.

A third student walked in, and that was when I understood: I wasn't sitting and waiting for the entire class to show up; I was in the midst of individually interviewing my students. This was W.A.A.R.

I wrote "*Long Ponytail*: B.G." and "*Angry Lobster*: B.G." in my notebook, then introduced myself to the new person in front of me. Despite the fact that I now knew what I was supposed to be doing, my interviews didn't noticeably improve. I couldn't get anyone to tell me his or her name (much less assess their abilities), and after three more interviews I didn't know anything about "*Crazy Perm*: B.G.," "*Swarthy Barefoot*: B.G.," or "*Giggly Glasses*: B.G." other than what they looked like.

The next person to enter the room was Mr. Horse.

"Hey!" I said. "Are you in my class?"

Mr. Horse smiled and gave a small bow. "Good night, Mr. Boyd. Yes, I am happy to be a student of you."

"It's good to see a friendly face."

"I do not know my face is friendly." He patted his cheek. "Thank you."

Mr. Horse sat with me for the remainder of the interviews, translating all of my questions into Puchanese and then translating the students' responses into English. I ended up putting everyone in the B.G., including Mr. Horse. He didn't really belong there, but there was no one else in the A.G., and I obviously needed his help.

After Mr. Horse left the classroom with the final student, I sat at my desk for a few minutes, delaying my return visit to Sam's office. Finally I stood up, switched off the light, and stepped outside.

All thirteen of my students stood there, clustered together and murmuring amongst themselves. They grew quiet as soon as they saw me. We stared at one another for several seconds, and then Mr. Horse raised his hand. I pointed at him and said, "Yes, Mr. Horse?"

"Excuse, but the class-time is one hour?" Mr. Horse bobbed his head apologetically. "We have thirty minutes remain for rest of class?"

"Oh, I didn't think we... I mean, I thought tonight we were only... never mind. I'm sorry." I *hai*-ed them and opened the door. "Please, come back in."

Once everyone was seated, I said, "Okay! Welcome. Let's see... what should we do? First of all, allow me to formally introduce myself. My name is Mr. Boyd." I went to the board and wrote: MR. BOYD. "My last name is *Darrow*, so you may call me Mr. Darrow, if you like." I wrote MR. DARROW on the board. "Or, you can just call me Boyd. No need to be formal." I wrote BOYD on the board, and waited for a minute as everyone printed my names into their notebooks. "Based on your interviews, I've determined that you all will be in the B.G.—the Beginner Group."

Mr. Horse raised his hand.

"Yes, Mr. Horse?"

"Excuse me," he said, getting to his feet. "Last year, I study in *A.G.* with Mr. Shawn. Not B.G."

I took a deep breath. "Well," I said, "I think this class will be sort of a *combination* of the Beginner and Accelerated groups. 'B.A.G.' That way, we can all learn from each other. We'll be like one single... *super*-group."

The students whispered to one another. Mr. Horse, still standing, raised his hand a second time.

I pointed at him. "Mr. Horse?"

"This class is 'super-group'—like Traveling Wilbury?"

"I guess so," I said. "Sure. We're like the Traveling Wilburys."

Mr. Horse nodded and smiled. "Very good!" He turned and addressed the class for a minute, and they listened to him with intense concentration. I heard him say "supergroup" and "B.A.G." Then he sang a few lines of "Handle with Care," doing a very credible imitation of Roy Orbison. The students nodded and murmured appreciatively.

After Mr. Horse sat down, a chubby young man with a wispy beard raised his hand.

"Yes, sir?" I said.

He got to his feet. "The Cream?"

"Excuse me?"

The man sang: "*In a white room, ba ba ba ba...*"

"Oh, *Cream*. Right. Cream is another supergroup. Good work." I went over to the blackboard and wrote:

"SUPER GROUPS"
The Traveling Wilburys
Cream

"Can anyone think of *another* supergroup that Eric Clapton was involved in?"

The students regarded me blankly. I hummed a few bars of "Layla," and Mr. Long Ponytail stuck his hand in the air. I pointed at him.

"Derek... and Dominos?"

"Correct! Derek and the Dominos, featuring Eric Clapton, and... I forget who else. One of the Allman Brothers?" I went and added *Derek and the Dominos* to our list. "Any more?"

"The Power Station," said a man in the back.

"Blind Faith!" yelled someone else.

"Asia!"

"Damn Yankees!"

After about ten minutes, we had a list of fourteen supergroups, including several Puchanese bands—"Gender 2000," "Devil Pile," "Team-Friends"—that I'd never heard of before. The class seemed to enjoy the exercise, and I now had their full attention. I checked my watch and said, "Let's finish up with something from the textbook."

I went around the room, handing out copies of *ENGLISH FOR EACH*, then glanced at the Table of Contents and selected a chapter called *PRACTICE TIME—Phrase Reading Example*. "Who would like to read aloud for us?" I asked.

Everyone kept their eyes on their desks except for Mr. Horse, who raised his hand high in the air.

"Okay, Mr. Horse. Very good. Let's turn to page thirty-seven. Mr. Horse, please read the first one—" I glanced at the title. "*The Spectral Zoo.*"

"Should I stand?" he asked.

"I don't think you need to."

"Mr. Shawn always say to stand when speak in the class."

I felt my jaw tighten. "Do whatever you want."

Mr. Horse nodded his head, considering his options, then smiled. "I will sit."

"Okay."

He cleared his throat and began to read: "High... above... the zoo... can... can-yons?... glides the... ayer?"

At that moment—as if on cue—the overhead lights began to blink on and off. The ceiling fan slowed and came to a stop. The classroom went silent and dark.

"Um..." I looked up at the lights, then back at my students. "It looks like the power's gone out."

"Yes," said Mr. Horse. "It happens sometime. To save the electricity. Do I continue?"

"I don't know." I glanced down at the page, waiting for my eyes to adjust. "Can you see to read?"

"I think yes."

Scanning the text, I said, "You know, this text sample is really hard, Mr. Horse. Maybe I should choose a different selection?"

"I want to try, please. It will be helpful to me." He held the book close to his face and then, slowly and stumblingly, pausing to sound out every word, he read:

High above the zoo canyons / glides the aerial tramway.
The skyfari whisks you / over grottos and mesas.
All of God's creatures / live lives of sweet harmony
and are now free of suffering / here in our special zoo.

The cotton-top tamarins / forage through leaf-litter
and white coatimundi / groom their young on the watercourse
as antic jerboas / frolic 'neath canebrakes
chasing the tails / of burrowing owls.

Patagonian cavies / stroll with peafowl and bearcat
and Scimitar oryx / nestle with mudhens.
Marmoset, civets, / sika, and scare-goats;
serval and pig-deer, / panthers and coy-dogs:

As they all roam here freely, / you may safely spy them
from the opposite side / of a deep-sunken ha-ha,
and if you look closely, / you might catch a glimpse of...

Mr. Horse smiled and paused dramatically, then finished:

... a small painted turtle / asleep in the sun.

With those words, the classroom door swung open, and in the dim light I could see a tiny, hunchbacked woman shuffle into the room.

The woman looked about a hundred years old, with a face like an apple left out in the sun. She was dressed in a tattered black tracksuit and wore an embroidered shawl draped around her neck. Her spidery fingers held a plastic picnic basket filled with Easter grass, chunks of honeycomb, and four brown whiskey bottles. She got down on her knees and began speaking in a rapid whisper. The students glanced at her as if she were a lizard that had skittered in across the floor, then turned back to me, waiting for the lesson to resume.

I awkwardly *hai*-ed the woman. "Can I help you?"

She ignored me, continuing to murmur under her breath like a sleepwalker. I looked to Mr. Horse for help.

"She is *malchak*. A honey-seller," he explained. "Not real honey; is made of sugar syrup, and then color is put in. Chemicals."

"Hmm." I looked at my watch. "Okay, everybody. It's basically seven o'clock. No homework tonight." I *hai*-ed my students. "Class dismissed."

They didn't move. Mr. Horse said a few words to them, and they began packing up their things and filing out the door, bowing to me as they left.

Mr. Horse approached my desk. "Thanks for all of your help," I said. "I'm new to teaching. Next class will be better."

"I'm happy to be a helper. The people in class are very shy. Also, some do not know much English words, and are stupid."

"Well, we're going to help them learn. I mean, *I* am."

"Yes." Mr. Horse turned to the *malchak* woman, who was still crouched at my feet. He spoke to her in Puchanese and pointed at the door. She studiously ignored him.

"It's okay, Mr. Horse. You can go. I'll take care of it."

After Mr. Horse had left, I looked down at the woman. It felt oddly intimate, standing above her there in the darkness. "Hi," I said. "*Ràp-naa ròp.*"

She grimaced and smacked her lips and didn't respond.

"How much for honey?" I asked, pointing at the basket.

"*Mà-tóo,*" she said, staring at a spot directly above my head.

"How much money?" I rubbed my thumb and forefinger together and pointed at a bottle. I didn't want to end up buying the whole basket again.

She looked me in the eyes and said: "*Prik!*"

I took out my wallet and handed her a brown bill, which is worth about three dollars. "Okay?" I said. "One bottle?"

She took the bill, and repeated: "*Prik!*"

I sighed, then handed her another bill, an orange one worth seventy-five cents. "How about that? That seems pretty fair," I said. She wrinkled her nose, then shrugged and offered me a bottle. I took it and held it in my hands. It looked as though it was filled with plasma.

Jungle honey.

"Thanks. Um, may I...?" I tentatively held out my hand to help her up, but the woman jumped to her feet and darted out the door.

I sat back down at the desk and closed my eyes, reviewing the evening's events. *The French... W.A.A.R... Angry Lobster... supergroups. The Spectral Zoo.* I pictured myself among the grottos and mesas, strolling with peafowl and bearcat... chasing the tail of a burrowing owl... riding on the back of a Scimitar oryx...

I was jarred awake by a loud noise from outside. I leapt up, instinctively grabbing the bottle of honey and brandishing it by its neck. The room was dark now, and I couldn't see much of anything. The door burst open and a beam of light shone into my eyes.

"Hello!" I yelled.

"What in the sweet name of Christmas are you doing sitting in the dark?"

Sam directed his flashlight at the bottle of honey in my hand. I was holding it over my head, as if about to hurl it at him.

"Sam," I said, slowly lowering my arm. "I... I bought some honey."

"Arrow. What happened?"

"Well, I wanted to report to you—"

"Mrs. Manarsumit just came to me. She said that nobody knew what the holy f-stop you were talking about, and that you had Máa translate for you during the E.L.A. assessment process?"

"Yeah, the thing is, the—"

"And then you left the entire class *standing outside* after the interviews were over?"

"Right, because I'd thought that we were just going to—"

"And then, when you brought them *back* inside, you informed them that they were all going to be smooshed together into one giant *super*-class, which you felt comfortable making up an *acronym* for?"

"That wasn't really official, I was going to consult you—"

"And then you spent half an hour discussing *rock* groups—"

"Actually, I think they enjoyed that—"

"—and *then* you spent the last few minutes having Máa read some crazy nonsense from the *advanced* section of the book—"

"I know, that was a mistake—"

"—and *then*, for the grand *finale*, you thought it would be a fun idea to invite a *honey-seller* in and use *class time* to make a sales pitch?" Sam pointed the flashlight at his face, so that I could clearly see his look of disbelief.

"I'm really sorry, Sam." I made a mental note of the name Manarsumit, wondering which one she was. Angry Lobster? "I'm still learning the ropes. I guess I just assumed that I could—"

"You *assumed*? Hold it right there. Let me give you a quick English lesson."

Sam walked over to the blackboard. I could hear him breathing through his nose as he inspected my list of supergroups, shaking his head. Then he erased the board, picked up a piece of chalk, and wrote the word ASSUME in huge capital letters.

"Now, what happens, Arrow, when you *assume*?"

Although I knew what he was about to say, I felt obligated to play along: "I guess sometimes, when you assume things, then, it's not an accurate prediction of..."

"Watch and learn." Sam violently slashed the word into three parts. "When you *assume*, Arrow, you make an *ASS* out of *U* and *ME*." As he spoke, he hit the board emphatically with his chalk, causing small bits of white shrapnel to splinter off. Then he leaned back against the wall, as if exhausted from his efforts.

"I'm really sorry, Sam," I said. "You can just tell me what to do and I'll do it. I'll take the book home tonight and..." I paused, trying to remember the acronym. "...R.L.T.?"

Sam gave me an approving nod and sighed. "Look. I'm not some kind of monster. But Y.E.S. has a sacred responsibility to its students." He wiped the chalkdust on his jeans and, studying his hands, said, "I sort of like you, Arrow. I don't know why.

Maybe I'm crazy—maybe I'm a gibbering madman. But, deep down, you look like you have a good head on your shoulders." He gazed heavenward, apparently seeking the strength to endure the trials I'd put him through. After a long pause, he continued: "I know you don't speak the local language, but you don't really need to. I'm a firm believer that, in this life, success is self-striven. Know what I'm saying?"

"Absolutely."

"Now, one final matter: you've heard about this thing that happens in the spring? The *Taang*?"

"Sure. My wife is working with Haraporn, helping to organize—"

"It's this big annual festival they have here. Fireballs shoot out of the river. People wear masks, get drunk, throw water-balloons at each other. *Etcetera*." He held up his finger. "Now, each year, one teacher is selected from the ranks of the Y.E.S. army to perform in the show. Said individual gets up and gives an eloquent speech based upon an essay title that I assign. The purpose is to provide the populace with a taste of what they'll get if they take a class with us. This year's title is, '*East is East and West is West: An Exploration of Socio-Cultural Differences Between the Gareng and Puchanese Worlds.*'" Sam patted the back of his head. "Pretty good, huh?"

"I like it."

"It should be no less than eight minutes and no more than fourteen minutes long. It's an advertisement for the school, so you want to really wow 'em. Two weeks before the Expo, I select the lucky individual. My Shiney absolutely refuses to participate, supposedly for political reasons—she can be stubborn as a horse when she wants to be—so this year, it's between you, Richie, and... what's-his-name. Black-beard."

I felt my stomach muscles tighten as I imagined myself standing on the stage of the P. Songpole Phammawattaana

Memorial Auditorium. Over the years, I've had any number of bad experiences that have contributed to my stage fright, but for some reason, the episode that flashed into my mind at that particular moment was the sixth-grade production of *Carousel*. (I know you remember the high-pitched fart I released during Justine Kalb's solo rendition of "You'll Never Walk Alone.")

I rubbed my eye with the palm of my hand. "It sounds great. But, I have to tell you, I'm just not honestly sure if I would be the *best* person to—"

"You and me both, Arrow. But it's a free country, so you're still in the running. I should emphasize that it's quite an honor to be selected. You'd be going on following the penultimate performance of the evening."

"You mean… it's the finale of the whole show?"

"That's right. We like to give the audience something to think about before they go off and have sex in the bushes. Haraporn lets us have that time slot every year. It's one of the benefits of being married to the organizer."

"The thing is, I get sort of nervous onstage…"

"I too suffer from a touch of *glossophobia*. You know what I like to do? Imagine the folks in the audience with their shirts off. Works like a charm." Sam pointed at me and added, "But I don't want you gawking at my daughter with that mindset. You know what? Just to be safe, I *forbid* you to use that trick."

"Okay," I said. "I promise."

"Also, for your information: in addition to the tremendous prestige conferred upon the selected individual, he or she will also receive an extremely generous bonus. Last year it was 9,000 *prik*."

"Really?" I did some quick math in my head: that was over three hundred dollars. I asked Sam to repeat the title of the speech, and as I wrote it down, I said, "Please keep me in mind. And thanks for giving me a chance."

"Okey doke. Second of two chances, Arrow." Sam stuck out his hand. "Give me your paw." We shook, and he turned to leave.

"Just one more thing," I said. "I wanted to ask you—at the end of each class, I assume that I should lock the—"

"*What*?" Sam's face twitched. "You *what*?" Then he chuckled and said, "I get it. You're razzing me."

"No, sir, I—"

"No respect for the elders." He smiled grimly and walked out of the room, leaving me alone in the darkness.

March 28
8:42 PM

Dear Hap:

My teaching gig is actually going pretty well—Sam has agreed to let me combine all the students into one single group, though he rejected my "B.A.G." acronym in favor of "M.G." (I forget what the M stands for. "Moderate"? Or maybe "Medium"?) Two of my students have dropped out already, which Sam wasn't happy about. He warned me not to make it a habit.

Sam loaned me a book that I'd spotted in his office: *Puchai—A Brief History of the Kingdom of Winks.* It contains a lot of information that the guidebook fails to mention. For instance, it goes into much greater depth on the topic of winking. Apparently, there's a different wink for every imaginable occasion and emotion, though I don't quite get how you're supposed to tell them apart. Now that I know that a wink doesn't mean simply "Hello, I like you," I'm a little worried about how my twitching eye has been interpreted by the locals.

Here is a partial list of winks and their meanings:

Príp johk: "I played a joke on you!"
Príp johk dtâ-lôk: "I am laughing at your joke although I don't find it funny."
Príp naâ raâk: "You're a cutie-pie. I want you."
Príp ràp róo: "I realize that I'm supposed to know who you are, but I'm sorry to say that I don't recognize your face."

Príp jóp hày: "I feel that, no matter how hard I try, no matter what I do, I am doomed to always stay exactly the same, trapped in a hell of my own devising."

Príp ngern: "I know I owe you a lot of money, but I don't have it at the moment."

Príp deng: "You're fired."

Príp wêrng wâang: "I am experiencing a keen sense of the inherent transience of all things, along with the understanding that this transience is the source of our world's beauty and sadness. However, this emotion is too vast for me to express in any way other than with this wink, which is meant to symbolize the relative quickness with which one's life passes by."

Príp jóot: "There's something in my eye. A piece of dust, or something. I don't know. Can you see anything in there?"

Príp pet sàm-pan: "I want to kiss your lips."

Príp jong nan glíat hee jong-chang: "I am trying unsuccessfully to fart."

Príp yíp: "It is as if my head is a camera, and my eye is the lens, and I am winking because I want to capture an image in my brain of the way that you look at this very moment, due to the fact that you are so incredibly beautiful to me."

Príp nong-nong: "I want many children. Do you have family wealth?"

Príp mor-rà lee: "I just realized that, one day, I shall be dead, my body rotting in the ground. I can't believe it. It's horrible."

Príp ràp-naa: "Hello and goodbye."

April 1
1:23 PM

Dear Hap:

Today is the third day of my new job. Not my job at Y.E.S.—my other new job. Mr. Yul has hired me to come to his office for a couple of hours daily and do some editing for him and his colleagues. Members of the Faculty of Gemology are supposed to stop by my desk when they need help phrasing something in English, but so far I've had very few visitors. Almost none, actually, except for Mr. Yul's gorgeous and aloof secretary—Ms. Pilopoblan—who brings me a small cup of *Express Dark* instant coffee every hour, as per Mr. Yul's instructions.

Right now I'm sitting in a large unfinished room in the bowels of the Faculty of Gemology building. In the corner of this room, two gray partitions are set up, creating a private nook for me. My only view around the corner of my partition is of the wall, and on that wall is a poster featuring the sickly face of an aging Yul Brenner. Below his image it states that he's dying of lung cancer, and recommends that everyone quit smoking cigarettes. I'm not sure if this poster was put up as some sort of office in-joke, or if Mr. Yul placed it there to make me feel as if he's watching me at all times.

I just received my first big check from Y.E.S.: almost 3000 *prik* for two weeks of work. Additionally, Mr. Yul gave me 600 *prik* for the editing I've done so far. Ulla has agreed to let me pay her back for the plane ticket in *prik*, with a decent exchange rate. I kept the 600 aside for spending money and gave her 3000, so now I only owe Ulla 26,460 additional *prik*—which means I'll have to work at Y.E.S. for another 17 weeks before my debt is paid. Maybe I need to look for a third job.

Ulla and I had a talk last night. We were playing dominoes, and neither of us had spoken for a while.

I said: "It's your turn, you know."

Ulla didn't say anything. Then she sighed and said, "It's your turn."

"Really? No."

"You've honestly been sitting here all this time thinking it was my turn?"

"It's definitely your turn."

"Whatever."

We both stared at the dominoes for a while. Then I said: "Are you okay, Ulla?"

She said: "Sure."

"You sure?"

"Are *you* okay?"

"You just seem really... I don't know."

She said: "Really what?"

"Far away."

"I can't imagine why."

"What's that supposed to mean?"

"What do you think?"

I said: "Ulla, all I did was get into a phone booth with some random person for a minute or two. You're the one with the secret White Sikh make-out sessions, and the secret—"

She said: "I'm too tired to fight with you. I just want to finish this stupid game and go to bed."

"We don't have to finish the stupid game at all if you don't want to."

"You want me to say that you're right? Okay. You win. You've done nothing wrong. I'm a bad person."

"Give me a break."

"I'm bad, and you're a perfect little angel. How's that?"

I didn't say anything.

She said: "You really, really look like you want to hit me right now."

I looked down at my hand. I unclenched my fist.

I said: "That's a terrible thing to say."

"I was kidding." Then she said: "Though it's kind of true, isn't it?"

"I don't like being like this."

"You think I like it?"

"It's hard enough living here, in this little room."

"I know it's hard. It's hard for me."

"It's been hard on both of us."

"I know."

I said: "At this point, we both just need to get over this stuff and move on."

She shrugged and drank her beer.

I said: "Maybe we should call a truce."

"A truce?"

I stuck out my hand.

"Fine." We shook.

"I'm serious. For real." I tightened my grip. "Truce?" I tightened my grip some more.

She said: "Yes! Truce! Uncle!"

She laughed, and her laughing made her suddenly appear blindingly pretty.

I released her hand. "I'm waving the white flag. Okay?"

"All right."

"We're on the same team here. We need to be a team."

"I know."

"I'm a man of peace."

"All right."

I said: "Make love?" I winked at her. "Not war?"

She winked back at me and picked up a domino.

"Let's finish this game first," she said. "I'm about to win."

April 2
3:22 PM

Dear Hap:

I've been trying to work on my Expo *Taang* essay the past few days, just in case Sam decides to give me the honor of representing the Young English School. This is what I've got so far:

A wise man once said: "East is East, and West is West, and never the twain shall meet." However,

I stopped by Y.E.S. this afternoon to talk to Sam, hoping to get some additional guidance on the subject.

As I walked my bike up the driveway, I saw Gabe sitting on a stool outside the office, reading a book and running his fingers through his hair. I thought I could detect a fleeting look of panic in his eyes when he noticed me.

"Hey," I said.

Gabe stifled an exaggerated yawn, as if I'd just woken him. "Darrow. What's up."

"Are you waiting for Sam?"

"Shiney."

I leaned against the wall and shoved my hands in my pockets. "I was going to see if I could meet with Sam."

Gabe bobbed his head, squinting off into the middle distance.

I pointed at his book. "What're you reading?"

"'*De Bartók aux Malchak: Culture Asiatique et l'Inquiétude de l'Ouest.*'" He flipped through the pages and added, "Critical theory bullshit."

"Do you take classes at the college?"

"This college here?" He snorted. "No. I go to I.U.D."

"I.U.D.?"

Gabe frowned and said, "*In*ternational *Un*iversity of *Da*khong."

"Oh. Right. That's how you know Shiney."

He nodded. "I was the TA in a class of hers."

"So you're just taking a break from school now?"

"I'm getting my Master's in Ethnomusicology. All I have left to do is finish my thesis." Gabe lowered his voice. "Sam basically fired all of his teachers last semester, then begged Shiney to move back home to help out. I decided to come with her and investigate the scene for a bit. There's a lot of research I can do here."

"What're you writing about?"

"It's... well... I'm not really used to discussing it in layman's terms." Gabe moved his tongue inside his mouth, as if trying to find a lost morsel of food. "Basically, I'm investigating the renovation of traditional *malchak panuk* music—as spearheaded by the *malchak* youth population— and its affinities with the avant-garde, particularly with contemporary experimental 'noize' compositions. The *malchaks*' unsuccessful... *mestization*, if you will... into this society has resulted in feelings of insecurity and isolation, against which music and dance are, of course, crucial bulwarks. However, much of their rich indigenous culture is in danger of being lost, due to modernizing influences, such as radio and television." Gabe reached up and thoughtfully stroked his beard with both hands, then grunted and continued: "In my paper, I plan to show that the *malchak* youth of today configure their identity—in both cultural and ethnic matrices—via musical expressions whose so-called authenticity is overdetermined, and that this reconfiguration enacts a dialectic in which cultural fluctuations in music and dance must be legitimized by an essentialized '*malchak*-ness.' The current generation is attempting to invert the power relations inherent in post-colonial thought by asserting their own grass-roots hegemony through a dramatic reconfiguration of the traditional *dtoom bpia noh*. They hold secret shows where they tap into the power grid, and hook up these crazy jerry-rigged speakers made out of stuff that they scavenge from the junkyard—"

"What's a *dtoom bpia noh*?"

"The *dtoom bpia noh* is a little metal piano-like instrument that you play mostly with your feet. It was traditionally acoustic, but just recently some kids have started to electrify and amplify them. They like it insanely loud—the sound makes your whole body numb. The music is like classic noisecore, mixed with *musique concrète*, mixed with... well, imagine BlackOxx and the dude from *Masturbierendes Musterbeispiel* doing a cover of a Steve Reich composition, and you get the idea."

"Have you actually seen them play live?" I asked.

"Yeah, totally."

"Do they have any shows coming up?"

"Umm..." Gabe massaged his temples, as if staving off a migraine. "Hard to say. The shows are usually illegal—due to the whole tapping-into-the-power-grid thing—and the *malchaks* are super-secretive about when and where they go down. They don't like having any non-*malchaks* showing up, much less some random white dude. But Shiney's been hooking me up. She's buddies with this one group—*Kati*

Na-Gareng." Lowering his voice, he added, "She used to fuck the lead singer, Pônge, back in high school."

"Really?"

He shrugged. "So?"

"I didn't think *malchaks* interacted much with the Puchanese. They seem pretty segregated."

"Dude, Shiney *is* a *malchak.*" Gabe glanced towards the door, then murmured, "Shiney's mom was full *malchaki-gai*—she was a *gà-roó-na* girl when Sam met her."

"Haraporn...?"

"Yeah, right." He laughed, spraying me with a fine mist of spittle. "No, Haraporn's her step-mom. Shiney's mom died years ago. I think Shiney and Pônge are even vaguely related somehow—kissing cousins, thrice removed."

"Isn't '*pônge*' a Puchanese word?"

"'*Pônge*' means 'alien.' He calls himself that as a way of re-appropriating the language of oppression. He's an intense guy." Gabe rolled his shoulders. "I actually got high with *Kati Na-Gareng* last weekend. It was pretty cool."

"What does '*Kati Na-Gareng*' mean? Is that '*gareng,*' as in... you and me?"

Gabe nodded. "*Kati Na-Gareng* means 'Kill Whitey.'"

The door opened, and Sam and Shiney emerged. Shiney looked at us and smiled. "Hello, men."

Sam mumbled a greeting, then said to his daughter, "See you later, alligator." He kissed the top of her head and walked briskly towards the dusty white Yugo parked next to the office.

"Excuse me, Sam?" I called after him. "Is now a good time for you to meet with me?"

"Now's no good," Sam said over his shoulder. "Got to see a man about a horse." He got into the car and slammed the door.

Shiney glanced at Gabe and said, "Hey, you know what? We should invite Boyd and his wife to that thing." She turned to me. "There's a music show tonight. Would you like to come? I think it would be interesting for you—it's a *malchak* group."

"*Kati Na-Gareng*?" I said.

"You know of them?"

Gabe tugged on his earlobe. "I was just telling Boyd about my thesis and all that," he explained. "I'm not sure if they'd actually find the show so interesting."

"I bet they would," said Shiney.

"Don't you think it might be a little weird if they came? I wouldn't want to piss off the band."

"Let me handle the band."

"Plus, Boyd already had that run-in with the *malchak*s, and he's probably afraid of getting attacked again. And I have to say, I wouldn't blame him." Gabe pointed his beard in my direction. "But, of course, it'd be cool if you'd like to join us."

"It'll be *fine*," said Shiney. "Nobody will be attacking anybody. We'll just stand in the back. We can all wear *tai-lans* and *bprà-jiats*. Boyd, what do you think? Want to come?"

I glanced at Gabe, who was squinting into the sunlight and tapping his book against his leg. I pictured myself in a smoky club, surrounded by *malchaks*. Then I looked at Shiney, who was staring up at me and smiling.

"Yes," I said. "I do."

April 4
11:58 PM

Dear Hap:

Ulla had initially informed me that she had no intention of going to the *Kati Na-Gareng* show, but when Gabe and Shiney showed up at our doorstep after dinner, her desire to leave the house won out over her dislike of Shiney, and she wordlessly put on her jacket and stepped outside.

Shiney carried a large duffle bag slung over her shoulder—she told us that she had to drop off some stuff at her Auntie Golli's house before the show. "It's on the way," she said, pointing at the trail leading into the woods. "We can travel by foot. We should have another half-hour of daylight."

When we reached the fork in the path, Ulla paused at the rotting dog-corpse. "This thing is so sad-looking," she said. "Shouldn't somebody do something about it? It must be a health hazard."

"This was Flip," Shiney said.

"Excuse me?"

"That was his name. Like the black American comedy star, Mr. Flip Wilson." Shiney bowed her head and said, as if in eulogy: "Flip was a pretty good dog." Then she stepped over him and continued down the path.

The four of us made our way single-file through the forest, and this time, I paid close attention to where I was going. We took a hard right at the egg-shaped rock, and soon we'd descended the stone staircase and emerged onto the ridge overlooking the river. We walked up the river road, passing old women who squatted on blankets and glared at us as they sewed scarves, and men who sat on stacked bags of black rice, drinking from a green glass bottle handed back and forth; and we passed a small boy who hovered, half-crouching, in the cold ashes of a fire pit. He wore a yellow sweatshirt and nothing else, and played with a bone tied to a piece of fishing line. Shiney greeted a few people here and there. They smiled at her, then murmured to one another: *gareng, gareng, gareng.*

As we approached a row of steaming oil drums, Gabe made a grunting noise in his throat—*ur, ur, ur*—that sounded like a robot coughing up a hairball. I gave him an inquiring look.

"*Ur-ur-ur.*" Shiney gestured towards the drums. "It's a kind of alcohol, made out of fermented *garongs.* Let's get a bottle."

She went over to the still and spoke to a slim teenage boy whose long, matted hair was woven through with green twist-ties. He gawked at us for a moment, unblinking, then handed her a stack of Dixie cups.

"First, we should have a taste," said Shiney, reaching into a barrel and filling her cup. The three of us followed suit. I'd expected the stuff to be clear, like moonshine, but it was cloudy white and smelled of perspiration and tangerines.

"*Páe laa jàak piang sàk,*" said Shiney, raising her cup. "That is the traditional *malchak* toast. Meaning, 'The pig dies but once.'"

We all took a drink. Ulla immediately spit hers onto the ground. "I'm sorry," she murmured. "It burnt my throat."

I drank my portion in two quick gulps. Going down, it felt like a mouthful of gasoline, but after I'd swallowed it, a rich flavor began to emerge on the back of my tongue. I tasted, in quick succession: beeswax, barnyard hay, and baby aspirin, with a *garong*/Creamsicle finish. I felt my face grow warm, as though struck by a passing sunbeam. When I exhaled, I breathed fire.

Shiney gave the boy some money, and he handed her a bamboo tube with a rubber stopper at the top. Shiney passed it over to me. "A gift for your household," she said.

We continued our walk along the river, passing the flask around and taking swigs. The last traces of the lowering sun clung to the orange sky above the water, and the air was thick with the sweet smell of woodsmoke and rotting *garongs*.

"Your aunt lives all the way out here?" said Ulla.

Shiney nodded. "My dad tried many times to make Golli move in with him and Haraporn, but Golli refused, so he had a small home built for her on the river. She's the only *malchak* in Mòk Bòo who has a strong house. I think that the jealousy of her friends makes her very satisfied. It's right up there—see?"

Up ahead was a tiny, perfectly square concrete dwelling that stood apart from the shanties. A blue plastic tarp hung in front of its door like a curtain, and in lieu of windows there were rows of glass bricks placed high up on one side. The building's roof was a single piece of corrugated green fiberglass. Though its design was simple, it looked completely out of place among the rows of haphazardly-constructed shacks, like a house that had fallen from the sky.

Shiney pushed the tarp aside, knocked once, then took out a key and let herself in. We entered a sparsely furnished room with a packed-earth floor and a ceiling so low that Gabe and I could barely stand up straight. A folding bamboo screen sectioned off the far corner; stacks of honey-filled brown bottles lined the opposite wall. There was a stone hearth with a fire smoldering in it, and a cast-iron pot hanging over the embers. It looked like the home of a fastidious sorceress.

Shiney disappeared behind the folding screen, and we could hear the creaking sound of someone being helped out of a hammock. After a minute, an old woman emerged. I was surprised to see that I'd met Auntie Golli before—she was the honey-seller who'd come into my class the other evening.

Golli blinked at us sleepily and frowned, then sat by the fire and began distractedly searching through the pockets of her tracksuit, pulling out used tissues and bobby pins. Shiney unpacked her duffle bag, placing a few groceries and bottles of water on the long wooden table in the middle of the room. I crouched on the ground and played with a small black kitten that was chasing my shoelaces. When I stood up, Golli gestured towards me and spoke in a raspy mutter.

"Golli says that you are a giant," Shiney explained.

I nodded and smiled at the old woman. "Yes. I am very tall," I said, stiffening my arms and swaying back and forth like Frankenstein's monster. Golli got to her feet and pointed at a spot directly above my head, flicking her fingers as though drying them off. Shiney frowned and asked her something, but Golli just turned away and went and sat back down.

"What?" I said. "What did she say?"

"Oh... nothing," Shiney said, smiling tightly. "We should get going."

Gabe bowed to Golli and said, "*Ràp-naa ròp, Golli-Hàa. Rao pa-waa Ngoo-pìk teo-da bàan krí-hât.*"

Auntie Golli gave him a stiff-eyed look and quietly responded, then broke into hysterical laughter. We could still hear her giggling as she shut the door behind us.

It had grown dark outside now, but our path was lit by kerosene lanterns that hung along the clusters of shacks.

After walking in silence for a minute, Gabe asked: "So, what was the big joke back there?"

"The *malchak* dialect is difficult," said Shiney. "Even for Puchanese people. It sounds very funny when you attempt to speak it."

"She said something about a flower?"

"Golli said: 'Go shit in your hat, pull it over your ears, and call it flowers.'" Shiney laughed. "My father taught her that expression."

"Hilarious," Gabe muttered.

"I think your aunt came into my classroom last week," I said. "I bought some honey from her."

"Really?" Shiney sighed and shook her head. "Well, don't tell my dad. He doesn't like it when she does that. Someday I'll show you—and you, Ulla—where they keep the bees. There's a long tradition of honeybee-farming with the *malchak* people."

JUNGLE HONEY.

Ulla turned to me. "Didn't someone tell you it was just sugar syrup and food coloring?"

"People say many lies about the *malchaks*," Shiney said. "'*Malchaks* are all drunks.' '*Malchaks* eat turtles.' '*Malchaks* sell bottles of river-water to tourists, pretending it's *garong-juice*.'" She paused, then added, "That one is sometimes true, I suppose."

We'd come to the end of the shantytown, and up ahead I could dimly make out the high school and the grove of *garong* trees. I half-expected to see the kids along the road, still throwing fruit at cars, but the sidewalk was empty. I looked out at the river. Near the opposite bank, a man in a flat-bottomed skiff pushed himself through the water with a long bamboo pole, whistling the same three notes over and over, as though perfecting a bird call. A lamp hung from the front of his boat, and if you didn't look too closely, it appeared that it was floating unsupported through the darkness.

"Do balls of fire really shoot out of the river during the festival?" I asked.

"Yeah, it's pretty cool," said Gabe. "The water level drops due to the lunar cycle, and the gas trapped at the bottom of the river is forced up to the surface. It combusts and creates a—"

"We believe there is a giant turtle," said Shiney, "the *ngoo*, residing on the bottom of the river. It is a very old spirit-animal that has lived there for approximately two hundred and sixty years. On the day of the full moon in April, the monks traditionally return from their forest retreat. The *ngoo* is a lover of the senses, and is annoyed by the life of the monks—their vows of chastity, their detachment from the world—and so it shoots up the red balls of light in an attempt to fill them with… longing."

"Go on," said Gabe. "You left out the best part."

Shiney shot him a look. "Supposedly," she continued, "the turtle is trying to tempt the monks into the water because it wants to make love to them."

Ulla laughed. "Yikes."

"How big is the turtle?" I asked.

"About the size of a compact car."

"And it's a lady turtle?"

"The turtle is said to have both a penis and a vagina."

"Have any of the monks ever gone into the water?"

Shiney paused, then said: "One man that I know of, yes."

"What?" said Ulla. "Come on."

"The brother of Mr. Yul."

"You mean the guy who the theater's named after?" Ulla asked. "'P. Songpole Phammawattaana'?"

"He obviously must've been crazy," Gabe said. "He basically just drowned himself on Festival Day. I don't think he was raped by any giant turtles."

"Who knows what happened," said Shiney. "There have been many stories."

"Like what?" I asked.

Shiney shrugged. "Sightings of him beneath the water, riding on the back of the *ngoo*. His arms around its neck..."

"Hey," said Gabe. "We're here."

We were alongside the fenced-in *mâdan* that I'd noticed on my first visit to Mòk Bòo. From this angle, I could see that its temple-like façade was as flat and two-dimensional as a stage set. The building itself was an ugly, industrial-looking concrete structure with smoke streaming out of its tall brick chimney. A warm wave of the fresh-bread smell hit us as we approached, and I inhaled a lungful. "What is this place, anyways? Some sort of high-security bakery for monks? It smells delicious."

Shiney made a face. "This is *Cherng Dtà-gon Mâdan*. It's a—what do you call it?" She wiggled her fingers. "A place where they burn the dead bodies?"

"Crematorium," said Gabe.

"Some band is playing a *show* in there?" asked Ulla.

"*Kati Na-Gareng* is friends with the night watchman here." Shiney stopped and fished around in her duffle bag, then handed us each a small flashlight. We switched them on and followed her along the chain-link fence, picking our way through weeds and piles of trash. She seemed to be searching for something.

"What are we looking for?" asked Ulla.

"This," Shiney said, pointing her light at the fence.

A black, dead-looking thing was tied there with wire. In the unsteady flashlight beam, I could just catch a few details: bits of fur and stringy flesh; a small claw; an eyeless face; a row of white teeth. When Shiney lowered her light, the dark shape stood out against the white spray of stars as if it were a hole in the sky.

I grabbed Shiney's elbow and then immediately released it. "What is it?"

"A *dtit-laa*."

"A flying dog?"

Ulla turned to me. "What?"

"It's a fruit bat," explained Gabe.

"Why'd they put it here?" I asked. "Some kind of warning?"

"To show people how to get in."

Shiney yanked on the fence, and a section of it peeled away where the links had been neatly cut. She held it back as we passed through the opening, then carefully replaced it and led us across the lawn, coming to a stop at the foot of the temple steps. A desk lamp glowed from inside, but otherwise it looked closed for the night.

"Before we enter, I have some clothes for us." Shiney unzipped her bag and pulled out four gunnysack robes, the kind I'd seen many *malchaks* wearing. "These are *tai-lans*," she said. She handed one to each of us, then put one on herself, tying the belt around her waist.

Ulla looked at her *tai-lan* dubiously. "I don't think I'll fool anyone in this."

"It's not a disguise," said Shiney. "It's a costume. Wearing it will show respect for the *malchaks*, and solidarity with their cause. You will maybe want to put this on, also." Shiney handed Ulla a square of blue cloth with pink and gray embroidered trim. "This is a *bprà-jìat*. You cover your hair with it, like this." She demonstrated by tying it around her own head, then helped Ulla with hers.

My robe barely covered my knees. Ulla looked at me and began to giggle. Shiney held a *bprà-jìat* out to me and said, "For you."

"Men wear these things?"

"Bend down," said Shiney. She rolled it up and tied it around my head like a sweatband, then stepped back and admired her work. "There. No one will ever suspect that you're not a *malchak*."

Shiney rang the silver bell that hung next to the *mâdan*'s entrance, and we waited in tense silence for a time. "Looks like nobody's home," I said.

"They're in there." Shiney balled up her fist and pounded on the door. Thirty seconds later, it opened up a crack, and a broad-shouldered, round-headed man glowered out at us. He was dressed in a military-style uniform and had a red *bprà-jìat* on his head. His khaki shirt hung open, revealing a yellow t-shirt with a silk-screened drawing of a clenched fist, its middle finger sticking straight up. A face was drawn on the finger, and a speech bubble coming out of its mouth said: "I LOVE YOU."

The man looked at each of us, curled his lip, and began to close the door. Shiney quickly wedged her body halfway inside and started yelling at him.

Gabe stepped back. "Too many *garengs*. I knew it."

Shiney shoved the door open and ushered us into a small office. A filing cabinet and a wooden desk stood in one corner; in the other was an altar decorated with flowers, incense, and a neat stack of turtle statues made from red clay. The round-headed man shouted something at us, then stormed out of the room through a door at the back.

"What's going on?" Gabe whispered.

"That guard is an idiot—I've never seen him before," said Shiney. "Acting like I don't belong here. I designed that *Kati* t-shirt he's wearing." She folded her arms and leaned against the wall. "He went to go get Pônge."

A minute later, a compact, dark-skinned man swept into the room, yelling over his shoulder at the chastened guard. He had the sinewy torso of a junkie and the severe but beautiful face of a consumptive starlet. His neck and chest were tattooed with tiny, symmetrical lines and dots drawn in dark blue ink. The only clothing he wore was a pair of green camouflage pants and a black *bprà-jìat* tied around his neck like a miniature cape. He cocked his chin at Shiney, then spun and cuffed the guard on the ear—a movement so quick and graceful, it almost appeared choreographed for our benefit.

"Pônge, these are my friends," said Shiney. "Boyd and Ulla."

Pônge took Ulla's hand and, exhaling slowly, said: "Yes. Good to meet *Ul-la.*" His voice was soft and deep and full of breath, and in his mouth, Ulla's name sounded like some kind of obscene act.

Ulla curtsied awkwardly, her face glowing. "*Ràp-naa lei.*"

Pônge stepped back and stared at her, as if admiring a painting he was working on, then murmured something to Shiney and ran his tongue across his teeth. Shiney frowned and spoke to him sharply as he turned and left the room, followed closely by the guard.

Gabe chuckled. "I think Pônge took a liking to you, Ulla."

"Really?" Ulla made her mouth small and rapidly blinked her eyelids. "Why, what did he say?"

"I'm pretty sure he said something about wanting to 'ride in the ivory canoe.' Is that the right translation, Shiney?"

"Pônge is a dog. *Worse* than a dog."

Shiney led us out of the office, and we silently followed her down a plasterboard hallway lit by banks of flickering yellow-gray lights. Pônge was nowhere to be seen. The *malchak* guard stood sentry at the far end of the corridor, and when we reached him, he nodded to us and opened a door, revealing a storage closet that was empty except for a mop and a few cleaning supplies. He squatted down and pushed aside a dirty pink mat, then lifted a wooden panel fitted into the floor.

I peered down into the square, dark hole. "Is that a laundry chute?"

"Don't even *tell* me we're going down there," said Ulla.

"It's okay," Shiney said. "It's safe."

"Aren't there any stairs?" I asked.

"We're going to a special part of the building, where no stairs lead," said Shiney. "The *Boon Jai*, it's called. 'The Pride.'"

Shiney explained that, back in the days when gambling was illegal, organized criminals would pay architects and contractors to build a secret room into the heart of a building during its construction—a room that couldn't be entered unless you knew it was there. "They would hold private casinos here in the night," she said, "playing *yuang baát*—'sticky dice'—and *tuâ tuâ*, the bean-counting game. Many buildings contain a Pride within them; a space that is now not used for anything. Most of the people who have worked in this building probably didn't ever know of the existence of this Pride." Shiney pointed her flashlight down into the hole, revealing a set of iron rungs along the side. "There will be lighting in the tunnel once we get to the bottom of the ladder. You will need your torches for the first part. Be careful going down."

She stuck her flashlight between her teeth, lowered herself into the shaft, and was gone. Gabe waited for a moment, then followed after her. As Ulla sat down on the edge of the chute, I said, "It's all right if you're scared. We can just wait up here."

Ulla tilted her face up to me. "I'm curious to see the band," she said. Then she took hold of the iron rungs, and I watched as the top of her head gradually disappeared into the darkness below.

I looked over my shoulder at the guard, who was leaning against the wall, staring at me impassively. I adjusted my headband, feeling ridiculous in my costume. "It is safe to go

down there?" I said, pointing at the chute. He wrinkled his
nose and said something, then reached into his pocket and
took out a small jackknife, opened it, and began to clean his
fingernails.

Just go.

"All right," I said. "See you around." I put the tube of *ur-
ur-ur* down the front of my *tai-lan*, and began to thread my
body into the hole.

I'd only descended a few feet when the guard replaced the
floor panel above me, sealing me in. I took a deep breath,
wrapped my arm around one of the iron rungs, and fished
around for the flashlight in my pocket. Its light was so weak
that all I could make out were four or five rungs directly
below me. I put the flashlight in my mouth, as Shiney had
done, and almost immediately gagged and spit it out, sending
it bouncing off the sides of the chute a few times before its
light went dead. Several seconds passed before I heard it
clatter to the ground.

I called Ulla's name. There was no response. I remained
frozen in place for a moment, then began rapidly climbing
downward, pressing my back against the wall, feeling the
concrete scrape against my spine. I began to sing at the top
of my lungs: "*There's darkness down the mine, my darling,
darkness, dust and damp, and I'm without my heat, my light,
my lantern or my lamp!*"

When my foot touched solid ground, I found myself
at the mouth of a low tunnel. Flickering yellow lights ran
along the ceiling, though many were burned out. The floor
was covered with thick shag carpeting that had once been
pink but was now mostly an ashen gray. I could only see
about thirty feet ahead of me; after that, I couldn't make
out which way the tunnel went. I called Ulla's name again,

but the sound of my voice diffused and deadened in the airless space. I crouched and scuttled down the passageway, following it as it turned to the right, and then to the right again, doubling back on itself.

A few moments later, I was confronted with a wall of rough-cut stone and a set of iron rungs that led straight up to another hatchway. I started climbing. When I'd almost reached the top, I paused, adjusted my robe and my *bprà-jìat*, then poked my head into the room. I was ankle-level with a crowd of *malchaks*—and none of the ankles looked familiar.

The Pride looked like an abandoned banquet hall that had become a haven for all sorts of clandestine activities. (Actually, it kind of reminded me of that place on Woodbine that you and Brooke-Ann used to sneak into.) The pink shag carpet was strewn with cigarette butts and bottle caps and playing cards, along with odd bits of ancient-looking ephemera that included a rusty corkscrew, a large black feather, several unopened condoms, a baby's pacifier, and an unspooled 8-track cassette of *Iron Butterfly's Greatest Hits*. The walls were painted canary yellow, with dark teak wainscoting running along the bottom. A series of symbols and icons were spraypainted in red across the ceiling, strung together like an unsolvable rebus: an eyeball, a figure-eight, a six-pointed star, a smoking gun, an X-ed out smiley face, and a bulbous penis with a pair of wings growing out of the sides.

"Boy-*duh*."

I turned and saw Shiney towering above me. The *malchaks* murmured loudly as she helped me out of the chute and led me to the corner of the room, close to where the musicians were setting up.

"People seem disgruntled," I said, glancing over my shoulder. "Are you sure it's okay that we're here?"

"They'll settle down in a minute."

"I don't know, they—*ow!*" I stumbled forward in surprise, then tentatively pressed my palm against the cinderblock wall that I'd just leaned against. It was hot to the touch.

"The ovens are on the other side," Shiney said.

"Jesus. This place is a total fire trap."

Shiney shrugged and looked around. "Should we go join our mates?"

We made our way over to where Ulla and Gabe stood. Ulla was saying, "It sounds like he blurs the lines between being a musician, a performance artist, a shaman, and a political activist. The Futurists used to explore a similar territory in their—"

"Hey," I said, placing my hand on her shoulder.

She jumped with surprise. "Boyd. Hi. What happened to you?"

"What happened to *you*?"

"What do you mean? I was—"

"Guys," whispered Gabe, holding his finger to his lips and pointing towards the musicians. "I think they're about to start."

Pônge sat on a stool, distractedly tapping on a small drum. A light shone directly onto his face, illuminating the layer of smoke that clung to the ceiling like a swath of spiderwebs. Several people stood behind him, tinkering with their instruments. A fine-featured *malchak* in a loose-fitting *tai-lan* sat on the floor next to Pônge, drinking water from a glass jar and looking incredibly bored. It wasn't until she stood up and removed her robe that I realized she was a woman. Hundreds of tiny bells tied to loops of string hung from her neck, and when she moved, it sounded like the distant noise of breaking glass. I'd begun to feel a ticklish sensation below my ankles, as if my socks were filling with ants, and then the itch became a vibration, and as this vibration grew stronger, it slowly crawled up my body, from the bottoms of my feet to the top of my head—numbing my face, my eyeballs, my tongue—and for a moment I thought that I was about to pass out again. But then the vibration became a sound, and I realized that *Kati Na-Gareng* had started to play.

The audience surged forward, the current of bodies pushing me in one direction and Gabe and Ulla in another. I looked back at them, and saw Gabe put his arm around Ulla's shoulder, flashing me a sour smile. An ambiguous expression flickered across Ulla's face as she and Gabe disappeared into the crowd.

The members of *Kati Na-Gareng* stood in front of several stacks of small black speakers that looked as though they'd been assembled in shop class. Three men crouched on the floor, playing a single, sustained note on their foot-pianos; another man held a large rubber mallet and was knocking it against a bedspring hooked up to an amplifier. A woman banged together a couple of PVC pipes into a microphone that hung above her head, while two other women—dressed in tight-fitting costumes embroidered with black and yellow beads—stood off to the side, swaying back and forth and hugging themselves as if they were cold. A tall man was lying on his stomach and fiddling with an acoustic guitar that had a car battery attached to the neck. Next to him was a chubby young *malchak* playing what looked like a stand-up electric bass made out of an oil drum, a boom box, and a rake. It was the fat boy—the kid who'd led the *garong* attack against me. Together, the band made the loudest noise I'd ever heard, the sound pushing against my eardrums as though straining to penetrate them.

I removed the container of *ur-ur-ur* from my back pocket and took a long pull; this time, it was much smoother going down. Pônge had wandered over to the speakers and was fiddling with the knobs, altering the pitch of the noise, nodding to himself and beating lightly on his small metal drum as if playing along to some inaudible rhythm. Impossible as it seemed, the noise grew even louder. I pressed my hands to my ears and glanced around. Everyone else in the room wore a look of rapt attention. Shiney had materialized at my elbow, and I opened my mouth and said her name, but my voice was swallowed up by the ocean of sound. I drank some more *ur-ur-ur*, and as I closed my eyes and listened to the noise surrounding me, a series of images flashed unbidden through my mind: a bucket of plastic apples; a dog dressed up like a pilot; an old man eating a candle; a gold watch floating in a toilet. I opened my eyes again. The drone had quieted to a barely audible hum, and Pônge was altering the volume on the speakers—he'd turned it all the way down, and was now slowly turning it back up. As the volume increased, the music began to mutate, becoming faster, more rhythmically complex. The two costumed women moved their bodies, not dancing exactly, but trembling to the beat. Pônge walked over to the spotlight and picked up the microphone. He began to sing a mournful, atonal melody, his vocals just slightly out of sync with the music, which in turn sounded completely unrelated to the percussion. His voice was rich and deep, and contained an uncracked sob that reminded me of a field recording I'd once heard of chain-gangs chanting as they broke rocks. The girl stood next to him, holding her string of bells and shaking them. The music swelled and ebbed, and the distorted, arrhythmic plonking of the toe-pianos grew louder. The girl with the bells had moved into the spotlight and was singing, though she didn't have a microphone. Pônge was standing off to the side, still singing into his mic, but now his voice was a high, womanly falsetto.

"Oh," I said aloud, though no one could hear me. "She's lip-syncing to his voice."

I looked around, wanting to share my realization with someone. Several people in the crowd held their arms out stiffly, their bodies shaking, as though experiencing some kind of collective fit. I leaned back down to Shiney. "What's everybody doing?"

Without taking her eyes away from the stage, she said: "Dancing."

I opened the tube of *ur-ur-ur*, had another drink, and then tapped Shiney on the elbow with it. She took it from me and swallowed several mouthfuls. I stepped a little nearer to her and asked, "What's he singing about?" Shiney began to respond, but I couldn't hear her. I bent down further, putting my ear directly next to her lips. "Sorry—what?"

"The song is based on a *malchak* legend," she said. "*Puthanawai Akkarat-Mee*. It's a very long poem about a famous warrior called Akkarat. This section tells about how Akkarat's jealous brother, Vichit, puts an evil spell on him. Akkarat is now living in exile from the village. He's on the verge of drowning himself in the river when he meets a young woman, Piam, who is washing her hair in the water. She takes pity on him and gives him some little snacks—dried fish, a boiled egg. Pônge is singing the dialogue between the man and the woman by the side of the river."

"It's cool how he's singing in her voice," I said. The girl with the bells continued to mouth Pônge's words, moving her hands above her head as though pulling on invisible strings. "Like Angel & Mann—you know?"

"This performance tradition is a typical example of *malchak* culture," Shiney said, shaking her head. "Never allowing the woman to speak for herself."

The music was becoming more and more frenzied, although Pônge's singing remained lilting and melodic. The crowd was spellbound, straining forward to hear every word, their bodies shuddering ecstatically. I looked back at Shiney, and saw that her body was beginning to tremble as well.

I touched her shoulder. "Sorry," I said, "but do you think... you could translate... just a little of it?" I was having trouble making my mouth function properly—it felt as if the *ur-ur-ur* had atrophied the muscles in my tongue.

"It's a courting song," Shiney said, squinting up at me. "I wouldn't want to make you uncomfortable."

"I can take it."

Shiney shrugged and took a sip of *ur-ur-ur*. She listened to Pônge for another moment, then spoke into my ear:

"Piam has taken off her clothes and is floating in the river. Akkarat is singing: '*I have not had a woman... since the long one I met on the road. The one who brought many men before me to fulfillment... and whose vulva is red as the mouth of a hound. You must come out of the water... come back to the swollen place on me. Crawling. Crawling. Crawl here.*'" Shiney looked up at me. I handed her the *ur-ur-ur* and she took another sip. Pônge was now singing in the voice of Piam. "'*I am ferried up to a cloud,*'" Shiney said, "'*my toes spread apart with wanting. Before we are married... I want to put my feet at their place around your neck. But I am no infant, and will not crawl. Slide into the river, and float over to my mouth. Bring me the fat fish that I'm starving for. River. River. Slithering river.*'" I felt my ears growing warm as Shiney spoke. She seemed to be enjoying herself now. "Akkarat gets into the water. He sings: '*Your nipples are protruding from the front of your body... like two long eyes that are surprised. You were shy with me, and yet... you are speaking boldly. My head is filled with flames, and I am the shy one now... with my dream of the soft inside of the vagina. The eight parts of your body tremble with desire. Hold up my penis and say... You are penis. You are body. Body. Fire. Body. Flame. Body. Urination. Body. River.*

Body. Ashes. Ashes. Ashes.'" The music was getting louder, and Shiney was almost yelling. One of the dancing women onstage was lying on her back, moving her arms and legs as though making a snow angel. The other woman stood above her, holding her hands in front of her and wielding a giant, invisible phallus. Pônge was singing as the woman. Shiney said: "'*A nice one... a nice one, a nice one. Now give a sound. A nice, a nice, a nice one, now give a sound, so it did.'"* Shiney laughed. "This is hard to translate."

"It's good," I said. "You're doing good." My throat felt tight. I took a swig of the *ur-ur-ur* and swallowed. "Don't stop," I said.

"The woman Piam is now floating on her stomach," Shiney said. "Pretending she is dead. Akkarat is saying: '*My maleness has been prepared for many seasons. Now it is ready... now that you have turned and sleep, snoring, face-down on the river. When you do not see me... may your bosom wobble. When you do not see me, may your vulva shiver. May my love's spell fill you with madness. I will kill a fresh black dtit-laa and two young ulukas once I have gratified my desire. A warm one with you will save me. No tricks. No tricks. No tricks.'"* Shiney was now shouting at the top of her lungs, and as I watched Pônge's lips move I almost believed that I could understand what he was saying. "'*Cursed! Cursed! Cursed!'"* Shiney shouted. "'*Curselifter!'"*

The music had reached a crescendo and I felt my hair stand on end and I turned to Shiney with my mouth hanging open and we looked at each other for a long, confused moment. The music was so loud, it was as if we were suspended in Jell-o. I could feel Shiney's breath on my cheeks. It smelled like the rind of an orange.

Kiss her, God damn you.

I closed one eye very slowly, then snapped it back open.

"Are you falling asleep?" Shiney asked, laughing.

"My head is a camera," I said, "and my eye is a lens, and I am winking because I want to capture your image in my brain."

"What do you mean?"

"It's a wink that I read about in a book."

"What?"

"Never mind. I think I'm drunk."

"I'm a little bit drunk, too."

The music had begun to taper off now, but I hadn't even noticed—I could still feel it pressing against my body. Some of the musicians were packing up their stuff, while others continued to play, more tentatively now, as if they weren't sure whether or not the show was over. The girl with the bells had sat back down on the floor, and Pônge stood with his back to the audience, looking down at her. Then he put out his hands and she stood up and came to him and he wrapped his arms around her and they began to kiss. People in the audience started talking quietly amongst themselves, and a line formed at the hatchway. By now, all of the musicians had stopped playing except for a guy shaking a tin can full of rocks and the bass player—the fat boy—who was grimacing down at the floor with intense concentration as he steadily plucked out the same three notes over and over and over again. The bell-girl and Pônge continued kissing, seemingly oblivious to the fact that they were on stage. The girl had a drugged, heavy-lidded look of abandonment in her eyes, and was gazing out over Pônge's shoulder into the audience. She appeared to be staring directly at me—suggestively, and almost mockingly—as Pônge ran his hands up and down her body.

"Is the show over?" I asked.

"This is basically the end," said Shiney. "There is usually a period of time when it's unclear if the show is still happening or not. A transition. That's part of it."

When I turned back to the stage, Pônge and the woman had separated, and she was removing the bells from her neck.

We couldn't find Ulla and Gabe anywhere in the Pride, so Shiney and I got in line to leave. Everyone stood back as Pônge pushed his way to the front of the crowd and climbed down the ladder.

"The people love Pônge," I observed.

"They do. Too bad he's such a dickhead."

"You used to date him?"

"Yes, but he was different then. He wasn't yet *Pônge*." Shiney sighed. "He was much nicer when his name was 'Handle-on-top-of-the-sticky-rice-basket.'"

Outside on the front lawn, a group of people had gathered around Pônge. They clapped and yelled as he addressed them in a fierce, emotional voice, pounding his fist on his open palm. A semi-circle of men stood in front of him, illuminating his face with the beams of their flashlights. I asked Shiney what he was talking about.

She listened for a moment. "He's giving a speech about the injustice of the fact that *malchaks* aren't allowed to perform in the Expo *Taang*."

"It sounds like he's doing some rabble-rousing."

"Something like that."

I looked around for Ulla and Gabe, and caught a glimpse of blonde curls poking out from under a blue headscarf. Shiney and I moved through the crowd until we reached them.

"Hi," Ulla whispered. "Sorry I left. I really had to pee. But I figured you were in good hands."

Before I could respond to this, a hush fell over the crowd, and we turned our attention back to Pônge. He was holding both of his arms out stiffly, tensing his entire body, and now spoke in a robotic monotone.

"Gabe, what's he saying?" asked Ulla.

"I don't know, exactly," Gabe said. "'My... balls?... are two... huge... hearts. Full of... something. My heart is like... a tiny... something. My blood...'" He looked at Shiney. "Can you give me a hand?"

Shiney stood on her tip-toes to get a better view of Pônge, then rolled her eyes. "Is he doing that stupid trick with the *hoong* again?"

The men were now training their flashlights on a mosquito that had landed on a ropy vein of Pônge's arm. As Pônge continued quietly speaking, he clenched his fist and allowed the bug to feed. No one breathed. I thought I could actually see the mosquito growing larger, its abdomen bloating and reddening as it filled with Pônge's blood.

"'The pain... growing,'" said Gabe. "'Making you... us?... fat with... tears?' Come on, Shiney, help me out."

"'Capitalist *gareng* are sucking the blood of Puchai,'" said Shiney, "'and the blood of the *malchak* people. They use the *malchak* man to risk his life... getting rubies from deep underground.'" She paused. "'And they use the *malchak* woman to satisfy their sick desires in the bedroom.' Very true. 'However... this same blood-thirsting greed shall one day lead to his wretched demise—'"

The mosquito exploded, misting Pônge's arm with tiny flecks of blood. The crowd stood in stunned silence, then broke into applause.

"That was *amazing!*" Ulla said.

"That's what I was telling you," said Gabe. "Pônge is a genius."

I looked around and noticed that the *malchaks* were staring at us. I heard the word *gareng* muttered somewhere behind me. "Should we maybe start heading home?" I asked.

"It's so cool how he takes elements from dialectical theater and infuses them with this radical political content," said Ulla.

"Totally," said Gabe. "It's like he has this instinctive ability to instill a Brechtian sense of *Verfremdungseffekt* into his audience. The mosquito serves as a—"

"It's just a trick," said Shiney. "The kind you do at parties."

Out of the corner of my eye, I'd been watching three of the flashlight-bearers having a heated conversation. They were now walking towards us. "I think we should get going," I murmured.

"Shiney, could you summarize Pônge's speech for me, while it's still fresh in your mind?" said Gabe, removing a small notebook out of his back pocket. "It could be really important for my thesis."

"Sometimes," said Shiney, "I think you should be dating Pônge instead of dating me."

"Oh, come on. You know this is all part of my research."

"Exactly."

The three *malchak* men hovered in front of us now. I smiled at them briefly, then looked down at the ground. "Gabe, Shiney—let's talk about this on the way home. What do you say?"

One of the men stepped forward and shouted at Shiney, pointing his thumb at Gabe and me. The two other men joined in, and we inched slowly backwards as their yells grew louder. I put my arm around Ulla's shoulder, and Gabe and I exchanged a nervous glance.

Shiney laughed and shook her head. "Let's go," she said, then turned and headed down the hill towards the hole in the fence.

We hurried to catch up with her. The men followed closely behind, still yelling. When one of them reached out and tugged at my *tai-lan*, I stumbled slightly and quickened my pace, clutching the tube of *ur-ur-ur* in my hand like a nightstick.

And then I heard Pônge shout something—a single word. I wasn't sure if it was directed at us or at the men, but the next time I glanced over my shoulder, nobody was there.

That all happened on Sunday. Now it's Monday night and I'm wide awake and sitting outside. Ulla is asleep. The Night Visitor was scratching around the basket earlier, and I just lay in bed, listening. When I closed my eyes, it felt as if someone's face was pressing against mine: small soft eyes pressing against my own eyes.

I wonder what Shiney's doing right now.

2:24 AM

Cursed. Cursed. Cursed.
Curselifter.

April 7
5:01 PM

Dear Hap:

This morning, when I went to the Faculty of Gemology, Mr. Yul looked me up and down and said, "Mr. Darrow, my intention is not to insult you, but I must observe that you do not look at all well. Your gills are veritably green."

I touched my fingers to my neck. "I guess I haven't been sleeping very well lately."

"You are an insomniac?"

"Sort of."

"And do you have a theory as to the source of this disruption?"

I thought about telling Mr. Yul about the Night Visitor, but decided it would sound too crazy. And besides, the Night Visitor isn't the main thing keeping me awake nowadays—it's Shiney. I lie in bed for half the night, reviewing every interaction I've ever had with her, replaying our conversations in my mind, obsessively sorting through these memories the same way I used to go through my comic book collection. Last night I had a dream that Shiney and I were in the Pride: her face was covered with striped yellow fur, and I wore a shirt made of the same fur. I was kissing her, and it seemed as real as anything in real life. Then I awoke with a start, and never managed to fall back to sleep.

"Maybe I'm still jet-lagged," I told Mr. Yul.

"Sometimes," he said, "the mind races." He looked at my face searchingly. "You have the visage of a man with a mind that is untamed."

"That's probably true."

"Mr. Boyd Darrow, may I say that you have a manner of familiarity that brings me contentment. I feel that I have a knowledge of your heart in a certain manner—as if, perhaps, I knew you, Boyd Darrow, in a previous time. There are several in this town whom I feel such a kinship with. The moment I was introduced to you, I understood you to be part of this cast of characters that have been drawn to Mai Mor—characters that are playing and re-playing out relationships and patterns that have been established hundreds and thousands of years previously." He frowned and winked at me. "Have you ever practiced any forms of contemplative meditation?"

"Not really," I said. "I read an article about it once in *Newsweek*."

"If you were to begin a practice, you would develop a greater sensitivity to these past-life scenarios. I think you would also improve your sleeping habits. It is a helpful thing to have an awareness of the ever-present moment that we exist in—'*every Moment has a Couch of gold for soft repose,*' to paraphrase Blake, the poet—and understanding that, with every moment of our existence, we may cease the passage of time with this awareness, seizing command of our destinies. Every passing second is an opportunity to begin anew." Mr. Yul went over to the bookshelf and removed a book. "Here," he said, handing it to me. "Allow me to present a gift from myself to you."

The book he gave me was *Suitable Exercises Pertaining to the Concentration of Meditation*, written by his brother, P. Songpole Phammawattaana. The following is an excerpt from the Introduction:

This book deals with concentration of the mind. After completing this program of exercises, you will achieve all of the myriad psychic benefits that are attainable via concentration, including—but not limited to—: the Eight Remarkable Powers and the Six Supra-Mundane Powers; the Super-Normal Knowledge Of The Divine Eye, Divine Tongue, Divine Nose, and Divine Finger; the Deep Comprehension Of The Four Formless States Of The Sphere Of Neither Perception Nor Non-Perception; the Power Of Clairvoyance; the Power Of Clairaudience; the Power Of Levitation Of The Body From The Ground; and the Power Of Walking Upon A Moving River As If It Were A Path In The Forest. Additionally, you will achieve: the Bliss And Delight Which Are Beyond The Ken Of Standard Mortals; the Power Of The Celestial Eardrum, by which you may hear Noises, both human and divine, both faraway and near; the Ten Concentrations On Corpses and the Ten Melancholic Remembrances; keen analysis of the Four Physical Elements and the Ten Devices, including the Earth-Dirt Device, Water-Liquid Device, Fire-Heater Device, Air-Wind Device, as well as the Blue Device, Yellow Device, Red Device, White Device, and Space Device; surpassing in the Suppression Of The Five Hindrances, those being Craving For Sense-Pleasures, Ill-Will, Sloth-Torpor, Restlessness-Worry, and Perplexity-Skepticism; and furthermore, obtaining Ecstatic Concentration upon Suppressing All Five Hindrances Simultaneously; until, at last, enjoying the Delight In Freedoms From The Worldly Shackle that manifest themselves daily.

In addition, you shall have the power to accurately predict the numbers of the Lottery within two-to-three digits.

Mr. Yul marked a page that features an exercise—*the Wooden-Sentry Concentration*—that he thought might help me to relax and sleep more peacefully:

Take up your meditation positioning, sitting in the "Turkish fashion" described in Chapter One. To begin the meditation, try the gimmick of short breaths, namely, short in-breaths and short out-breaths: the sensation of impact should be continuous, as is the case with a cine-film, which consists of separate pictures, but when projected on the silver screen at a certain minimum number of pictures per second, the persistence of vision produces the illusion of continuous scenes. As you focus your mind on this continuous breath sensation, you may find that your phlegm is thrown up, and you should have a square of tissue-paper at the ready in order to capture this.

Continuing on with this breath, allowing your sub-conscious mind to do the breathing in lieu of yourself, you will progress to the matter at hand. Eyes shut four-fifths of the way—so that the lashes on your upper lid are the distance of the thickness of a bobby-pin from the lashes on your lower lid—you will now visualise the following portrait: A standing figure, like a night-guard or "sentry," that is carved from wood (approx. 30 centimetres in height) standing within your own body, from the top to the bottom of the sternum. Picture, in your mind's eye, this standing sentry floating within you, and picture that it is creating a kind of equilibrium that is unshakeable within. It stands balanced inside your chest, always upright, like a compass pointing towards Magnetic North. If you lean slightly to the left or to the right, you will feel that this Sentry is continuously straight. Focus on it, running your thought-hands across its form, feeling its smooth, polished surface.

Perform this meditation for 15-25 minutes, and then, throughout the course of your day, you should un-consciously feel its presence with you at all moments. It is a truly intriguing and productive Exercise which you can practise in any location and at any moment. You will be surprised after a few weeks how keen your sense of calm equilibrium will become and it

*will have been worthwhile and may be of true value to you
sometime as you explore your life-path.*

*Note: During the Exercise, you may experience Joy in many
forms and intensities, ranging from the Joy that raises the hair
of the body, to the Joy that raises you off the ground, sometimes
to the ceiling. You must recall that this Joy should not carry
you away, nor should be clung to, in fact it would be best to not
grasp it whatsoever. Rather, allow the Joy to float away from
your person like a cloud in a summer-time sky.*

*Additionally, as you sit, your mind might wander, and if you
meet a friend in your thoughts, put out your hand and greet
your friend warmly, 'Hello.' Then, tell your friend: 'Goodbye.'*

Ulla doesn't get home for a little while. I'm going to go sit
in the Turkish fashion and see what happens.

April 8
10:31 PM

Dear Hap:
When I showed up to teach this afternoon, the only person in the room was Mr. Horse. I sat down at my desk to wait for the other students, and Mr. Horse smiled and told me that today was a Special Day—"Old-Sport Day"—and that no one else would be showing up.

"There is picnic at the soccer field," he explained.

"I don't get it. We only meet a few times a week—why would they choose to go to a picnic instead of coming here to study?"

"Because of Old-Sport Day."

"Right." I sighed and checked the time. "Well, I guess we'd better get started." I took out my copy of *ENGLISH FOR EACH*. "I actually had a pretty fun lesson planned for today."

Mr. Horse stared down at the book on his desk, then tentatively raised his hand. I pointed at him. "Yes, Mr. Horse?"

"Today... is... *Old-Sport* Day," he said, speaking very slowly and patiently. "There is *picnic*... at the soccer field."

We gazed at each other for a few moments, then I closed my book.

"You know, I was thinking that today we should cancel class," I said. "In honor of Old-Sport Day."

"Yes?" Mr. Horse made a show of considering my suggestion. "Very good."

*　　*　　*

When we arrived at the soccer field, Old-Sport Day was in full swing. Students and faculty members crowded the grass, playing a variety of different games: volleyball, Frisbee, hacky sack, whiffle ball, soccer, and something that resembled Red Rover. Along the sidelines stood long tables covered with cardboard tubs of pink ice cream. Mr. Horse saw some friends playing badminton and ran over to join them. I decided to wander around a little and see if I ran into anybody I knew.

My heart skipped a beat when I heard a woman's voice behind me call my name. I spun around—but it was only Miaw, sitting on the sidelines with Dicksplash.

"Hey, guys," I said. "Happy Old-Sport Day."

"*Hola, amigo*," said Dicksplash. "Take a load off." He held up a bottle of *Gong*. "May I wet your whistle?"

"Thanks." I lowered myself onto the grass. "Is Ulla here?"

"Ulla… at office," said Miaw. "Ulla work very *hard*." She and Dicksplash both laughed.

"Yeah, Ulla's a total workaholic." I drank half my beer, then leaned back and closed my eyes. "I like Old-Sport Day," I murmured. "It's very relaxing."

Miaw sighed. "I think I must go back to office now?"

"No, don't go," Dicksplash said. "We never get to just chill out together like this." He paused. "Mr. Boyd wants us to keep him company."

I lifted my head. "No, that's okay. I was thinking about taking a little nap. I mean, if Miaw needs to go back to work—"

Dicksplash put up his hand and, turning to Miaw, said: "Mr. Boyd should go to sleep, and we will stay and watch him and make sure he doesn't stop breathing." He turned back to me and blinked his eyes several times—I think he might've been winking. "That's cool, right, Boyd?"

"Um, sure."

"Awesome." He patted me on the leg. "We'll be right here if you need anything."

I lay back and shut my eyes again. After about ten seconds, I heard Dicksplash stage-whisper: "Mr. Boyd go to sleep. We sit here together."

"Okay," said Miaw. "We be silence now?"

"I think it's cool for us to talk, if we're quiet. Mr. Boyd looks so peaceful, doesn't he? I think he's dreaming now."

I felt obligated to mimic the slow, steady breathing of someone in a deep sleep as I lay there and listened to Miaw and Dicksplash's conversation:

DICKSPLASH: [*clears throat*] Try not to think of me as your teacher right now, Miaw. I'm just a friend. A friend with… potential.

MIAW: [*giggles, remains silent*]

DICKSPLASH: Hey, I have a great idea. Let's play a game.

MIAW: Game?

DICKSPLASH: Yes. A fun game. I learned it at a couples healing workshop that I attended with my wife. My first wife, that is. The game's called: "Are You Perfect?" What we do is, we take turns explaining why we are *not* perfect. Admitting our faults. It's fun, I promise. You want to play?

MIAW: [*giggles*] Yes?

DICKSPLASH: Cool! [*claps his hands together*] First, *you* ask *me* if I'm perfect.

MIAW: Mr. Richie… you… perfect?

DICKSPLASH: No, I'm not. At night, when I'm in bed, sometimes I have to pee, but I don't feel like getting up because I'm a lazybones, so I just hold it in. And when I wake up in the morning, my bladder hurts. And I think this is wrong, because the body is a temple. [*pause*] Are you perfect, Miaw?

MIAW: No. Not perfect, because... I not speak English, and... I want learn to speak. [*pause*] You perfect?

DICKSPLASH: I just want to say, I think you speak English *very* well. But, anyways—no, I'm not perfect, Miaw. God knows. My wife has been much less sexual with me for the past two and a half years, which makes me get very upset with her. I guess it's wrong to be angry. But sort of understandable, at the same time. I may be old, but I am still a sensual man. [*pause*] Miaw, are you perfect?

MIAW: No, Mr. Richie. Sometimes... sometimes Haraporn shouting at me, want me to work with English, and I get afraid, and I... become sad. And I make anger, and thinking, "I not *like* Haraporn!" And, one month ago? I sleep and have dream of office, and Haraporn yelling: [*lowers voice*] "Miaw, you need speak English, you stupid Miaw!" And I become very sad in heart, and I crying. But then, in dream I say, "You not yell at me, Haraporn! I am *good* worker!"

DICKSPLASH: That's cool that you stood up to her. Dreams are the way that our subconsciousness tells us—

MIAW: And then, I take the... what do you call, snipper? Scissor! I take scissor, and put it into *eyes* of Haraporn! I cut the eyes of Haraporn—*snip snap*—and... I *eat*! [*laughs*] I eat the eyes! In the dream—not real! [*laughs some more*] And blood come from Haraporn face, and Haraporn crying, "*No, Miaw, I sorry, I love Miaw*," but I laugh and I say, "I *hate* you! You *dead*!" And I take blood of Haraporn and I draw on face... like this? Like a cat. What do you call? "Whispers"?

DICKSPLASH: [*pause*] Um... whiskers?

MIAW: Yes! Yes. I make this with blood, and I dancing on Haraporn. I screaming, "*Miaaaaaaaw! Miaaaaaaaw! Miaaaaaaaw!*" [*pause*] Mr. Richie, you are perfect?

DICKSPLASH: Um... [*long pause*] Sorry, I'm still blown

away by your dream. It was... [*pause*] You haven't had any dreams like that about *me*, have you?

MIAW: [*giggles*] No, Mr. Richie!

DICKSPLASH: Okay. [*pause*] Okay. Anyways... no, Miaw. I'm not perfect. Sometimes, I think I have... well, feelings for you. I want to hold you, and caress you. I know you're my student, but you're also a full-grown adult, capable of making decisions for yourself. So, if it's wrong for a red-blooded man to feel this way about a beautiful, intelligent, lovely woman, then no, Miaw, I am *not* perfect. [*pause*] Are you perfect?

MIAW: [*extremely long pause*] No. I have... [*pause*] I have secret. Secret love. [*pause*] A love-feeling that is bad. Wrong. And... I don't know. People *say* is wrong, but it is my heart. And I... [*pause*] I not sure... [*sound of crying*]

DICKSPLASH: Oh, Miaw. Wow. Hey. Don't cry, Miaw. Let me just tell you, these feelings are not wrong.

MIAW: [*sniffles*] No?

DICKSPLASH: The heart is *never* wrong, Miaw. What you're feeling is so natural, so beautiful. Two people can be very different, speaking different languages, but deep down, their hearts are beating together, in a perfect union. *Ba-boom. Ba-boom.* Give me your hand. Do you feel my heart? Do you understand?

MIAW: Yes. Heart... not wrong. Thank you.

DICKSPLASH: The heart is *never* wrong.

MIAW: Oh, Mr. Richie, *thank* you!

FEMALE VOICE: Uh... hi. Am I interrupting?

I opened my eyes. Ulla had her hands on her hips and was frowning down at me. I sat up and said, "Hi."

"We go back to office now?" Miaw asked, getting to her feet.

"We're supposed to go to the stage." Ulla gestured toward the far end of the soccer field. "People from the Faculty are performing, or something."

"Ah!" Miaw clapped her hands. "It is time for show of song!"

The four of us headed over to the P. Songpole Phammawattaana Memorial Auditorium. The entire Faculty of Theatre Drama had gathered there on the grass, watching and listening as Haraporn stood onstage and sang something in an eerie, undulating tone that sounded like a sea shanty played backwards.

Ulla ducked behind me when we sat down. "Everyone in the Faculty of Theatre Drama is supposed to do a song," she said, "but there's no *way* I'm getting up there." She snorted and shook her head. "We should totally be in the office right now—only three weeks left until Festival Day, and they're eating ice cream and singing. Oh, and get this: Haraporn just told me that, next week, me and Miaw and her and a few other Faculty members are going on some kind of retreat into the mountains! For *six* days!"

"Really? Why?"

"Maybe because they're totally *insane*?"

Haraporn had finished her song and was now addressing the audience. As she looked out over the crowd, our eyes briefly met, and a frown flickered across her face. Then she pointed her finger at me and spoke my name.

Out of the corner of my mouth, I muttered, "Did she just say 'Boyd Darrow'?" Haraporn was now making the shooing-away motion with her hand. "And why is she doing *that*?"

"I guess it's your turn to sing a song," Ulla said, scrunching down even lower.

"But… I'm not a member of the Faculty." The *àep-sôn* incident flashed into my mind, and I said: "Wait—did you ever tell Haraporn that I have stage fright?"

Ulla hesitated. "I might've mentioned it. Why?"

"You sing!" Miaw said, grabbing my wrist and getting to her feet. People were now staring at me with intense interest.

I reluctantly stood up. "Ulla," I whispered, "what should I do?"

She shrugged and winked at me. "Knock 'em dead."

As I made my way through the crowd, I could feel my legs grow tingly and cold, as though someone had jabbed me in the lower back with a fast-acting local anesthetic. I tried to dredge up a memory of some previous onstage experience that hadn't been traumatic, and a succession of images paraded through my brain: tripping and falling into the audience while dressed as a dandelion when I was five; accidentally yanking the cord out of my guitar amp while doing my big solo on "Season of the Witch" during the Battle of the Bands in 10th grade; and my drunken, nonsensical speech at Maury's wedding. None of these memories brought me any comfort.

I climbed onstage and *hai*-ed Haraporn. She smiled grimly and announced into the microphone: "Mr. Boyd Darrow!"

There was a smattering of applause.

I murmured to her, "I'm sorry, but I don't think I can do this."

"You will sing a song." She bowed and took a step backwards. "Any favorite song from your country."

I faced the audience, holding my hand above my eyes as though shielding them from the glare of a spotlight. There was a sound in my ears that I knew wasn't coming from the crowd—it sounded like the staticky roar of the ocean as heard in a conch shell. I found myself thinking about the "Jabberwocky" incident in 4th grade, and how I'd barely made it to "*all mimsey were the borogoves*" before hitting the floor. That wasn't the first time I'd ever passed out, but it was the first time it had happened in public. And now, standing up on that stage, I had the terrible feeling that it was going to happen again.

I gazed out at the crowd and caught sight of Dicksplash and Miaw, along with Ulla's watchful eyes behind Dicksplash's shoulder. And there—next to Miaw, smiling up at me—was Shiney. Gabe crouched above her, his hands gripping her shoulders. He whispered something into her ear, and she laughed, and then—very quickly—tilted her head back and kissed him on the neck.

I looked away and fixed my eyes on the floor, as though I'd been caught spying on them through their kitchen window. The scene replayed itself, its afterimage burned into my brain: *whisper, laugh, kiss*. Something about the casual intimacy of that kiss—its amiable sweetness, and the familiarity that it implied—made me feel like I'd been stuck in the gut with a sharpened screwdriver.

I put my hand to my stomach, holding it there as if to keep the blood from gushing out, and I experienced an awful moment of clarity. I saw that my feelings for Shiney—the tiny seeds of hope that I'd allowed myself to slowly and secretly cultivate over the past few weeks—were, in fact, the symptoms of a delusional fantasy brought on by ennui, culture shock, and an overactive imagination. I also saw that, if Shiney was the kind of person who would date a person like Gabe, she must have some kind of hidden character defect, and would most likely never be interested in being with someone who wasn't an asshole. Shiney and Gabe were together, and Ulla and I were together. And that was the way it was going to stay.

I was momentarily staggered by this realization; but then—like someone who, during a crisis, spontaneously accesses a hitherto unknown wellspring of resolve and fortitude—I found myself accepting my fate. I saw that Ulla and I were together for a reason, and that, despite our unhappiness, we belonged together, deserved each other, and that allowing myself to want Shiney was simply wrong; not morally wrong, but intrinsically, inherently, fundamentally *wrong*, out of step with the natural order of things. I understood all of this, and, through this understanding—this surrender—I was unexpectedly set free.

I looked out blankly at the sea of faces, my breathing slow and steady. I could feel the numbness that had once been in my legs now spreading up to my brain, filling me with a preternatural sense of calm. I could actually sense the Wooden Sentry inside of me, standing there, stock-still. I *was* the Wooden Sentry.

Haraporn cleared her throat behind me. "A *song*, Mr. Boyd?"

I smiled at her, then brought the microphone to my mouth and said, evenly: "Today I'll be performing 'Wall of Water,' originally recorded by Freddie Church & the Sinners." I had no idea what made me think of this song—it just emerged, unbidden, from the depths of my foggy mind. I guess I remember Dad singing it to Mom. (Did I just make that memory up? Somebody's father used to sing it to somebody's mother. Maybe it wasn't ours.) I wasn't even sure if I knew any of the words past the first verse, but I opened my mouth, and I sang it as if I'd been practicing for months:

There's a wall
wall of wa-a-ter
falling from the sky...

Yes, a wall
wall of wa-a-ter
'cuz you love some other guy

And I...
can't see...
the forest for the trees

And I...
can't see...
you standing next to me

Through this wall...
wall of wa-a-ter...
Falling from above...

I paused. Like a superhero whose powers were mysteriously wearing off just when he needed them most, I felt a nervous twinge skitter up my chest, and I sensed a shadow above me. I imagined the Jabberwocky hovering there, waiting for me to fall.

Swallowing a mouthful of dry spit, I continued the verse:

Yes, a wall
wall of wa-a-ter
between me and my love

Well, if...
I lived...
for another thousand years

I'd still...
be here...
trapped behind this wall of tears...

I stopped abruptly and bowed. "That's it. Thank you very much. *Pranoo ròp.*"

There was a confused pause, then a brief round of applause. I handed the microphone back to Haraporn, and she began to say something to me, but I just smiled blandly and stepped off the stage.

When I approached Ulla and the others, Dicksplash slapped me on the back and said, "That was super-beautiful, Boyd."

Gabe flashed his teeth at me. "Mel Tormé of Mai Mor."

"Your voice is very... *unique*," Shiney said.

"Thank you." I put my arm around Ulla's shoulder and looked down at her. She gave me a surprised glance, then took a half-step closer to me.

"Yeah," she said. "Nice work."

I nodded my head and remained silent. I was still enjoying the aftereffects of my epiphany, along with my newfound ability to stand in Shiney's presence without feeling like a spaceship about to be sucked into a black hole.

"Any of you want to meet us for dinner later?" asked Shiney. "We're going to this place I know that does *malchak*-style barbeque."

Ulla and I glanced at each other, and she gave a small shrug. I turned back to Shiney and said, "Thanks, but maybe some other time?"

"All right," she said. "Some other time."

As I walked with Ulla back towards the Faculty of Theatre Drama, I remained silent, lost in thought. After a minute, Ulla asked: "You didn't want to get dinner with them? I wouldn't have cared. I'm over the whole Shiney thing."

"I know. I just thought we could go get some *uluka pai mong* at Golden Cowboy."

Ulla studied my face. "Are you okay? You look a little... weird."

"How so?"

"You kind of look like your dog just died." Ulla paused, then added: "And you also kind of look like you took a bunch of Valium." She reached over and brushed my hair behind my ear, resting her hand on the back of my neck for a moment. "We need to get rid of that rat-tail. Maybe I'll give you a haircut tonight."

I nodded absently. "You know, Richie taught me a game today."

"A game?" Ulla scrunched up her eyes. "What kind of game?"

I laughed and took her hand in mine. It felt comfortably warm and limp, like one of those steamed towels they hand out on airplanes.

"Ulla," I said, "are *you* perfect?"

THE JABBERWOCKY
(AFTER TENNIEL)

April 13
3:56 PM

Dear Hap:

~~God damn me~~

Okay. Sorry about that.

So—first of all, Ulla's gone. On her trip with Haraporn and the rest. And today I was walking home from the cafeteria and I decided to stop by the Faculty of Theatre Drama to see if they had any mail for us—I was expecting a care package from Mom. I wasn't even sure if the office would be open, but Mrs. Manarsumit was there, sitting at the front desk. She disappeared into the back room, and emerged a few minutes later with a postcard.

The image on the card was a detail from a painting by Hieronymus Bosch: a naked man and woman, standing on their heads and facing one another. On the other side of the card, written in blue ballpoint pen, it read:

Mrs. Ulla Darrow
c/o The Faculty of
Theatre Drama
Mai Mor College
Mai Mor, PUCHAI

The message area had been left blank.

When I got home, I propped the postcard on the windowsill and made myself some ice coffee, then sat down at the table and opened *The Dain Curse*, by Dashiell Hammett. I spent a few minutes trying to read, but I was having trouble concentrating. I kept glancing at the postcard, mulling it over. I recognized the distinctive, typewriter-like handwriting from a letter Ulla had received a few weeks ago—I'd been in the office when Mrs. Manarsumit had handed it to her. Ulla had told me that it was from her father, and put it in her purse without opening it. It now struck me as odd that her father would be sending her a postcard with no message written on it, especially one that featured a detail from a Bosch painting; Ulla's dad seemed like more of a LeRoy Neiman kind of guy.

I went outside and knocked on Mr. Horse's door. He wasn't around, so I sat on the grass and read some more. *The Dain Curse* is a pretty weird book, and I couldn't really decide if I liked it or not. Judy came over and sat near me for a while, until he saw a cat in the woods and went chasing after it. I tried to take a nap but couldn't sleep. I felt the way I sometimes feel when I've had too much coffee—as though my spirit was about to slip out of my body and drift up into the clouds.

I went back inside and picked up the postcard and studied it again. "Mrs. Ulla Darrow." Would Ulla's father address a postcard to his daughter like this? Did he even know that we were pretending to be married? It wasn't the sort of information that Ulla would normally share with him. I lay on the bed and closed my eyes and thought for a while, then got up and went over to the desk.

It couldn't hurt just to look.

I opened the drawer where Ulla kept her stuff. There was a bunch of junk in the drawer—lotions, paperclips, pens, jewelry, candy—along with some forms from the Faculty of Theatre Drama, and an old copy of *People* magazine. I stood reading the magazine for a minute, then put it back and closed the drawer.

Under the bed.

I knelt down on the floor and looked under the beds. There was nothing there but a dirty sock and a small orange lizard.

The closet.

I went to the closet and searched through Ulla's clothes. I took down a shoebox from the top shelf and looked inside. It was filled with underwear. I was beginning to feel like a jerk, and told myself I had five more minutes and then had to stop. I flipped through a stack of books next to Ulla's bed, then lifted her mattress and checked beneath it. I looked through the medicine cabinet in the bathroom. I looked under the bed again. My five minutes were up.

I decided to try and perform my daily Wooden Sentry meditation. I sat on the floor in the Turkish fashion and closed my eyes four-fifths of the way shut. I began to focus on my breathing, the continuous stream of in-breaths and out-breaths, in-breaths and out-breaths. I visualized the standing sentry floating within me, rigid and upright...

The blue tin behind the eggs.

I untangled my legs and went and opened the fridge. I took the blue cookie tin from the bottom shelf and set it on the table and lifted the lid. The tin was filled with homemade mint crisps that Ulla's grandma had sent to her. I can't stand Ulla's grandma's mint crisps—they taste like nougat-flavored toothpaste. Apparently Ulla wasn't so crazy about them herself, because only a couple of them had been eaten since they'd arrived in the mail several weeks ago. I removed two layers of cookies and two sheets of tinfoil. At the bottom of the tin was a small pile of letters.

All of the letters were addressed to *Mrs. Ulla Darrow c/o the Faculty of Theatre Drama.* All of the addresses were printed in the same handwriting as the postcard. None of the letters had a return address. I opened one up and looked at the signature.

Motherfucker.

I checked the postmarks, arranged the letters on the table, and read them in chronological order.

Feb 24

My one & only "Ooh-la-la"—

It's almost three o'clock in the morning, and I can't get any rest. Partly because of Devasheesh's snoring—but mostly because I'm going crazy with missing you, and cursing myself for sending you away. And yet, it still makes me grin to think about you there in my old stomping grounds. I picture you in the rice fields, rallying the malchak workers, fomenting revolution. You're dressed like "Tania," in a hand-knit black beret and a tight, body-hugging green jumpsuit. The zipper's pulled halfway down, revealing your bare, porcelain skin... the dark umbra below your clavicle hinting at your proud, full breasts. You slide the zipper down a little farther, and I glimpse the downy, peach-like fuzz above your navel, the tiny blonde hairs forming the shape of a downward-pointing arrow that's invisible to everyone but me...

But there I go, getting myself all worked up again. To tell you the truth, I can't stop thinking about you, and haven't been able to keep my hands off of my poor, abused cavalryman, who consistently rises to the occasion. (Maybe I shouldn't be telling you that. Or—maybe you like it? Maybe, as you read this letter, you're exploring your own secret garden with those lovely pianist's fingers of yours?) The bottom line is, I can't shake our "team-building" experience in Brattleboro together. On that night, the parking lot of the Hunan Garden converged with "Sach-Khand"—the Realm of Truth. I can't forget your soft, warm fingertips, fluttering like a million hummingbirds on my flesh, seeking out nectar to suckle on. During those moments, it felt like all of the birds in the world exploded inside me, a golden shower of feathers and musical tweeting. Just talking about it again is making me hard as a railroad spike.

These memories are the sweet succor that enables me to endure our separation. I think Deva is starting to notice that I haven't been myself lately, though she hasn't said anything yet. Even Giaanroop, Nripinder, and baby Dylan seem to know that Papa is out of sorts. I know I need to let go and move on, focus on my family, my faith—but I feel like my time with you has "fomented" my desire to shrug off this foreign religion, with all its trappings that now appear weird and ridiculous to me. But I need to be near your joy, your light, your laughter— sweet anodyne that it is—to give me the courage to strike out on my own.

And how are you doing there in that wild country? I hope that you are laughing. You are my laughing girl, Ulla, and you deserve to have laughter in your life. I'm afraid that your white light has been hidden for too long beneath the bushel of your partner. How are things with Boyd? Are you still feeling like he's a placeholder—a stop-gap measure? I understand that my age and my situation, etc., don't make me seem like an ideal mate to you, but I believe that our powerful and mutual attraction—along with our shared interests and parity of intelligence—make us, in many ways, perfect partners. Maybe, in some alternate reality, we're married and enjoying a life of travel, theater, cuisine, and lovemaking. In that world, you're my queen—and I'm no longer wearing this fucking turban.

I know we'd agreed to cut off all communication, but I felt that I had to send this letter out into the world, not even daring to hope for a response. "I too am not tame, I too am untranslatable, I sound my barbaric 'YAWP' over the rooftop of the world!!" I hope you can hear this barbaric yawp loud *and clear. I also hope you're thriving there in Puchai. I'm sure that with your youth and beauty and intelligence, you'll have many more exciting adventures in your life (amorous or otherwise), and may soon enough forget about an old man like me. But you should know that, when and if you do return to this dirty old town, I'll be here, waiting.*

With love & hope,
Your "Shawn-na-na"

I read this letter three times, and when I was done, I folded it back up and returned it to its envelope.

The second letter read:

Mar 16
Dear Ulla,
Great to get your letter yesterday! I'm sorry to hear about your unhappiness there in "The Kingdom of Winks"—I'm guessing that you're just in the throes of culture shock, and will settle in soon enough. I have to disagree when you say that Puchanese people are "lame." Maybe you just need to be introduced to the right folks? I found Haraporn and Miaw to be really wonderful—the salt of the earth. Have you met Haraporn's step-daughter, Shiney? She's a very appealing young woman who I bet you could be "bosom" buddies with—no pun intended. Send her my warmest regards.

I have some sad and confusing (but also exciting) news to share with you: Devasheesh and I have separated. Additionally, I've renounced some of the more formal aspects of my Sikh-hood, and have (literally) cast my turban aside! It feels like several albatrosses have been simultaneously lifted off my neck. Deva and the kids are moving back to Albuquerque, and I'm trying to figure out my options. My career has taken some fresh twists and turns (last week, Andrea promoted me to Executive V.P. of Client Services!), and—though it breaks my heart not to be near my "three angels"—I don't think I can leave the city right now. My decision-making process would also be influenced by knowing if/when you're planning on returning to the Tri-State Area. If you have any new thoughts regarding where you and I stand on things, please share them with me. The letter you wrote me was warm and friendly, but its overall tone was hard to read. However, the smiley-face that you drew next to your signature did have a randy little twinkle in its eye, unless I'm mistaken!!

I realize that you first need to resolve things with Boyd. I'm obviously biased in the matter, but, from an outsider's perspective—and this is coming from a man who has had his fair share of experience on this crazy blue marble called Earth—I feel compelled to say that you two just aren't good for each other. Mustard-oil and rosewater both serve important functions in life, but not when they're mixed together!

There, I've said my piece; now you must find your peace. Three final words: I MISS "U."

Shine on,
S.

P.S. I was thinking I might send you one of those special secret postcards sometime in the near future, so be on the lookout for it. (Remember, that thing I read about in <u>A Century of Spies</u>? "Every man carries his own ballpoint pen with him at all times!") I like to imagine the postcard sitting there on your coffee table—my feelings for you hiding in plain sight. Five minutes in the oven (low heat) should do the trick. **WINK!**

I re-read the P.S. several times before putting the letter away.

The third letter read:

Apr 10
Ulla—
Your last letter, which took so long in arriving, made your stance regarding our future together painfully clear. Luckily, it dovetailed nicely with some amazing developments in my own life: Deva and I are back together, and are stronger than ever—as is my Sikh faith. She and I attended a series of White Tantric workshops that allowed us to connect on a deeper level (emotionally, spiritually, and physically) than ever before. It truly is a blessing to be basking once again in the warm glow of my wife and children. Although I went through a momentary phase of chafing at the bonds of domestic bliss, I'm now embracing my identity as a "family-man" with newfound relish. I plan to join my three angels (and Deva) full-time in N.M. within the month, and look forward to a fresh start. I'm particularly excited to fulfill my lifelong dream of building an anagama-style kiln.

Good luck to you, Ulla, in finding your one true path.

Sut nam ("I am Truth"),
Shawn Talbot-Singh

P.S. This is awkward, but: Deva has asked that I cut off all communication with you, and so I'd like to formally request that you refrain from writing to me or calling me from this point on. I hope that you will respect the wishes of my family.

P.P.S. If you feel, for some reason, that it is <u>absolutely necessary</u> to convey a message to me, I could theoretically

be contacted at the P.O. Box written on the inside flap of
this envelope. However, if you have something important to
communicate, I would recommend that you do so immediately
because I will be leaving on the evening of April 17th to start
my new life!!

I put this last letter back into its envelope and sat there
for a while, staring at it, my mind empty. Then I returned the
letters to the cookie tin and went and retrieved the postcard
from where it had been sitting in the sun. I examined it
closely, and in the empty message area I could now just
barely make out the ghost of a word. An *F*, and a *T*, and also
maybe an *M* and an *NG*. I walked over to the toaster oven,
turned it to 200° F, and placed the postcard on the rack.

A few minutes later, I held the warm piece of cardboard
in my hand. The nine brown, wobbly words that had
materialized on it looked as if they'd been hurriedly written
using a small paintbrush. I stood in the middle of my room
for a long time, reading those words over and over again, and
wondering if they were true.

MY DEVA HAS LEFT ME.
I'M COMING FOR YOU.

April 14
5:28 PM

Dear Hap:

Words and phrases from the White Sikh's letters have been playing and re-playing in my head all day long. *Proud breasts... my barbaric YAWP... your secret garden... sweet succor... an anagama kiln...*

Brattleboro.

Ulla's company had gone on a corporate retreat to Brattleboro about a month before we left for Puchai—what the hell happened in that Hunan Garden parking lot?

And: *I'm coming for you.* Is that a promise, or a threat? Everywhere I go now, I see his face.

Ulla comes home in three days.

I didn't sleep much last night, and almost didn't even bother dragging myself to Y.E.S. today. Mr. Horse led the class in a game of Hangman while I sat and stared catatonically out the window. I barely noticed when my students filed out of the room at the end of the hour. Mr. Horse handed me a note that had been slipped under the door in the middle of class: *ARROW SEE ME ASAP SAM.*

Sam was on the phone when I arrived at his office, speaking excitedly to someone in Puchanese. After a moment he hung up and said, "Guess how much it costs to pasteurize a horse in this country? Eleven hundred *prik* a year—*minus* feed!"

I nodded my head, waiting for him to elaborate. When he didn't, I asked, "Did you just buy a horse?"

"Me?" Sam chuckled. "No thank you very much. People say pigs are dirty, but I personally would prefer a pig on my pillow to a horse beneath my heinie."

"Horses are—"

"But, enough with the horse-talk. I'm sure you know why you're here." Sam opened his desk drawer, took out an unsharpened pencil, and began tapping it against his knee. "As you might've noticed, six of your students have dropped out of your class in the past month. Six students to whom Y.E.S. had to give partial refunds."

"I'm sorry. I'm not sure why that happened."

"No?" Sam inserted the pencil into the electric pencil sharpener on his desk: *rurrrrrrrrr, rurrrrrrrrr, rurrrrrrrrr.* "It seems like we have some bad kismet here," he said. *Rurrrrrrrrr.* "My wife keeps bugging me about the relic that she's convinced you shrunk..." *Rurrrrrrrrr.* "...and Mrs. Manarsumit gives me weekly reports concerning your various transgressions..." *Rurrrrrrrrr.* "...and, I hear tell that you cancelled your class in honor of Old-Sport Day?" Sam removed the sharpened pencil and blew on the tip, sadly shaking his head. "Arrow, although it pains me to say so, I think that it's time—"

"If there's anything I can do to be a better teacher, Sam, I'm willing to do it. No matter what it takes. Just tell me what to do."

Sam eyed me, twitching his moustache. "God help me, son, you're just a hiccup away from a fart." He removed his sunglasses, and spent a minute polishing the lenses with a piece of Kleenex. Then he placed them back on his face and sighed. "Tell you what," he said. "We have a teacher here—a fellow name of... you know him. Lurks around my daughter. Looks like that Serpico actor?"

"Gabe Sloat."

Sam snapped his fingers. "His name is Sloat." He wrote something on an index card and handed it to me. "I think maybe it was a mistake having you train with Richie. I'd like you to schedule a time so as to observe Sloat teaching a class. It might be beneficial towards opening your educational faucets."

I shoved the card into my back pocket. "Apart from that, is there anything else you could recommend—"

"His class is finishing up right now," Sam said, consulting the schedule on his wall. "Room Four-Panther. Grab him!"

Classroom 4-P was empty when I arrived. I spotted Gabe at the opposite end of the walkway, talking to Dicksplash.

"Here comes Mel!" said Dicksplash, grinning at me as I approached. "That's your new nickname. As in, Mel Tormé."

"Cool." I nodded at Gabe and said, quickly: "Sam thinks I need a little more training, and he wants me to observe one of your classes, so... I wanted to ask you when would be a good time for me to do that."

Dicksplash let out a low whistle. "Studying at the feet of the master," he said. "'*Patience, young grasshopper.*'"

A smirk flickered across Gabe's lips. "Well, I don't have any more classes until next week—"

"What about tonight?" said Dicksplash. "He should come to the class *tonight*."

Gabe gave Dicksplash a dead-eyed stare.

"Oh, don't worry. Mel's cool." Dicksplash turned to me. "Gabe volunteers at the hotel once a week. A conversation class, with the ladies." Lowering his voice, he added: "It's kind of a secret class. But you should come. It's pretty awesome. You *have* to come."

"I don't know, Richie," said Gabe.

"Do you teach a class there, too?" I asked Dicksplash.

"I guess you could say that." He paused and thought about it for a moment. "It's like, you know how people say, 'The baby is the father of the man'? In this case, it's like, the *teacher* is the *baby* of the *student*."

Let's go.

"Okay, what the hell," I said. "I'll go."

Gabe's face fell, then he forced a tight-lipped smile.

"You won't regret it." Dicksplash winked at me and added: "*Goo-goo gaa-gaa.*"

Sloat

April 16
11:54 AM

Dear Hap:

I met up with Gabe and Dicksplash at the cafeteria last night around seven o'clock and we hailed a *pini-mini*, the three of us squeezing into the backseat. As we sped down the Friendly Highway into town, I clutched the armrest and braced myself as best I could—Mr. Horse tells me that people get thrown from *pini-minis* all the time. It was already dark out, and I couldn't see much apart from the occasional glow of a shack in the fields. I had the sensation of being trapped on an asteroid, hurtling through space, rapidly approaching some unseen planet that would probably kill me on impact.

"Hey, Richie!" Gabe shouted over the engine noise. "You got any...?" He put his thumb and forefinger together and held them to his lips.

"Oh, yeah." Dicksplash removed a tightly rolled joint from his shirt pocket, lit it up, and took a hit. "Sometimes, my brother, I think you just hang out with me for my bud," he said, passing it to Gabe.

"Sometimes I think you might be right." Gabe exhaled, and offered it to me.

"No, I'm good, thanks."

"Come on. This stuff is the best—*Rainbow Faceplant*." Gabe held the joint up to my nose. "I insist."

I thought back to the last time I'd smoked pot: I was fourteen, and you and Jef and Mike Tuminello got me so incredibly stoned that I had that massive panic attack and spent the whole night running in circles around the T.C.B.Y. parking lot, saying the Apostles' Creed over and over: *I believe in God, the Father Almighty, the Maker of Heaven and Earth...*

"I kind of had a bad experience once and swore off the stuff," I said.

"I'm sure you just smoked some bad shit," said Dicksplash. "One time I smoked something that was spiked with PCP and, like, *Drano*. I spent an hour trying to pull nightcrawlers out of my tearducts." He shuddered. "That was the night I asked my first wife to marry me."

"You think that's bad?" said Gabe. "I was in Zambia, hanging out with some *kankobela* players—street kids, poor as dirt—and they turned me on to the most fucked-up drug *ever*. They fill a soda bottle with raw sewage, put a balloon over the top, and leave it in the sun. The balloon fills with fermented sewer gas, and then they take the balloon off and *inhale* that shit. Dude, you have the most intense hallucinations—I did some with them one night, and spent half an hour fucking a bumblebee the size of a schoolbus." Dicksplash and I began to laugh, but Gabe held up his hand and said, "I swear to God, I touched its fur. I made it *come*."

"Wow," said Dicksplash. "That sounds beautiful."

"It was the most fucked-up experience of my entire life."

"I think you just convinced me to not smoke any pot tonight," I said.

"This is totally different," Gabe said. "There's basically no way to have a bad time on Rainbow Faceplant. It's like... imagine a warm glass of mother's milk that's been boiled down to a pure, tender nugget. Then, imagine infusing that nugget with one hundred percent unadulterated THC."

"Then," said Dicksplash, "imagine that the most beautiful woman in the world took that nugget and carried it around in her underpants for, like, a whole week." He smiled dreamily at the thought.

Gabe took another drag, then continued, "Imagine that that woman hands you the nugget, and you put it in your pipe and smoke it. At first, you don't feel anything. But, after a minute, you begin to feel eerily calm, yet all-powerful. You feel like Jesus H. Christ himself."

"And *then...*" Dicksplash gazed at the night sky and blinked thoughtfully. "Imagine that you and the woman go out and have an amazing dinner. You go back to her apartment—she lives with her parents, but they aren't home, because they had to go to a family reunion—and you have a ton of crazy, totally consensual sex with her. You fall asleep in each other's arms, and when you wake up, she's cooking you this amazing breakfast. And she's still nude, except she's wearing shoes and socks. And a chef's hat. And—"

"The point is," said Gabe, "it's basically physically impossible to have a bad reaction to Rainbow Faceplant."

"Yeah. I don't think I'll have any. But thanks."

Come on. That was ten years ago.

Gabe pushed the joint into my hand. "Come on."

It'll be okay. You're not on those meds anymore. It wasn't even the meds that messed you up that time—it was you worrying about the meds.

"Go for it!" said Dicksplash.

A little toke won't kill you.

"Okay, fine," I said. "Just a little."

"That's the spirit!" Gabe slapped my knee. "*Carpe diem.* Pluck the goddamn day."

I took a shallow hit and held the smoke in my lungs, watching the headlights pass us on the Friendly Highway, then exhaled and handed the joint to Gabe.

"How do you feel?" asked Dicksplash.

"I don't know. Pretty good."

"Did you even *inhale*?" Gabe passed the joint back to me. "Have some more."

I took another drag, getting a deep lungful this time, and held it in until I began coughing violently. As I gasped for breath, the effects of the drug hit me like a warm, gooey wave. It felt as if my skin was undergoing some kind of chemical change—transforming into pudding, or maybe galvanized rubber. I reached up and probed my face with my finger. The skull beneath my skin felt as if it was made of stainless steel.

Gabe and Dicksplash both watched me, grinning. "How do you feel *now*?" asked Gabe.

I didn't respond, too preoccupied with trying to count how many people were riding in our *pini-mini*. I was having trouble because I wasn't sure if I was supposed to count myself just once, or maybe twice—being both the subject and the object, the counter and the counted—or if, very possibly, I wasn't supposed to count myself at all. Then it occurred to me that I should count the driver, too. Why hadn't I counted him in the first place? Was I a racist? I closed my eyes to help my concentration, and an image of a yellow slug popped into my head. Someone was sprinkling salt on it. I opened my eyes.

"Dude, what are you doing?"

I turned and looked at Gabe. I really wanted to touch his beard just then—it seemed as if it would be incredibly soft. I held up the joint, which had burnt down to almost nothing. "I believe that this check... has been cashed."

"Look at him!" Dicksplash laughed his deep-throated, honking laugh—*huhn huhn huhn huhn*—and pointed at me. "He's totally stoned!"

Choosing to ignore him, I leaned forward and said, "So, Gabe—I'm really excited to observe your teaching techniques tonight!" It was difficult for me to tell if I was being sarcastic or not. "You know, I think Sam wants to fire me."

"Probably. He's axed two teachers since I've been here. It's his favorite pastime." Gabe glanced at Dicksplash and added, "Richie has a pretty good thing going, though. He's basically fire-proof."

Dicksplash shrugged and gave a sly grin. "Sam has... you know... what's it called?" He twirled his fingers in front of his eyes.

"You mean, he's insane?" I said.

"Sam has glaucoma," said Gabe, "and one way you treat it is by smoking pot. Richie here provides the man with his weekly dosage of Rainbow Faceplant."

"The ancient Mayan culture used hemp for treating tons of maladies," said Dicksplash. "Psoriasis... sinusitis... simple chronic halitosis... vertigo... almost everything. They used to say, 'Marijuana is Mother Nature's band-aid.'"

"Wow, look at that—it gets me every time," said Gabe, pointing up ahead. "'*In Xanadu did Kubla Khan / A stately pleasure-dome decree...*'"

We'd passed through the center of town, and as our *pini-mini* crested the hill of a winding, freshly paved driveway, a building rose out of the blackness, shimmering like a mirage. It appeared to be a replica of a medieval castle, except that its exterior was shiny and wrinkled, as if it had been hastily covered in tinfoil. Red and blue spotlights illuminated the facade, giving it a purplish glow. In the center of the circular driveway was a fountain featuring an elaborate, semi-abstract sculpture of a group of translucent swans in the throes of a vicious battle. The black vinyl banner that hung above the doorway read:

HOTEL TEL-HÔ WELCOME TO HATTANAI PROVINCE NITELIFE TOUR!!

The *pini-mini* came to a stop and we all sat there, watching the hotel glimmer and flash. I felt a sudden impulse to reach beneath my t-shirt and rub my nipples. I sat on my hands and said: "Let's go inside."

The hotel's lobby—replete with bearskin rugs, yellow marble floors, mock-Tudor furniture, and mirrored walls—looked like some kind of Rococo palace gone horribly awry. The vaulted ceilings were decorated with murals depicting eagles and angels cavorting in the sky, and the air-conditioning was cranked up so high that my teeth began to chatter.

Gabe led us up the grand, *Gone-with-the-Wind*-style staircase, and when we reached the second floor landing, we paused and gazed down at the lobby below.

"What a weird place to teach a class," I said. I hesitated for a moment, then casually looked over at Gabe. "Did you know that guy who was in town last year—Shawn? I think he used to volunteer here."

"I only met that bastard one time," Gabe muttered. "He got drunk at a Y.E.S. barbeque and tried to put the moves on Shiney in the Angel Nest."

"Mr. Shawn is a *legend* around here," Dicksplash said.

"The girls won't shut up about him," Gabe agreed. "One of them told me he had balls the size of coconuts."

Coconuts.

Gabe pushed open a door marked *Employees Only*, and we followed him through an empty and disused-looking industrial kitchen, then across the floor of a large banquet hall. We emerged onto a corridor lined with offices, the nameplate on each door listing the occupant's job title in English: *Rooms Division Manager, Uniform Services Detail, Club Lounge Agent, Night Auditor.* One of the doors was ajar, and I glimpsed a woman inside. She wore a beige business suit, and was speaking softly into the telephone as she moved her hands across the keys of an electric typewriter. Our eyes met, and she regarded me blankly for a moment before looking back down at the page.

Gabe stopped in front of a door near the end of the hallway. The nameplate next to it was different from the others I'd seen—it appeared custom-made, hand-carved and inlaid with brass:

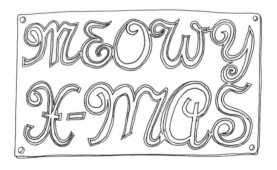

I reached out and traced the engraving with my finger. Touching it set my teeth slightly on edge, as if a low current was running through the metal. "Meowy Christmas?"

Dicksplash put his hands on his belly and said, quietly, "Ho, ho, ho."

I could hear a muffled throb coming from the other side of the door. Gabe pushed a small white button on the wall next to the nameplate, and there was a soft buzz from within. Gabe yanked the door open. "Welcome to my classroom."

Gabe and Dicksplash walked inside, but I hung back at the threshold for a moment, gazing in at the *gareng* men and *malchak* women crowded around the bar. Meowy X-mas looked as if it belonged to a different building altogether: the scuffed walls were cheap fiberboard painted black; overhead, a few bare pink lightbulbs illuminated a hazy blanket of cigarette smoke. The floor was covered in warped gray linoleum and was slick with spilled beer. Some kind of music—so distorted that I couldn't tell if it was techno or salsa or swing—was blasting from blown-out speakers. There was something unconvincing about the bar's seediness, and I had the distinct impression that the hotel's architects had spent a lot of time and money to create a detailed, theme-park simulation of a rough-and-tumble roadhouse.

I found Dicksplash alone at a table in the corner. He greeted me with a wordless grin, and I sat down next to him and surveyed the room. Two tables away, a beautiful young woman in a white nightgown was surrounded by a cluster of middle-aged *garengs* wearing matching khaki shorts and black socks with sandals. Their skin was the color of Styrofoam coffee cups, and dark pink gin-blossoms bloomed in their cheeks. They looked as if they could be related to one another, possibly gathered for a family reunion. One of them—a hulking, baby-faced man—was brushing the girl's hair with a pearl-handled brush. The other men leaned towards her, murmuring to her gravely as though trying to convince her to do something, something that would be for her own good. The girl sat smoking her cigarette, ignoring them completely, gazing off into the middle distance.

"Where's Gabe?" I asked, scanning the room.

Dicksplash shrugged. "I think he's rounding up our students. Or maybe he's with Dairng."

"Who?"

"Oh, that's his Meowy girl." Dicksplash winked at me. "Gabe's super-monogamous—Dairng is the only girl he'll be with here." He lowered his voice and added, "Myself, I like to play the field."

Over by the bar, three men in matching rugby shirts stood around a petite but sturdy-looking woman. They held their pints above her head, and as they drizzled beer down on her, they sang:

We cheer the Gold and White,
We never fear a fight!
Always a-winning
Always a-grinning
Always a-feeling right!
Z-I-P! Z-I-P! Z-I-P!
Gooooooo... Zippers!

The woman was squealing, mouth curled into a snarling smile, her small breasts glowing through her damp t-shirt as she rubbed her hands sleepily up and down her body. I felt my flesh creep with a mixture of disgust and excitement as I watched her—and when I looked down at my arms, my skin appeared to be the same bloodless tint as that of the other *garengs*. I hoped it was just a trick of the light.

Dicksplash nudged me in the ribs, and I nodded absently as the girl lifted her beer-soaked shirt and caressed her stomach. "Holy mackerel," he said. "I'd like to fill *her* belly button up." His voice was thick, and he was breathing wheezily through his open mouth.

"She's very pretty," I murmured.

He laughed and shook his head. "We're such pigs, huh?"

"Well, I didn't mean it like—"

"Hey, brother, it's cool. I'm not exempt. Guilty as charged. *Oink!*" Dicksplash smiled and leaned back in his chair. "I mean, I'm man enough to say that I consider myself a feminist. I'm all for bringing down the patriarchy, and I believe in the veneration of the Goddess, 'She of Twenty-five Thousand Names.' I believe in the Fellowship of Isis... vagina worship... Dianic craft. Plus—I *am* a married man." He pointed at me. "As are *you*. But still, sometimes... you know what it's like. You see a gorgeous female animal coming down the street, and you can't help but look at her. Let's be honest: you stare at her. Did you know, science has determined that if you glance at a woman's breasts, even for just a fraction of a second, she's aware of it? But it's not your fault—you can't turn it on and off. You can't make your mind go blank. 'Mother Nature abhors a vacuum,' right? So your brain floods itself with pictures and images of her nude body. But it's okay, Boyd. That's nature. It's handed down to us from the cavemen."

I nodded toward the bar. "I think I might go get myself a—"

"And it doesn't just happen to you on the street. It's everywhere, in the most inappropriate places. Man, these Puchanese girls... I'm telling you, I'm ruined for *life*. It's like, with white women, sometimes they're so big, you can't even get their clothes off! You know what I'm saying?"

"Um...." I replayed the sentence in my head. "Not exactly."

"I know how it is for you. I mean, for instance, you'll be teaching your students about how to make an adverb or whatever, and then you'll just glance at that little minx, Miaw, and: *boing*! You're in a state!"

"Actually, Miaw isn't one of my—"

"I totally agree," he said. "It's not like she's so beautiful or anything; but she has that kind of giggly, feral, primitive thing that just *does* it for you. But it's so confusing, because she's totally confessed that she's into you, but then when you try to move things along, she acts all conflicted. *Totally* teasing you, driving you crazy! And so, you're trying to teach, and right there in the middle of class, you disappear into fantasyland. Your students are like, 'Where'd he go? Earth to Boyd! Come *in*, Boyd!' But you're just sitting there, picturing yourself eating dinner with Miaw. Walking around, holding hands with her. Then, cut to: you're in her bedroom. She's smiling at you. You tickle her a little. She takes off her shirt. She starts to take off her jeans. She has trouble taking them off. You help her. Then you start kissing her, tenderly. She's never had a gentle white lover before. And then, as if by magic, you're totally nude! Except for your socks. For some reason, the socks always stay on."

"Hey, what happened to Gabe?" I asked, craning my neck and looking around the room. "Maybe I should—"

"It begins slowly," said Dicksplash, his voice hushed. "She plays with your ponytail while you remove her brassiere. Her body is incredible, like—" He paused, closing his eyes. "Like some kind of car. A perfect car from the future, made out of soft, heavy gold. You rub your hands on her skin, and it feels like it's made out of butter. She gets bold, starts playing with your privates—sort of, like, *flicking* at them with her pointy fingernails. *Ow*, Miaw! It kind of hurts, but it feels good, too. Pain and pleasure; lace and leather. It's a gray area, right? Next thing you know, you're heading south of the border. The six becomes a nine—"

"Listen, I—"

"—and, let me tell you, nature definitely doesn't abhor *this* vacuum! So then, finally, you decide to go for it. The sexual intercourse feels amazing. But after a minute, you realize you should really be wearing a prophylactic. So you pull out, and then what happens? Your member turns bright red, swells up like a popsicle, and—*ka-boom*! Your seed flies everywhere: on the bed, the walls, in her hair. You both just laugh and laugh. She gets some in her eye, and you have to wipe it out with a piece of toilet paper. Then you explain to her about how that's the most humiliating thing that a Western man can experience. But, you know what? She tells you it doesn't matter. She tells you how incredibly… *happy* you've made her." Dicksplash took a slow, thoughtful sip of his beer. "The crazy thing is that that entire fantasy scenario flashed through your mind in one single split second while you were sitting there in the classroom, trying to teach those poor people some English. It's no wonder you have to spend so much time hiding behind that desk! But my point is, it's not just *you* who thinks those thoughts while your innocent, trusting students are waiting for you to teach them. We *all* have these thoughts. It's healthy. You know what I like to say?" He put his hand on my shoulder and looked at me intently. His eyeballs were enormous and perfectly round, and they glistened as if they were sweating. "Shame on the shameful, my friend."

Before I could respond, Gabe walked up to our table with six girls and three gigantic mugs of beer. His hair was slicked back, as if he'd just taken a shower, and he moved in the overly exact manner of someone trying to hide their drunkenness. Setting down the drinks, he said, "Ladies, allow me to introduce these two very, very special guests. *Dtrong mee nae-nam kóp.* I think most of you know Mr. Richie here." Dicksplash gave them a cheerful wave. "And this is Mr. Boyd. He's fresh off the boat." Gabe chuckled, as though laughing at a private joke, and added: "He is a *má-làt-tá-ná!*"

The girls all began shrieking and talking excitedly to each other. One of them walked up to me and touched my hair, then gasped and ran back to the others.

"Everybody grab a chair," said Gabe. "Let us enjoy some English conversation practice."

Dairng, a bony girl with dyed-blonde hair and a pierced eyebrow, sat near Gabe and whispered into his ear as he sipped his beer and smiled down at the table. The girl who took a seat next to me was tall and voluptuous, and her exaggerated features—wide mouth, full lips, heavy-lidded eyes, slightly oversized teeth—gave her face a kind of ugly beauty. She wore a short pink skirt and a tight gray t-shirt with a brightly-colored photograph printed on the front. When I looked more closely, I saw that she herself was the subject of the photo: it was an image of her posing awkwardly on an inflatable camping mattress, reclining with one hand behind her head and the other resting on her inner thigh, pulling her legs slightly apart. She was staring up at the camera and frowning, as if the photographer had just insulted her. She was wearing nothing but a pair of argyle socks.

The girl saw me staring at her shirt and grimaced—mirroring her expression in the photo—but then winked at me and patted my leg. A man walking past our table yelled, "Show of hands—who here wants to shave my *pushy*?"

I turned to Gabe and said, in a low voice: "This is the class I'm supposed to observe?" I glanced involuntarily over at Dairng.

Gabe nodded, not saying anything. Then he licked his lips and said, "First of all: unlike your buddy Mr. *Shawn*, my primary motivation for coming here isn't to get laid. I come here because I actually want to do some good for the *malchak* people, and this is one way I can help them. Second of all: Shiney's not stupid. She grew up in this town, and she knows the score. Every *gareng* who comes to Mai Mor ends up at the hotel at some point. So—although I haven't explicitly told her that I come here—I would say that Shiney and I have a tacit understanding." Gabe stuck a cigarette in his mouth and dragged a wooden match across the tabletop. The match flared up brightly and went out almost immediately. He removed the cigarette from his mouth and tapped it against his knuckle. "You know, I have to say, at first I was worried about you coming here. I thought you might rat me out." He struck another match, lit his cigarette, and continued, "But then it occurred to me that you wouldn't want your wife knowing about your visit here. It also occurred to me that we're both in the same boat—that *neither* of us would want Shiney to know we're here."

"What're you talking about?"

Gabe exhaled a plume of smoke and leaned forward, putting his mouth next to my ear, and said, softly: "I was watching you at the *Kati* show. Shiney whispering to you, translating the sexy bits. Hot stuff, huh? Did you get a little stiffy? Half-mast, at least?" He laughed and wiggled his finger. "However, if you're looking to sample the women of Puchai—"

"I'm not looking to sample anybody."

"—then I would recommend that you start here, at Meowy." He gave Dairng a sideways glance. "Shiney is an incredible person, but—the thing about this girl here is, she doesn't *judge* me. I can tell her things I wouldn't tell anybody else in the world. And even if she doesn't always understand exactly what I'm saying... it's like, she *understands*. She feels for me." Gabe squinted up at the ceiling and worked his fingers through his beard. "What's that line from *Beyond Good and Evil*? '*Mitleiden wirkt an einem Menschen der Erkenntnis beinahe zum Lachen, wie zarte Hände an einem Zyklopen.*'" He raised his mug into the air and said, "'Pity... has a strange effect upon men of knowledge. Like tender hands... on the face of a Cyclops.'" Then leaned towards me, putting his face close to mine, and murmured: "*Nietzsche.*" It sounded oddly like a threat.

"Gabe, I'm not—"

"You could have any one of these girls here. They're nice girls. And you're a nice guy." Gabe picked a piece of tobacco off his tongue, inspected it, and flicked it away. "Shiney's not a nice girl. She just feels sorry for you." He seemed genuinely sad about it.

"So, you and me—we're both Cyclopses, huh?"

Gabe laughed. "The plural is *Cyclopes*. Not 'Cyclopses.'"

Fuck you.

I pushed my chair back and got to my feet. "I think it's time for me to go."

"Whoa," said Gabe. Everybody at the table was watching us now. "Easy there, big fella."

"Enjoy the rest of your class," I muttered, throwing some money on the table and turning to leave.

"Guys, what happened?" said Dicksplash, looking confused. "Boyd—you don't want to just chill out a little longer?"

"That's right," Gabe purred. "Take a chill pill." He said something to the girls, and they made sad faces and shook their heads. "Don't be rude, Darrow. You're upsetting the womenfolk. Have one more beer." Gabe snapped his fingers at a passing waitress. "*Hai-hai! Gong* beer! Three big ones. *Dtree bia gàp lòt.* With straw." Then he looked up at me and said, "Take a seat."

"Hey, speaking of Cyclops," said Dicksplash, "did you guys ever hear this one? 'Why did the Cyclops get fired from his teaching job?'" He began to chuckle.

Gabe said, "What the hell are you talking about?"

"Why did he get fired?" I asked, lowering myself back into my chair. I had a feeling that the answer was going to be important in some way.

Dicksplash closed one eye and opened the other wide. "Because he only had *one pupil.*"

The waitress returned with three icy bottles of beer and three straws. I pointed at my mug and said, "I haven't even finished my first beer yet."

"That's okay," said Gabe. "Observe my technique." He took his straw, bent the end of it, and stuck it in the bottle. "The straw provides a steady flow of air into the bottle, so that its contents can shoot down your throat with tremendous force and speed—like this." He lifted the beer to his mouth, keeping the bent tip of the straw outside the bottle, and downed its contents in about fifteen seconds. All the girls cheered and clapped when he was finished. Gabe grinned at me and said, "Your turn."

"I might just drink mine the old-fashioned way."

"Jesus, Darrow. My Aunt Molly parties harder than you."

"I want to try," Dicksplash said. "Come on, Boyd. Let's you and me both do it."

Just one.

"Okay, fine." I put the straw in my beer. "Just *one*."

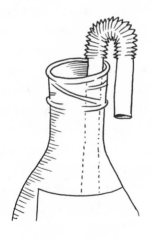

Sometime after consuming my fourth large beer in this manner, I found myself in the middle of an intense and bewildering conversation with the t-shirt girl. She had taken a proprietary interest in me, chasing away several other ladies who'd wanted to practice their English. As she sat there talking, she rubbed the inside of my leg, digging in with her fingernails as though massaging a cramped muscle. I could only understand bits and pieces of what she was saying: something about her family... nine sisters... their legs are all broken? Broken eggs? No mama, no baba. Two babies. Something about JFK. A relative with no face. A hospital. Something about her breasts. Something about a bird. She occasionally grew angry as she spoke, as though discussing a sensitive subject, and would raise her voice threateningly. Then she would smile and press down harder on my leg and ask me to buy her another *sip-drink*. She told me something about her teeth... oral surgery... she was catching a rock and it broke her tooth. Her babies eat rocks in the river. Her father was a doctor in the river. Giving birth to a fish. I just kept smiling and nodding and trying to concentrate on not looking at her t-shirt, though out of the corner of my eye I couldn't help but see it: the image of her body, naked and inviting, and also her eyes flashing with anger, staring up at me reproachfully, as if to say: *What are you looking at?*

I'd just ordered another round—and decided that this beer would definitely be my last—when Gabe came over, bent down, and whispered into my girl's ear. Then he patted her on the shoulder and murmured to me, "You only have one pupil, Darrow," before turning and walking away.

The girl stood and said, "Excuse me. You to come with now."

I blinked my eyes and thought for a moment. "No, that's okay. I think I'll just sit here. You can go if you need to, though."

"I want to make you... television."

"Television?"

"We go television, very funny. Then come here."

"I'm sorry, I don't understand. We will watch television?"

"Yes, watching." She took my hand and said, "Please to come with."

"Television," I repeated, getting to my feet. I hadn't watched television once since I'd arrived in Puchai. I'd almost forgotten about television. You just sit there and watch the people talking to each other. You don't have to do anything. It sounded perfect.

The girl held tightly onto my hand and dragged me across the room. "I'm sorry," I said, "but can you please tell me your name again?"

"My name—*Pêt*!"

"'Pêt,' like… 'delicious'?"

"Ah, yes! Thank you! You speak Puchai, very good!" She leaned her face close to mine and yelled, "What your name?"

For some reason this sounded like a trick question, as though she was asking me for my Social Security number. "Uh… *Hap*," I said.

"Ahap?"

"Ahab. Call me Ahab."

"Ahab!" She giggled. "Pretty name!"

"Thank you. Your name is also very—" I paused, staring at the crowd of people at the bar. "Hang on a second," I said. "There's someone I know back there…"

I thought I'd caught sight of a white man wearing a white turban.

"No, Mr. Ahab. You come now!" Pêt interlaced her fingers with mine, yanked me through an orange velvet curtain, then led me down a narrow hallway, stopping in front of a white door. "Television den," she said, unlocking the door and herding me inside.

The tiny room was empty except for a low, unmade cot that filled almost the entire space. I noticed a series of pencil markings running up the doorframe, as if a small child had measured its height against it for several years. A shoebox-sized television was bolted to the ceiling in the corner.

"Listen, Pêt," I said, as she shut the door and locked it. "I don't think—"

"Please sit, Mr. Ahab." Pêt tapped me on the shoulder, and I collapsed backwards onto the cot. "Mr. Gabe say you like watch television."

I looked up at her. From that angle, she appeared exquisitely beautiful. I lay back even further on the bed, and discovered that the further I reclined, the more beautiful she became. A fresh wave of drunkenness washed over me, coupled with a renewed sensation of being stoned. I pictured the Rainbow Faceplant as a powerful creature, lying dormant at the bottom of the ocean for thousands of years, only to be reawakened by the atomic blasts of alcohol flooding my system. I rubbed my face and sat up. "Television," I said.

Pêt smiled at me indulgently, then climbed onto the cot and switched on the T.V. She sat back down next to me and we watched as a grainy black and white image materialized on the screen. It looked like a tableau from a snuff film: a static, airless overhead shot of a man and a woman sitting on a bed, staring off into space, waiting for their fate to be decided.

"We watch us on television!" Pêt slapped my knee. "Very funny."

I studied the televised image of Pêt wearing a picture of herself on her body, and thought (or possibly said aloud): *It's like infinity*. Then Pêt said, "Watch," and on the screen the televised Pêt peeled off the Pêt t-shirt, threw it on the floor, and turned to face me, the tip of one of Pêt's televised and naked breasts pressing softly against my elbow; and I watched as the televised Pêt put her hand on the back of my head and said: "Number one show for *má-làt-tá-ná*."

"I think maybe I need to leave now," I said, carefully staring directly into her eyes. "I'm sorry. I had a lot to drink."

I pretended to chug a beer and made a sad face. Then I held up my hand and said, "Also, unfortunately, I'm married."

Pêt leaned forward and took my hand, staring at my ring and furrowing her brow, as though attempting to divine some sort of esoteric knowledge from it. She was very close to me now. Her skin smelled like coconut milk and calamine lotion. "I have wife at home," I elaborated. "Wife, and... children. Many beautiful babies." I stood up. Pêt continued to hold onto my hand. "I go home now," I said. "But it's been very nice to meet you. Good luck with your education."

Pêt shook her head. "Mr. Ahab, you do not leave."

"I'm sorry, I really have to."

"No. Wait. I want make... laugh." I tugged on my hand, and she gripped it even more tightly. "Mr. Richie teach me joke. Very funny." She tapped her forehead. "Yes, I know. Yes. Question: can you say, do you know... what is different between cock-sucker and ham sandwich?"

I gave my hand another yank. "What's the difference between a cocksucker and a ham sandwich? I don't know."

"You don't know?"

"No idea."

Pêt opened her mouth, looking up at me with large eyes. "Okay. Then now it is time for *lunch*."

"What—"

Pêt brought my hand up to her face and began to delicately lick the tender spaces between my knuckles. I inhaled sharply and held my breath as she took my ring finger and slowly put her lips around it, first only the tip, and then—gently—the entire finger. The sides of her mouth felt soft and warm, like the interior of a tropical plant, and she closed her eyes and dreamily suckled on my finger. I closed my eyes as well, and felt the entire room shift slightly to the left; I had to pause for a moment and try to remember if we were on a boat.

Then I felt Pêt bite down on my finger, and I opened my eyes and watched as, in a single deft motion, she dragged her teeth along the entire length of my digit. I looked at my hand and saw that there was now only a pale tan-line where my wedding ring had once been. Pêt made a show of swallowing, then opened her mouth wide, proudly showing me that it was empty, as if she'd just performed a magic trick.

I stammered: "You… you ate my wedding ring."

"Now, what kind of show you like?" Pêt reached up and undid the buckle of my belt. "Fucking show?"

Secret garden.

"No," I said. "I'm not feeling very well right now."

"You like sucking show?" She unbuttoned my pants.

Succor. Like a million hummingbirds.

"No. I need to get out of here—"

"No?" Pêt unzipped me slowly. "What you like? Is okay." She looked up at me. I felt her fingers caress me lightly. "You not married now, Ahab."

Pianist fingers. Seeking nectar.

"Don't," I said helplessly.

Succor. Coconuts. Succor. Ham sandwich.

I felt the blood shoot up from the bottoms of my feet to the crown of my head.

All of the birds in the world.

"I have to go," I said, and then:

I'm in the dark. I'm still the same stone figurine, but huge now—a statue carved from the side of a mountain. Tiny birds are sitting on me. I'm surrounded by tiny animals on the ground. The hovering thing above me has grown closer. It's black, flat, spade-shaped. Then its blurry form begins changing: it's like an hourglass, then a canoe, then a seed. A manta ray, a Jack-in-the-Pulpit, the head of a bird. A flying dog. It floats closer, and it comes into focus. I can see it clearly now. I know exactly what it is. I just can't remember the word for it.

I opened my eyes. A cluster of women were looking down at me. One of them topless. I was on the floor, covered with ice cubes. A large *malchak* man was standing next to the women. He was wearing bright orange sweatpants and a black tank-top with the words

P.U.M.P. H.A.R.D.

printed across the front. His arms were folded and his mouth was wide open, as if he was silently roaring. I found myself wondering if P.U.M.P. H.A.R.D. actually stood for anything.

I lifted my head a little higher and caught sight of Gabe. He was holding an empty plastic pitcher and scowling at me. My shirt was soaking wet. I felt for my pants, and was relieved to still be wearing them—though my belt had gone missing.

"Darrow," Gabe said. "What happened."

"Not sure," I muttered, picking an ice cube out of my hair.

The girls all chattered excitedly and crowded around me. I struggled to my feet and shook my head back and forth. I could feel my brain sloshing around inside my skull like a wet sponge in a cigar box. I buttoned my pants and told the crowd: "I'm fine. You all can go back to doing... whatever you were doing."

P.U.M.P. H.A.R.D. barked an order at the girls, and as they reluctantly shuffled out the door, he and Pêt launched into a heated argument. Gabe spoke to both of them in soothing tones, then said to me through his teeth, "You need to give her some money. *Now*."

I glanced around. "Did I break something?"

"For her services."

"What services? I didn't receive any services. That I know of."

"Darrow." Without moving his head, Gabe's eyes darted toward the big *malchak*. "Come on."

I couldn't bring myself to look at P.U.M.P. H.A.R.D., but I could hear his ragged breathing. He sounded as if he'd just run a four-minute mile. I opened my wallet and handed Pêt two bills.

She scowled at Gabe. "Mr. Ahab *má-làt-tá-ná*?"

P.U.M.P. H.A.R.D. took a step closer to me. The three of them began to argue again. I heard the word *má-làt-tá-ná* repeated several times.

"You need to pay more," Gabe said.

"What exactly does *má-làt-tá-ná* mean?"

"Darrow, now isn't the—"

"Tell me."

He sighed. "It means, like… Daddy Warbucks. A wealthy man. But—"

P.U.M.P. H.A.R.D. shouted something and then snatched the empty beer pitcher from Gabe and hurled it at the wall. It narrowly missed hitting Pêt in the nose before clattering to the ground.

Gabe leaned towards me and said, "It was just a joke and I tried to explain that to them, but it doesn't matter at the moment because this guy is *not* a joke, so just give them whatever money you have and let's get the fuck out of here."

I shook my head as I took all of the money out of my wallet and gave it to Pêt. She counted it and showed it to P.U.M.P. H.A.R.D. He said something to me, and I showed him my empty wallet. He spat on my shoe, then grabbed Pêt by the arm and stormed out of the room.

Gabe and I were both quiet as we stood listening to their footsteps recede down the hallway. Then he said, "What's the deal with all the passing out, anyways?"

I sat down on the bed. I felt like I wanted to die. I tried to think about something else.

Pêt Undresses My Pain.

"You want me to call Shiney?" Gabe said. "Have her blow some bubbles into your mouth?"

Please Understand My Pleasure.

Gabe kept talking, but I could barely hear him. I was thinking about P.U.M.P. H.A.R.D.—trying to match words to the letters. It made my brain feel better, for some reason.

Holding A Rabbit-Duck.

Ulla comes home tomorrow.

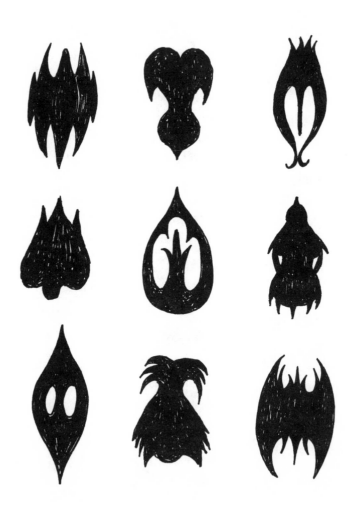

April 17
7:26 PM

Dear Hap:

I was sitting outside, but it was too lonely out there—*Home Kwan Home* is deserted at the moment because everybody's attending a concert at the auditorium. It's part of "His-Majesty's-Blues Day," the Special Day that celebrates Puchai's king and his love of jazz piano. (I'm told that the king plays fairly well himself, and recorded an album of Thelonious Monk compositions that has topped the Puchanese charts for the past three years.) Now I'm lying on the bed, drinking *ur-ur-ur* mixed with tamarind soda and listening for the sound of Ulla's key in the lock. For some reason, I'm having trouble remembering what she looks like—when I close my eyes, all I can see is a bunch of curly blonde hair, and that little silver earring high up on her ear.

Part of me is also waiting for the White Sikh, coming to find his Ooh-La-La.

When I learned about Ulla and the White Sikh, the first thing that flashed through my mind was that I wanted to stab him in the throat with a ballpoint pen. The specificity of this image is weird to me: why "ballpoint pen"? Why "throat"? Now that I stop and think about it, isn't a ballpoint pen to the throat the way you give someone an emergency tracheotomy? It's as if my first instinct wasn't to kill the White Sikh—it was to save him from choking to death.

We've never actually met, but I did see a photo of him once

in the Gelder & Ventry newsletter. On the cover was a collage of pictures that had been taken during the Brattleboro retreat, and in the center of the collage was a snapshot of Ulla and the White Sikh. The caption read: *IN 'SHAWN' WE TRUST—Junior staff member Ulla Liptauer performing a trust fall with Shawn Talbot-Singh.* In the photo, Ulla's eyes are closed, and her arms are crossed over her chest. She's smiling nervously, about to tip backwards into the White Sikh's arms. There's a cartoon thought bubble above her head: *I guess now's not the time to ask for that raise?!* The White Sikh is looking directly into the camera. He's handsome in an old-fashioned kind of way—lantern-jawed, with shiny white teeth that are just a touch too large for his mouth—and, although it's a black and white photograph, his cheeks still somehow manage to appear ruddy with good health. I'm pretty sure that Sikhs have some strict rules against beard-trimming, but the White Sikh's facial hair is sculpted into a tidy goatee. The turban and beard actually give him a glamorous look, like the hero of some exotic B-movie. *Starring Tyrone Power as the Crimson Sheik!* He has a mischievous grin on his face, and is sort of shrugging, as if asking the viewer: *Should I catch her? Or should I let her drop?*

Shawn. "Sean" somehow wouldn't be as bad. Try saying it yourself. *Shawn.* Is there an uglier name in the English language?

Sometimes I like to imagine that, after I'm dead and buried, these letters to you will be discovered in a desk drawer and eventually collected and published. Maybe the White Sikh will still be alive, and maybe he'll pick up my book in the store—maybe because he likes the cover, or the title (*The Hap Letters*?)—and, on a whim, maybe he'll buy it. As he sits in the den of his Upper West Side apartment, reading my words, he'll quickly realize that he *knows* these people in this book, and that he's part of the plot. Maybe after he's done he'll set this book aside and try to forget about it. Maybe he'll attempt to distract himself by doing the crossword puzzle. And then maybe, after a little while, he'll begin to cry, and his three blonde angels will gather around him and say, *Daddy, what's wrong?* And he'll tell them: *My angels, I have deeply wronged a man—a good man, who did not deserve the pain that I caused him. If only I had the power to give the gift of renewed life to Boyd Darrow, and climb into his moldering grave, so that I might take his place and have him rise again and enjoy the bounty of this world—lo, I would do so in an instant.*

And then the White Sikh will calmly set aside his crossword puzzle, and stab himself in the throat with his own ballpoint pen.

9:49 PM

Where the hell is Ulla?

I feel very alone here now. And lonesome. It's just you and me versus whatever. I'm thinking that maybe I actually did die on that airplane, and now I'm stuck in some kind of ridiculous afterlife.

P.S. I am drunk.

I've been hearing noises outside the door, but when I get up to look out the window, nobody's there. The Night Visitor must be early tonight. It's funny—I keep having the idea that *you're* the Night Visitor, and that one night I'll open the door and you'll be standing there, grinning at me. Do you want to hear something terrible? Sometimes I think there's some part of me that's actually jealous of you. I realize that that's a fucked-up and ignorant thing to say. But it's kind of true, and I'm being honest now. And something else, a theory I have about myself: when I black out, it's like I'm trying to get to where you are. Hanging out in the spectral zoo. Eating your stupid jungle honey. In oblivion.

What the hell is wrong with me: I'm jealous of a dead man—

Hang on. I hear someone at the door.

YOUR FINALE VOYAGE

Our company will do its very best to advocate your own, personal sentiments and emotions. FUCHAI FANG KOTE LTD.

Some say that *life* is a journey in a straight line.................

......but I believe that life is like a *voyage* around a sphere; you will end where you *begun.*

#3

Dear Hap:

You're probably wondering why I'm writing this letter on the back of a blood-stained paper bag.

I'll explain:

Last night, when I heard a key in the lock, I put down my notebook and watched and waited as the door swung slowly open. Ulla lingered in the doorway, speaking to somebody over her shoulder, then stepped inside.

I said: "Hey. Where have you—"

"Hi, hang on, I'm about to wet my pants!" she said, throwing her bags on the floor and hurrying past me into the bathroom. She shut the door halfway and, over the sound of her peeing, I heard her begin to sing quietly: "*I... fall... to pieces... each time I see you again...*"

"Ulla," I called. "Who were you talking to outside?"

"It's nice to see you too," she said, emerging from the bathroom. "My trip was great, thanks for asking."

"Why were you just singing that song?"

"Singing?" She came over and gave me a quick kiss on the mouth. "What're you drinking?"

"*Ur-ur-ur* and *Puchalicious*."

"Yuck." Ulla opened the fridge, stared thoughtfully into it for a moment, then got herself a beer.

"Who were you talking to outside?" I asked again. I was impressed by how sober and casual my voice sounded. I felt like I wanted to punch my fist through the wall.

Ulla gave me a look and frowned. "Jooey. He helped me carry my bags." She went to the sink and squirted liquid soap on her hands. "Have you noticed that all the soap here smells like cilantro? It's funny—the reason I hate cilantro in the first place is because it *tastes* like soap." She laughed and began washing her face.

"Who's 'Jooey'?"

"You know—*Jooey*. The guy who drives the van? He's actually really sweet, once you get to know him. Miaw told me last night that she's in *love* with him, but he's a *malchak*, and so she doesn't know what to do. Her family would totally freak if they found out. Even Haraporn has a problem with it. Haraporn's a total racist, I've decided."

"Ulla," I said. "I need to talk to you."

Ulla turned off the water and patted her face with a towel. "What's up?"

"Could you come sit down?"

"Sure, just let me just finish getting ready for bed. I'm exhausted. It took us eight hours to drive two hundred kilometers. The roads here suck—this country has, like, *zero* infrastructure." Ulla massaged some lotion into her face, then stood in front of the mirror and brushed her hair. "You'd love Reoi. It's really pretty in the mountains. Super-peaceful. I want to go back sometime, without Haraporn— traveling with her was a *nightmare*. The first thing she said to me when I got in the van was, 'Ulla, your face is looking very round now, like a moon! Puchai food make you fat!' She thinks she can say anything she wants, as long as it's with a smile and a big wink." Ulla bared her teeth and gave an exaggerated wink into the mirror. "And she's so *mean* to Miaw! You know, Miaw can speak English much better than you think. She's just shy about—"

"Can you just come here for a second. Sit down."

Ulla lowered herself onto the bed, studying my face. "You look so serious," she said, smiling tentatively. "Am I in trouble?"

I didn't say anything. Ulla's smile faltered, and she said, "Boyd, you're starting to—"

"I found the letters."

Ulla stopped brushing her hair for a moment. "What letters?"

"What letters do you think?"

She started brushing her hair again, more energetically now. "Boyd, I have no—"

"What happened in Brattleboro?"

Ulla put down her hairbrush. She placed her hand on her forehead, as if checking to see if she had a fever.

"I don't understand," she said, quietly.

"'Shine on, Ooh-La-La. I MISS U.'"

"Why did you—"

"And there's a new one," I said. "*I'm coming for you.* Have you seen him yet?"

The whites of Ulla's eyes slowly expanded like two eggs frying in a pan. "What are you talking about?"

I went and got the postcard from the desk. "Invisible ink," I said, handing it to her. "I had to put it in the toaster oven."

Ulla held it by the corner and read the message several times, speaking the words under her breath as if trying to make sense of them. Then she dropped the card on the bed and murmured, "I can't believe he actually did that. He wrote it with his... *ew.*"

"His what?"

"His... sperm. I think. He read about it in a book."

"Jesus. And that's supposed to be sexy or something?"

Ulla flipped the postcard over and studied the image on the other side. Then she said in a low voice: "Boyd, I don't know." She moved her head back and forth. "I can't go through all this with you again. I don't know if we can do this anymore."

"Do what anymore?" It now sounded as if someone else was projecting their voice through my mouth. "Do *what* anymore?"

"This isn't working. We both know that."

I got to my feet and took a step backwards. "You have to tell me what happened in Brattleboro."

"What would be the point."

I was staring at a flat black water bug that was crawling across the floor. Ulla followed my gaze and we both watched the bug trying to make its way around my copy of *ENGLISH FOR EACH*, which I'd left at the foot of the bed. It kept bumping into the book and then backing up and trying again. Finally it turned around and started climbing up the wall. I took off my shoe, walked over to the bug, and raised my arm to kill it. Then I turned to Ulla and dropped my arm. "Tell me," I said.

She gazed back at me for a time without blinking, her eyes bulging and wet. The room was so quiet that it seemed as if the silence around us was permanent, irrevocable. Then Ulla folded her hands in her lap and began to speak.

"We went out—the whole group—on the last night of the retreat, to a Chinese restaurant. We had dinner and then hung around chatting. People started leaving, and after a while, Shawn and I were the last ones left." Ulla paused, then said: "He wanted to quit. Being a Sikh, I mean. He needed someone to talk to, so I listened to him. We had some drinks and talked until they turned out the lights and we had to leave. We went out to the parking lot and were still talking, and the whole time, he was looking at me like…" She shook her head. "I don't know. You never looked at me like that." Ulla was crying now. Then she stopped crying and sat very still, as if waiting for me to say something.

"So you were talking," I said. "What else?" I was standing above her, feeling very light. My bones felt thin and hollow, like a bird's.

"We were talking and after a while we stopped talking. We were standing next to the car, leaning against it and just sort of looking up at the sky. Except there was nothing to see, because the lights in the parking lot were really bright. And then the lights went out, and you could see everything. The whole Milky Way. And then—I don't even remember how it started—but he was kissing me. I didn't stop him. I… I felt like I owed it to him. I was leaving in a couple of weeks, and I was probably never going to see him again. And—" Ulla stopped abruptly and sucked in a mouthful of air between her teeth. "While we stood there, he was pressing himself against me. He was rubbing himself on my leg. I started laughing, I don't know why. Your face popped into my head for a second, then went away. I decided not to think about it. He opened his pants and he took my hand and guided it to him. I was still laughing, but then I stopped. I held it."

Ulla grew quiet. She seemed to have forgotten that she'd been talking.

"You held it," I prompted.

She nodded. "I sort of just put my hand under it and held it lightly. Like I was weighing it. It's different from yours: long and skinny, perfectly straight, like a... Lincoln log." Ulla laughed. "This is what you want to hear?"

I didn't say anything.

"I'll tell you," she said, "if you want to hear. I remember feeling very sleepy. All I wanted to do was go back to my hotel room and get under the covers. But it was too late for that. So I started moving my hand. I remember his breath smelled like plum sauce. He was saying something in my ear. Chanting. It sounded like Pig Latin. It was like he was praying to me. He began to get soft, but he told me not to stop. And then he made a face and tipped his head back. I stepped out of the way, and he said my name, and then he came on the side of my car. My rental car. It was a Toyota Celica."

"And that's all," I said. "That's all that happened."

Ulla was crying again, though she didn't have any tears on her face. "We'd been seeing each other, Boyd."

"Seeing?" I said. The word sounded meaningless coming out of my mouth.

"You know. We'd been..." She pressed her hands against her eyes. "I felt horrible about it the entire time. I feel horrible. It makes me sick. But that time in the parking lot was the end. I'm so sorry."

"Okay. That's enough. I understand."

Ulla reached up and touched my wrist. "Are you all right?" she whispered.

I swallowed a mouthful of spit. "I understand," I said. "Thank you—"

I was falling forward but it seemed as if I was standing still and the coffee table was rushing up to meet my face. I remember noticing the pattern etched around the edge of the table's glass top. A cursive loop of upside-down hearts. I opened my mouth to say Ulla's name, but it was too late.

The black thing above me is your bat kite, I see it clearly, and it drifts down and covers me, and I'm soaked in darkness, and then I am the kite. There's a sound like the sound of water, and I'm floating down the river on my back, my two round yellow eyes staring up at the fast-moving sky. Then I'm slipping beneath the river, and then the water is on top of me and my face is slick with wetness and I spit and suck in air and I'm on the floor of our apartment. Ulla is making squeaking noises. I touch the wetness and look at my hand. Blood. My nose. And inside my mouth. There's blood on my shirt, the floor, Ulla's hands. Ulla opens the door and runs outside. I hear her yelling. I put my head back and close my eyes. She's going to get help. She comes back alone. No one's around. His-Majesty's-Blues. She brings me a washcloth and tells me to press it to my face and asks if I can stand up. I stand and then the room tips and I sit down in the chair and close my eyes. My breathing feels strange. I cough and then I spit blood onto the floor. I move my tongue in my mouth. I'm missing a tooth. A canine. I bare my teeth and show Ulla. She helps me stand up and tells me we're going to go get a *pini-mini*. It's dark outside and it's not raining anymore but the ground is still wet. We go out to the road and I sit down in the wet dirt. Ulla runs out into the road and flags down a *pini-mini* and we get in and Ulla says, *Hospital*. I say, *Hospital*, but I'm not sure if any sound comes out of my mouth. Ulla shoves some money into the man's hand and he stares at me and then puts the money in his pocket and starts driving. We take a left onto the highway instead of a right and Ulla yells,

Hospital, pointing behind us. We pass the *malchak* school and the grove of *garongs* and turn onto the river road. We're driving towards Mòk Bòo. We pass the crematorium and stop in front of a small white building with a big black cross painted on the front. It's dark except for one dim light in the window. Ulla says, *We want to go to town. To Mai Mor Hospital. Big hospital.* The driver yells something and gestures towards the blood on his seat and then shakes his fist at us, and we climb out of the *pini-mini* and he drives away. Ulla and I stand there in the dark for a few moments and then we turn and walk into the building. We enter a small office that's empty except for a bench and a cot and a desk with a woman behind it. She's wearing a t-shirt and jeans and is slightly plump and has a round pleasant face and is reading a comic book. She jumps up when she sees us and brings me over to the cot in the corner. I take the blood-soaked washcloth away from my face and show her my nose. She nods her head and says, *Stay*, and hurries out. I close my eyes. My heart is jumping around inside my chest like a bird trapped in a house, throwing itself against the door. The woman comes back and now she's wearing a tight gray uniform and has her hair pulled back into a bun. She looks very nice. She has a basin of water and a dirty-looking sponge and she gently cleans my face, squeezing the bloody water into the basin. I thank her and say, *Are you the doctor?* and she says, *Doctor come.* She lights a kerosene lamp and takes my arm and leads me out the back door. Ulla follows silently behind. We walk outside through a small courtyard and enter another building, and the nurse leads us into a small room with yellow brick walls. There's a bench against the wall and there's a bed frame but no mattress. White bugs swarm around the light on the ceiling, leaving bright trails behind them. The nurse leaves but soon returns with a small man wearing a bathrobe. They are carrying a mattress. They put the mattress on the frame and I see there's a dark yellow stain on it. It's shaped like an S, like a body curled up on its side. The man's name is Dr. Pisanu. Beneath his robe he's wearing a t-shirt with shiny pink lettering on it that reads: *80% HUMAN*. I can tell that it's supposed to be funny but I don't understand what it means. He has a pencil-thin moustache and slicked-back hair and black eyes. He looks like a card sharp from an old movie. He's flustered and sleepy. He says something to me in Puchanese and I assume he's asking me what happened, so I mimic slamming my face on the edge of the table. He studies my nose and then he carefully puts a thumb on either side of it and he says something I don't understand and he pushes, hard. I hear it make a small, bony *click* and I let out a yell. The doctor steps back and nods to himself, admiring his work. The nurse hands me a mirror and I study my reflection. I look terrifying. My face is caked with dried blood and my nose is swollen and misshapen and there's a mouth-shaped gash across the bridge. The doctor dips a cotton ball into a jar of something and wipes it on my nose. It stings and smells like limes. Some of it drips into the back of my throat. It tastes like limes too. I think it might actually be lime juice. The doctor takes a needle and thread and begins to sew up the wound. I grit my teeth and breathe through my mouth. It hurts but it doesn't take long. Then he puts some Vaseline on it and steps back and admires his work once again. He doesn't look so impressed this time. Ulla asks if I want her to stay and I say, *Maybe*. She says she'll go home and get a little sleep and then come visit me in the morning and bring me a change of clothes. She pats me on the head and asks if I'll be okay and I say, *I don't know*. The doctor puts his arm around Ulla's shoulder and indicates that he'll help her get a *pini-mini*. I

ask him if I could have some soap. I make a hand-washing
motion with my hands. He nods his head, and he and Ulla
leave. The nurse is still with me. She sits down on the bench
and asks me how old I am. *24*, I say. *You look like 18*, she
says. I say, *Thanks, I guess*. I ask her, *How old are you*? She
says, *Very old*, and laughs. *32*, she says. *You also look like
you're 18*, I say. She blushes and laughs and shakes her head
and says, *No*. She says, *Are you married*? *No*, I say. Then I
remember that I'm married and I say, *Yes*. Then I remember
everything that's happened and say, *No*. The nurse laughs
and asks my name and I tell her. She tells me her name is
Ken. She turns off the light and leaves, and I look out the
window and watch her kerosene lantern float through the
darkness of the courtyard as if it's being carried by a ghost.
It's very dark in the room and I get up and turn the light
back on and then try to sleep. I feel like I'm falling into a
cold deep space and I have half-waking dreams that are so
strange that I'm woken up by the sound of my palpitating
heart. I feel as if I'm dying for real and I don't like it. I don't
want it any more. I feel like wherever I'm going to is
somewhere flat and empty and I don't think you're there.
Someone has placed a long pink cylindrical pillow next to
me on the bed. I lie on my side and wrap my arms around it
as if it's a person. I go to sleep and wake up coughing. My
mouth fills with liquid and I don't want to swallow it so I spit
it into my empty water glass. It's mostly saliva with some
blood. It's pink. The next time I wake up the room is pitch
black. It's so dark and so quiet that I think maybe I'm dead.
All I can hear is the wet sound of my breathing. I sit up and
say, *Hello*? I get out of bed and stagger over to the light switch
and flip it up and down. Nothing happens. I turn in the
direction of where I think the window is and shout—*Hello*?
and I can't see anything at all. But then I see a light. I watch

it float across the courtyard and then Ken comes into my room. She's changed clothes again. She's wearing a robe. I apologize for waking her up and I flip the light switch up and down, demonstrating that it doesn't work, and she explains that they turn off the generator at night. She leaves and comes back with a kerosene lantern for my room. She points at my big pink pillow and says, *Bolster. Bolster,* I say back to her. I wish Ken would stay in here with me. She leaves. I feel something digging into my leg and I reach into my pocket and find my ballpoint pen. I clutch it in my hand and place that hand beneath my pillow, as if the pen is a knife or a gun and I am now armed against whatever might come for me in the night. I wrap my other arm around the bolster pillow and don't wake up again until the morning.

Ken just came in a few minutes ago and brought me some breakfast: a plate of roasted fish and some rice with sweet coconut milk and sliced *garong*. I asked her for something to write on and she brought me this stack of paper bags. I haven't seen the doctor yet today, but there's a bar of soap on my bedside table, so maybe he stopped by at some point. The soap is covered with dusty brown grease. I think I'm improving, though I still have this cough. And every time I cough, I cough up blood.

April 19
8:51 AM

Dear Hap:

Ken brought me a book to read yesterday—*The Lady with the Lamp: The True Tale of Florence Nightingale*, by William Studebaker Hall. Ken brings me delicious snacks and tall cold glasses of tamarind soda and cups of hot green tea and warm wet towels for my face, and sometimes when she has time she sits on the bench in my room and just stares out the window, humming under her breath. I love Ken.

My face looks like something someone dropped a cinderblock on top of, and I'm still coughing up some blood. I asked Ken if the doctor could take a look at me, but I didn't really understand her response—she kept pointing at her foot and gnashing her teeth.

Ulla's supposed to visit this morning. She came twice yesterday, before and after work. We didn't really talk about what happened. I wonder if we're broken up now. It's hard to say. I feel too tired to think. Maybe I'll stay in this little yellow room forever.

I'm wondering if Shiney's heard about my situation. I picture her appearing here in the doorway, wearing a white dress and holding a single yellow daisy plucked from the roadside. I tell her that I've never seen her wearing a dress before, and that it looks nice. She sits at the foot of my bed and we talk. I tell her all about you, Hap, and she is visibly moved. She's silent for a bit, studying my face, then tells me that my injuries make me look tough—like a Portuguese boxer. I ask her, *Why Portuguese?* and she just smiles enigmatically. When she gets up to leave, she gives my foot a light but friendly squeeze that sends chills down my spine. At the doorway she pauses and says: *Boyd, this is kind of awkward, but... there's something that I really need to tell you. I realize that you're married, but I just want you to know that I can't stop—*

Ulla's here, got to go.

5:41 PM

Ulla brought a card signed by what appears to be every member of the Faculty of Theatre Drama—even Mrs. Manarsumit. She also brought along a surprise guest: Mr. Horse. He presented me with a tin of peanut brittle and told me he was sorry for my tragedy, then went on a long tirade about this filthy *malchak* clinic and about how they were going to move me to the hospital in town as soon as possible. When he was done ranting, he stormed out to track down the doctor.

A few minutes later, Dr. Pisanu hobbled into the room on crutches, his ankle wrapped in bandages. Mr. Horse and Ken came in behind him, in the midst of an intense conversation— discussing my case, I assume. (I think that Mr. Horse might have a little thing for Ken.) The doctor escorted me to the main building and gave me an X-ray using a contraption that looked like a time machine from the 1950's. After the X-ray was developed he brought it into my room and held it up to the window and pointed at a small dark shape in one of my lungs. He spoke to Mr. Horse for what felt like an eternity, and finally Mr. Horse turned to me and explained that I had inhaled my tooth, and that it was now in my left lung. I don't know how—

7:55 PM

I had an immediate sense of *déjà vu* when Shiney appeared in the doorway. Except she wasn't wearing a dress: she was in black jeans and a worn yellow *Kati Na-Gareng* t-shirt. She let out a gasp when she saw me and held her hands up to her face. "Oh no!" she said. "Look at you!"

"Hey," I said, sitting up. "Come on in." I lowered my chin to my chest, taking a discreet sniff at my armpit.

Shiney began to laugh, her hands still covering her mouth. "I'm sorry, but—you look *horrible*! Your nose! And your tooth?"

I opened my mouth wide and showed her the hole where my canine had been. "Apparently, I inhaled it. It's in my lung."

"Your *fang* is in your *lung*?"

"A serious case of *fang-in-lung*. They're having a specialist come down from Dakhong with some kind of robot-telescope device to get it out." I inhaled a deep, wheezy breath, and added, "What do you think they'll do if I can't pay my hospital bill—put me in one of those prisons?"

"Can you really not pay it?"

I shrugged and looked down and smoothed the blanket over my legs. "How're things in the outside world?"

"All right." Shiney held up a plastic bag. "I brought you some *garongs*." She placed the bag on the ground, still remaining just inside the doorway, as though afraid of catching something. After staring at me vacantly for a few moments, she started laughing again.

"What?"

"I just had a strange image come to me." Shiney paused, then said, "There's something that you keep reminding me of. But it doesn't make sense, exactly."

"What is it?"

"It's hard to explain."

"Try." I had the distinct impression that she was going to say something about a Portuguese boxer.

Shiney pressed her eyes shut, then opened them. "There's a type of very large bird here. The *uluka*. Do you know it? It's like an owl. With a very big head and big beak."

I touched my face. "I remind you of a big-headed owl?"

"No, let me finish. The *uluka* flies very high above the fields, and when he sees a rodent, he comes down and eats it. But, he can't digest the entire animal, so anything that is extra he coughs up in a little pellet. The bones, the fur, the teeth; they're all mixed up together. Like a mixed-up animal. All the parts of the animal, without the body of the animal." Shiney gazed up at the ceiling and frowned for a moment. "Imagine that this pellet is a copy, made out of spun sugar—a piece of candy that is cast from a mold of a pellet from the *uluka*. You are walking through the woods, and you see this piece of candy on the ground. You pick it up. It is hard, but at the same time, you could crush it between your fingers. On an impulse, you put it in your mouth. And it melts on your tongue—and then it's gone."

I cleared my throat, waiting for her to continue. When she didn't, I said, "That's it?"

She nodded.

"Do you think maybe something's been lost in translation here?"

"Probably not. I'm very comfortable with speaking in English." She shifted uneasily on her feet and glanced at her watch. "I should go now. You look tired."

"You're welcome to hang out."

"No, thank you." Shiney hovered there for a moment, as though considering saying something more; then she *hai*-ed me and walked out the door.

April 20
7:17 PM

Dear Hap:

When Ulla entered my room this evening, I almost didn't recognize her. Her lips were pulled back into a toothy grimace, and her eyes were two pink horizontal slashes in her face. "I look like a *rabbit*," she hissed, "crossed with a *duck*?"

"What?"

Ulla rushed up to me and leaned over my bed. I could see specks of white spittle clinging at the corners of her mouth. "And, that dirty little black-eyed bitch? Whispering dirty little *fuck*-poems into your ear?"

"Wait, what—"

"I should rip out her eyes and shove them up her dirty little snatch, so she can see just how dirty she is!" Ulla took her ring off and threw it at me. It bounced off my forehead and *pinged* on the floor. "Oh! And some *whore* ate your wedding ring?"

"Ulla..."

Ulla opened my backpack and flipped it upside down, spilling its contents onto to the floor. "I found your *letters*, Boyd!"

I blinked at her and opened my mouth to speak. Nothing came out.

"I always wondered what you were doing," she said, "sitting out on your little garbage can for hours and hours, scribbling into your little notebooks. Carrying them around in your backpack, like they were top secret *documents* or something." Ulla looked down at the pages on the floor and gave them a kick. "I figured it was just the typical sort of travel-journal bullshit. Which it basically is: '*Today I ate something weird at lunch. Then I saw a big weird bug. Puchanese people don't speak English and so we had a funny misunderstanding.*'" She wiped her mouth with the back of her hand. "You didn't have any problems reading *my* personal correspondence, so I figured it wouldn't be so bad if I took a quick peek at yours. Though I guess *you* didn't get around to putting *your* letters in the mail, huh? I can't *believe* we're going through this bullshit again."

"Ulla..."

She sat down next to me on the bed and I scooted away from her, towards my bolster pillow. "And, I'm sorry," she said, "but you have to admit, it's a little creepy. Spending so much time, writing letters to—"

"All right—"

"—someone who isn't—"

"*All right!*"

Ulla flinched and got to her feet and took a step away from the bed. Neither of us spoke. After a moment, Ken appeared in the doorway and asked if I was all right.

"Yes," I told her. "Sorry. Thank you."

Ken lingered for a time, gazing at my notebooks scattered across the floor, then retreated down the hallway. Ulla stood there uncertainly, her arms held out at her sides, as if to keep her balance. We didn't say anything. I laid my head on the pillow and closed my eyes.

The next time I opened them, Ulla was back on the bed. When she saw that I was awake, she reached out towards my face; for a moment, I thought she was going to shove my nose into my brain with the heel of her palm.

"You're warm," she said, placing her hand on my forehead. She straightened my covers and looked at the floor. "You have to understand... those letters were really hard for me to read. The things you said. I just don't get why you write to him." She looked up at me. "I know it seems like I'm jealous or something. But—it's like you can say anything to him. I want to be that person. I'm *here*. You know?" Ulla bit her lip and glanced out the window. "We both fucked up. But I think maybe we need to forgive each other. Start over—for real, this time. I'm willing to try." She looked into my eyes. "Are you?"

The room hummed with silence. Outside, I could hear a dog barking, and a song playing on the radio—the sad voice of a woman singing in Puchanese. Time seemed to slow, then congeal, then come to a complete halt.

No.

Ulla tapped her fingers on my chest. "Boyd? I'm asking you if—"

"No," I said.

"No?" Ulla pulled her head back. "No, you can't forgive me?"

"I just mean—I'm done. I've had enough." I looked around the room. "Enough's enough."

"What's wrong with you?" Ulla asked, following my gaze. "Did that nurse give you some kind of drugs or something?"

"No."

"I don't understand. You're breaking up with me?"

I looked over at my bolster pillow. After a long pause, I looked back at Ulla. "I feel like we both sold each other a bill of goods when we first met. Not on purpose, but... it just happened. You know?"

Ulla's eyes widened. "A *bill* of *goods*?"

I nodded.

"So that's it? You're done? Just like that?"

"Don't you think it's the right thing?"

"You're seriously going to just abandon me here?"

"No, I'm not—"

"I can't believe you." Ulla stood up and brushed her fingers across her lap as though it was covered with crumbs. She slowly walked towards the door.

"Where are you going?"

"What do you care?"

"Are you going to be okay?"

Ulla paused at the doorway. She didn't look back at me. "I'll be staying with Miaw, if that's what you're asking."

"I could stay with Mr. Horse, if you want."

"No. You can have that shitty apartment. I went over to Miaw's place last night, and she was really sweet to me. She has a house off campus with a spare bedroom, and she said I could stay with her whenever I wanted. I don't really feel like being alone right now."

"Okay."

"And don't tell anyone about this. About us. I couldn't deal with Haraporn finding out." Ulla looked over her shoulder in my direction. Her face was like a mask made of hard, shiny plastic. "Maybe you're right," she said. "When I first met you, I thought—I don't know. You just looked so... tall."

After Ulla was gone, Ken came in and began to pick up the papers from the floor. She stacked them as neatly as she could and placed the notebooks next to me on the bed, then left the room. I slowly went through my letters to you, trying to put them back into order. Some of the pages were ripped and dirty, with Ulla's footprints on them. My heart was flapping against my ribcage, and I could feel my tooth sitting at the bottom of my lung, like a bullet at the bottom of a well. I put the notebooks down and rested my head back and stared at the crack in the corner of the ceiling for a minute, and then I closed my eyes and had a short and very vivid dream. You were there. I started crying in the dream, crying like a kid—heaving and shuddering and gasping—and then I was awake again, and my entire body was shaking, and I pressed my face into the pillow to try and quiet the noises coming from my mouth, and the next thing I knew I'd flung myself out of bed, filled with the desire to tear my room apart.

Then the blood rushed to my head and things began to get soft and gray around the edges, so I crawled back under the sheets. I lay there and imagined myself picking up my blood-filled glass and hurling it against the wall, and imagined flipping my dirty mattress onto the floor and dousing it with kerosene and setting it on fire; I imagined upending the bench, smashing it to pieces, and imagined taking a heavy piece of this wood and opening my mouth wide and smashing out the rest of my teeth; I imagined pushing my fist through the window and grasping a shard of the broken glass and dragging it along my neck; and I imagined dipping my fingers into the wetness of the cut and writing something on the wall—some kind of message. A message for someone who would come to this godforsaken place and see it.

But I couldn't for the life of me imagine what that message would be.

April 23
Approx. 2 PM

Dear Hap:
I'm back home now. *Home Kwan Home.* My stitches have
been removed from my nose, and, yesterday afternoon,
my tooth was removed from my body. The procedure was
extremely uncomfortable and involved sticking a fiber optic
filament and a small grabbing device down my nostril and
into my lung—like one of those games at the fair where you
try to snag a stuffed animal with a remote-control claw.

After they got the tooth out, I had Mr. Horse ask Dr. Pisanu
if I'd be able to pay them using some kind of installment
plan. Mr. Horse informed me that the bill had already been
settled the previous evening by an anonymous donor.

"I don't understand," I said. "The clinic doesn't know who
paid my bill?"

Mr. Horse nodded. "Someone call Miss Ken and ask what
is amount, and then they send the money at the post office.
We do not know name of the giver." He winked at me and
said, solemnly: "Some person is your friend."

I thanked everybody and promised Ken I'd come by to visit
her sometime, and then Mr. Horse gave me a ride back home
on his motorbike. When I entered my empty apartment,
the room had a slightly disturbed air to it, as if it had been
carelessly ransacked: the desk drawers were all pulled out, the

bed was unmade, and the bathroom floor was covered with baby powder. An ashtray containing two crushed cigarette butts sat on the table. Did Ulla start smoking again? Does the White Sikh smoke cigarettes? I couldn't remember.

I made myself an early dinner of noodles and eggs and then went outside and drank a cup of *Express Dark* instant coffee. I had no idea what I should do next. It felt pointless being out there on my trash can when I knew that Ulla wasn't inside. I sat staring at the picture on the *Express Dark* packet that I held in my hand—an illustration of the silhouette of a farmhand making an ambiguous gesture towards a young girl. Below that reads the legend: *KEEP IT DARK.*

I went back inside and sat on the edge of the bed and methodically stapled all of my paper-bag letters into this new notebook. When I was finished, I lay down and watched the restless movements of the lizards on the ceiling for a while. Then I curled up and I shut my eyes.

When I opened them, I was in darkness. I sat up and looked around, reaching out for the bolster pillow. Something had tugged me back into consciousness—a sound outside the door. I got up and walked quietly over to it and stood there, listening. It sounded like a bird dragging its beak back and forth on the other side. *Click tap scratch scratch scratch tap tap click.* My heart grew still and I felt the hair prickle and rise on the back of my neck and I took a few steps back and grabbed the broom from the corner and held it close against my chest. Then I leaned in and put my mouth to the edge of the door.

"Hap?"

The sound stopped.

I hesitated, my hand hovering at the doorknob. Then I opened the door.

It was Shiney. She was wearing a flowered peach-colored dress with a black Spanish-looking short-sleeved silk jacket over it. The dress was cut low and straight across her chest and the skin below her throat was the color of burnished wood. Her canvas knapsack was on the ground and she was holding a ballpoint pen and a piece of notebook paper. She folded the paper, took a step backward, and said, "Hi."

"Hi." I put the broom down. "How's it going?"

"I was dropping off some more healthy foods for your recovery," she said, holding up a plastic bag.

I looked out into the darkness. "Were you scratching on my door?"

"Your lights were off—I was writing you a note." She showed me the folded piece of paper. On one side, in large letters, was written:

To BODY

"'Body'?"

Shiney inspected the piece of paper and laughed. "Whoops. That was an accident." She folded the note several more times and placed it in her knapsack.

"Can't I read it?"

She shook her head.

"Well... would you like to come in?"

"Okay." Shiney stepped into the room, then glanced over her shoulder and said, "It was very strange. There was a man outside, standing in the woods. When he saw me, he ran away."

I leaned out the door and looked around. I couldn't see anyone out there. I closed the door and locked it. "What'd he look like?"

"He was a *gareng*. He looked like that man Shawn—the Sikh." She patted the top of her head. "But this man did not have a turban on."

"I think that might be him," I said, absently. I went over to the refrigerator and opened it.

"Really? He's visiting?"

I didn't respond for a moment. "Would you like a beer?"

"Yes, please."

We sat at the table together, and I handed her a bottle of *Gong*. "You're so dressed up," I said. There were grass stains on her bone-colored pumps, but apart from that, she looked like she was on her way to a cotillion.

She shrugged. "I just felt like it. I never get to wear this."

"You look nice."

Shiney nodded and smoothed the dress over her knees and glanced around the room. "Ulla is out?"

Tell her you've broken up. You weren't actually married.

"Ulla's working," I said.

"I saw her yesterday, at the Hi-Fi." Shiney paused, then added, "I don't think she likes me very much."

"What do you mean? Ulla likes you."

"No, she doesn't." Shiney took a sip of beer. "It's funny— Gabe is so jealous of my friendship with you."

"Really?"

"Very silly, don't you think? He's such a paranoid."

I swallowed a mouthful of *Gong* and held the bottle close to my face and studied the label, as if admiring its elegant design. "I haven't officially heard, but I assume Gabe's giving the Y.E.S. presentation?"

"I think so."

"I'm probably too scary-looking to go on stage now, anyhow." I bared my teeth and gently tapped the side of my nose.

"I'm sorry for acting so odd during my visit with you at the clinic," Shiney said. "I wanted to tell you that."

"You weren't odd."

"I have a terrible dislike of hospitals."

"I don't like them either."

"Yes, but I truly am phobic. It's from when I was young, and had to visit my mother." Shiney stared down thoughtfully at the backs of her hands. After a few moments, she began to laugh. Then she lifted her head and explained: "I'm remembering something funny that happened to me once—another reason why I hate hospitals."

"Yeah?"

She chewed on her lip and said, "Gabe hates this story. He has a morbid fear of the functions of the body. As you know."

"Now you have to tell it to me."

"May I smoke?"

"Sure."

Shiney fished a pack of *Cowpokes* out of her knapsack and lit one. "Three years ago," she said, "Pônge was sick with cancer of the lymph. I was home from university for the summer, and I visited him in the hospital. Every single day, for two months. This is during a time when we'd become lovers again." She blew a ring of smoke at the floor and took a breath. "The doctors had told him that the radiation therapy would make him unable to have erections, and he was very upset by this. One day, when I was visiting him, he asked me to perform oral sex on him. Right there, in the hospital! His prognosis was bad, and I felt that I couldn't refuse him. I wanted to do it very rapidly so that the nurses wouldn't see, but it took a long, long time. It was not pleasant for me after a while, and my neck and jaw began to feel very sore. Finally, as he was achieving his orgasm—" Shiney paused and looked at me. "Wrong end," she said.

"What? Oh." I removed my cigarette from my mouth—I'd been trying to light the filter. I broke it in half and put it in the ashtray.

"Where was I?" Shiney asked.

"Pônge was… *achieving*…"

"That's right. So, I took my mouth away from his penis, and the semen spilled all over his stomach. The sperms were repulsive to look at, all gray and dead because of the radiation. When he looked down at it, he was filled with disgust and nausea, and, instantly, he vomited! Onto my head!" Shiney put her hand over her face and laughed. "I had very long hair at that time, and it was full of the vomit! And *then*, I was so disgusted that I vomited onto *his* stomach! It was truly the most disgusting time in my life!" She was laughing so hard now that tears were making her cheeks shine. "That day, I cut my hair, and it's been short like this always after that. A few months later, when Pônge became healthy again, and when he knew he wasn't dying any more, he broke up with me." She stopped laughing for a moment and wiped her eyes. "When I say he is a dog, I mean it truly. Anyhow, that's why I don't enjoy the hospital. It reminds me of my dying mother—and of vomit, mixed with sperms." She dropped her cigarette into her empty bottle of *Gong*. It let out a short, wet hiss.

I cleared my throat and stood up. "Another beer?"

"Please."

I went and got two more. "You know, it's strange. Someone paid my entire hospital bill for me. Anonymously."

"Really?" Shiney raised her eyebrows and blinked.

"Wait—was it *you*?" I asked, sitting back down.

"Oh, no. I don't have money to be paying the bills of *garengs*." She shrugged and took a sip of beer. "I did, however, mention your concern to Mr. Yul..."

"Mr. Yul! Of course."

"But you mustn't say I told you it was him. He's very modest." Shiney lit another cigarette and squinted at me. "I was wondering about what happened to make your accident? Haraporn tells me you were drunk and fell down on your face?"

"I wasn't drunk. Not too drunk. I just had a... you know. I conked out for a second."

"Conked?"

"Passed out. Like after the *garong* thing."

"Is it some kind of medical condition that you have?"

"Sort of. Yes. But there's not much they can do about it. I mean, ultimately, I think it's more—" I twirled my finger next to my head and whistled like a cuckoo clock. "You know?"

"Psychology?"

"Right."

"Has it always happened to you?"

"As a kid, I'd pass out and have seizures. I was on meds for years. Phenobarbital, mostly. When I was sixteen, the doctors decided I'd outgrown the seizures, and I went off the drugs. But I never totally outgrew the passing-out." I looked up at the ceiling. "It's funny—my brother always said I looked really happy whenever I was down on the ground, twitching. That it looked like I was smiling. He used to do a pretty good imitation of it."

"He doesn't have these problems? They're not genetical?"

"No," I said. "He was healthy." I clicked my teeth against the mouth of the beer bottle. "But... he passed away, actually."

Shiney lifted her chin and looked at me. "I'm sorry."

I nodded to her.

"When did he pass?"

"Nine years ago."

"Were you close?"

"Kind of." I stared down at the table, rubbing my tongue back and forth across the raw area in my mouth where my tooth had once been, my eyes tracing the border of upside-down hearts. "His name was Adam," I said. "But my parents always called him Hap."

Then I told Shiney about you: about how no one ever believed us when we said we were brothers because I was tall and pale and you always looked like you'd been in the sun and had those dark eyes and thick eyebrows and how you always said that Mom must've had sex with a Mexican or a Cherokee because you looked unlike any other Darrow. I told Shiney about your predilection for trouble, and how pissed you'd get when I wouldn't go along with whatever trouble you had in mind. I told her that in a certain way we were best friends despite the fact that you were four years older and we often hated each other. I told her about some of the stuff you used to do to me when I was little, like that time with the fire-ants, and putting the laundry detergent on the orange slices, and freaking me out with your bat kite at night above my bed. I also told her how if anyone ever messed with me you went ballistic, and how you broke Jon Tolliver's collarbone and ended up getting sent away to Holderness. I told Shiney how I wrote to you almost every day and also how in a certain way Mom and Dad and I were secretly relieved to have you gone because we could all finally relax—Dad compared it to having a chainsaw running for sixteen years straight and not noticing the noise until someone shuts it off. I told Shiney about you coming back home to finish high school after getting kicked

out of Holderness, and how you could tell that we were all
skittish around you after your absence. And I told Shiney
about that all-ages show at the Mabuhay, and how you gave
me a couple of beers, even though you knew I shouldn't be
drinking on the meds, and I passed out and seized right
there in the front row and fell on the laps of those girls,
and then you took me outside to get me some air and sat
with me on the curb for a while until one of the girls came
out to see how I was and you two started talking and then
you told me you'd be right back and went inside; and you
didn't come back and I felt pretty sick so I got a ride home
from Suzy Plant without telling you, and when you came
out and found me gone you freaked and called Mom and
Dad and told them you'd lost me and you were drunk and
crying and by the time I got home there were two cop cars
in the driveway and you felt terrible about it but also hated
me for getting you into trouble and barely talked to me
for a couple weeks afterwards. But it was always something
like that. And I told Shiney that you hadn't even bothered
applying to any colleges for the fall and we all figured
you'd just end up working at Rit's forever, or—best-case
scenario—studying Geology at Indian Valley, but then one
night late in August you came into my room and woke me
up and showed me the ad:

EARN THOUSANDS OF DOLLARS — SEE THE WORLD —
LIVE YOUR DREAMS — JUNGLE HONEY.

Shiney said: "Jungle honey?"
    "They were looking for Americans to go to Suriname,
in South America, and work with the natives, trekking into
the rainforest and collecting honey from these enormous

beehives. The honey supposedly has amazing medicinal properties—you give a teaspoon to a baby when it's born, and it's healthy for life. The ad said that jungle honey was worth more than gold. Hap asked me to go there with him, though he must've known I'd never do it. I think what he really wanted was for me to try and stop him. I think he was scared. Hap was always daring himself to do things, and then he'd be forced to follow through with whatever stupid idea he had." I rubbed my thumb against my temple. "He left in the middle of the night. Didn't tell my parents. He called us a few days later from Paramaribo, asking for money. The jungle honey thing turned out to be some kind of pyramid scheme, but he liked the place and wanted to stay. I think a girl was maybe involved. He was there for a couple of months, just hanging out, tending bar at some tourist hotel. I sent him ten letters, and he sent me only one postcard. He was a shitty correspondent." I put my hands in my pockets and then took them out and folded my arms. "And one day we got a phone call, and it was someone from the U.S. embassy saying that Hap had been swimming somewhere at night with some people and he'd been drinking and he…"

I stopped talking and looked at Shiney. I felt as if all of the words and all of the breath had been squeezed out of my body. I uncrossed my arms and slid my hands beneath my legs and waited for her to say something.

Shiney frowned vaguely towards the door, then brought her eyes back to me. "'Hap,'" she said. "That's what it sounded like you said before, when you heard me outside."

"Did I say that?"

"I think so."

I rubbed my face and let out a silent yawn. "This is going to sound kind of weird," I said, "but—there have been these noises at night in our apartment. A scratching noise at the door. Inside, too. Something moving around. I thought... I don't know what I thought, exactly."

"You think the ghost of your brother would come all the way to Puchai?"

I shrugged. "He liked to travel."

"I have a question." Shiney was now staring at a spot in the air just above my head. "Since you've been in Mai Mor, have you felt particularly unlucky?"

"What are you looking at?"

"Since you've been here, have you..." Shiney paused. "Have you, by any chance, killed a turtle?"

"What do you mean?"

"When you came into Auntie Golli's house, she saw a thing hanging over you. She also saw it in your classroom. A black tooth, about the size of a *garong*."

"A black tooth," I repeated. I tried to smile, but it felt as though my face had gone slack.

"Yes. Black and sticky, like road-tar."

"Hanging over my head?"

"Yes."

"And she told you this *before* I knocked my tooth out?"

"She told me about it that same evening when we all visited her house. I mean, she described the shape to me. It was after your accident that I was able to interpret what the shape represented."

"And she thinks it's because of some turtle curse?"

Shiney shrugged.

"Golli, Golli, Golli." I took a sip of beer and drummed my fingers on the table. Then I shut one eye and gazed carefully down into the bottom of the bottle and said, "You know, actually, now that I think about it—there *was* a situation in which I accidentally stepped on a very, very small turtle. It was completely unintentional. It did die, though, I guess."

Shiney bobbed her head up and down excitedly. "And did you leave any sort of offering at the turtle shrine?"

"It was an accident."

"It doesn't work like that."

"Don't they understand that I'm not from here?"

"You must pay honor, regardless of the circumstances. *'The turtle spirits water their gardens with the tears of the unrepentant turtle-slayer—'*"

"What's that? Turtle scripture?"

"'—and they drink those same tears like sweet liquor, giving them strength to make love for many days.'"

"Turtles drink my tears and have *sex*?" I sat down on the bed and gazed at the floor. I was surprised to find myself missing Ulla. It gave me comfort knowing that she would laugh in my face if I told her about my turtle curse. "You shouldn't be saying all this," I said. "I tend to believe in this sort of thing."

"I believe as well. That's why I'm saying it to you." Shiney snapped her fingers. "We must go make an offering to the shrine."

"Isn't it too late?"

"If you present the offering with an open heart, they'll receive it with their hearts open as well. But you should give them something good." She stood up. "Do you have any pork?"

"No. I have some ramen noodles."

Shiney walked over to the fridge and opened it. "There's nothing much in here that a turtle spirit would want to eat." She took out a bag of eggs. "Haven't you got anything tasty?"

"Didn't you say that you brought me some food?"

Shiney fished a plastic bag out of her knapsack. "Some *garongs*. The turtles will like those." She looked around the room and asked, "Any other snacks?"

I went over to the basket of *fae-dongs*. "What about these?" I asked, holding up one of the bags. "They're very *pêt*."

"Why do you have an entire *brà-boong* of *fae-dong pikachai*?"

"It's a long story," I said. "They're some kind of *malchak* snack, right? What's *pikachai*?"

"*Pikachai* is…" She made a fluttering movement with her hands. "The type of giant moth—like the one we had to catch in the *Rák-Wá-See*."

"Seriously?"

"You have eaten a great deal of the fried moths," she said, looking into the basket. "Very impressive."

I frowned. "The dog ate some, too. Also—the thing that comes into our room at night. I think maybe he eats the snacks."

"The turtle spirit is the hungriest of all spirits. They are gluttonous."

"So, that's what you think that noise was?"

"Certainly." Shiney picked up a bag of the *fae-dongs*. "In Puchanese culture, the moth is a death-symbol," she said. "You know, as when they say: 'the moth of death'? Do you use that saying?"

"I don't think so."

"Puchanese people don't eat the moth because of this superstition, but the *malchaks* make it into a delicious snack. We eat the moth and we say: 'Fuck thee, Death. I am *digesting* thee, Death. And now I am *shitting* thee.'"

"'Thee'?"

"We use the informal pronoun when addressing Death, to display our disrespect. Now, what else do you have for the turtles?" Shiney looked around. "*Ur-ur-ur*," she said, pointing at the bamboo tube on top of the fridge. "That will be good." Shiney opened the canister, took a swig, and handed it to me. I had some and handed it back to her and she put it into the *fae-dong* basket, along with the eggs and the *garongs*.

"What else does a turtle spirit like?"

Shiney sat down on the bed and ticked off the items: "Beef. Pork. Money. Shiny things. Gadgets. Games. Amphetamines. Beer. Booze. Trinkets. Cocaine."

"My brother and the turtle spirit have a lot in common."

"They also like sweet things—pastries, cakes. Things with a lot of color. Pink things. Red things. Smelly things. Perfume. Bubble gum. Ganja." Shiney opened the basket and helped herself to a little more *ur-ur-ur*. "Do you have some money to give them?"

"Seriously?"

"Whatever you can spare."

"Fine." I looked in my wallet. I only had a 300 *prik* bill. I put it in the basket and took another slug of *ur-ur-ur*.

"Leave some alcohol for the turtles," Shiney said. "And let me have just one more little sip."

I got up and went into the bathroom and came out holding a jar of vanilla-scented face cream that Ulla had left behind. "This stuff is pretty smelly, in my opinion."

"Excellent." Shiney pointed at my wrist. "How about that?"

"My watch? No way."

"They would love it. It lights up, right?"

"But I need it. I like to know what time it is." I pushed a few of the buttons. "Also, it has a calculator, and an alarm clock. And—" I paused. "Ulla gave it to me."

"I see."

I pressed the side button, starting and stopping the stop watch. *Beep. Beep beep.* I sighed. "Fine, they can have it. I don't care." I took the watch off my wrist and tossed it into the basket, then lay down on the bed, crossing my arms across my chest.

"Do you have any music?" asked Shiney. "They enjoy hard rock and rapping."

I groaned and sat up and retrieved the *BLACK-EYE SOUL* cassette. "I have this. Though I'd kind of like to hang onto it."

"Why?"

"To *listen* to it."

"All right." She began rifling through the desk drawers.

I tossed the tape into the basket. "Maybe the turtle spirits should just back their van up to my door?"

Shiney didn't respond. I went over and helped her go through the contents of the desk. We found some gum, a pack of cigarettes, a deck of cards, and a perfume sample. I also threw a ballpoint pen into the basket. Shiney looked at me questioningly.

"In case they want to write me a letter," I explained.

"You know what they would like?" Shiney went to her knapsack and searched through it. "My note to you." She added it to the pile.

"They're allowed to read it, but I can't?"

Shiney shrugged. "Sorry."

I thought of something else, and pulled a small plastic bag out of my pocket. "Would they like this?"

"What is it?"

"My tooth. The doctor gave it to me as a souvenir."

"What would a turtle spirit do with a tooth?"

"I don't know." I began to put it back in my pocket, then asked, "Do you want it?"

Shiney laughed and took the bag from me. "Thank you very much," she said, slipping it into her knapsack. She walked over to the windowsill and picked up the jar of honey that I'd bought from Golli. "How about this?"

Jungle honey.

"Okay," I said. "Give it to him."

Shiney put it in the basket and reviewed its contents, murmuring to herself. I stood very still and watched her profile for a moment. The mark around her eye looked particularly dark, and I noticed for the first time that her hair was now dyed a reddish-black. I found myself flooded by a wave of desire, and let out an involuntary groan.

Shiney looked up at me. "Are you in pain?"

"No."

"Okay." She picked up the basket—disappearing behind it almost completely—and shoved it into my arms. "Let's go lift your curse."

We made our way across the dark courtyard of *Home Kwan Home*, Shiney lighting our path with one of my water-bottle lanterns while I staggered behind her, bearing my basket of gifts. Up ahead I could see the silhouette of the giant wooden turtle, illuminated by the yellow Christmas lights wrapped around it. We didn't speak until after we'd reached the shrine and I had set the basket down. Shiney instructed me to kneel and light a stick of incense.

"Now say a prayer to the turtle spirit, presenting your offering and asking for forgiveness," she said softly. "Push your chest forward and speak from an open heart. And when you're done, bow your head low so it touches the ground."

Shiney knelt and said a few quiet words, then took the lantern and walked over to a tree stump and sat down with her back to me. I got on my knees and folded my hands together and began:

O Great Turtle Spirit. Hello. Ràp-naa ròp. I'm here to tell you that I'm sorry to have offended thee. I'm very, very sorry that I killed one of your children in the parking lot. I don't know if you remember—it happened several weeks ago. I guess you probably do remember. It was an accident, but it was wrong. I find it hard to believe that I should be punished for this act, because it was clearly unintentional, but I'm sure that thou hast thy reasons for creating such an unfair and arbitrary-seeming system. I guess it's no more arbitrary than the rules of many world religions. I hope that my plentiful tears have made thy garden bloom brightly, and provided thee with considerable staying power during thy sexual adventures. I present to thee a beautiful gift basket that includes garongs, money, alcohol, cigarettes, music, a digital watch, and a bottle of honey. I hope that thou, Turtle Spirit, enjoy all this stuff. Please lift off my curse. Lift off my curse, Curselifter! I wonder if I'm drunk right now. Sometimes it's hard to tell. I don't know what's wrong with me. But I'm done with all that. Please don't hurt me. I don't want to die. I'm sorry you're dead. I've done my best here. It's hard. I'm trying. I feel like I've tried to do what you said and it hasn't gotten me anywhere. But maybe it has and I can't see it. Lately I haven't really been hearing you like I used to. Or it's like I can't tell if it's my voice or your voice anymore. I'm sick of wanting to disappear. It's a sin to think like that. I should've tried harder to stop you. I didn't think you'd actually go. You can't hold that against me. What the fuck do you want from me? Enough already. I'm sorry. I don't know what I'm talking about. I don't know what to do. Maybe I should go to school for Gemology. I wonder if Shiney's watching me right now. I'm not really sure how long

I'm supposed to kneel here. Five minutes, or half an hour? My knees hurt. Maybe I should stand up and walk over to Shiney and kiss her. I might get hit by a bus tomorrow and never have another chance. I don't know. Anyway—are you still there? Okay. In conclusion, I'd like to say: please accept this offering, and please stop coming into the apartment during the night, whoever thou are, because I'm not sleeping very well. I don't know what's going to happen with Shiney, but if thou can help me out at all, I'll bring you a beautiful piece of pork. I swear to God. Though I'm probably not even supposed to ask thee for those kinds of favors. I'm unclear how this religion works exactly.

Amen.

I crossed myself and bowed low, pressing my forehead into the dirt. It felt nice and cool there and I think I would've stayed that way for a while if I hadn't known that Shiney was waiting. I forced myself up and went over to her and said, "All done."

"Are you okay?" she asked, holding the lantern up to my face.

"Yeah."

"Your eyeballs look funny." She handed me the container of ivory chopsticks. "Shake these until one falls out. Then we will learn the advice of the turtle."

I rattled the container, tilting it as I remembered Miaw had done, and a chopstick slid out and fell to the ground. Shiney picked it up and stuck it into the hole on top of the altar, pushing down on it so that the side panel popped open and the key-drawer appeared. She found the drawer that matched the number on the chopstick and opened it with the key. She read the piece of paper, then put it back in the drawer.

"What did it say?" I asked.

314 Matt Dojny

"'*You must submerge... your physical shell... into the awful, happy realm of...*' No, wait. It's complicated to express in English. '*... the turtle-spirit-cursed joy of...*'" Shiney shut her eyes and ran her tongue across her upper lip, then opened her eyes and said: "'*I command you to bathe your body in the... in the god-damned joyfulness of the earth.*'"

"The *god-damned* joyfulness of the earth."

"The turtle-spirit philosophy is slightly different from the Buddhist teachings," she said, shrugging. "Hey—what happened to your brow?" Shiney stood on her tiptoes and brushed her fingertips against my dirty forehead. Then she laughed and said, "Mr. Pig-Pen! That's your nickname!"

The spot where she'd touched me was still warm after she took her hand away. "Please, not that," I said.

"No?"

"How about... 'Mr. Body.' Like you wrote on my note. Maybe that's a better name."

"That's pretty good." Shiney smiled at me, and as we looked at each other, her smile began to change into something else. "Body," she said, quietly.

At that moment a stillness descended upon the world, and I opened my mouth to speak and could feel my breath being drawn out and disappearing into the stillness. I saw that the stillness was a wall in front of me that I had to step through to reach Shiney, and all I had to do was lift my foot and move my body forward through time and space and I would be there.

I took a step toward her.

"Do you know what time it is?" she asked, glancing up at the sky.

I touched my bare wrist. The stillness was gone.

"No," I said. "I don't have a watch."

"I should probably go." Shiney continued staring up at the stars, blinking her eyes. "I told Gabe I'd just be going on a short visit. He likes to worry." She looked back at me. "Congratulations," she said. "You have now been curse-lifted."

I walked Shiney over to her motorbike and watched as she rode away. The wind had extinguished the candle in my lantern, and I remained standing in the darkness for a while. I reached up and smacked myself on the forehead with my open palm, then turned and headed back inside.

"KEEP IT DARK"

April 25
Early evening

I still haven't seen Ulla since that time in the clinic last week. I went over to the Faculty of Theatre Drama yesterday to talk to her, but just before I went inside, I lost my nerve and decided to write her a note instead:

Dear Ulla—

Hi. I just wanted to get in touch and make sure you are doing OK. You know where to find me if you feel like talking. I think it might be a good idea. Otherwise, I'll see you at the Festival show. Stay in touch. Hope you're OK.

— Boyd

P.S. I know I still owe you that money, and just wanted to say don't worry, I still plan on paying you back.

I hung around outside until I saw someone I knew—Mrs. Djiinippiwai, the Associate Director of Theatre Lighting Studies—and gave her the note to deliver to Ulla. She doesn't speak English very well, so I figured she wasn't likely to read it, and she has the air of someone who knows how to be discreet.

When I arrived at the Faculty of Gemology this afternoon for my scheduled editing session, Mr. Yul was in the front office, sitting on the desk of his secretary, Ms. Pilopoblan. He was smoking a cigarette and Ms. Pilopoblan was laughing a full, deep-throated laugh, and she didn't stop laughing even after I'd entered the room. Ms. Pilopoblan is so intensely attractive that I want to turn and run in the opposite direction every time I'm near her.

Mr. Yul invited me into his office for a cup of *Express Dark*. Ms. Pilopoblan brought us a tray of coffee, and as she glided silently out of the room, Mr. Yul said to me: "It brings me great joy to witness your good health, Mr. Boyd Darrow."

"Thanks," I said. "I want to thank you for helping me out with my hospital bill. It was very generous, and I—"

Mr. Yul held up his hand. "I humbly accept your proffering of gratitude. It brought only pleasure to my conscience to be in a capacity that would assist an honored guest of Mai Mor College. And, although I do not wish to be viewed as being immodest in your eyes, truthfully I can say that I have been blessed with a situation of comparative wealth, thanks to my arduous labors in my chosen field of Gemology, and that the sum I paid to ensure your positive health was, in fact, a non-significant amount to me. So I say to you: '*Saát teè prôm aa-haàn glaang wan.*' The meaning of this expression— commonly used by individuals such as myself, whom fortune has shone upon—might translate into English as: 'I spilled as much at lunch.' That is to say: the cost of the thing you refer to is insignificant to me, and I am so wealthy that, when I ate at my luncheon today, the drops of brandy that I dribbled upon my lap are greater in value than the thing that you refer to; in this case, the bill for your hospital tenure. The entire gift gave me a warm feeling to proceed upon it, and so I beg of you, do not mention this again in my presence."

I *hai*-ed him. "*Pranoo ròp*. I hope to someday be in a position to say those same words: 'I spilled as much at lunch.'"

"I have no uncertainty that one day you will. Particularly if you continue to pursue your burgeoning interest in the fascinating and lucrative field of Gemology." Mr. Yul rubbed his hand over his perfectly smooth head. "My only regret is that my secret was revealed by our mutual friend—I had hoped to remain nameless. Shiney informed me of your scenario, and so I was happy to throw my hat into your ring." He paused, then added, "She is a good friend to you. I believe she has also been an instrument in advising her father to continue your employment at his school."

"Really?"

"She has told me so in confidence, yes. Shiney has a strong heart. I have known her since she was a young girl, and think of her as... almost as an offspring to me. I was once close with her mother." He frowned down at his desk. "It has been a grand pleasure to have Shiney visiting in Mai Mor. I will miss her powerfully upon her imminent departure."

I sat up a little straighter. "What do you mean?"

"She has purchased a ticket to travel to the south, to visit an island there. Sing-ren is its name. Following that, she will be returning to Dakhong to live."

"With Gabe?"

"Currently, I'm led to assume that she and Mr. Sloat are no longer functioning on friendly terms."

I touched the corner of my mouth, holding it there, and said, "Do you mean they broke up?"

"It is not my place to discuss the affairs of the love of two people other than myself and another—but, yes, confidentially, I think her heart is no longer with Gabriel Sloat."

I felt a warm prickling rising in my chest. "Okay," I said, nodding. "That's good to know. I mean, I'm sorry to hear about her trouble. I should maybe try to talk to her. See if she's all right. Or, I don't know. I guess she has friends she can talk to. Though I consider myself a friend to her at this point. I don't know." I braced my hand beneath my chin to stop my head from nodding any more.

"I'm sure she'd appreciate the comfort of friendship from you." Mr. Yul adjusted the black handkerchief over his eye, then removed two cigarettes from a wooden box on his desk, offering one to me. I lit it with his gold Zippo and sat back down. Mr. Yul was moving his lips, tracing a finger on the blotter on his desk. We both sat there for a time, quietly smoking. Then he said:

"I knew the mother of Shiney many years ago, in her youth. Her name was Noi. I met her simply by introducing myself at the market one day—she was selling unripe mangoes, and I approached her and informed her that she was the most splendid-appearing woman I had ever seen. And in this I did not lie. She was just twenty years, I was almost of thirty years. Although she was *malchak*, I nevertheless began to court her. I was studying in Dakhong in the field of Gemology, but would return to Mai Mor when I could afford the time. It was difficult to steal moments to be with Noi and to share myself with her, and so I constructed a plan. I invited her to travel with me to that island of Sing-ren—the island which Shiney is planning to explore forthwith. To my absolute pleasure, Noi agreed to come with me. An elaborate deception was fabricated for the sake of her family, and then, that same evening, she and I boarded the night-train to the south. Truly, my memory of this time on the isle of Sing-ren remains powerful and unchanged in my mind up to this moment, eternally standing out in sharp relief from the rest of my days. One might compare it to the phenomenon of when the noonday sunshine flows directly onto a boulder from above, causing no shadows to obscure or confuse one's view."

Mr. Yul removed a white handkerchief from his suit pocket, coughed into it, and continued: "Noi and I lived for eight days in a small bamboo home on the beach, and developed an exquisite regimen during our stay. We would sleep until the late morning and then swim in the ocean that was very warm and was covered with smooth white sand on the bottom. Noi had never been to the ocean before, nor even viewed it with her eyes before, and so wanted to spend hour after hour floating upon the water—water which was so perfectly still and clear it almost was as if we were flying on our backs, held up only by the air. After the swimming we would lay under the sun until our bodies became warmed and dried and then we would stroll along the beach of Sing-ren and feast upon the incredible foods of the vendors on the sand. We ate cakes made of steamed and sliced squid with hot chili and small yellow seeds sprinkled upon them— cakes that were fragile and soft in the mouth, melting on your tongue, and the squid of a supreme delicateness. We purchased plates of tiny yellow crabs, twice-steamed and eaten with a pepper sauce. They were hot and sweet, and you could eat a whole crab in a single bite. We also devoured the meat from large blue crabs, soaked in the juice of citrus and then sprinkled with the crunchy pink salt and presented on a warmed bun. Then we consumed black fish-skin fried in oil, and oysters in the shells, and the gonads of urchins. We ate a luncheon lasting for two hours in duration, grazing along the vendors in the sand as the cow is known to dine on the grassy expanse of fields. And always while eating we were drinking a rice-wine that was flavored with the juice of the banana and served very cold in a jar rimmed with sugar. This beverage was delicious and cost so little that we consumed it as one would drink water from a spring. And lastly, we devoured fresh and ripened *garong* sliced and covered with sea-salt and red flakes of chili. We would sit and consume these and our bodies were so warmed from the sun that our skin was hot to the touch, as with fever. We would then return to our room during this time of day when the sun was most overbearing and we would lay together on the cooling sheets of our tiny hard bed, holding one another and listening to the *bailam* music outside our window until submerging into a deep sleep without any dreams. We did not have to dream, because during those slow and empty days on Sing-ren, we were truly living within the golden mist of a dream. It was the happiest time that I have ever known."

Mr. Yul looked at me and then leaned forward and pushed a heavy black ashtray in my direction. My cigarette had burned down while he was speaking, and I'd been ashing into my hand.

Mr. Yul said, "After, I had need to continue my studies in Dakhong. Noi remained here in Mai Mor. In this period, I believe she began working as a *gà-roó-na* girl. Not soon following, she met Samuel, and later she sent me a letter saying that she would be wed to him." He paused. "My heart has been broken three times in this life. The first time was the day I received that letter." Mr. Yul reached up and once again adjusted the silk handkerchief that covered his face, and I caught a glimpse of his shriveled, empty eye. "The third time was years later—the day that Noi passed. These are sorrows that burden me wherever I travel to. But I understand that I have truly done something in a former life to bring these griefs upon me, and I am at peace. I carry the memory of Sing-ren always, and I may visit this memory whenever I desire—like a light switch that I can put to the on position, illuminating me. Sing-ren is now inside me."

I nodded. I found it difficult to speak for a moment. Then I said: "'Memory makes the absent present.'"

Mr. Yul tapped his lips with his finger. "That is a truly beautiful truism. Is it a saying in your land?"

"I think it's maybe a Puchanese expression." I stood up and *hai*-ed him. "I've taken up enough of your time. I'll go to my office now."

Mr. Yul gazed at me unseeingly. Then he blinked and said, "If you would like to find Shiney, I believe she has a class at the school now. You need not stay in the office today. There is no work for you here."

I left Mr. Yul sitting there at his desk, staring into his hands and murmuring to himself as the afternoon shadows slowly filled his room.

There was no answer when I knocked on Sam's door, but it was slightly ajar, so I pushed it open and entered. Sam was fast asleep in his chair, snoring softly. A silver thread of drool hung between his lower lip and the puzzle on his desk: a half-completed picture of a bulldog snoozing in front of a roaring fire.

As I began to retreat, Sam groaned: "No knocking?"

I stepped back into his office. "Sorry?"

"You're not a knocker, apparently."

"No, I'm a knocker. I knocked."

"Maybe that's what woke me up." Then he studied my face and said, "You look like the wreck of the *Hesperus*, Arrow."

"I can come back later, if now's not a good time."

Sam let out a high-pitched yawn and beckoned me inside. "I was just having the most wonderful dream. I was in a majestic redwood forest, drinking cherry wine with Joey Heatherton. She was dressed like a *courtisane*." He fell silent, staring mournfully at his puzzle.

"Sorry I woke you. I just wanted to let you know that I can start teaching again. Also, I was wondering if Shiney—"

"I wasn't *sleeping*, Arrow. Just giving the orbs a little rest." Sam adjusted his sunglasses. "So, you're back amongst the land of the living? I hear you went on some kind of bender and swallowed your teeth?"

"I tripped and fell in our apartment, and—"

"Oh, before I forget: someone came by here today. Former employee of mine—very popular teacher... Don is his name, I believe. Or... he's a white man, used to walk around in a turban? Has three tow-headed little kids. Ron? John?"

"Shawn."

Sam snapped his fingers and pointed at me. "Maybe." He shrugged. "Anyway, he wanted me to get this to your wife." He took an envelope from his desk drawer and handed it over.

I folded the letter and put it in my pocket. "Did he say anything else, or was—"

"Okay, shall we move on to more pressing matters?" Sam brought his finger up to his nose, seemed to consider picking it, then placed his hand flat on the desk. "I had Richie teach your class while you were off on your lost weekend, and during that brief period of time, three more of your students dropped out, leaving only *two* students remaining: Mrs. Manarsumit, and your buddy Máa. This morning, Mrs. Manarsumit informed me that she, too, was permanently excusing herself. Leaving you with only *one* student." Sam licked his lips and smiled grimly. He had the look of a starving old lion on the verge of devouring a wounded zebra. "Now, I think that the time—"

Just then, there was a knock, and the door swung open. Shiney walked into the room and dropped a stack of books onto Sam's desk, muttering something to him in Puchanese. She was dressed in a cream-colored linen skirt suit with an off-white silk blouse, and she had the detached air of a secretary bringing a memo to her boss during a board meeting. I tried to catch her eye, but she brushed past me as if she had no idea I was there—as if I was some dumb ghost of a dead man who had yet to realize that he was dead. Before I could even speak, Shiney was gone.

Sam moved his shoulders back and forth. "As I was saying, Arrow: I think the time has come for you and I to—"

"Excuse me." I went and stuck my head out the door. Shiney was walking briskly down the driveway. "Shiney!" I yelled. She didn't look back.

"Arrow! Stop ogling my daughter and get in here."

I watched Shiney for another moment, then stepped back into Sam's office. He pointed at my little blue chair and said, "Take a seat."

"Is she all right?"

"She's fine. Now, I think that the time has come for us to—"

"I'm sorry," I said, glancing over my shoulder. "Let me just… I'll be right back."

I heard Sam yell something at me as I ducked out the door, but I have no idea what it was.

I called Shiney's name several times as I jogged after her down the driveway, but she ignored me. I jogged a little faster and then I started running. When I reached her, I walked alongside her for a minute. She continued staring straight ahead. I was panting slightly. Neither of us spoke.

"I heard about you and Gabe," I said, finally. "Are you doing okay?" Shiney was walking even more quickly now, and I struggled to keep up. "Do you want to talk about it, or...?"

Shiney stopped and glanced around, as if she wasn't sure who was speaking. Then she removed a flattened pack of *Cowpokes* from her pocket, shook out a cigarette, and lit it. She held her elbow cupped in her hand and smoked, staring straight down at the ground. As if she were all alone, waiting for the bus. I watched her and wondered whether she had lost her mind.

"Gabe told me about your visit to the hotel," she said.

I replayed her words in my head: they sounded important, full of meaning, but I wasn't sure what that meaning was, or what exactly it had to do with us at that moment. I cast my mind back to that night. "Do you mean he told you about how I passed out?"

Shiney's eyes darkened, and she looked away and murmured: "I always knew, deep down, that he was going there, but I didn't really want to believe it. Whenever I asked him, he acted like I was crazy. But last week a girl I know saw him in the bar. I confronted him and he denied it, but then I told him I had a witness. That's when he started talking." She threw her cigarette on the ground and stalked away.

I hurried to catch up with her. "Wait—I bet Gabe thought *I* was the witness. Right? And then he probably told you some bullshit story."

"Are you saying you *didn't* go to Meowy?"

I took a deep breath. "What happened was, your dad wanted me to sit in on one of Gabe's classes. Richie told me that Gabe taught a conversation class at the hotel—"

"And you went to a room with that *gà-roó-na* girl to teach her some verbs? Is that it?"

"No, I—I was drunk, and I'd smoked this really strong pot Richie had, and... I was dealing with some personal things... and, the girl said something about *television*, and I just thought we were going to watch it." As I tried to explain myself, I began to understand that Gabe might've simply told Shiney the truth, and that the truth might be damning enough. "Let me just tell it from the beginning. I was—"

Shiney pressed her hands over her ears. "I don't care! It doesn't matter." She shook her head. "I don't know what made me think you weren't like every other *gareng* here— looking for *malchak* pussy."

"That's not fair," I said, slowing my pace. "I didn't come here looking for *any* type of pussy, particularly!" A few passing students glanced in my direction. I nodded to them and smiled, then ran after Shiney. "Would you just listen to me for a minute?"

Without looking back, she said: "How could you do that to Ulla?"

"Ulla is something else I need to talk to you about. It's complicated, but Ulla and I—"

Shiney turned to face me, and I fell silent. "I don't understand what you want from me," she said, and reached up and touched her eyelid with her thumb. I couldn't tell whether she was wiping away a tear, or a piece of dust, or if she was forcing her eye into some kind of indecipherable wink.

"I don't want anything from you. I just wanted..." What I wanted from Shiney was too big to put into words.

"Just leave me alone," she said. Her voice was brittle and dead-sounding. "I want to be left alone."

*   *   *

I watched Shiney slowly climb the hill until she reached the cafeteria and disappeared from sight. Then I lowered myself onto a rock by the side of the road and lit a cigarette. As I smoked it, I pretended to myself that I was supposed to be meeting someone there. A medium-sized turtle sat on the ground next to me, and I reached down and touched its shell, murmuring, "I just finished teaching my class. I'm waiting here for Ulla and then we're going to go eat lunch at the cafeteria." The cigarette tasted like dirt in my mouth, but I finished it and then got up and said, "I guess she's not coming," and slowly walked back to *Home Kwan Home*.

As I passed the turtle shrine, I sucked at the hole in my teeth and muttered: "Fuck *you*."

The idea of unlocking my apartment door and entering my little empty room made my skin crawl, so instead I sat down on my garbage can and smoked another cigarette. Judy appeared around the corner and approached me. "Judy," I said. He lay down at my feet and in a low voice I told him what had happened. Then I stood up and said, "I have to get out of here." I bent down and patted his head and then turned and walked into the forest. After a moment, I heard the crunch of his footsteps behind me.

I didn't have a destination in mind—other than, possibly, the Golden Cowboy Place—but when I reached the fork where the trail split in two, I stepped carefully over Flip's rotten body and took the path on the right, heading downhill. Judy stopped and sniffed at the dead dog and then ran to catch up with me.

The forest was warm and filled with the smell of sunlight on the trees, along with the more distant odors of rotting fruit and gasoline and the baking-bread smell of ashen bodies. Judy stayed by my side, occasionally looking up at me and wagging his tail as if wondering where we were going. Once we reached the egg-rock, I followed the path on the far left, and after a few minutes Judy and I were making our way down the stone staircase. We emerged from the trees onto the hill overlooking the Ngoo-pìk, and I sat there on the grass for a time, smoking and watching the river and watching the people who lived alongside the river. And then I got to my feet and walked down to the road and headed towards Golli's house.

I hesitated for a minute before knocking. I thought I could make out a faint scuffling sound from within, followed by the hum of voices.

"Ms. Golli, it's me," I called. "Boyd Darrow. Shiney's friend."

I leaned my ear against the door to see if I could hear anything more, and at that same moment it swung inward and Golli's face appeared next to mine. We both let out a yelp of surprise, and Golli hurriedly pushed the door shut.

"Wait! Sorry, I was just... can I please talk to you for a minute?"

The door re-opened a crack and Golli peered out at me.

"*Ràp-naa ròp,*" I said, *hai*-ing her. "I don't know if you remember me, but a couple of weeks ago I came here with Shiney? I was the one with the..." I gestured above my head. "...sticky black tooth, or whatever?"

Golli's expression remained impassive, though I think I might've seen her lift an eyebrow.

"Is the thing gone now?" I asked. "I gave a bunch of stuff to the turtles, so it should be. But I'm not so sure. Anyway, I was just wondering if you knew where Shiney was."

Auntie Golli licked her lips and scratched at a small blister on her cheek.

"You don't have any idea what I'm saying," I said.

She stepped aside, holding the door open.

"Are you… inviting me in?"

Golli made an ambiguous movement with her chin and muttered something, then retreated into her home, leaving the door ajar.

I looked down at Judy, who was wagging his tail and staring into Golli's house with interest. "No dogs allowed," I said. I patted him on the head and walked inside.

The room was empty and perfectly still, and the only sound was of a kitten mewling from behind the bamboo screen in the corner. I felt a wave of disappointment crash over me—I think I'd been expecting to find Shiney there at the table.

"Do you mind if I sit down for a second?" I gestured toward the bench in front of the fireplace. Golli rolled her shoulders, and I took a seat.

Looking around, I said, "You have a very nice home. Very clean." Golli didn't respond. "Did *Shiney* visit you recently?" I asked, raising my voice. I traced a circle around my left eye. "Your niece. *Srisuriyokhai*. Was she *here*?" I pointed at the floor.

Golli wrinkled her nose and stood up. She removed a stone bowl from the cupboard and rummaged through some coffee tins on the table, occasionally taking something out of a tin and placing it into the bowl.

I nodded my head, as though she'd responded. "That's too bad. I wanted to talk to her. I thought she might be here."

Golli glanced in my direction, then back down at her tins.

"Shiney and Gabe broke up," I said. "So that's good news. You didn't like that guy, right? The *gareng* with the black beard?" I wiggled my fingertips beneath my chin. "Let me ask you something: why do you think someone like Shiney would ever date a guy who—oh, thanks. *Pranoo ròp*."

Golli had filled the bowl with hot water and placed it next to me on the bench. Floating in it were small clusters of black twigs and dried yellow leaves, along with a few pink spongy globules that looked like the testicles of a small rodent. Golli sat down on the bench and began poking at the fire again.

"This thing with Shiney is really bothering me," I said. "She's acting like I'm some kind of—*whore*monger." I rubbed my eyelid and sighed. "I guess it was stupid to go to that place. I didn't know what the deal was. I mean, I knew that Gabe's class was in a *gà-roó-na* bar. But I really honestly thought that the focus of the evening would be more on education."

Golli waved her hands in front of the bowl, pushing the steam toward me as if trying to tempt me with its delightful odor. It smelled like a hot burp, with a hint of black licorice. I picked up the bowl and looked into it. "Is this some kind of tea, or... soup?" I lifted it to my lips, pausing as its garbage-like scent filled my nose. Golli widened her eyes expectantly and broke into a grin. Holding my breath, I took a sip. The liquid tasted the way it smelled—literally like opening my mouth and filling it with someone else's burp. There was also a lingering flavor of tree bark, goldfish-bowl-water, and the faintest hint of *Good n' Plentys*.

As I gagged and then swallowed it down, Golli clapped her hands and laughed. I placed the bowl on the bench and said, "I guess I was pretty drunk that night. I was also just sort of freaking out. I'd just found all these letters that the White Sikh had written to Ulla—including a postcard that he wrote using his *penis* as a *pen*."

An indistinct noise came from behind the screen. Golli and I looked at each other, then turned and looked toward the corner of the room. After a moment, the black kitten appeared. I whistled between my teeth and called, *"Kitty kitty kitty."* The kitten jumped into the air and began playing with a bottle cap.

"Anyways," I continued, "nothing happened with me and that girl. I only went with her in the first place because she told me that we were going to watch television. I don't even *like* television." I picked up the bowl and took another sip. I was beginning to get used to the taste; I tried to focus on the licorice flavor. "Basically, she took her shirt off and told me a dirty joke, and then I passed out. When I woke up, I had to give all my money to some guy. Her pimp, I guess? I don't know what his exact title was. Gabe had told them all that I was a millionaire. Asshole."

Golli didn't seem to be listening; she was busy rolling a small cigar made from a dried banana leaf. She lit it, exhaled a cloud of white smoke, and offered it to me.

"No thanks. I've got some." I took out my pack of *Cowpokes*, then decided I didn't want one and put them back into my pocket. "And, get this—the girl *ate* my wedding ring. Sucked it right off my hand and swallowed it!" I pointed at the tan line on my finger. Golli took my hand and inspected it, flipping it back and forth and frowning. "I mean, I only paid ten bucks for it, so it's not such a big deal." I took another sip of the stuff in the bowl. Golli smiled. "You know, we're not actually married, me and Ulla," I said. "We're not even together anymore. I don't know why we stayed together in the first place." I gently touched the bridge of my nose. "It's like... we just got used to it. I think that when we first met, Ulla liked taking care of me. Organizing my life. It gave her a purpose. And, I guess I must've liked having her tell me what to do. But I think we both outgrew those roles—you know?"

Golli nodded her head and pointed at the bowl, and I took another sip. It tasted very strong now, and I struggled not to make a face.

I put the bowl down and said, "The thing is, I really do like your niece. I just enjoy being around her. I wish I could just… be her *employee* or something. Her driver, maybe, or her cook. For a little while, I even thought…" I shook my head. "I don't know."

I heard another *meow* come from the corner. I didn't see the cat anywhere. When I turned back to Golli, she was staring at me, her nose in the air and her eyes hard and sharp, like a dog catching a scent. Then she winked. I nodded my head, although I wasn't really sure what was going on.

Golli stood up and walked over to the door.

"Time for me to go?" I said, getting to my feet. I glanced at the spot on my wrist where my watch had once been. "Yeah, I should probably head out. I've got some stuff to do." But I didn't move. I just stood there in the middle of the room, staring at the stacks of brown bottles against the wall. Then I pointed at them and said, "That's all honey, huh? How do you say 'honey' in Puchanese?"

Golli's eyes went narrow, and she moved her head slightly.

"Never mind. I'll look it up. Shiney said she was going to take me sometime to where they keep the bees. I would've liked that."

Golli opened the door and waved her hand.

"Okay, sorry, I'm leaving." I stepped outside and said, "Thanks for letting me come in. And thanks for listening to me. I find you very easy to talk to, for some reason. You remind me of my grandmother."

Golli exhaled a plume of smoke and bowed, then shut the door in my face.

May 3
Late evening

On the morning of April the 30th, just after sunrise, I awoke to the sound of a scream.

I sat bolt upright in bed, heart pounding. The room was quiet and dark and I thought for a second that the scream had been part of my dream—that maybe it had even come out of my own mouth—but then I heard it again. I ran over to the window and yanked the curtains open, certain that someone was having their throat slit in the courtyard. But what I saw out there was quite different. In the woozy light of dawn, I watched as a Valkyrie chased a half-naked boy across the silver-green lawn.

The Valkyrie was a stocky young girl wearing a Viking helmet and a wig of long blond braids; the boy had nothing on but his running shoes and a pair of white underpants. His hair was long and black, and his slender body was inked with *malchaki-gai* tattoos. The boy let out another loud shriek as the girl paused to lob a red water-balloon at his head, missing him by mere inches. They ran three laps around the courtyard, the girl hurling balloons and missing with every throw. Finally, just when the boy had reached the edge of the forest, one of the balloons hit him square in the back, exploding and soaking him with white, milky liquid. He turned around and let out a loud whoop and the Valkyrie ran straight into him, grabbing his shoulders and shoving him against a tree, her helmet falling to the ground as she leaned down and pressed her mouth against the boy's slender neck. His body went limp and the two of them remained like that for almost a minute, perfectly still, until the girl raised her head and bounded away down the path into the woods. The boy ran his hands up and down his body, staring up at the sky dreamily, then roused himself and went after her.

This was the morning of the day of the Festival of *Taang Lôke Kwaam Ban-terng Sumitchanani*—the Festival of Earthly Delights.

I lingered by the window for a while, waiting to see if any further apparitions were going to materialize, then climbed back into bed and closed my eyes. I had barely set foot outside of my apartment since my fight with Shiney a few days earlier, and my room had devolved into a squalid disaster area that reeked of cigarette ash and greasy sweat and festering laundry. Sleep was now my primary pastime, and I'd learned to enjoy the banal, epic-length dreams of home that were the by-product of my marathon sleeping sessions: dreams of mowing Mr. Golinsmith's lawn, or of riding my bike up and down Kent Way, or of working the cash register at Rit's. The hour of the day had become insignificant to me—Ulla had taken the alarm clock, the turtle spirits had my watch, and I'd been keeping the curtains closed, relishing the sensation of being untethered from the passage of time. I divided my non-sleeping hours between staring at the ceiling, playing solitaire, and methodically reading the stack of *People* magazines that Ulla's father had sent to her. There was only one magazine left, and the question of what I'd do with myself after finishing it filled me with dread.

I was avoiding almost everyone I knew in the town of Mai Mor, including: Sam (whom I hadn't seen since I'd run out of his office); Gabe, for obvious reasons; Ulla (whom I hadn't

heard from since our breakup); and, of course, the White
Sikh. The only person I wanted to talk to was Shiney, but I
didn't anticipate her stopping by. I felt lost and adrift, with
no idea what to do next—all I knew was that, now that the
Festival of *Taang Lôke Kwaam Ban-terng Sumitchanani* had
arrived, I was definitely not in the mood to celebrate any
delights, earthly or otherwise. As I lay there in bed, drifting
back to sleep, I resolved to spend Festival Day at *Home
Kwan Home*, drinking beer and watching the action unspool
outside my window.

I was in the middle of another splendidly boring dream—
Poppy and I were in his garage, sorting nuts and bolts into
cigar boxes—when I was jarred awake by the sound of a
heavy thudding outside my door. A voice barked, "*Hello!*"
and I found myself leaping out of bed before I was even
fully conscious, like a sleeping soldier reacting to a volley
of mortar fire. My foot slipped on one of Ulla's magazines—
THE PRIVATE PAIN OF KITTY DUKAKIS!—and I stumbled
sideways, crashing into the pyramid of empty beer bottles
stacked against the wall. Shards of brown glass skittered in
all directions across the floor, and then the room fell silent.
I held my breath and stood there, stock-still and naked,
listening.

The knocking resumed after a few seconds and I heard the
voice bellow: "I need to have some *words* with you, Arrow!"

I covered my nakedness with my hands and hopped over
to the closet, carefully avoiding the broken glass. As I pulled
on a pair of shorts, Sam said, "I just want to talk—I'm not
gonna *hurt* you, son."

I yanked on a t-shirt, then hurried into the bathroom and
shut the door. It hadn't occurred to me that Sam had dropped
by with the intention of doing me harm, but his reassurance

made me reconsider. I went over to the tiny window that faces the rear of *Home Kwan Home No. 3*, wondering if I could possibly squeeze through it. Maybe if I took off my clothes, covered my torso with Vaseline, and dislocated both of my shoulders—

"I can hear you crashing and flopping around in there! The gig is up, Arrow. Let me in."

I unlatched the window and stuck my head outside. A boy and a girl were sitting on a pile of gravel behind the building, locked in a passionate embrace. The boy was dressed as a fried egg, and the girl was dressed as a shepherdess. They both turned and gave me a withering look.

I shut the window and glanced at myself in the mirror. I looked like hell. I didn't feel so great, either: my mouth was coated in a slimy, beery film, and my skull felt like a porcelain vase packed in a bed of Styrofoam peanuts. I smiled sadly at my reflection, nodding my head as if bidding farewell to a dear old friend. Then I went to let Sam in.

On Festival Day, everyone is supposed to wear a costume representing his or her individual *goo fán dee* (a Puchanese term that doesn't have a direct English equivalent, but might loosely be translated as "dream-self"). Sam was already dressed up: he wore a red- and white-striped shirt, a fringed leather vest, ripped blue jeans, a string of yellow beads around his neck, and Jesus-style sandals on his feet. His mustache had been dyed to match the wig of shoulder-length black hair on his head, and in place of his aviator shades he had on a pair of round, pink-tinted sunglasses. A black beret sat perched atop his head. Sam's *goo fán dee* appeared to be a French hippie.

"You want to stand there all day gawking, or you want to invite me in?" he growled, stepping inside. "I'm not inclined right now to get pummeled with one of those damn balloons."

I shut the door behind him, suddenly self-conscious about the sorry state of my home: the shards of glass, the half-eaten bowls of ramen, the mounds of dirty clothes. "Sorry about the mess," I said, grabbing the broom and pushing the broken beer bottles into a pile against the wall.

Sam looked me up and down skeptically. "That's some serious bed-head you have there. Don't tell me I woke you up?"

"Can I get you a cup of coffee?" I asked. "Or, I was thinking of making some breakfast, if you'd like something to eat."

"Breakfast?"

"Or—brunch?" I looked at my wrist. "What time is it, anyway? I don't have any clocks in here at the moment."

"Have you honestly not been outside today? It's almost three o'clock PM. The festival's already half over."

I went to the window and lifted the curtain. The courtyard was littered with exploded balloons, ribbons of toilet paper, empty bottles, and detritus from various costumes. The only people in sight were two male students—one dressed as a cowboy, the other dressed as an Indian—lying on the grass next to a sunbathing turtle. They had their arms wrapped tightly around one another, and were passed out cold.

"There's not too much to see anymore," said Sam. "Most folks are heading over to the auditorium." He lowered himself onto a chair, and said, quietly: "Take a seat, Arrow."

I nodded absently and sat down. "I wanted to apologize about the other day. Running out like that. I assume—"

Sam glanced at me sharply.

"I mean... I don't assume anything, but... I would imagine you're here to inform me that I'm no longer a Y.E.S. employee, and—"

"Take it easy, Nostradamus. You're not fired till I say so." He twirled his love beads around his finger and tugged on them thoughtfully. "Here's the question I'm looking to pose to you: do you have something prepared for the show tonight?"

"The Expo *Taang*?"

"No, the *other* show. The Smothers Brothers Comedy Hour."

"I thought Gabe was—"

"Sloat is currently *persona non gratis* in my book. And Richie is clearly unsuitable. I'd give the speech myself, except—as I think I've mentioned—I happen to be a victim of chronic stage fright. So, *ergo*, you're my only option, if you're willing and able." Sam adjusted his wig and added, "I think you'll be quite pleased with this year's bonus."

"The bonus," I murmured.

"Now, I ask once again: *do* you have something prepared?"

Yes.

"Yes?" I said.

"Yes? You have a speech?"

You can just write something, I thought. *You need the bonus—and maybe Shiney would like seeing you up there. Maybe it would impress her. Maybe it would make things all right.*

"Yes," I said.

"And you're willing to get up there and give it?"

"Yes." I pressed my fingers against my eyelid, overcome with the urge to rip out the twitching nerve once and for all.

"What's wrong with your eye?"

"Nothing."

"Good." Sam got to his feet and headed toward the door. "You're scheduled to go on at one-nine-one-five hours. That's 7:15 PM. I recommend showing up backstage at least sixty minutes early, to avoid any snafus." He turned and waggled his finger at me. "And a word of advice: do *not* get drunk before your performance."

"Of course not."

"Everybody will be offering you a little sip of this, little sip of that, but I want you sober when you give that speech." Sam looked at me over the tops of his sunglasses and added, "Your bonus hangs in the balance. *Comprenez-vous*?"

"I understand."

He offered me his hand. As we shook, I found myself staring down at his arm. "I've always wanted to ask you, Sam—about your tattoo..."

"What about it?" he said, frowning and releasing my hand.

"I was just wondering what it's a picture of."

Sam slid his sunglasses up onto his forehead and brought his arm to his face. "I guess it has gotten a little bit blurry," he muttered, lifting his chin and looking at me. His eyes were small and watery and red-rimmed, with bright green irises. It occurred to me that it was the first time I'd actually seen them.

Sam was quiet for a moment, then glanced around the room. "I don't mean to pry into your personal life, Arrow, but it seems like you might be down on your luck a little bit."

I followed Sam's gaze to a stack of *People* magazines in the corner. They were weighted down with an egg carton filled with a mixture of beer, cigarette butts, and balled-up Kleenex. "A little bit," I admitted.

Sam nodded his head, then rubbed his thumb on his arm and said: "The origin of this design here is related to an odd thing that befell me after I got back home from the war. I was sitting by myself on my parents' front porch one night, smoking this old meerschaum pipe of mine and trying to figure out what to do with myself in the future days ahead. I'd had a few drinks, I'll admit—typically, I can take it or I can leave it alone, but that night I'd been sipping from my father's bottle. I guess I must've dozed off for just a minute or so, I don't know how long. Then a car backfired down the street, and I got jarred back into consciousness. But, the thing is"—Sam lowered his voice to a whisper—"*I couldn't open my eyes.*" He blinked at me, shaking his head, then continued: "I recall all of the hairs on my entire body standing straight up on end, like they each knew that something very unnatural was in the midst of occurring to my person—a phenomenon that my own semi-aware mind wasn't even fully privy to yet. I don't know how to describe it, other than to tell you it was like two small cold bony little hands were covering my eyelids." Sam lifted his fingers to his face and demonstrated for me. "Like a game of Peekaboo-I-See-You, but without the peeking. And I could hear something behind me, breathing. Even worse, I could feel its *presence*. It really was the damnedest thing. So I just sat there—still clenching that pipe between my teeth— frozen stiff. I was pretty much scared out of my wits, to be honest. I might've just sat like that till sunrise, but after a bit, I got to thinking about everything I'd just been through: the jungle, the chopper crash, the deaths. I thought to myself, I'll be *damned* if I let this thing master me, and what I did was, I let out a yell. A true holler, an ungodly screech that would've made the devil himself turn from black to white and back again. And when I let out that yell, the pipe fell from my mouth and broke into about fifty thousand pieces. A real tragedy. And at that same moment, I could feel that the thing behind me was gone. *Bamph!* Just like that. I opened my eyes and turned my head, and I thought I heard a noise in the bushes, but I couldn't see much due to the darkness. Well, my folks came running out when they heard me make that noise, assuming I must've been killed or been having some kind of serious post-action stress or something. And, who knows, maybe that's all it was. When I told them what had happened, Mother said it must've been 'Grim Reaper' himself come to steal me away—she was always a conceptual thinker, God bless her. But Dad, he was less of a philosopher in such matters. He said he figured it must've been a raccoon in heat. The next day, I went to Seawall Boulevard and told the man what I wanted." He traced the tattoo with his finger. "See? This here is the skull. And this here is the raccoon. *Peekaboo*."

I bent down and inspected it closely. "I think I can see it now," I said. For a moment, the cluster of blurry lines did in fact appear to organize themselves into the shape of a raccoon holding a skull, before dissolving once again into a formless blue blob.

Sam leaned a little bit closer to me. His breath smelled like damp paperbacks and root beer. "However, to be perfectly frank with you—I'm not so sure it really was a raccoon, at that."

He gave me a big wink, then slid his sunglasses back down over his eyes.

*   *   *

After Sam left, I finished getting dressed and then took out my old notebook and paged through it. I vaguely remembered having at some point written a rough draft for the speech— or, at the very least, an outline. When I found the page I was looking for, I was chagrined to see that all I'd jotted down was the following:

> *A wise man once said: "East is East, and West is West, and never the twain shall meet." However,*

"However," I said aloud, hoping that the sentence would complete itself in my mouth. I found my pen and crossed out *However*, then added a new sentence:

> *A wise man once said: "East is East, and West is West, and never the twain shall meet." ~~However,~~ This may very well be true. And yet,*

"And yet," I said, turning to gaze out the window. The Cowboy and Indian were no longer there, though I noticed that the Cowboy had left behind his Peacemaker cap-gun. At the far end of the courtyard, a small group of students sat huddled around a burning pile of stuffed animals, passing a bottle back and forth and singing a Puchanese folk song at the top of their lungs. They were dressed in dirty, loose-fitting clothes, their faces smudged with black soot; a few held makeshift bindlestiffs slung over their shoulders. I think they were supposed to be a clan of hobos.

Judy was lying on the grass and watching the students with an expression of mild alarm. I went and retrieved two eggs from the fridge, cracked them into a bowl, and brought them outside.

Judy wagged his tail when he saw me and came over, leaning his hip against my leg. The hobos were now singing "The Reflex," by Duran Duran. I crouched and patted the dog's greasy white fur as he wolfed down the food. "You might want to lay low today," I said. "The humans are acting sort of crazy."

I went back inside and sat down and picked up my pen. I could still hear the hobos singing, and I sat there trying to ignore them and concentrate on my empty piece of paper until I gave up and yelled at the top of my lungs: *"EVERY LITTLE THING THE REFLEX DOES LEAVES YOU ANSWERED WITH A QUESTION MARK!"*

I was silenced by the sound of knuckles rapping against my door. I shut my mouth and held my breath, waiting and listening. Amidst the din of singing, I thought I heard the muffled voice of a woman saying my name. I lifted the curtain and peeked outside, catching a glimpse of the embroidered sleeve of a *malchak tai-lan* robe. I jumped up and yanked the door open, certain that it had to be Shiney.

It was Ulla—dressed in full *malchaki-gai* finery. I blinked my eyes, too stunned to speak.

She adjusted the blue *bprà-jìat* on her head and *hai*-ed me. "*Ràp-naa lei*," she said.

"Hey." We awkwardly hugged, then I took a step back. "I almost didn't recognize you in your costume."

"It's not a costume, actually. It's a very special kind of *tai-lan*. It's called a *tai-lan kuoi*." Ulla's eyes were round and clear and had the rapt intensity of someone who'd undergone a religious conversion.

I nodded, not understanding. "It looks nice," I said. To tell you the truth, Ulla did look very nice, dressed up like that. Seeing her in the doorway of our home made me aware of just how lonely I'd been over the past few days. I took another step backwards and invited her in.

346 ● Matt Dojny

Ulla entered the room and stood there, surveying the mess. I waited for her to comment about how I'd trashed our apartment, but instead, she just smiled wistfully and shook her head. "Ah, this place," she murmured, sitting down at the table. "So many memories here."

I glanced around at the broken glass and cigarette butts on the floor. A lizard climbed out of the egg-encrusted wok in the corner and skittered up the wall. "Sorry it's such a wreck. I... well, I've been going through a bit of a rough patch."

Ulla clasped her hands together, nodding and continuing to smile as if she hadn't heard me. "Sorry I haven't been in touch since you got out of the hospital. We've been so insanely busy at work! I actually can't stay very long—Miaw and Jooey are waiting to drive me to the auditorium." Leaning forward, she put her hand on top of mine. "How *are* you? Your nose, and your lung?"

I frowned down at our entwined fingers. "I'm okay," I said, my voice slow and thick. "How are *you* doing? You seem very—I don't know." I scrutinized her face. "Happy?"

"It's true. I am *very* happy." Ulla forced her lips into a pout and added, "Of course, our breakup has been really hard for me." Then she brightened again: "But, I do think it's for the best. Don't you?"

I nodded.

"Good." Ulla dropped her chin and stared into her lap. "Boyd... I came by because I need to tell you something. Something I didn't want you to hear from anyone else."

"About you and Shawn?"

"'Shawn'? Don't you mean, 'the White Sikh'?" Ulla laughed and shook her head. "No, this has nothing to do with him."

"He's been lurking around here, you know. That reminds me..." I got up and went to the desk. "I have a note for you that he left with Sam."

"What does it say?"

I handed her the envelope. "I didn't read this one."

Ulla put it in the pocket of her *tai-lan* without glancing at it. "It doesn't matter. I just saw him a few hours ago."

"So he really is here," I said, easing myself back into the chair. For some reason, I hadn't actually believed that it was true.

"Oh, he's here, all right. He tracked me down at Miaw's this morning. He was already pretty drunk. Caused quite a scene." She clucked her tongue and undid the belt of her *tai-lan kuoi.* "Do you mind if I take this thing off?" she asked, shrugging off the robe. "It's so hot in here."

"So," I said, "you and Shawn aren't...?"

"*God*, no! He's forty-two years old, with three little kids! It would never have worked. I'm not here to talk about *him.*" Ulla rested her elbows on her knees and leaned her body towards me. She was wearing a pair of pink shorts and a thin cotton camisole top, and her skin appeared lit from within. "I want to talk about—well, I'm not sure the best way to say this to you."

I took a deep breath—inhaling the familiar smell of the vanilla-scented perfume that Ulla had dabbed between her breasts—and experienced a terrifying premonition that we were moments away from getting back together. I looked away, fixing my eyes on the pattern of upside-down hearts that ran along the edge of the table, steeling my resolve.

"Boyd," she said, softly, "I'm with Pônge now."

I nodded my head, squinting at her. It took a moment for me to process the meaning of her words. "Pônge?"

"The lead singer of *Kati Na-Gareng.*"

"I know who Pônge is, I just—"

"Pônge and I are together, Boyd." Ulla clapped her hand over her mouth and began to giggle. "Isn't that incredible?

And I have *you* to thank. It never would've happened if you hadn't dumped me the way you did."

"I didn't 'dump' you…"

"No, don't you see? It was actually helpful that you were so… well, *callous*. It forced me to really think about things—about how I always take the path of least resistance, and how I needed to take more risks. Move outside my comfort zone. Explore this incredible culture." Ulla smiled at me sadly. "I didn't want any more secrets between us. I'm sorry if it's upsetting for you to hear this. But, I have to say"—she clutched my arm—"it's been *so* amazing with Pônge! I didn't know how it could be, you know? At one point, when we were together, I just closed my eyes, and it felt like I was riding across the ocean on a giant sea horse!" Ulla's face began to flush pink, and she turned away, adding, "I know it sounds crazy, but I think he's serious about things. He gave me this *tai-lan kuoi* to wear today—it's the traditional *malchak* courting outfit, which I guess is kind of a big deal in his culture. And look at this!" Ulla jumped up and lifted the back of her shirt. Near the base of her spine was a cluster of inflamed-looking blue squiggles, oozing blood.

"Jesus, what happened?"

Ulla laughed. "It's a tattoo, *duh*." She patted it gingerly and winced. "It's still healing right now, but it's going to be totally awesome-looking. Pônge designed it especially for me. He drew it with a safety pin attached to a stick! Can you believe it?"

"Shouldn't you put some Neosporin or something on there?"

"He rubbed the juice from a *garong* leaf onto it. The pain is already starting to subside."

I bent down and studied the tattoo more closely. It looked like a drunken child had used a dull icepick to carve a string of Puchanese characters into Ulla's lower back. "What does it say?"

"It means: '*Many blessings unto you, most beautiful maiden of the village. We are fortunate to have the opportunity to bask in the glow of your fleeting presence. May your spirit always be harmonious, and may your light always shine brightly. You are the white angel-flower of smiles.*'" She shrugged. "Or something along those lines."

I sat back down. "How did you two...?"

"*Well,*" said Ulla, "a couple of nights ago, Jooey came over to Miaw's house, and Pônge was with him. We all got high, then Pônge and I went out for a walk to give Miaw and Jooey some privacy. We had this amazing conversation—his English is pretty good, better than you'd think—and he told me all these cool stories about his life. The struggles his people have faced." She took a deep breath and brought her fingertips to her lips. "And it was just this totally amazing coincidence that I was the *one* person who could help him with his plan!"

There was a knock on the door. Ulla and I exchanged a meaningful glance—meaningful of what, I wasn't sure—and I went to go see who it was.

The person on my doorstep wasn't wearing a mask, but it still took me a few seconds to recognize Miaw. She had on a low-cut green velvet gown, and her frizzy hair was teased up into a *Bride of Frankenstein* beehive. Long blood-red whiskers were painted across her cheeks. Jooey stood a few feet behind her, dressed in the same gray military-style uniform that he always wore. When he saw me, he grimaced and blinked down at the grass.

Miaw gave a small curtsey. "Is Ulla...?"

"Coming!" called Ulla, slipping back into her robe and walking quickly over to the door. She turned to me and said, "You're going to the show later, right?"

"I'm the grand finale."

"You mean… you're doing the speech for Sam's school?"

"Apparently."

Ulla considered this for a moment, then leaned forward and murmured into my ear: "You might be extremely useful to us, Boyd."

"To the Faculty of Theatre Drama?"

"I don't have time to explain right now," she said, glancing at Miaw. "Come find me backstage before you go on. Do you promise?"

"Sure."

"We'll be counting on you." Ulla gave me a quick kiss on the cheek, then hurried away.

I shut the door, locked it, and went and got a bottle of *Gong* from the fridge. After taking a long swallow of beer, I sat at the table and lifted the curtain to see what was going on outside. The courtyard was deserted except for an old man in a tuxedo t-shirt who was shuffling unsteadily across the grass, moving his arms and hips as though part of an invisible conga line. He had a garland of paper flowers draped around his neck, and he wasn't wearing any pants.

Two girls—one in a leotard and a hockey mask, the other in a skimpy blue hospital gown—appeared from around the corner the building. When they saw the old man, they whistled loudly between their teeth and ran towards him. The man froze in place and remained perfectly still as the girls lobbed three red water-balloons in his direction. One of the balloons exploded against the side of his head, soaking him in a gooey paste of flour and milk. The girls laughed, and—without breaking their stride—continued down the path into the forest. The man stood and watched them go, smiling ruefully as he wiped the back of his neck with his flowers.

I opened my notebook, lit a cigarette, coughed, put out the cigarette, and did some more editing:

> Someone
> ~~A wise man~~ ^ once said: "East is East, and West
> is West, and never the twain shall meet."
> ~~However, This may very well be true. And yet,~~
> However, as I look out at your faces today,

Off in the distance I heard some people drunkenly screaming the words to "Take Me Home, Country Roads." I put my hands over my ears to drown them out and said: "However, as I look at your faces today, I see that you... I realize that we are, each and every one of us... I know that, in my heart of hearts... that, truly, our twains shall, as a matter of fact..."

The singing was growing increasingly distracting. I kept my eyes fixed on the notebook and tried again: "As I stand here today, looking out at your beautiful faces... your kind faces... at your wise and mysterious... mysteriously wise and smiling faces... as I look at your faces, it makes me think about... the idea of belonging. What does it mean to truly belong somewhere?" I pressed my hands against my ears and shouted over the sound of the singing, "I AM REMINDED OF THE SONG THAT SAYS, '*COUNTRY ROADS, TAKE ME HOME, TO THE PLACE WHERE I BELONG. WEST—*'"

There was a knock from outside, and I heard a voice say: "Mr. Boyd?"

After a moment's hesitation, I went and opened the door, and was greeted with the very welcome sight of Mr. Horse. He was dressed in tight black plastic pants and a puffy red silk shirt that was unbuttoned halfway, revealing a gold chain necklace and an unnatural-looking thicket of

352 ● Matt Dojny

black curls on his chest. A caterpillar-like mustache was glued to his upper lip, and his hair had been permed into a floppy Afro. Standing next to him was none other than Ken, who was wearing a long white lab coat, a nurse's hat, and a stethoscope around her neck. Her coat was hanging open slightly, and I caught a glimpse of a Wonder Woman costume underneath.

"Mr. Boyd!" said Mr. Horse. "You are still home!"

"Hey, guys. *Ràp-naa ròp.*" I *hai*-ed both of them. "Long time no see, Ken."

Ken smiled at me, then peered over my shoulder into my wrecked apartment. "Are you... good?"

"Healthy as a horse."

"Excuse me?" said Mr. Horse.

"Do you two want to come in for a minute?" I glanced back at the room. "Or, maybe we should just stay out here, actually."

"We are going to show now," Mr. Horse said. "Will you join our walk?"

"I'd like to, but I don't think I can. It turns out I'm actually going to be giving that speech thing later on, so I should probably stay home. I still kind of need to write it."

"You are in Expo *Taang*?" Mr. Horse sighed and pressed his fingers against his mustache. "That is a blessing."

"You know, Mr. Horse, you look really familiar to me," I said. "Your costume, I mean."

"Because I am famous." He thrust his chin forward and sang: "*Because I'm easy... easy like Sunday morning...*"

"You're Lionel Richie!"

Mr. Horse bowed and smiled shyly. "Yes," he said. "I am Lionel Richie. Who are you?"

I glanced down at myself. "Nobody, at the moment."

"No? But, you need have the *goo fán dee!*" He turned to Ken and the two of them had a brief discussion in Puchanese, then Mr. Horse said, "We can help to make one—but we must be fast. Please invite us to enter the home now."

They came inside and sat down at the table, both looking around wide-eyed at the condition of my apartment. "Your home is very wild," observed Mr. Horse.

I kicked aside the pile of bed sheets on the floor and pulled up a chair. "Can I get you guys anything? A beer, maybe, or some scrambled eggs?"

"We have no time for egg, thank you." Mr. Horse squared his shoulders and looked into my eyes. "Let me ask you— have you understanding the idea of *goo fán dee?*"

"It's supposed to represent my secret self. Or, my true self. Something like that?"

Mr. Horse nodded. "Tell me, what do you think the secret person to be?" He lowered his voice, speaking in the velvety purr of a hypnotist, and said, "Close the eyes and make a picture and dream of *goo fán dee.*"

I squeezed my eyes shut and took a deep breath. "*Goo fán dee,*" I murmured. "*Goo fán dee. Goo fán dee...*"

"Dream of what you are, and what you love. What do you love? Please be thinking quickly, and with truth."

"What do I love," I said. "I love... food. Fried chicken... tacos... pickles. I love coffee. I love dogs... bears... bats. Various animals. I love swimming. I love... um..." I laughed. "I love *angels.*"

"You are an angel-lover?" exclaimed Mr. Horse.

I opened my eyes. "Sorry, that was kind of an inside joke."

Mr. Horse and Ken had a brief, animated discussion, then Mr. Horse asked me: "When you say you love 'angel,' you are meaning the ghost-man who is helper to Christ, and who is with a round golden hat, and wearing the white dress, and has arms like a bird to fly?"

"Actually, now that I think about it, there's another—"

"We will make you the beautiful angel *goo fán dee*," said Mr. Horse. Ken smiled at me and winked.

"The other thing I just thought of is… a bat kite."

"'Bat-kite'?"

"Like a *dtit-laa*. But a kite—you know, the toy on the string that you fly in the air?" I made a fist and stretched out my arm, waving it back and forth.

Mr. Horse conferred with Ken for another minute, then nodded his head. "We will make you become both," he said, getting to his feet. "The angel and the bat. Let us labor hard and quick—the Expo show is soon begun!"

Mr. Horse and Ken ran out to grab some supplies from Mr. Horse's apartment, and when they returned, the two of them set to work. I removed my shirt, and Ken made me a pair of angel wings by attaching badminton birdies along both of my arms with rubber bands. Once she was done with that, she took out a jar of greasepaint and painted my upper torso white. Mr. Horse forged a halo from a wire hanger and clipped it into my hair with bobby pins, then fashioned two heavy-duty black garbage bags into a pair of bat-wings and used duct tape to attach them to the undersides of my arms. Ken cut my bed sheet in half and I went into the bathroom, removed my pants, and tied the half-sheet around my waist like a toga. For the finishing touch, Ken opened a container of shoe polish and, carefully avoiding my nose, painted my entire face black.

I checked myself out in the mirror when they were done. "Wow," I said, flapping my wings. "I look really… interesting. Very nice. Thank you." I touched my hand to my cheek. "Are you sure it's okay having my face painted like this? It's not too much like… blackface?"

"Black-face?" Mr. Horse shrugged. "Black is beautiful."

Pamarassam Road was a river of people flowing slowly up the hill in the direction of the P. Songpole Phammawattaana Memorial Auditorium. Ken gave me a bottle of banana-brandy-flavored rice wine, which is the traditional beverage consumed on Festival Day, and I decided it would be rude if I didn't drink at least a little bit of it. Everyone was jostling one another and drinking and singing songs, and there was the constant motion of small red water-balloons arcing above our heads and then falling back down towards the earth and exploding onto whoever happened to be there. The sun hung high and hot in the sky and I could already feel my greasepaint and shoeshine beginning to melt and run, and everything was wet and sticky and dusty and loud and warm, and all around me were human bodies of every possible size and shape, all wearing costumes. I saw a man covered head to toe in masking tape being pushed in a wheelbarrow by a fat woman dressed as E.T.; I saw a group of tiny children dressed like orange treefrogs; I saw a slim pretty girl dressed as a jellyfish holding a clear blue umbrella from which hung green sparkling plastic streamers. I saw an old woman dressed like His Majesty the King of Puchai. An old man dressed like a turtle. A man dressed like Spicecat—a popular Puchanese cartoon character—holding hands with a woman dressed as an all-black version of the Statue of Liberty. A zombie, a chimpanzee, a demon, a toadstool, a caterpillar, a unicorn. A girl dressed like a bullet. A man in a nightgown wearing a tiger's mask; a man in a coffin made of heavy cardboard carried by six men wearing baby-blue tuxes. I saw a man sobbing on the ground, fake-looking blood running down his face. I saw a woman in a tight rubber dress perched on a milk-crate and cackling as she lifted her hem and showed the crowd that she wasn't wearing anything underneath. Everyone was attacking everyone else with red balloons and waterguns and bags of flour, whooping and cat-calling and screaming bloody murder as they dodged and feinted and ran circles around each other, and several people stood on the sidelines and held turtles high above their heads, providing them a view of the chaos. A balloon burst on the front of my toga, covering it with a dark sticky substance that looked like blood but tasted like tamarind syrup. A handsome woman dressed as a tree sprite ran up and dumped a bag of glitter over my head before slipping away. The small shiny pieces of silver and gold clung to me and made me sparkle all over. Mr. Horse saw some friends of his and one of the guys was dressed as a camel and there was a spigot coming out of his hump that dispensed banana-brandy-flavored rice wine, and I decided I was allowed to have just one additional final drink and filled up my empty bottle. The banana-brandy-flavored rice wine wasn't making me feel drunk, exactly, just sort of light-hearted and giddy and slightly dizzy. One of Mr. Horse's friends had an acoustic guitar and Mr. Horse took it and played it as we walked, singing several Lionel Richie songs to Ken as she smiled down into her cup of banana-brandy-flavored rice wine, and we all joined in as we walked up the hill singing "All Night Long (All Night)" at the top of our lungs, though I hardly knew the exact words, and the whole time I kept thinking about how much you'd have liked all of this. I was soaking wet, covered in paint and soda and sweat and milk and glitter, and one of my bat-wings was torn, and the duct tape itched and my halo was barely hanging on, but I was still feeling pretty good, probably better than I had a right to be feeling; I was surrounded by people, and I felt all alone in the world, but at that exact moment I felt wonderful.

As we crested the hill and approached the soccer field, my throat grew tight and my eyelid began to twitch as I saw what appeared to be thousands or possibly tens of thousands of people huddled together on the grass, their heads bent back as they watched an overweight man standing alone on the stage of the P. Songpole Phammawattaana Memorial Auditorium. The man was dressed as a rainbow and the air was filled with the amplified sound of his voice singing along to a pre-recorded version of "The Devil Went Down to Georgia." He sounded scared out of his mind.

"Is it always like this?" I asked Mr. Horse, speaking loudly to make myself heard above the noise. "So many people?"

"Oh, yes. All the student of college, and all teacher, and all the people from the town come. And people from other town. And, parents of the student. And tourist from all Puchai—and from other countries. Everybody love the Expo *Taang.*"

I turned back to the stage. The rainbow guy had dropped his microphone, and looked like he was about to have a stroke.

"I don't think I can go up there," I said.

"What? Yes you are. It will be good!" Mr. Horse produced a bottle from his knapsack. "For your thirst?"

"No, thanks."

"For your courage," he said, handing it to me.

"I probably shouldn't drink anymore." I unscrewed the cap and took a long swallow of the banana-brandy-flavored rice wine. "Do you know what time it is?"

Mr. Horse shook his head. "Lionel Richie wears no watches."

"Mel," I heard a voice say. "Is that you?"

Behind me stood a *gareng* wearing a long white beard, a pointy wizard's cap, and a purple robe embroidered with gold stars and crescent moons. He was holding hands with a dark, veiled woman dressed as a genie.

"Richie," I said. "How's it going?"

"Oh, you know." Dicksplash was staring distractedly at something off in the far distance. He sighed and turned back to me. "Is your *goo fán dee* the Creature of the Black Lagoon? That's cool." He looked as if he was about to start crying.

"Are you okay?"

"Yeah. I don't know." Dicksplash heaved another sigh and glanced at the woman next to him. She was bending down and fussing over a young child in a Snoopy costume. Dicksplash leaned towards me and murmured, "I guess you heard the news—Miaw totally ditched me for some *malchak* dude. That stupid van driver."

"No, I didn't know. Sorry."

"That chick is seriously confused. She doesn't know her own *mind*." He hit himself on the side of the head, as though trying to knock water out of his ear. "However, lucky for me, I've been generously consoled by my friend here. I think you guys have met?" Dicksplash tugged on the woman's hand. "Hey, babe. You remember Boyd, right?"

The woman turned to us with frowning eyes, then lifted her veil. It was Pêt.

"I am hungry," she said.

"Say hello to Boyd, sweetie."

Pêt held up the child. "Off is hungry."

"I'll get you two some *bplaa ràa tong* in just a second. Do you remember Mr. Boyd? From the place—you know? Say, 'Hello, Mr. Boyd!'"

Pêt squinted at me and pursed her lips, then replaced her veil and looked back up at the stage.

Dicksplash shrugged. "Hey, can I offer you a shot?" He picked up a bottle from the ground and pressed it into my hand. "This is some kick-ass ouzo that my cousin just sent me. He lives on the isle of Euboea, which is in Greece." As I took a drink, Dicksplash glanced over at Pêt and said, "Can I just tell you, this girl here is *amazing*. Total mind-blower. Unfortunately, she's costing me a fortune." He slapped me on the shoulder. "Speaking of fortunes—I hear you're giving the big speech tonight! That's awesome."

"I'm a little worried about it, actually."

"Well, let me know if you need a last-minute sub—I sure could use that bonus cash. But, I'm totally psyched for you. I hope you break a leg up there."

"Thanks. I probably will."

"I mean, I've basically got two mouths to feed now," he said, gesturing toward Pêt and her child. "Or three, if you count my mouth."

"You've also got a kid back home, right?"

Dicksplash shrugged. "Teddy's got a job at the movie theater, so he's not about to starve. You can eat all the popcorn you want if you work the concession stand. This situation here is different: these people *need* me. Which is kind of a cool feeling." Dicksplash removed his hat from his head and said, "I hate to ask you this, Boyd, but—any chance I'd be able to get a small personal loan from you?"

"Well, I—"

"Just a sliver of your bonus. Like, approximately a hundred and thirty-five bucks?"

"I wish I could help you out. I actually have an outstanding debt that I really need to pay off."

"I hear that. It's cool. No worries." Dicksplash licked his lips and, lowering his voice, said: "The reason I ask is that I have a new business plan, and I need a little capital in order to implement it. I'm considering buying some horse. Just to see how it goes."

I nodded, unable to fully hear him over the George Winston piano piece that was now blasting over the speakers. "I'm told it's pretty expensive to take care of a horse here," I said. "Or, maybe it's really cheap. Something about putting them out to pasture. You should ask Sam about it."

"No, I mean... you know—" Dicksplash tapped his arm and bugged out his eyes.

"Oh," I said. "*Horse.*"

"It might be a real cash cow. No pun intended."

"You sure that's a good idea?"

"I'm not looking to turn people into junkies, or whatever. I just think the tourist boys would pay good money to have a cool and safe Third World hard-drug experience. What do you think? Silent partner?"

"No. I don't even want to know about it."

"If you invested a hundred and thirty-five dollars' worth of your bonus *prik*, you'd get a thousand dollars back in three weeks. I guarantee it on my honor."

"Sorry. I'm not going to do it."

"Promise me you'll just *think* about it."

I looked at Richie and Pêt and at Pêt's kid dressed as Snoopy. "I'll let you know if I change my mind," I said. "Okay?"

Richie grinned. "Minds change every day. It's a proven scientific fact." He clasped my hand in his and shook it. "My friend, you and I are going to be very rich men in the future. And the future is just around the—"

"Mr. Boyd!"

I looked behind me and saw Mr. Horse waving his arms. He pointed toward the stage and yelled, "We are moving up close to show!"

"Hang on, I'm coming with you!" I patted Richie on the shoulder and said, "I should go. See you guys around?"

Pêt was staring at me strangely now, tilting her head to the side. She handed her child over to Richie and lifted her veil again. "*Ahab?*"

I winked at her and bowed. "*Ràp-naa ròp.*"

As I turned and made my way towards Mr. Horse, Richie yelled after me, "Boyd! I forget to tell you something!"

"What?"

He cupped his hands around his mouth and yelled, "I said I *forgot* to *tell* you something!"

A group of teenagers dressed as skeletons had swept me up into their midst as they pressed toward the stage. Two of them seemed to be trying to tickle me. "*What* did you forget to tell me?" I yelled.

"Watch out for *Gabe!*"

"What do you mean? Is he—"

But Richie had already been swallowed up by the crowd.

I extricated myself from the skeletons and started scanning the immediate area for Mr. Horse's Jheri-curled head. After a few minutes of searching, I located Ken and Mr. Horse about halfway towards the front. They were standing with four young women—friends of Ken's, I guessed—and Mr. Horse was playing some songs for them. Ken winked at me and handed me a paper cup. "Good *ur-ur-ur,*" she said. "Try." I took a small sip, just to cleanse my mouth of the nasty ouzo taste, and joined the group in singing "Lucky Star," by Madonna. When that song was over I planned to excuse myself from the group to go work on my speech, but Mr. Horse started playing "American Pie," and I felt obligated to stick around because I happen to know all of the lyrics. I drank a little more *ur-ur-ur* and we sang "Yellow Submarine,"

"Raspberry Beret," "Puff, the Magic Dragon," and—at my request—"(Don't Fear) The Reaper." Dusk was falling and the stage lights went on as seven middle-aged men launched into a dangerous-looking acrobatic routine, and Mr. Horse started playing Culture Club's "I'll Tumble 4 Ya," and we all sang it as loud as we could. I kept promising myself that I was going to leave to go do my work but was finding it hard to pull myself away, particularly because Ken's friends had linked arms with me during my heartfelt rendition of "Your Song" by Elton John and were now refusing to let go.

The people in our vicinity made us quiet down when a man in an elephant suit appeared onstage and started singing a beautiful a cappella rendition of "Memory" from *Cats*. Someone placed a cup of whiskey in my hand, and I sipped it while I watched the show. A group of women dressed in ruby-encrusted costumes performed a traditional Puchanese dance that involved making nearly imperceptible movements with their elbows and chins, and then two guys did a dramatic re-enactment of Darth Vader's "Luke, I'm your father" scene from *The Empire Strikes Back*. I wasn't able to tear my eyes away from the stage until three teenage boys came on and started doing some lackluster rope-jumping tricks, at which point I removed my speech from my underpants and took another look at it.

Someone ~~A wise man~~ once said: "East is East, and West is West, and never the twain shall meet." ~~However,~~ ~~This may very well be true. And yet,~~ However, as I look out at your faces today,

I made a disgusted noise and muttered, "What the fuck is wrong with you?"

"Excuse me?" said Mr. Horse.

I showed him my piece of paper. "This is my entire speech."

Mr. Horse examined it and handed it back to me. "It is a tiny speech," he admitted.

"I'm an idiot." I made a fist and began to punch my forehead, gently at first, then less gently. "Stupid," I said. "Retard. Idiot."

Mr. Horse watched this display with concern. "Mr. Boyd," he said, reaching up and taking hold of my wrist. "You are the man who can speak with open heart, and of the soul. You are the *soul*-man. You do not need writing for speech." He slapped me on the chest. "You must tell from your heart! All right? Do not cry now like baby girl. You are lucky man to be go on stage. You do not know the luck. *I* should be on the stage! Me! Máa! *Máa!*" He slapped my chest again, making a sweaty handprint in the white greasepaint. "Say the name!" he said, staring fiercely into my eyes. "*Máa!*"

I was beginning to understand that Mr. Horse was even drunker than I was.

"Máa?" I said, tentatively.

"*Máa!*"

I looked up at him. "Máa."

"Yes!" He shook me by the shoulders. "Máa!"

"Máa."

"Again! Yes!"

"Máa!"

"Again!"

"Máa!"

"Yes!"

"Máa!" I said, my voice rising. "*Máa!*"

"Yes," he said, wrapping his arms around me, pulling me close to him, resting his chin on my shoulder as he held me tight. "Yes. *That* is how you say my name."

"Hey, excuse me? Sir?" I said, trying to catch the eye of a passerby dressed as a mermaid. "Can you tell me what time it is?" I gestured towards his wristwatch with my chin. "Time?"

The man held his watch up to my face. It was just past 6:30 PM.

"Oh, shit!" I pried Mr. Horse's arms off me. "How did it get so late?"

Mr. Horse burped and gave me a lopsided smile. "What is your problem, Mr. Boyd? You always frown!"

"Don't go anywhere. I'll be back." I reached up and adjusted my halo. "I just need to go find my wife."

As I staggered through the crowd towards the stage, two independent but not unrelated ideas began gestating in my brain. The first was the realization that I had to inform Ulla there was simply no way I could get up and give my speech; the second was the realization that I had somehow become extravagantly drunk, and was growing exponentially drunker with every passing moment. It dawned on me that I hadn't consumed anything all day other than beer, ouzo, *ur-ur-ur*, whiskey, and banana-brandy-flavored rice wine, so I stopped at a food stall and purchased a plate of rice noodles, scarfing them down as I continued to walk. The noodles had an intense flavor and were oddly stringy and elastic-seeming, and as I chewed them up and forced them down my throat I dimly recalled that something called *bplaa ràa tong* (pickled fish-stomach) was the traditional good-luck dish served on Festival Day—a dish that Mr. Horse had warned me to avoid at all costs.

I'd just swallowed my final bite when I spotted Mr. Yul sitting by himself on a folding chair at the edge of the crowd. He didn't have a costume on, and yet, despite his lack of *goo fán dee*, there was something distinctly unsettling about his appearance. Then it dawned on me: he wasn't wearing the black silk handkerchief he normally wore draped across his missing eye. Even more unsettling was the fact that he now appeared to have two eyes in his head.

"Mr. Yul?"

"Yes? Ah, is this Mr. Boyd Darrow?" he said, smiling. "I did not recognize you in the midst of your outfit. You look affectively strange to behold." He studied me for a moment. "Unless I am mistaken, you appear to be a Moorish character—or, perhaps the member of some pagan mystery cult."

"I see that you... um..." I gestured vaguely towards his face.

Mr. Yul laughed and winked at me. "I do not typically insert this ersatz eye into my head, but it handily serves as my annual *goo fán dee*. However, it always has an uncanny effect when viewed by acquaintances." He tapped his eyeball with his fingernail and added, "It is crafted from Venetian glass."

"It's very realistic."

"This is a kindness for me to hear you to make that claim, my friend. Now, may I ask: is the grapevine honest in proclaiming that you will be the performer of the spectacular ending for our Expo this evening?"

I hugged my arms to my chest and nodded.

"Your face looks unwell," said Mr. Yul. "Is your health waning?"

I opened my mouth to respond, and let out a noisy hiccup. The metallic taste of bile, accompanied by a small chunk of fish-stomach, rose in my throat. I swallowed it back down and said, "I think maybe I'm just a little nervous."

"Allow me to say, my friend, that I am fully confident of your inevitable triumph on the stage. I highly suggest you to draw upon your meditative practice with the Wooden-Sentry Exercise—in doing so, you will discover that the power and stillness you require dwells within you, much like an inextinguishable match-flame. The Wooden Sentry shall grace you with all of the courage necessary to fulfill your greatest and truest dreams."

"I'll remember that." I placed my hand on my sternum. "Thank you, Mr. Yul."

"Additionally," he said, reaching into his coat pocket, "this Very Superior Old Pale brandy is rumored to be quite efficacious in terms of bolstering one's fortitude as well." He held up a small flask. "My tradition is to slowly consume an entire bottle over the course of the Festival Day, in honor of the memory of the anniversary of my brother's untimely passing. Would you care to try some, to bolster your own fortitude? It is imported."

I looked at the flask for a moment, hesitating, then said: "Thanks, but I don't think I need it."

"No?"

"No." I took a deep breath. "To tell you the truth, I'm pretty sure that the Wooden Sentry will be all I need—"

There was a loud squeal of feedback over the PA system, and then a familiar voice intoned: "Boyd Darrow, will you please immediately report backstage. Repeat: Mr. Boyd Darrow, you must report backstage. Right now."

"It sounds as if your wife is urgently requiring your services," said Mr. Yul.

"It does," I murmured.

Mr. Yul wordlessly handed me the flask, and I removed the cap and took a long, open-throated drink from it. When I was done, I wiped my mouth with the back of my hand and let out another loud hiccup. The brandy was delicious, and made my entire body feel as if it had been submerged into a warm, grape-scented bath. It was premature to judge whether this was a good thing or not.

"Mr. Yul," I said, handing the flask to him, "I feel like I need to tell you something. Regarding me and Ulla—I haven't been totally honest with you about the nature of our relationship. The thing is, she's not technically my *wife*, per se."

Mr. Yul nodded. "I did in fact suspect that she was not your actual betrothed. It is common that young visiting *gareng* couples will feign marriage for the sake of propriety. I was merely using the term 'wife' just now in the colloquial— ah, Sibbi. *Ràp-naa ròp.*"

Ms. Pilopoblan appeared out of the crowd dressed in a sheer silver gown covered with enormous white ostrich feathers and holding a bag of sliced pineapple. She smiled politely at me, then sat down on Mr. Yul's lap, crossing her legs and leaning back into his arms.

Mr. Yul placed his hand on Ms. Pilopoblan's thigh and looked up at me. "Go forth and spread your wings, Mr. Boyd Darrow," he said. "All of us here on the ground shall be watching your voyage with great interest."

When I reached the rear of the auditorium, it took me a while to wade through the clusters of people waiting in line for the Port-a-Sans before I found Ulla. She was standing at the bottom of the metal staircase leading up to the staging area, consulting her clipboard and talking into a walkie-talkie. She let out a small gasp when she saw me approach.

"Boyd?"

"Sorry I'm late."

"Where have you been? And what are you wearing?" Ulla covered her mouth with her hand. "That costume is terrifying."

"I love angels." I hiccupped and flapped my wings.

"Oh, no—you're *drunk*, Boyd!"

I hiccupped again. "I have the hiccups," I explained.

"You're supposed to go on in"—Ulla looked at her watch—"eleven minutes! And you're totally *wasted*!"

"No, I'm not. I did have a couple drinks... or, technically, a few drinks... but mainly I just feel sort of sleepy, and a little nauseous—I think I accidentally ate a bowl of that fish-stomach stuff. But I'm fine. I might just sit down, though, for a second." I began to lower myself onto the grass.

Ulla glanced around, then grabbed my elbow, yanking me back to my feet. "This is really, really important. I need you to focus." She leaned toward me and whispered, "*Kati Na-Gareng* is going to crash the show."

"Crash this show?"

"Yes."

"Seriously?" I looked around. "Where are they?"

"Behind you—all the way to the right. But don't stare."

I glanced over my shoulder and saw a group of nine men and women huddled together next to a Port-a-San, clutching duffle bags and nervously smoking cigarettes. Pônge stood in the middle of the group with his arms folded, staring straight ahead. He was dressed in a white housepainter jumpsuit covered with tinfoil and silver duct tape, and his hands and face were painted bright green, rendering his tattoos invisible. His long black hair was pinned up and hidden beneath a green swim cap. Every member of the band was wearing an almost identical variation of this costume. I didn't get at first what they were supposed to be—but then it clicked.

"Aliens," I murmured. I turned back to Ulla. "When do they go on?"

"That's what I needed to talk to you about. They're going to start playing during your speech."

"My—wait, what?"

"That night that Pônge and I first hooked up, he told me about his plan to crash the Expo and asked me to help him. I couldn't figure out how to make it all work until you told me that you were going to be doing the finale. So here's the deal: while you stand there and give your speech, the band sets up in the unlit area downstage. When they're ready to go, I'll bring up the lights, and you run offstage. It'll be great."

"Won't Haraporn see them backstage and figure out what's going on?"

"Haraporn watches the show from down on the ground, with everybody else. We keep in touch with this." Ulla held up her walkie-talkie. "By the time you're done talking and the band starts to play, it'll be too late for her to do anything to stop it. It's the perfect finale! We'll make *history*!"

"The thing is, I don't really have a speech prepared." I reached into my underpants and took out my piece of paper. "I actually came to tell you that I can't go on."

"Say whatever you want up there. We just need you to distract the audience long enough for the guys to set up their gear and plug in."

The door at the top of the stairs opened and Miaw appeared, waving her arms. "Ulla!" she yelled, flashing four fingers. "Time!"

Ulla waved back. "We're coming!"

"Another thing," I said. "If Sam thinks I'm in on this whole thing, I definitely won't be getting the bonus—and I was planning on paying you back with that money."

Ulla put her hands on my shoulders and gazed into my eyes. "Boyd, if you do this thing for me now, your debt to me will be totally erased forever. This is so much more important. It could be a crucial blow in the struggle for *malchak* civil rights."

I didn't say anything for a long moment. Then I opened my mouth, hiccupped, and said, "Okay."

"Oh, Boyd!" cried Ulla, embracing me. "You'll never be forgotten. No role, no matter how small, is insignificant in this battle!"

A loud, staticky screech burst from Ulla's walkie-talkie, followed by the sound of Haraporn's voice: "*Hello!*"

Ulla rolled her eyes and raised the walkie-talkie to her mouth. "I'm here."

There was a crackle of static, and Haraporn muttered something to herself. Then she said, "*Ulla?*"

"Yes!" yelled Ulla. "I'm here! I can hear you, Haraporn, loud and clear!"

"*Ulla, if you can hear the sound of my voice, please tell me: what is the current status of the show?*"

"The Chairman of the Department of Public Health is almost done with his song."

"*Did your husband come to you?*"

Ulla glanced at me out of the corner of her eye and pressed her lips together. "Yes, he's with me now, ready to give his speech. Over."

"*I'd like to review some final items of business with you before—*"

Ulla shut off the walkie-talkie. "All right," she said, looking grave. "We're officially off the grid. I'm no longer an employee of the Faculty of Theatre Drama at Mai Mor College. And *you* are no longer working for Sam."

"I'm not?"

"No." Ulla placed her walkie-talkie on the grass. "We only have one remaining allegiance," she said, taking me by the hand. "You and I, Boyd, are working for the aliens now."

Ulla marched me up the stairs with a firm grip, as though afraid I might cut and run at any moment. When we reached the top of the platform I looked back over my shoulder at the members of *Kati Na-Gareng* down on the ground. Pônge was standing there, staring up at me with a steady gaze. He raised his chin and made a movement with his hand, beckoning me towards him. I hesitated for a moment before realizing that he was doing the opposite of the backwards wave: he was telling me to go on. I gave him a quick nod and then followed Ulla through the door that led backstage.

I could dimly hear the applause of the crowd outside as Miaw escorted an elderly gentleman dressed as a caveman off the stage. Ulla briskly steered me over to the stage-right wing and whispered, "Once the audience settles down, Sam will give you a quick introduction, and then you'll go out and do your thing."

"Sam's onstage right now?"

"No, he's there." Ulla pointed to the opposite side of the room, where Sam sat perched on a stool at the edge of the curtain, holding a microphone and squinting in our direction.

"Why is he looking at me like that?" I whispered.

"He can probably smell the rice wine on you from over there. Just try not to sway back and forth so much. We're almost—oh, no."

Sam had dropped his microphone onto the floor and was now striding towards us. As I stood there watching him, a sickly wave of nausea passed over me, and another bilious hiccup emerged from my throat.

"Just be cool, Boyd," said Ulla. "Hold yourself together."

Sam was halfway across the room and picking up speed when the back door opened and Miaw appeared. She rushed over to Sam, grabbing his elbow and leading him back into position. He reluctantly climbed onto his stool, still grimacing as Miaw handed him the mic and patted him on the arm. Holding up her hand, she counted down on her fingers—*three two, one*—and pointed at Sam. He twitched his mustache, shrugged his shoulders, then brought the microphone to his mouth and began to speak.

"*Ràp-naa ròp* and good evening, ladies and gentlemen. Welcome to the 159th annual Expo *Taang*. It's been a great show tonight, don't you think? The answer is yes, it certainly has. Let's give another big round of applause for the nice work done by Mrs. Haraporn Leekanchanakoth-Young and her team at the Faculty of Theatre Drama. Great job, everybody. *Chai-glíat raeng deung dóot!*" He rapped his knuckles against the mic several times, then continued, "My name is Samuel P. Young, and I am, as most of you know, founder and president of the Young English School. You can't see me right now, but I'm sitting here behind the curtain, and, obviously, you can hear my voice. You know what they say in the Land of Oz—'Pay no attention to the man behind the curtain'—but we're not in Oz anymore, folks." He cleared his throat noisily, then continued, "I'm here with one of our best Y.E.S. teachers, Boyd Arrow, who is this year's"—he widened his eyes and jabbed his finger in my direction—"*rep-re-sent-a-tive* of the Young English School. Tonight, Mr. Arrow will be giving a presentation entitled..." He fumbled in his pocket for a moment, then took out an index card and held it up close to his face. "...'*East is East and West is West: An Exploration of Socio-Cultural Differences Between the Gareng and Puchanese Worlds.*'" Sam paused, then said: "End of introduction."

There was a smattering of applause from the audience, followed by utter silence.

"Okay—go!" Ulla hissed.

I looked outside at the dark stage and at the empty spotlight and at the waiting crowd. In the encroaching darkness, all I could see was a vast and restless movement—a movement that seemed to extend infinitely all directions. I felt as if I were a man on a boat in the middle of the night, staring out at the unending ocean, searching for a sliver of land.

I took a step backward. "I need a minute to collect my thoughts."

"No! You're on!"

Ulla turned and we both watched as Sam handed the mic to Miaw and started heading in our direction.

"Damn it!" said Ulla, gripping my arm and pulling me towards the stage. "Get out there! If he sees that you're drunk, he'll stop the show!"

I struggled to wrench out of her grip. "Let go! I'll be ready as soon as I—"

"There's no time!" Ulla had managed to get me out onto the darkened downstage area, and was now pushing me towards the edge of the spotlight. "Go!"

"I'm going!" I whispered, reaching into my underpants. "Just give me one second to take out my—"

"Now!" yelled Ulla. She placed both hands on my back and, with a powerful shove, sent me flying into the circle of light.

I was greeted by a confused burst of applause as I took several stumbling steps forward and came to an abrupt stop at the tall silver microphone in the center of the stage. I remained frozen in place for a few seconds—mouth open, hand still down my pants—before coming to my senses. As I yanked out my speech, the crowd emitted a collective gasp, followed by murmurs of relief when they saw what I held in my hand. I unfolded the piece of paper and waved it high above my head, displaying it to the people like a Roman senator presenting a new set of laws. I took another step toward the microphone and leaned into it, shielding my eyes against the glare of the lights and gazing out at the crowd.

This, I quickly realized, was a mistake.

My eyes had started to adjust to the darkness, and I could now see the upturned faces of the people in the audience staring back at me, watching and waiting for me to do something. Their eyes felt like damp black bugs crawling across my body, and I could hear their papery voices as they whispered to one another—*hshhhh, hshhhh*—and I could smell their warm breath floating up to me from the ground in fetid waves. An oily sweat began to cover my hands and face, and I became aware of a blurry roar in my ears like the roar of water heard from a great distance, and I murmured, "No, come on, please, not now," clenching my fists and steeling myself for what was going to happen next—and then I noticed Ulla.

She was standing on the grass in the front row, staring at me with the pop-eyed look of someone watching a matador being gored by a bull. As I stared back at her, a ridiculous idea occurred to me, and I heard Sam's voice saying: *You know what I like to do? Imagine the folks in the audience with their shirts off. Works like a charm.* I blinked my eyes, and Ulla was instantly, miraculously topless.

As my eyes lingered on the familiar and reassuring sight of Ulla's full, naked breasts, I dimly realized that almost every person I knew in the town of Mai Mor was watching me from the front row of the crowd, and also that—in my momentary state of self-hypnosis—every single one of them was naked from the waist up. I calmly gazed at the blindingly perfect form of Ms. Pilopoblan; the powerful shoulders of Mr. Yul; the voluptuous, nut-brown body of Ken; Mr. Horse's remarkable chest-wig; Mrs. Manarsumit's wrinkled torso; Miaw's small, slightly asymmetrical breasts; the heaving, matronly bosom of Haraporn; and—

Shiney.

A remote sector of my brain registered the costume she wore—a blue, futuristic-looking nun's habit—but all I could see was the dizzying vision of Shiney's unclothed body. I kept my eyes on her for a long, breathless moment, feeling like a superhero abusing his powers, before forcing myself to look away. The next person I saw was Sam, who had placed his arm protectively around his daughter's shoulders and was staring daggers at me. He alone appeared fully clothed.

I quickly glanced down at the piece of paper I held clenched in my hand. My eye throbbed horribly as I looked at the words on the page and saw that the sweat-soaked writing on it was now just a smeary, barely-legible blur. Not that it mattered—I knew the one-and-a-half sentences by heart. I took a deep breath, said a brief but fervent prayer, and then, in a halting voice, began to give my speech.

"Someone once said: 'East is East, and West is West, and never the twain shall meet.'" I nodded sagely and glanced around at the crowd. "However—" I paused and stifled another hiccup. "However," I continued, "as I look out at your faces today..."

I had reached the end of my prepared remarks. I closed my eyes and opened my mouth, waiting for additional words to spill forth from the depths of my innermost heart, just as Mr. Horse had promised me. My tongue remained inert. I opened my eyes again. "I look out at your faces today," I murmured, and I looked out at the faces of the people of Mai Mor: I looked at the turtles and the robots and the ghosts and the kings and the dogs, and I looked at a little girl dressed as a *garong*, and at a woman wearing a dinosaur costume, and at a person dressed as a hot dog, and at the face of a man attired as Dolly Parton. I looked at Ulla as a *malchak*, at Sam as a hippie, at Mr. Horse as Lionel Richie, and at Shiney as a beautiful blue nun from another planet—and, all at once, I knew exactly what I wanted to say.

I crumpled the piece of paper and dropped it to the floor. "You know," I said, "I had prepared a speech to read to you this evening. The speech was going to talk about the ways in which you and I are so different from one another; about how we're from two different worlds, speaking two different languages, with two very different cultures." A few excited murmurs percolated throughout the crowd. "However—I'm not going to give that speech right now." I glanced down at the balled-up speech and kicked it, watching it bounce and roll off the edge of the stage. "As I look out at your faces today, I realize that—instead of reading my prepared remarks—what I really want to say is something that can't be contained on a simple piece of paper. The words I want to say to you are words that come from in here." I tapped my chest. "My heart." The murmuring was growing louder now, and a few people were pointing at me with mild alarm. I smiled, raising my hand to quiet them. "Truly, there are many ways that you and I are different. But what I think you should understand is that, deep down, I am—"

"You mother*fucking* angel-loving *freak*," said a tired voice behind me.

Standing in the shadows—gently and unsteadily rocking back and forth on the heels of his wingtips—was Gabe. He wore a pair of white surgical gloves on his hands and had a red bandana tied around his face like a bank robber in a Western. He looked even drunker than I was, and had the shaky, unwashed appearance of someone at the tail-end of a bender. Seeing him like that made me feel an odd sort of kinship with him, and—although I knew that something very bad was about to happen—part of me was glad to have Gabe with me up on that stage.

We stood there, woozily regarding one another like a pair of exhausted boxers nearing the end of a fight. Then Gabe stepped into the spotlight, pointed his finger at me, and said: "Fuck *you*." His voice was slurry and slightly muffled by the bandana over his mouth, but his words were unmistakable.

Over Gabe's shoulder, I spotted the figures of *Kati Na-Gareng* scurrying around in the darkness as they hastily set up their equipment. I'd almost forgotten they were there. I watched them distractedly for a moment before turning back to Gabe. I felt no anger towards him, for some reason—only curiosity.

"*I* should've been giving this speech," he said, taking another step towards me. "I *needed* that money." A third step. "I know you ratted me out to Shiney." He was just a couple feet away from me now—he smelled like flop sweat, Old Spice, and ouzo. "I should've done this a long time ago," he mumbled, and I watched as he bent his elbow, raised his fist to his shoulder, and—like a young girl throwing a baseball for the first time—shoved it forward, aiming in the general direction of my broken nose and shouting, "*This* is how we do it in Connecticut!"

I took a stutter-step backwards, shielding my face with my hands and turning my head to the side as Gabe's knuckles glanced off the bony edge of my eye-socket. A hot throb of pain shot up my skull and the audience let out a swooning gasp as I staggered, began to tip over, then righted myself. I pressed my hand against the side of my face—when I brought it away, there was a jagged pink smear on my palm. I tried to open my eye, but it had already swollen shut.

"You bastard," I said. "You *hit* me."

Gabe rubbed his knuckles, looking a little shocked himself. Then he squared his shoulders and said, "That's right, I did."

I stepped up to him, reared back, and took a swing. Despite the fact that he didn't try to dodge my punch, I still somehow managed to miss him altogether. The momentum spun me around in a graceless 180-degree pivot, and I was once again face to face with the audience. We exchanged a surprised look, and then the crowd let out a yell as Gabe came up behind me and clamped his forearm across my windpipe. He put his mouth next to my ear and said, "So, did you screw her yet?"

"*Mmnnghh,*" I said.

"Tell me!"

"*Uggghhnn…*"

"That little slut," Gabe snarled. "I bet you just can't *wait* to get into that—"

"*Gggrrrnngghh!*"

My fingers found Gabe's ear and I pulled and twisted it while at the same time jamming my elbow into his stomach. He roared and released me and I turned to face him. His bandana had slipped to one side during the struggle, and I saw that he'd shaved off his beard. I took another wild swing at him, hitting him directly on his knobby, hairless, obscenely tiny chin. He staggered for a moment and then rushed me, grabbing my arm and bending my wrist backwards. I reached out and took hold of his jaw, and Gabe tightened his grip and gave my hand another twist, sending a queasy black wave of pain up my arm, and I felt my entire body growing slack and tingling, my throat constricting like a pupil in the sunlight. The floor was pitching and buckling beneath my feet and the familiar sickly absence of color was stealthily creeping in around me and blurring the corners of my vision into a dull gray smudge, and as I felt myself blacking out, I remember observing that it wasn't really the pain or the alcohol or the stage fright or some mysterious undiagnosed affliction that was forcing me into unconsciousness; it was that I was *willing* it to happen, that I *wanted* to disappear into that blackness, that in fact I wanted more than anything to escape to a dry flat airless place where I was a statue made of stone.

Gabe folded the fingers of his free hand into a fist and I let go of his chin, bringing my arm up to protect my nose. I knew that all I had to do was release my grip and I could fall into the soft waiting blackness and be done with all of this.

"Do you want some more?" Gabe spat out.

Yes, I said.

The next thing that happened was that Gabe slammed his fist into my sternum as hard as he could—hitting the exact anatomical location of the Wooden Sentry—and a hot pinkish-gray geyser of vomit shot directly out of my mouth and into his face.

Gabe staggered backwards and crumpled to his knees as he let loose a high-pitched, keening wail, like the Wicked Witch of the West melting into a puddle of water. I stood above him, doubled over, my hands on my knees, gasping for breath.

"*Aiiiiiiiggghhhh!*" Gabe screamed, rubbing his face with his shirt and picking bits of pickled fish-stomach out of his hair. "*Eeeeiiiiiihhhhhhhh!*"

I shook my head and opened my mouth. "*Hhhhhh*," I said. I still couldn't breathe.

"*Nooooooo!*" said Gabe, curling into a ball and rolling from side to side, as though he were a beetle trying to right itself.

"*Kkhhhhh…*"

"Get it *off*, get it off of me!"

"*Kkhhhnnn…*"

"*Nooooo…*"

"*Kkhhhonnnnnn…*" I groaned, taking in a deep, gasping breath. "*…nnecticut*," I sighed, and another half-gallon of bile and tripe and banana-brandy-flavored rice wine vaulted out of my throat and onto Gabe as the air around me quivered and shuddered and then was split in two by an enormous sound—a sound that sounded like a flat-lining EKG amplified a thousand times, combined with the sound of an electrified gong struck by a cannonball, combined with the sound of the windshield being ripped off of a car by an ungodly wind. The stage was flooded with light from above, and I turned around and saw that *Kati Na-Gareng* had begun to play their first and only song of the evening.

I stood for a moment watching them and feeling the noise wash over me, and then I felt a hand slap me on the back and I heard a voice yell in my ear: "*Hot dog!*"

It was the *garong*-throwing fat boy, looking truly alien in his shiny green face paint, but also undeniably regal in his silvery unitard. He grinned at me and raised his chubby fists, punching the air.

"Fight!" he yelled. "*Fight!*"

I nodded my head, still trying to catch my breath. I stood all the way up and wiped my mouth with the back of my hand and smiled.

The fat boy pointed at my face. "*Pow!*" he yelled.

I touched my eye. It was swollen and there was a small cut on the side, but I could still see out of it and it didn't really hurt too much; also, the twitch was gone. I was actually feeling pretty good, all things considered: my drunkenness, my hiccups, my stage fright, my dizziness—they'd all been vomited right out of me.

"It was a cheap shot," I said to the fat boy, yelling to be heard above the noise.

We both looked down at Gabe, who was writhing around and struggling to remove his vomit-covered shirt. He appeared to be weeping. The fat boy nudged Gabe's shoulder with his foot and spat on the floor. "Shit-head!" he said, raising his boot in the air as though preparing to stomp on Gabe's kidney.

"Hey, no. Maybe you shouldn't do that right now."

The fat boy frowned. "No?"

"You need to go play." I gestured toward the band. "Music!"

Out of the corner of my eye, I noticed some kind of commotion over by the side of the stage. Haraporn—dressed as the Queen of Hearts from *Alice in Wonderland*—was waving her hands and shouting at three gray-uniformed *malchak* security guards. They watched her impassively for a minute, then began approaching us. Two of them headed for the fat boy, and the third walked over to me. As he grew closer, I realized that I knew him.

"Jooey," I said. "*Ràp-naa ròp.*"

Jooey nodded and smiled at me, then grabbed me by the elbow and began pulling me away from the spotlight.

The fat boy yelled something at Jooey and pointed down at Gabe, and Jooey yelled back at the fat boy, then shrugged and released me. Jooey and another guard each grabbed one of Gabe's ankles and dragged him offstage, leaving a trail of my vomit in his wake. The third guard had taken a seat on the floor and was watching the band as it played. The fat boy winked at me and punched my shoulder, then ran over and joined the other musicians.

The music wasn't as loud any more, and patterns were emerging from the sheets of noise: intricate ping-ponging rhythms and snatches of melody that floated above the cacophony and briefly distinguished themselves before changing and then vanishing, like when a cloud in the sky forms the shape of a dog or an elephant for a moment before once again becoming just a cloud. The frog-colored faces and silver bodies of *Kati Na-Gareng* were glowing and shimmering beneath the hot white and yellow and blue lights, giving them the appearance of creatures that truly were from some other world altogether. Pônge held something that looked like a microphone attached to a car battery and was waving it like a wand in front of the speakers, creating sculptural peals of feedback that made my skin prickle. The three dancing women shook their bodies in unison, and the girl with the bells around her neck whom I'd seen in the Pride was standing all alone, perfectly still, staring out at the crowd as though she were the carved figurehead on the prow of a ship. Some people clapped and yelled and a few were booing but most were just watching, wide-eyed and slack-jawed with amazement. And the funny thing was, although I knew that I was now free to leave, I didn't want to get off the stage anymore.

Pônge marched back and forth, yelling instructions to the musicians and beating on his little metal bongo drum with a rubber mallet. He caught sight of me and yelled something and pointed at the microphone in the center of the stage. I nodded and stepped up to the mic, though I wasn't exactly sure what he wanted. Pônge pointed at me again and I leaned forward and said, "Ladies and gentlemen—*Kati Na-Gareng!*" The band began to play faster and there was some more applause and yelling and I stood watching them and listening to the music. It sounded as though I was listening to the music of an entire building: in one room of that building, a one-armed man was learning how to play the drums; in another room, someone had hooked their Moog synthesizer up to a gas-powered generator and played it with their elbows; in another room, someone had turned on their garbage disposal and was shoving forks and knives down the drain; in another room, an old woman played a sad waltz on the singing saw; and, way deep down in the basement, I could just barely make out the sound of someone listening to a warped old 8-track tape of a long-forgotten R&B song. I put my mouth against the microphone and, very quietly, began to sing the words to that song. I began to sing a little louder and I glanced back at Pônge and he nodded to me and then I began to sing for real. I was singing a melody that seemed to lock perfectly into place with the sounds that *Kati* was making, and as I sang I heard myself singing in the low rich baritone of Mann—

Humans... they act so funny some days
They say the world is a hell,
a foul sty, no place to stay

and then I sang in the quivering falsetto of Angel—

Yeah, people—they're always troubling each other
Go to war and fight their brothers
Keep their lovin' under covers...

and then I was singing a duet with myself:

I have a message
yeah, I'll write it in the sky
Look up there people,
learn the way to live your life...

Black and white, unite
You're the coffee in my tea
I'm the bitter in your greens

I heard the preacher say
There's a dark and there's a light
There's a pink and there's a gray...

And when I reached the part of the song where the solo was supposed to be, I leaned forward and hummed it into the mic, and as I hummed, it was as if I was actually hearing a guitar playing the "Black + White" solo note for note. I turned around and there was Mr. Horse—like an unexpected character appearing in a dream—standing on the stage. He was wielding an electric guitar that perfectly matched his red shirt, and his long curls were soaked in sweat, and he twisted his lips into a cruel smile as he moved his fingers up and down the frets; and I watched, astonished, as he fell down onto his knees, the three *Kati* dancing girls surrounding him and undulating their bodies as he hammered away on his instrument, broken strings dangling, thin ribbons of blood running down his hand. He wasn't the only audience member who had climbed onto the stage: a large group of *malchak* guards were sitting on the floor and watching the band, and a fat Buddha was dancing with the bell-girl, and the group of skeletons were gently slamdancing with each other, and the guy dressed like Darth Vader had taken off his mask and was playing a set of bongos, and a woman dressed like a polar bear had plugged in another mic and was playing the electric flute, although you couldn't really hear her at all. Mr. Horse's solo was still going on and had mutated into what sounded like Jimi Hendrix's version of "The Star-Spangled Banner," and the noise he made was now just a part of the collective noise that pushed forward like a dark gooey wave, flowing slowly and inexorably onto the audience and expanding out into the night sky. I could feel myself getting lost in that noise, lost in the same way that you get lost inside a forest or a river. I felt a hand on my shoulder and turned and it was Pônge, and I knew what he wanted and I nodded and moved away from the mic. He stepped up to it and spread his arms wide and opened his mouth and began to sing. He wasn't singing in the high delicate voice of Piam or the throaty growl of

Akkarat, but in a voice that I hadn't heard before—his own voice. I stepped to the edge of the spotlight and stood there, my body moving now, jittering and shaking as the bodies of the *malchaks* had shaken that night in the Pride: shaking as though I was grasping onto an electrified fence with both hands and refusing to let go. As Pônge sang I had the uncanny sensation that I could understand his words, and that Pônge was telling a story, and that the story was a story about me, told in my own voice: the story of why I'd come to Mai Mor, and about what had happened after I'd arrived, and also what was going to happen in the future. I listened to Pônge sing about how I came to be standing on a stage in this small, strange country, sweating and broken-nosed, angel-winged and black-eyed, shitfaced and in blackface and broken-hearted. He sang the story of how it all had begun, back when I'd first met Ulla:

I am the Beholder, the one
who was chosen to stay;
cursed with life;
in the world,
but not of it;
and I am lost—

I rise from my foamy bath
and put on my father's clothes
and put on my pointed teeth
and set forth into the night
to discover she who is both rabbit and duck:
The snake-haired girl—

And as Pônge sings I begin to move, acting out his words: I open my eyes wide, beholding, and I open my mouth, baring my fangs; I hop like a rabbit, I flap my arms like a duck, and I wiggle my hands in my hair like a nest of snakes; and now Pônge sings of the White Sikh, and I swirl my finger above my head, an invisible turban, and I hug my arms to my body and pucker my lips—*the White Sikh makes love to the face of my woman / and makes love to the hand of my woman / and makes love to the body of my woman / and all of the birds in the world fly from the tip of his long straight member / and my household is secretly shamed and torn asunder*—and I shake my fist in the air and rub my eyes like I'm crying, and Pônge sings, *The woman and I journey to the land of Newark / and enter the silver bird / and flee to the opposite face of the earth / pushing through the clouds / that form the shape of my name*, and then I stretch out my arms, an airplane circling the globe, and the music is playing faster now and as I move my body the *Kati* dancers come to me and move around me, mimicking my movements, anticipating them, as if they know the story and are helping me to tell it, and now I am doing the twist, crushing the baby turtle into the earth—*And I unknowingly and unseeingly / destroy the turtle-child beneath my boot-heel / and now I am cursed / cursed / cursed*—and I lift an invisible jug to my lips and drink, the turtle-spirit drinking a gallon of my tears, and *I am set upon by a band of scoundrels / who bring me down with forceful fruit / until I am vanquished and prostrate on the ground / vanished to another world*, and I fall to the ground and stretch out as though dead, and *I am saved / by the tiny woman / the one who walks like a cat / the one with one dark eye / the one who puts her lips together / and blows balls of air into my mouth / to make me rise*, and I rise to my feet, and now the story is moving more quickly and I'm wiping my body with the child-shroud—*I cannot be touched / I cannot be felt / what am I?*—and I am the lizards crawling across the ceiling, I am a dog running through the forest—*I dwell within a man and woman / not in a girl or a boy / what am I?*—and I am the Pleasurely Beast, I am a frightened moth trapped in a glass box—*the snatch of desire*—I am the bat on the fence, I am the cow in the barn, I am the jerboa, the scare-goat, the raccoon *on the opposite side / of a deep-sunken ha-ha*, the pea-fowl, the hummingbird, and all of the birds in the world, *what am I*, I am a resident of the Spectral Zoo, and I am the zookeeper, and I am the keeper of the hive of *jungle honey*; I'm clutching my hands over my head, fondling the furry smoke-black curse-tooth hanging there in the air, *what am I? / cursed / cursed / cursed / curse-lifter / what am I*, and I am the Night Visitor crawling across the floor, I am the Wooden Sentry standing stock-still and always upright, and I am a giant glass eyeball in the sky, beholding, winking, opening, closing, I am *80% human*, I am *the big fish you're hungry for*, I am bathing my body in the god-damned joyfulness of the world, I am *Body / Body / fire / Body / flame / Body / urination / Body / river / Body / ashes / ashes / ashes* in the water, and *my name / is a cloud*—and I'm standing on a stage and I make a circle with my thumb and forefinger and look through it and I wink. I wink at everybody I can see and also at everybody that I can't see. I wink at Hap, and I say *Hello and goodbye*—

The stage was now filled with people dancing underneath the colored lights, and the music was so loud that my bones were beginning to hurt. I caught a glimpse of Mrs. Manarsumit, who was dressed like Marie Antoinette and was doing the Mashed Potato and grinning maniacally, and I saw Mr. Yul and Ms. Pilopoblan laughing and shaking their bodies together, and I saw Miaw and Jooey, slow-dancing and making out as if they were the only two people on the stage. Pônge wasn't singing now, exactly, but was making a sort of rhythmic panting noise into the microphone, and Ulla stood behind him, smiling serenely with her eyes closed and holding his long blue-black hair behind his head as she rocked gently back and forth. All of the *malchak* guards were onstage watching the band or dancing, except for one who was off at the side arguing with Haraporn. I looked over at Mr. Horse and although I couldn't really hear his guitar anymore I saw that he was still playing. Ken had taken off her lab coat and was standing there in her Wonder Woman costume, watching him and hugging her arms to her chest and singing wordlessly. And then I saw Shiney.

She was just a few feet away from me, her hands folded together prayerfully as she dipped and swayed in time to some backbeat in the music that I couldn't quite hear. Our eyes met and she smiled and I took a step towards her and then I felt a hand on my shoulder. I turned and saw that the hand was attached to a broad-shouldered light-skinned man in a police uniform, not one of the security guards and not someone in a costume but an actual, bona-fide *cop*, and I also saw that he looked pissed. He grabbed my greasy white wrist and I saw that the stage was flooding with cops and that a group of them were heading towards the band, nightsticks drawn. My cop watched enviously as his comrades struggled with the members of *Kati Na-Gareng*, and his grip loosened just a little bit, as if he was contemplating giving up on me and heading over to where the action was. I looked back at Shiney and saw she was trying to make her way over to where I stood but was stuck in the crowd of people that now clogged the stage. Then I saw a red blur out of the corner of my eye and watched as a water-balloon sailed through the air and exploded onto the ground next to a cop that was wrestling with the fat boy—and then there was a second balloon, and a third one, and the fourth balloon hit a policeman square in the face, covering him with milk, and the music was still sort of playing although the band was focused mostly on fighting. My cop loosened his grip a bit more, glancing around as if he was worried about getting smacked by a balloon. He and I stood and watched as the Mai Mor police force was pummeled with balloons that were now flying in from all directions, and the *malchak* guards had linked arms and formed a wall in front of the band to prevent a fresh wave of cops from getting to them. One of the *Kati* dancers had taken off her shirt and draped it around a cop's neck, and then the two of them began to dance, and my cop watched this and I felt his grip loosen just a bit more, and then I caught a glimpse of Shiney again, waving at me, and I yanked on my arm to try and make a run for it and my cop tightened his grip and boxed me on the ear and then he took something from his utility belt and looped a pair of plastic handcuffs around one of my wrists, twisting my other arm behind my back—and then, there was what sounded like the sound of a gunshot a few feet away from us, and we looked and saw the fat boy grinning and holding a roman candle above his head, shooting it straight up into the air. My cop shouted at the fat boy and took a step towards him and at the same time let go of me completely. I froze in place, not being accustomed to running from the police, and then I felt a tug on my arm. "Come on!" yelled Shiney, grabbing my hand, and I could hear my cop screaming as we squeezed and slithered our way through the crowd. A balloon bounced off the back of my head but didn't break and another one hit my shoulder and soaked me in root beer. I held on tightly to Shiney's hand as we ran backstage and out the stage door and down the back stairs. We ran around to the front of the auditorium along the edge of the crowd, pushing through people on the grass, both of us laughing or maybe just screaming, I couldn't really tell. After a minute there was nobody chasing us and we stopped running and stood there, panting, and then Shiney let go of my hand and I said, "Is anyone coming?"

"No," she said, standing on her tip-toes. "I don't think so."

I held up my handcuffed wrist. "If I have a handcuff on, does that mean I'm officially under arrest?"

"Yes," said Shiney. She took my arm and tugged on the handcuff and I pulled and managed to slide my hand out. There was a series of whistling explosions behind us and we turned and watched the red flares of dozens of roman candles shooting into the sky. Shiney turned back to me and said, "I enjoyed your presentation."

"Thanks."

"Your song was very good… and the dancing… and the part when you were speaking from the heart. Oh!" She kicked my shin. "And the part when Gabe was beating you up, and you vomited on him? That was crazy!"

"He sucker-punched me."

"Yes—I see you have a shiner." She tilted her head and reached towards my face but didn't touch it.

"I'm a Cyclops," I said, winking my bad eye shut. "I only have one pupil."

"What?"

"Forget it." I took a step back and studied her outfit. "What's your *goo fán dee*—the girl on the Blue Nun bottle?"

"My great-grandmother was with the Daughters of Charity of St. Vincent de Paul. I also based the costume on an old Balenciaga bridal gown."

"Cool," I said. "I don't really know what you're talking about, but it looks amazing."

"Thank you." Shiney took out a tube of *ur-ur-ur* and offered it to me. "To cleanse the vomit taste?"

I poured some into my mouth, swished it around, and swallowed. Then I handed the tube back to her and said, "Listen, Shiney. I wanted to talk to you about—"

"*Arrow.*"

We turned around. Sam's arms were folded across his chest, and he was moving his head slowly up and down and back and forth, as though he had a crick in his neck. He still had his sunglasses on.

"I simply do not know what to say," he said.

"What did you think, Dad?" asked Shiney. "The show was really wild, huh?"

"I'm literally struck dumb by the sight of what just occurred on that stage." Sam reached into his pocket and took out a crumpled ball of paper: my speech. He tossed it over his shoulder. "Son, I believe that that was truly one of the most remarkable performances I've ever had the privilege to bear witness to."

Sam spoke with such a quiet, coiled intensity that it took me a moment to absorb the meaning of his words. "You mean... you liked it?"

He placed both hands on my shoulders and broke into a grin. "It was *incredible*, Arrow! It almost made my old noggin blow a gasket! I think I had some kind of outer-body experience watching you up on that stage: something about the way the lights combined with the music—I don't know why, but it made it seem as if I was up there at the same time you were, dancing around, while simultaneously I was down on the ground, watching the whole crazy thing through the eyes of the crowd! And your costume's pretty magnificent—you look like some kind of *will-o'-the-wisp* or something."

"Dad," said Shiney quietly. "Are you high?"

Sam patted her on the head. "That's an impolitic question, sweetheart."

"I'm glad you enjoyed it," I said.

"These folks will not be forgetting you very soon, sir. You threw a real *ing-bing* up there. Keystone Cops and all."

Up on the stage, five policemen were struggling to handcuff Pônge. He head-butted one and slipped out of their grasp, then ran up to the microphone and yelled, "*Pônge!*" with his fist raised high into the air, "*Pônge! Pônge! Pôn—*" and then my cop whacked him with his billyclub and Pônge fell to his knees, arms outstretched, and the cops all dove on him and the crowd began to chant, "*Pônge! Pônge! Pônge!*" as he was dragged offstage by his long black hair. The entire sequence of events was so well orchestrated, I found myself briefly wondering if they were actual cops at all.

"Total anarchy," Sam said, admiringly. Then he sighed. "I should go look for Haraporn. She must be having a conniption right about now. But I got to say—and don't dare tell her I said this—it's about high time we had some *malchaks* up on that stage. It was a sincere delight to be able to see such a thing occurring in my own lifetime, and you helped make it happen, Arrow." Sam shook his head and laughed. "Which is why it pains me all the more to have to fire you."

Shiney laughed. So did I, though not as hard. "Fire me?"

"That's right," said Sam, beaming. "It never gives me pleasure to let someone go. No, sir. But in this instance, unfortunately, it's unavoidable."

"Dad!" said Shiney.

"Shiner, it's one thing if he's an incompetent in the classroom. But after that show, he'll be forever associated in people's minds as the Y.E.S. employee that destroyed the Expo *Taang*. From a P.R. perspective, it's simply untenable." Sam turned to me and said, "Strike two, shame on you; but strike three, shame on me. You understand. No hard feelings?"

I shrugged. "I guess not."

"However," he said, raising his finger in the air, "this is a case of good news/bad news/good news. The good news is—you still get your bonus."

"I do?"

Sam nodded. "Despite whatever negative and damaging repercussions this may have on the Y.E.S. brand, we're resilient enough to shrug them off. And your performance was such a remarkable achievement, I feel duly obliged to reward your efforts." He produced a small green plastic bag from his pocket. "Here you are."

I opened the bag, then reached in and took out Haraporn's *àep-sôn*. It was folded into a small rectangle and there was a hard lump in the middle. I carefully unfolded it, half-expecting to find a small bottle of Sam's urine. In the center of the cloth lay one of Haraporn's angels—the small Batman figurine that had been painted white. I cupped it in the palm of my hand and studied it, holding my breath as though the figurine was a small bird that had mistaken me for a tree. Then I looked up at Sam and closed my hand around the figurine and nodded.

Sam coughed into his fist. "I know you were admiring that other figurine with the dentist and whatnot, but I thought the wife might miss that particular model. This one, I figured she wouldn't mind parting with. And she's convinced that shroud artifact is ruined, so I figured I'd give it to you and find a replacement." He shrugged. "Now you have some souvenirs to take home with you."

I wrapped the angel back up in the cloth. A cheer came from the crowd and, off in the distance, a red ball of light soundlessly arced into the sky and disappeared.

"That was the *ngoo*," said Shiney. "We should go to the river."

Sam nodded. "You kids go ahead. I think I need to stay and soothe my wife."

"That wasn't from a roman candle?" I asked.

"No," said Shiney. "It came out of the water."

I looked over at Sam. He tilted his head and said, "You should go see the phenomenon with your own eyeballs. I've always personally suspected that it's a *malchak* prank—some kind of underwater bamboo-and-gunpowder contraption. They are a clever people." He pulled Shiney against his chest. "Take care of my girl. It's dark down there by the water."

"I'll keep an eye on her."

"And no funny business, Arrow—you hear?"

Shiney wriggled out of Sam's grasp. "Dad, how many times have I told you, his name is *Darrow*. Boy-*duh*... *Dar*-row."

"I'm well aware of that." Sam patted her on the head, then turned and began to walk towards the stage. "Arrow," he said over his shoulder, "is just his nickname."

I followed Shiney out to Pamarassam Road and we joined the stream of murmuring people walking slowly down the hill and through the darkness in the direction of the river. Neither of us spoke for a while, and then I said: "About the other day, Shiney—I just wanted to apologize." I glanced over at her. She had her chin pressed to her chest and was staring at the ground, smiling strangely.

"I heard you visited with Auntie Golli," she said.

"Yeah, I stopped by her place." I paused, then added: "I was looking for you."

"Golli says you drank the entire *dtui-dtui*?"

"You mean that soup she gave me?"

"The *dtui-dtui* is something that we use to make the room smell pleasant—it's not intended for drinking. I think Golli was trying to disguise your hot-dog smell." Shiney laughed. "It is as if she offered you a stick of deodorant, and you thought it was a candy bar."

"She could've stopped me," I muttered. "I just assumed she was a terrible cook."

"I believe that you two had a lengthy conversation."

"It was pretty one-sided. Does she understand any English?"

"Not too much."

"I was just wondering, because—I don't know. I thought Golli might've told you what we talked about."

Shiney gave a vague shrug.

"Look," I said. "I need to be clear about this whole Meowy X-mas situation. I understand why you'd be upset that I went there, but it honestly was more due to stupidity than anything else. I'd be happy to give you a blow-by-blow account—or, not blow-by-blow, exactly, but... I just want to tell you what really happened."

"You don't need to," Shiney said quietly. "I think you were just maybe a little simple in your thinking."

"Exactly! I'm a simpleton. That's my main crime, more or less."

We'd reached the end of Pamarassam and began walking with everybody else down the Friendly Highway. "Another thing," I said. "About me and Ulla—"

"You're not married, correct?" Shiney gave me one of her half-winks. "I will keep your secret safe."

"I'm starting to think it wasn't much of a secret."

"I'm sorry to see that she's fallen in with Pônge now." Shiney whistled between her teeth and shook her head. "That tattoo!"

"You saw it? It's pretty nasty-looking, right?"

"She's lucky, actually. Pônge must truly care for her. The last time he gave a tattoo to a visiting *gareng* woman, it said:

'The scrotum of Pônge is equal in volume with the bladder of an elder male goat, and his testicles may be favorably compared to two ripened *garongs* in the spring-time.'"

"Wow. So, Ulla isn't the first foreigner he's hooked up with."

"Pônge is obsessed with *garengs*—he thinks they're very exotic, and he appreciates their loose sexual morals." Shiney snorted. "Last year, his relations with Devasheesh created some awkward complications."

"Shawn's wife?"

"Pônge was particularly proud of that conquest."

I groaned and shook my head. "I think maybe it's time for me to go back to my own country."

Shiney and I had now reached the edge of the ridge overlooking the Ngoo-pìk. The hill was lined with vendors selling balloons and glow-sticks and food and beer, and groups of people sat at child-sized chairs and tables, staring out at the pitch-black river. Down below, I could just make out the dark forms of people crowded along its banks. A warm breeze floated up to us from the water, and the moon hovered in the sky, looking like the cold blue stone that it is.

"Do you mean that?" Shiney said after a moment.

"What?"

"That it's time for you to go home?"

I shrugged. "I don't have a job here anymore. I have no savings. All I've got to my name is a return plane ticket."

"I'm sure you could find other work." Shiney chuckled and added, "I might have a job for you, in fact."

"What kind of job?"

"I'm currently looking to hire a driver," she said, pressing her lips together. "Or perhaps a cook."

Her words rang a dim bell in my brain. I pointed at her

and said, "You were there, weren't you? You were in Golli's room that whole time. You heard everything I said."

Shiney didn't answer; she was staring at something past my shoulder with a look of intense concentration. I followed her gaze to a little table next to a beer stand.

"How weird," said Shiney. "Isn't that—?"

"Yeah. It is."

A broad-shouldered *gareng* was sitting at the table alone, sipping from a bottle of *Gong* as he looked out over the river. He wore shorts and a tight white t-shirt with a red soda stain running down the front, and—although he was clean-shaven, and turban-less—I had no doubt who he was.

I stared at the White Sikh, and he stared back at me as though he were blind; but then a light of recognition began to shine in his eyes, and he sat up straight and put down his beer and stretched out his arm, raising it halfway into the air.

The crowd made a noise just then and Shiney grabbed my elbow. "Look!" she said, and I watched as a ball of red light moved soundlessly up through the sky above the river, hovering for just a moment before fading away.

"Let's go," said Shiney, her hand still cradling my elbow. "We should stand down by the water."

I looked back at Shawn and winked, and then turned away from him and followed Shiney to the river's edge.

Everybody was speaking in hushed tones and watching the black water and we all waited for a minute and then two minutes, and then another red glowing ball broke the surface and floated into the air. My arm was brushing very lightly against Shiney's and we stayed like that for a while, not speaking, just watching as the small red balls of light emerged from the river. I don't know how long we stood there, but after a time the red balls began to appear with less frequency, and people started talking again, and I said, "That's amazing."

"Isn't it?"

"I still don't understand what it is."

"There's nothing to understand."

"But—where do they come from? Could it really be that there's some kind of river-gas that just happens to be released on the same day every year? Or, is there actually some guy under the water shooting off roman candles, like your dad said? Or some giant magical turtle swimming around, trying to get the monks to have sex with him? What *is* it?"

"Look," said Shiney, pointing at the water as another ball broke the surface, "Just look at it," and I made a circle with my thumb and forefinger and held it up to my face and looked through it, and the night sky looked like a big black eye looking back at me, and the red pinprick of light hovering at its center was the pupil of that eye; and then the light began to fade, and after a few seconds there was only the blackness and the dead white spray of stars behind it.

I nodded my head, then asked Shiney if she wanted to go for a walk.

We make our way upriver, away from the people. It's dark on the river road but the moon is high and we can see well enough. We walk down to the edge of the water and sit there on a flat rock and Shiney removes the thing she's wearing on her head and we talk for a while, and then, at some point, we stop talking. From the way she speaks to me I understand what will happen next, and now Shiney is looking out at the water, her face turned away from mine, and I look down at her as though looking down from a great height, and I feel dizzy as I lean forward and I kiss her on the neck. Her shoulders move and she doesn't look at me and then she turns her head toward me and she's smiling. She puts her hand on my leg and says, *Do you know how to swim?* We separate in the darkness and remove our costumes. I fold the shroud carefully around the thing that it holds and place them both on a pile with my bat-wings and my halo and my toga. I hear the noise of water and in the corner of my eye I watch Shiney as she moves into the water, and I look away from her but then I look straight at her. I can just see her slip of a body in the flat light, her body looking like something carved from white stone, and then she laughs and raises her arms and dips down into the water and stands up again, dripping. Her back is to me and my pale white body is glowing as if it's on fire and the water is exactly the same temperature as my body. I enter the water and lower my body into it and reach down and pick up a handful of silt and rub it against my body and my face, scouring away the sweat and the soda and the paint and the glitter. I go out farther and try to stand and the current is stronger here, the rocks slick with growth beneath my feet, and I slip and float for a moment and I'm caught in the current, moving downriver quickly, my arms and legs knocking against the rocks, the water holding me down. I can't stand up and I can't breathe and I reach out my hand and touch something sliding past me through the water, something large and hard and alive-feeling, although maybe it's just the river that I'm touching. I let out a yell and push away from it and I slip into an eddy where the water is still. I get to my feet and wade back upriver, sucking in lungfuls of air. Shiney stands in the moonlight and she says laughing, *Body, I was calling your name, where did you go? Float over to me.* Her silhouette is a slim dark flashing shape above the white moving water and I move towards her, hiding my body beneath the current as I slowly push against it. *Body,* she calls, *come quickly,* and then I stand up in the darkness where it's shallow and I'm not hidden and I move towards her. She laughs and says *Body, I want to show you something. Come here, Body,* she says, and so I do.

THANK YOU:

Brooke Costello; Doug Dibbern; Maury Dojny; Morgan Dojny; Brian Gillett; Josh Golin; Andrea Grodberg; Alex Halberstadt; Bill Hall; Justine Kalb; Corin Hewitt; Kirsten Kearse; Philip Leventhal; Molly McFadden; Sarah Russo; Sarah Sarchin; Jean-Guy Simard; Peter Schmul; Jenn Smith; Michael Tuminello; Susan & Parry Young. Thank you John Henderson, to whom these letters were first addressed. Thank you Mom & Dad, for your perpetual support. Thank you Katherine Fausset. Thank you Matt Bell, Steven Gillis, Steven Seighman, and Dan Wickett. And: Thank you, Sybil.